Tony Aued

The Vegas Connection
Blair Adams
An FBI Thriller

by

Tony Aued

Copyright © 2012 Tony Aued

Blair Adams Books

This book is a work of fiction. Names, characters, places, and incidents are products of the author's imagination or are used fictitiously. Any resemblance to actual events or locales or persons, living or dead, is entirely coincidental.

All rights reserved.

ISBN:10-1479281883
ISBN-13:978-1479281886

DEDICATION

This novel is dedicated to my son Blake and his wife Merritt. Following their journalistic careers gives me inspiration to do my very best.

ACKNOWLEDGMENTS

I wish to express my thanks to Carol Dean for her editing assistance. Carol along with many members of my Shelby Writer's group have been an outstanding resource and help. I want to especially thank Carl Virgilio, a member of our writers group who created the cover for this novel.

Writing the Blair Adams Series has been great fun for me and I certainly hope that you have also enjoyed the adventures of our brave heroine. This is the third book in the series and I hope to have more adventures for my loyal readers.

The research used in completing this novel included traveling to many locations and using the actual geography to describing those places. I thank the people who allowed me insight into their cities.

Other Novels in the Blair Adams Series

By Tony Aued

The Package

The Abduction

Watch for soon to be released

The Blame Game

Prologue

Hunter Adams served in Iraq as an Army Special Forces soldier. He was killed by a sniper's bullet and died a war hero. His wife, Blair, wasn't unaware that he was working in an undercover assignment with the government while serving his country.

Blair's life was turned upside down once the revelations of her husband's activities were discovered. She was thrust into a world of espionage and intrigue that sent her on a mission of solving the mystery of a package that another soldier had sent her from Hunter's foot locker. She joined forces with a rogue FBI agent, Allisa Jones, during that search and won the admiration of the director of the FBI.

Those events opened new opportunities for Blair and she joined the FBI's training program at Quantico in Virginia. She unknowingly became a target of the men that escaped from the safe house in New York. Al Yawer, an escaped terrorist, tracked her down and attempted to avenge the killing of his friends due to her involvement. He planned a trap and *Abducted* her friend Allisa hoping to reel Blair in and kill both women. The devious plan worked that left Blair critically injured.

The FBI captured Yawer in Falls Church, Virginia and along

with his supporters they were imprisoned after a lengthy trial. Terrorist's cells were found operating in Michigan along the Canadian border. The director of the bureau, John Franklin Martin, was able to use the evidence to foil plots designed to cripple the United States by attacking the power grids from New York to Michigan along the Great Lakes.

Blair Adams spent months recovering from her injuries at Bethesda Medical Center while being protected 24/7 by the FBI. Would she recover and become a viable agent? Was she still a target? Where will she be sent after her recovery? What new adventures lie ahead for her?

One

Two security officers stood stunned looking at the nude body on the ground. It was dark when they approached, at first they could hardly make out the figure on the pavement. Streaks of red flashed on the cement like the opening brush strokes of a Picasso painting. Blood was splattered over the facing of the building. The night had cast a dark shadows across the landscape. The officers were making their normal rounds when they saw what appeared to be the body on the ground. They usually walked in pairs this time of night, often escorting nurses to their car. Neither of them had experienced any problems since working at the Medical Center.

One of the officers held his hands to his mouth he didn't know what to do. The side of the victim's face had been crushed by the fall. His partner pressed his hand along the side of her neck feeling for a pulse, but none existed. He reached down searching for any identification. He found a hospital bracelet on her right arm and he turned it over. The information read, Sandy Thorpe, blood type B positive, room 405. Her blond hair was sticky and matted with blood and her body was surrounded by bits of shattered glass.

The lifeless body lying on the harsh pavement seemed an unjust treatment for someone obviously so young. Sandy Thorpe was a patient of the Bethesda Medical Center. The officers radioed it in to their chief, and he in turn called it in to the local police. They covered her body with a tarp that was pulled from the trunk of their vehicle. It just seemed like the right thing to do.

The information was called in to both the Bethesda and Maryland State Police Departments. Orders came back to rope off the scene and wait. Officers started to string the area with yellow tape. You soon could hear sirens screaming out in the night like an animal in anguish. They were coming from down the street, and two vehicles were seen approaching.

It was one-thirty-six a.m. and lights started coming on in the Medical Center. The shrill screams and volume of sirens had awakened many of the patients. The medical staff personnel could be seen peering out to catch a glimpse of the action. There was a dense fog that covered the grounds' and it was hard to tell exactly what was going on. It wasn't unusual to hear sirens this time of night but these didn't appear to be coming toward the emergency entrance.

"What's going on?" a Doctor asked the group standing at the window.

"Not too sure, but it appears that something is up near the west wing of the Medical Center," a nurse answered.

The doctor and nurse watched for another minute as two more emergency vehicles were seen coming down the street. Flashing red and yellow lights turned the landscape into a beacon of orange flames. Officers were putting up blockades around the area and ringing it with crime scene tape.

On the second level of the atrium, medical personnel had gathered, trying to get a peek at the action. You could hear each new bystander asking the same questions.

"What's happening?"

The only answers were inconclusive. No one knew what had happened except that a lot of unusual action was taking place near the west end of the Medical Center.

Blair Adams had been watching the action outside her window. She could see emergency and police vehicles gathering a few feet from the corner of the building. It was dark and a layer of fog covered the ground. It appeared that there was something covered on the ground just a few feet from the base of the building. It was so close that details were hard to make out. Blair could see police gathered around the area as she stood closer to the window overlooking the Bethesda Campus. She had been at the Medical Center for months recovering from surgery and was close to being released.

Many people had sent well wishes, and her room was always filled with flowers. She loved Gerber Daisies, and her parents had a standing order to have fresh ones delivered to her room every week. Her blond hair had been cut short when she entered the FBI training program, and she decided to keep it that way. Her brilliant blue eyes looked as deep as the ocean, and when she smiled, people just naturally smiled back. She had started a work-out regimen at the Medical Center and was in her best shape. At five foot four inches tall, she was described by one of the agents as a blond stick of dynamite. She was very muscular yet obviously beautiful. Many doctors had hoped to make an impression on her, but she never showed any interest. She just wanted to get better and go back home to Southern California.

Her room was located on the fifth floor of the west wing of the Medical Center. She had been moved there after her initial surgery that took place in Arlington. Her move to the Center was per the request of the director of the FBI.

Blair continued to watch the gathering outside of her room as flashing lights lit the night sky. The brilliant glow from the police vehicles shining through the fog cast an eerie shadow in her room. She wondered what had happened. She had been up and couldn't sleep. The doctors had informed her that she would be released at the end of the week and the excitement kept her awake. She had talked to her parents and looked forward to being able to go back to her home in Southern California.

The action of the past few months finally were coming to an end. Blair was recovering very nicely from the injuries she received in the bomb blast at the motel in Virginia. Her friend, Allisa Jones had been killed in the blast set by Al Yawer. He was an escaped terrorist and planned to kill both Blair and Allisa Jones. He had tracked them from his hideout in Canada and was able to abduct Allisa in a plot to lure Blair to the motel. His plan had worked. Blair followed Yawer's orders and drove to the secluded motel where he had planted a bomb. He set a bomb to detonate as Blair came closer to the room where Allisa was being held. She had been tied up to the bedpost unable to warn her friend and helpless.

It was only through the efforts of FBI special agent Johnny Amari that Blair survived the blast. Her recovery was touch and go for the first few days, but the doctors at Arlington General Hospital did a great job making sure she got the best care possible. Once Blair had started her recovery, the director of the FBI moved her to the Bethesda Medical Center so that he could provide a 24/7 protective detail. He knew that it would be best having her closer to Washington and to keep protecting her. Although she didn't want the extra attention, he felt it was necessary.

Flashing lights from the emergency and police vehicles again filled her room with a continuous stream of red and yellow streaks. Blair wanted to gather more information on the events below. Her FBI training caused her to want to be more than just a bystander. She watched as two more vehicles arrived on the scene. What could have happened she wondered? As she moved closer to the window there was a knock at her door.

"Who is it?"

"Ms. Adams, its Robert. Sorry to bother you but I saw the lights on in your room. I just wanted to make sure you're okay."

Robert Sampson was one of the FBI security guards assigned to protect her. He shared the duty for the past few months with another group of agents. They kept a 24/7 security detail on her room and each group had a twelve hour shift. Robert was part of the Washington Bureau, and although the detail had been boring, he enjoyed the time talking to Blair. She was always friendly and very smart.

"Yes, I'm fine. I was just wondering what was happening outside." Blair answered while still standing near the windows.

"We've sent a man down there to check it out. I'll let you know once he comes back."

Blair continued to watch the action. Her thoughts were about going home. It had been over a year since she left her home in Santa Monica, California. Her life had seen so much turmoil since her husband Hunter had been killed in Iraq. Hunter was on a special mission when he was killed by a sniper. It was his last mission that caused terrorist to travel to California to search their home. They knew that an American soldier had discovered a package of documents that was critical to Saddam's war plans. Once they didn't find it, they followed his wife, Blair, hoping to discover the missing package that might unravel Saddam's' supporter's plans.

When the package was discovered and delivered to the director of the FBI, the United States used that information to bring down the regime. Blair and her new friend Allisa Jones had helped to foil the terrorists. The director suggested that Blair join the bureau. He was impressed with her performance during the search and wanted her on his team.

She joined the bureau's training program at his suggestion. The terrorist was captured after the blast at the motel and his trial was front page news for over a month. John Franklin Martin had successfully captured a terrorist, foiled a plot on the life of the president and turned over the documents that Blair found, all in one year. His success could lead to his being promoted to a cabinet position. He gave orders to make sure Blair Adams would always have a protective detail.

The noise and action below was now in full steam and as Blair watched the action below, she saw one of the policemen pointing up toward her room. She wondered what he was pointing at. She slowly backed away from the windows. There was a knock again at her door. What had happened? Why were they looking at her room?

Blair moved toward the door, "Who's there?"

"Ms. Adams, its Robert. Not sure what's going on yet but it might be safer for you to stay back from the windows until we do."

"Okay, but now they are pointing up here. You better find out why. I saw two of the men looking up here a minute ago."

Robert hadn't talked to his man that headed down to the scene below. "My man hasn't returned, but one of the nurses said that a woman might have jumped from her room." He kept watching down the hall for his partner to return. He hoped to get details on the action below. "Ms. Adams, I'd appreciate it if you just stayed back from your window." Robert wasn't taking any chances.

"Sure," she answered.

The men on the ground had been looking up toward the corner of the Medical Center. They could see the windows broken on the fourth floor above. It appeared that it was a gaping hole from a room on that floor and the drapes were blowing out into the wind. The local police chief dispatched two officers into the building to check it out. "The glass in that building is pretty thick, it would be impossible for someone to have jumped through the window." One of the officers stated that the glass must be at least two inches thick.

The Maryland state police officers entered the building and pushed the elevator for the fourth floor. The hallway was dimly lit, probably set on an evening timer they figured. The walk toward the corner room was about twenty-five feet. They approached room 405 and saw that the door was ajar. The call went back to the chief before they entered. The instructions were to proceed with caution. The room was dark, and they could hear the wind rushing through the opening in the glass wall. The officers had guns drawn and moved slowly toward the opened door.

"Police!" they called out.

There was no answer. One of the officers was a ten year veteran of the Maryland force. His partner was a rookie. He had never been in the Bethesda Medical Center but knew that many military personnel were treated there. They slid around the opened door and crouched low as he again announced his presence.

"Police!" they called out again.

Still there was no answer. The two men held their guns in their right hand and a small flashlight in the left hand. The flashlight was positioned over the top of their gun so that they could respond if needed. The room was dark and cold. The first officer could see bits of shattered glass on the carpet as he shined his flashlight toward the window. The room was empty. He called back to the chief to fill him in.

"Nothing up here, Sir," The officer said. "It looks like someone went through the glass, Boss. I'm not sure why the door to her room was opened to the hallway. That doesn't make any sense." The breeze was blowing the curtains straight out and the hallway was considerably cooler in that area.

The chief agreed and gave him further instructions. "Let's rope that room off and I'll get the CSI team up there. We need to rule out any foul play."

He was right. Dan Moss was the local police chief and he was well respected. The two men moved out of the room and secured it waiting for further instructions. They were now needed to make sure they secured the scene for the CSI team to investigate. The room would be checked for fingerprints and any evidence that could help with the investigation. As they stood near the doorway they noticed a large chair covered in glass lying sideways against the shattered window. If only they could check it out further but they didn't want to compromise the scene. Their instructions were clear, wait for the crime scene team.

Dan was made aware that a team of FBI agents had been on a special detail in that wing of the building. One of their agents had been down at the scene gathering details from the men at the base of the building. The agent didn't tell the chief why they were on special assignment. It seemed that the bureau never shared anything with the local cops. Chief Moss knew that the bureau guys were nothing but a pain-in-the-ass. They wanted full control of every event and never gave any help to the local cops. The troopers could see that their chief was angry and frustrated. It was best to stay away from him.

Moss radioed his men to make sure no one, and he meant no one got any information unless it was cleared through him.

Robert saw his partner coming down the hallway. Maybe now he would find out what had happened downstairs. Robert had been with the FBI for five years and assigned to the D.C. Bureau since last May. He was familiar with the events surrounding Blair Adams and the chase for the abductor last fall. He was pretty excited to be assigned to the protective detail at Bethesda and had been able to talk to Ms. Adams quite a few times. She was always very nice and quite intelligent. She would often give the guys food and items that people sent to her. She once told Robert that she'd weigh three-hundred pounds if she ate all the candy, cookies and fruit that people sent. She appreciated the gifts but felt that she didn't deserve all the attention. His partner was hurrying down the hall and waving his arms.

"Holy shit!" Robert's partner called out. "We need to call this in. Looks like someone tossed a young female out of the 4th floor window."

"What do you mean tossed her out of a window?"

"The local guys are up in the room right now. There is no way someone could jump through that plated glass. I'm sure it was foul play. Hell, Robert they're in room 405, just below Blair's."

"Christ!" Robert got on the horn right away. He knew this was going to be a problem. Blair had been at Bethesda for over two months without any issues. Why now, he thought. Robert called it into his bureau chief. "Boss, we have a 187 here," He continued. "It appears that a young woman might have been killed at the Medical Center. We heard from the local police that it appears that she was in the room below Blair's on the fourth floor."

The D.C. bureau chief, Andrew Jackson, dreaded this news. His team of agents had been on protective duty at Bethesda for months without an issue. Now, when he had just been informed that Blair would be going home, something had to happen. He would call it in to the director. It was almost two-fifteen a.m. He wondered if it would be better to wait until he had more information before calling. Jackson ordered a second detail to Bethesda and quickly dressed. It was critical in his mind that he was on the scene before calling it in.

Blair called out again to Robert when she heard the loud conversation in the hallway. "Robert, do you know what is going on down there?"

She had been watching from the big overstuffed chair in the corner of her room. It seemed that more officers had been called to the scene, and her natural instincts figured this was something serious.

Robert didn't want to tell Blair what they had heard, or that he had called it in to his bureau chief. "Miss Adams, it looks like a possible suicide."

She didn't buy his answer. "Maybe you need to call it in," she suggested. "I'm not sure the local cops and Medical Center people can do a thorough investigation."

Robert knew Blair was a smart cookie. Talking to her before, it was obvious that she had a keen knowledge of operating procedures, and solid investigation skills. He pressed closer to the door and answered her. "I agree and called it in to my chief a few minutes ago," Robert hoped that she would remain calm and away from the windows. He continued, "I really don't think it is related to us here, but better be safe than sorry." He was just hoping to appease her.

"That's a good idea," Blair responded. "What can we do in the meantime?"

His bureau chief would get there soon and direct the investigation. He followed the procedure that had been set-up in the event of a problem. The west wing of the 5th floor had been secured and one man was stationed at each end of the floor. He called it in to the Bethesda officers to inform them that the FBI was locking down the wing of the 5th floor. Robert took charge and handling everything according to procedure.

"Ms. Adams, we've got men stationed along the corridor and everything is under control. I'm right here at your door, and if you need anything just call out to me."

Just then the door opened. Blair looked out into the hallway and addressed Robert. "I think you should have someone else at my door and maybe you come in here with me."

Robert agreed that it was a good idea. "I'll call down to one of the guys to come up here," he said.

Blair suggestion was solid. If someone was trying to get to her, they might have created this as a diversion. She wasn't paranoid but now all the action below was causing her to plan for the worst. "I'd feel safer if you were in here." Blair also wanted to get all the information she could, and by having Robert in her room she could question him further about the events below.

He positioned a man outside her room and went in with Blair. They would wait for the bureau chief together. Robert knew that his Jackson would want to handle the investigation himself.

"I'm sure everything will be fine," Robert tried to reassure her.

Blair wasn't sure if he was trying to comfort her or himself. "I'm sure it will be okay," She responded.

The two of them watched out the window as flashing lights continued to appear on the horizon. Blair asked him to see what was going on when they noticed a team again flashing their lights along the facing of the building. When he moved closer to the windows checking the action below, he could see the State Police CSI team gathering evidence on the ground. They were also looking up toward the area of Blair's room. He wondered if they know that she was there. He hoped they would discover the identification of the dead woman soon and the cause of her death. He didn't know that they already knew who she was.

Two

There were police officers everywhere and the building's staff on the West end were in a state of commotion. The Bethesda Medical Center officers had been relegated to traffic duty as the Maryland State Police department took over the investigation.

Robert Sampson waited for his bureau chief to arrive. He had been sitting with Blair in her room, per her request. They talked about the action below as streams of bright lights continued to filter through her window. She questioned Robert on the investigation below. He didn't want to alarm her, but Blair's questions caused him to give her more information than he had planned. He hoped there wasn't a connection to the dead girl on the pavement and his protective detail.

Once Chief Dan Moss of the Maryland State police department had found out that the FBI was on the scene he ordered his men not to talk to anyone. He also found out that the local bureau chief was on the way. He dreaded the confrontation that was sure to take place. Nothing good had ever happened when the FBI was involved. Moss had been involved in an incident a few years back with FBI agents from the Washington Bureau, and they were a real problem. He planned to take this investigation over, and freeze the FBI out. He was determined not to let the bureau take over again.

Dan Moss was a twenty year veteran of the state police department. He had risen through the ranks and was liked by his men. He had been promoted to police chief five years ago and had a great record of success. He was a big man, six foot four inches tall and about two-hundred-twenty pounds, causing people to cower when meeting him for the first time. Although he had a gruff exterior, his men knew he would do anything to help them.

He was a pragmatic individual and always followed the standard procedure during an investigation. The men in his unit respected Dan and he always took care of them.

Moss had his men positioned on the fourth floor of the Medical Center in the dead girls room, and below at the crime scene. He had confirmed with the Medical Center that a Mrs. Sandy Thorpe was indeed the patient in room 405. He waited to make sure that the CSI team confirmed that the body was Mrs. Thorpe. Just because she had a hospital bracelet with that name he wanted a positive identification.

The CSI team completed collecting evidence. They noted that the glass around the broken window in the dead girl's room had unusual jagged edges. It matched the shards of glass on the ground. The glass was an inch-and-half thick, and they agreed that it would be almost impossible for someone to have jumped through it. Something must have been thrown out of the window before the woman was tossed out. Upon further investigation in the room it was suspected that the large chair in the room could have been used to shatter the glass. They also noted that the chair had scratches on the legs and a piece of sheered glass stuck in the fabric. They planned to inspect it for prints.

A black Suburban was seen pulling up to the roadblock. Chief Moss was sure it was the FBI bureau chief. Might as well face the music, he thought. A tall dark skinned man got out from behind the driver's seat. He was wearing a black suit and carrying a small leather case. Dan decided to head over to the vehicle and introduce himself. How he hated these sorts of things.

"I'm Chief Dan Moss, Maryland State police." Dan held his hand out to greet his guest.

"Andrew Jackson, Federal Bureau of Investigation," was the greeting from the new arrival. Andy looked at Dan whose hand was extended and gave him a handshake that Dan would say felt like holding a dead fish. "Fill me in," Andy said.

Just as Dan thought, the FBI was on the scene and all will be solved. What an asshole, Dan thought. He turned and walked toward the tarp that had covered the body on the pavement. Jackson was now talking to one of his agents as he followed, when Dan turned and addressed him.

"My team has the room closed off and our CSI guys are up there gathering evidence. It appears we are dealing with a murder. The perpetrator may have used a chair in her room to break the glass before tossing her out. Maybe he hoped to make it look like suicide." Dan stood waiting for a response but Andy just stared at him.

"Is that it?"

"No, that's not it!" Dan was really pissed now. Who in the hell did this shit think he was. "We were on the scene in less than five minutes. This is our case. Do you understand?" His face was flushed and breathing hard. He wanted to scream.

Andy looked at him with a puzzled glare. "Sure, this is your case," He answered. "I'm just here to observe. We have a protective detail that the director and I are involved in. I need to make sure your case doesn't affect ours. I need to get with my team and see what they have. I'll be back with you after talking to them." Andy walked away and left Dan standing alone, flabbergasted.

What a sarcastic asshole, Dan couldn't believe it. He thought about the FBI bureau chief's name. Does he think he is special because of that name? Wonder if he's any direct descendant to former President Andrew Jackson. The chief remembered back to his American history classes. President Andrew Jackson, known as Old Hickory, was a bloody fighter in the Creek Indian wars. He was also known as an asshole to many. He caused a major split in the Democratic Party when he went head to head with John Quincy Adams. Often portrayed as a crude bar brawler, it would follow that this FBI guy would be related to him. Maybe he comes from a long line of assholes.

Dan shook his head as he made his way back to the crime scene. He walked toward a group of men near where the medical examiner was talking pictures of the dead body. He didn't quite know what to do.

The FBI bureau chief had gone into the Medical Center.

Dan stood among his men pacing. All of a sudden he yelled, "It's my case". The men standing near him jumped as they heard Dan holler, with fist clenched starring into the dark night. He blurted out, "The FBI sucks," and walked away.

Blair had now been talking to Robert for about a half-an-hour before Andy arrived. When he walked into her room, Robert jumped up.

"Sir, I was just telling Ms. Adams that you would be here to take over the investigation." Andy smiled, and moved into the center of the room.

"Hello Blair."

Robert was surprised to hear his chief call her by her first name. Blair returned the smile and gave him a kiss on the cheek. "Long time since I've seen you," She said. "Guess it was in the hospital in Arlington."

Andy smiled. "I didn't know if you would remember me. I know you had so many members of the bureau on the scene that it must have been confusing." Andy looked at Robert and asked. "So tell me, what's the status out there?"

Robert planned to fill his chief in. Before he could answer, Blair said, "Seems that the dead girl was tossed out of the window right below mine." Andy looked at Robert. Blair knew too much already. Robert just shrugged.

"Yeah, it appears that she might have been strangled and tossed out of the window," Robert added.

"I sent our men down to the investigation site to gather as much information as possible. The victim is a young blond woman who had been in the Medical Center for a few days. She had just been moved to that room yesterday afternoon. I was concerned that someone might have thought it was Blair's room. It seems that the woman wasn't listed in that room yet." Robert was hoping that Andy wasn't going to blame his team for the incident. Andy moved closer to the window and watched as the State police continued their work below.

"Robert we need to put as much together as quick as possible," Andy stated. "If someone thought that they had gotten to Blair, they might still be around making sure that they had succeeded."

That made sense. Robert asked the chief, "How do you want us to proceed?"

"I'm going back downstairs and talk to the state police chief first," he said. "The guy seems to be freaking out, and I need to get him on our team."

Andy didn't plan on getting into the case with Blair, but now he didn't have a choice. She obviously had probed Robert for answers and now he needed to fill in the blanks.

"Blair, once I get some information from the State Police, we'll sit and talk."

Andrew Jackson had been with the bureau for close to twenty-five years and knew that local and state police often felt threatened by bureau officers. He hoped to calm down Chief Moss. He also knew he would have to eventually deal with the name thing. It always came up. He wished his parents weren't such history buffs. His dad was a college professor and loved American history. Hence the name for each of his two sons became Andy and Jessie. His brother always got weird looks when people met him. Better to be named Andy then Jessie he thought. When he reached the scene outside two State police officers approached him. "Can we help you?"

"Yes, I need to talk to your chief."

The two officers were surprised at the request. In the past when the FBI was involved, their agents never asked, they just demanded. Andy had been in the Washington Bureau for a few years and never had worked with the Maryland State Police before.

"I'll get him for you, Sir," One of the officers answered.

Dan stood talking to the officer who had delivered the message. He looked over toward Andy who was standing on the other side of the crime scene tape. What the hell is he after now? "Tell him, I'll be there in a minute," he told his officer. He had a few run-ins with the FBI guys and he was going to make Andy wait. After a few minute Chief Moss took a deep breath and strolled over to where Andy was standing.

"What can I do for you now," Dan asked. He was adamant that the FBI would not take over his case. His face was flushed and Andy could see that Dan's jaw was clenched.

"We might have connecting cases here." Andy started to tell him.

Yes, just as he thought. "Now just wait a damn minute," Dan blurted out. "I told you this is our case and I don't give a shit what you think!"

Andy smiled, and that seemed to piss Dan off even more. "Maybe we need to start over." Dan stood there, lips pressed together and eyes glaring at him. "If you'd just listen, you would see that we need to work together on this," Andy continued. "I'd like to have you come with me into the Medical Center so I can fill you in on our case."

Dan didn't know exactly what to think. The men standing around tried to make it look like they weren't paying attention, but they were eaves dropping in on the whole conversation. Andy waved to Dan to follow him. He reluctantly followed as both men headed toward the Center.

The two officers that were listening commented to each other, "Seems like the chief is about to blow his top." They laughed as they watched the two men walking into the Medical Center. They knew their boss, and he wasn't about to take any shit from the FBI guys today.

Andy knew that he had to get Dan away from the scene to share details of the situation. He usually spent time working with the Secret Service and other FBI bureau's, so working with the Maryland State police would be a little different. He also realized from earlier conversation that Dan wasn't fond of the FBI, so it would take a little extra effort to get his cooperation. The two men walked without talking until they reached the elevator in the west wing of the building.

"Dan, I'd like to give you some information, and I would appreciate if you kept it to yourself." He was hoping by making the first overture that it would set the tone for the conversation.

Dan seemed to be much calmer and surprised at the tone. He looked at Andy and asked, "Okay what have you got?"

Andy pushed the button for the fifth floor and waited for the elevator doors to open. "I want to introduce you to someone." The two men got into the elevator and headed up. When the elevator doors opened on the fifth floor, an agent greeted the two men with his gun drawn. "What the hell!" Dan jumped back.

"Everything is okay," Andy said to his agent. They got out of the elevator and headed down the hall toward Blair's room.

"You see Dan we have a special protection detail here. One of our agents that had been recovering for the past few months is a patient. The director wanted to make sure that she was okay and she was placed in the west wing of the Medical Center. It seems that there may be some people interested in hurting her."

Dan nodded as Andy continued his story.

"Have you heard of Ms. Blair Adams?"

"Yes, we know who she is," Dan responded. "I think if you asked anyone in the D.C. area who Blair Adams was, they would know the answer."

"Well when she was recovering after surgery in Arlington, it appeared that someone was in her room one night. We haven't been able to confirm that, but the director wanted to be on the safe side. She's been here for months without an incident. Your case seems too close of a coincidence to ignore." Andy had given Dan all the information that he would need to see why the cases might be related.

"I see," Dan answered. He felt like an idiot for his earlier response to Andy. "How can we help," He offered.

Andy was pleased that Dan was coming around. He turned to him and said, "I want to introduce you to her."

They continued down the hall and Andy greeted the agent that was stationed in front of room 505, Blair's door.

"She doesn't want any special consideration, but the director was insistent that we continue the protective detail."

They opened the door and Robert and Blair stood up. She had a yellow robe on and although she had been awakened by all the action below she looked great. Dan wondered how someone could look so good in the middle of the night.

"Ms. Adams, this is Chief Dan Moss of the Maryland State Police. Dan, this is my agent in charge, Robert Samson."

Dan shook Roberts hand and greeted Blair. "Ms. Adams my team of men would be very proud to assist the FBI with any mission that might be helpful to your safety." Dan Moss like many people had read the accounts of the bombing at Falls Church and the bureau's capturing the suspect.

She moved toward Chief Moss and clasped his right hand.

"I feel very fortunate to have so many nice looking men protecting me." She knew how to work the room. "I'm sure that I'm safe here, but having your team along does help me feel more comfortable."

Dan was immediately impressed by her. She had been sitting with Robert for quite a while since the flashing lights and glaring sirens below woke up everyone in the Medical Center. Blair had gathered all the details that the FBI had gotten from the state troopers on the scene. She had been made aware that the woman may have resembled her, and that all precautions were being taken to protect her.

"Chief Moss, have you been able to identify the dead woman?" She asked.

Dan was taken aback by her question. He didn't expect the woman being protected to want to start asking him questions. "My men have had her fingerprints confirmed and are in the process of contacting her nearest relative."

This was new information for Andy and Robert.

"What's her name?" Blair asked.

"Sandy Thorpe," Moss stated. "She was a patient in room 405, directly below yours."

"Was she married?" Blair was on a roll.

Dan Moss looked at Andy and then back at her. "Yes, it seems that she was just coming out of a nasty divorce. Her ex-husband had reportedly raped and beaten her sending her here to the Medical Center. The personnel said that they had moved her to the room below yours yesterday. She was in the emergency room before that."

"That's terrible. What a shame." Blair was still gripping Dan's hand.

"Ms. Adams, we will do everything possible to help clear this situation up," He told her.

"Thanks!" She moved back to where Robert was standing.

Dan had just told Blair everything that Andy had hoped to find out. Andy smiled. The director had told him that she was a very smart woman and more than extremely capable. Andy and Robert just witnessed her investigative skills.

Dan turned toward Andy and asked how his team could help.

Andy took a deep breath, "You can see that our concern was that someone may have assumed that the woman on the pavement below was Ms. Adams. If so, he or she might still be around, to see if they were successful."

Dan nodded. It all made sense to him now. The FBI was protecting Blair, and the woman below was in the same room number, just one floor below, and resembled Blair. It only made sense that they would think that someone was after her.

Dan stood and again extended his hand toward Blair. "We won't rest until we have all the answers on this, Ms. Adams."

Blair smiled and leaned in and gave Dan a hug. "Thank you," She said.

Andy thanked Blair for her time and said that he would walk with the chief back downstairs. They walked out of the room and headed back down the hall toward the elevator.

"You got a real smart cookie there," Dan said. "Just point her toward the case and she'll find out what you want to know."

Andy laughed. "Yes, she has been very easy to protect. Our men love this assignment."

"Have there been any incidents since she's been under your protection?"

"No nothing!" Andy answered. "We just don't want anyone to know she is here."

The two men headed back down the elevator to the ground level. Dan walked over to the crime scene that was still being worked by the state police. Dan called out to his men.

"I want you all to make every bit of evidence available to Mr. Jackson and his FBI team."

The two men stood talking for a few minutes then Andy headed back into the Medical Center. The local guys turned and laughed. What the hell happened? It was all yelling and the damn FBI, now they're working together? Wish we could get the captain to soften up like that with us.

Three

Moss and the Maryland State Police continued their investigation into the apparent murder of the young woman at the Medical center. Her ex-husband became the main suspect. Ryan Thorpe and his wife Sandy had a long list of marital difficulties. Sandy had a restraining order limiting her ex to be at least five-hundred yards away from her. Their divorce was a nightmare. Police records show many calls from neighbors because of loud fighting from the Thorpe home. Ryan had been released from jail just yesterday morning after the hearing and he posted bail. Records showed that bail had been posted at six p.m. That meant that he had been out of jail for about seven hours before Sandy Thorpe was killed. The CSI team placed Mrs. Thorpe's death around twelve-thirty a.m. That gave Mr. Thorpe plenty of time to get to the Medical Center.

Family members and friends were thankful that there were no children involved. So many times they begged Sandy to leave him. No matter what they said she always came back. It wasn't unusual for women to think that it would get better. Police often cited that it was difficult to get wives to press charges against their husbands. Neighbors knew that Ryan was trouble. His constant yelling often brought them out of the house to see what was going on. Records showed that many calls by them brought the local cops to the Thorpe door.

The state police were in contact with the local authorities and Dan had his men accompany the Bethesda Police to the home of Ryan Thorpe.

It was close to noon when the squad car pulled along Elm Street. Elm Street was in a beautiful quiet neighborhood with towering trees lining both sides. The entrance to the subdivision had a grand island with dazzling strips of bright blossoms, clumped together in enormous mounds. The sign at the entrance had a notice that a deaf child lived on the street, please drive slowly, it read. It was an idyllic area of Bethesda, Maryland. Records showed that Mr. Thorpe had a new yellow Hummer and it was parked in the driveway.

The Thorpe home was a small bungalow that sat about two hundred feet off the street. The front was brick veneer and had a large wrap-around porch. There was a large Oak tree in the front yard and two overgrown shrubs along the driveway. The large picture window off the porch brought a lot of sunlight into the home and offered a great view of the neighborhood.

Two officers approached the house cautiously hoping to question Mr. Thorpe. It was normal procedure to question the spouse first in this type of investigation. With the previous marital history it became more apparent that they needed to talk to Mr. Thorpe. He was their prime suspect. The officers knocked on the door and waited for an answer. It was close to five minutes without a response. The officer at the front door knocked again and called out to anyone inside. The other officer moved around to the side door as the first officer continued knocking on the front door. Just then shots rang out from inside, piercing the front door. The sound of bullets broke the silence of the afternoon. The trooper hit the ground and grabbed for his weapon. More shots came from inside and the officer that had gone around the side was on the radio calling for back-up.

The state trooper and Bethesda officer had moved away from the home and positioned themselves where they could cover both doors. A third officer was dispatched around the back to make sure that the person inside could not escape.

One of the police officer grabbed his car's radio and called it in to the Bethesda Chief. "Sir, we've got a situation here. Upon approach, someone inside the Thorpe home started shooting at us."

The local police chief was stunned at the events. He figured that they would question Mr. Thorpe and check out his alibi. They were also waiting to get a search warrant from the District Attorney. Now he had a situation with someone held up in the Thorpe home shooting at his officer's and the state police. They could only surmise that it was Mr. Thorpe.

Another call went out to Dan Moss from his trooper. "Boss we're at the Thorpe residence and someone inside is shooting at us.

If it's Mr. Thorpe, guess that answers our question about his involvement."

"Not too quick," Dan stated. "Let's try to take the person alive so we can sort this out."

"Yes Sir," came the trooper's answer. He relayed the message from his chief to the local police on the scene and said that they should wait for re-enforcements.

Just then the quiet suburban neighborhood came alive with the sound of sirens and flashing lights. It was like a scene from *"Law and Order"*. All that was missing was the SWAT Team. It seemed that only seconds had passed when three local police cars and two State troopers came around the corner. Neighbors came rushing out of their homes to see what had happened. Officers blockaded the area and warned people to stay back. Shots again rang out from the Thorpe house.

The lead state trooper now moved to the car closest to the home and called out with a bull-horn. "This is the Maryland State police! Drop your weapon and come out with your hands up!" His call went un-heeded.

Another trooper decided to try to move closer. He slid out around the side of his vehicle, and moved toward a large overgrown shrub along the driveway. Once he made it to the shrub he called back to the rest of the unit. "I've got a solid position on the north side of the driveway just past the Hummer. Let's get someone around the south side. We have men still in place at the rear of the home. We might be able to force him out." It looked like a good plan. Surround the home and the person or persons inside won't be able to protect all sides at once.

The local police chief had arrived on the scene. His officer filled him in on the events. It was becoming obvious that whoever was inside shooting at them was more than likely involved in the death of Sandy Thorpe.

Dan Moss was still at the Medical Center working with the FBI and he monitored the calls from his men at the Thorpe house. He would relay the new events to the Bureau's guys. If Mr. Thorpe had been involved in the death of his wife, it might help to let them know that there was no relationship to Blair being at the Medical Center and the murder of Sandy Thorpe. The Chief knew this information would be critical to the bureau.

The scene along Elm Street had now grown into a major confrontation with someone held-up in the Thorpe home. Both the state and Bethesda Police had moved into positions and had the home surrounded. It had been quiet for the past twenty minutes without any gunfire coming from the home. The Bethesda police chief was coordinating efforts with the state police to gain access into the home. There were now close to thirty officers from both units involved and local news team had taken a position just east of the blockade.

The evening anchor, Gina Warren was very popular with the viewing audience. Gina covered the viewing area from Northern Virginia to suburban Maryland. She was armed with a microphone and had her camera crew filming the events as they unfolded. Gina was a beautiful brunette who once was Maryland's representative in the Miss America Pageant. She had the highest TV ratings the past two years since she joined the channel 7 news team. Gina was in the newsroom when the call came in and she grabbed a camera crew and headed out to the scene. She would often handle stories that would normally belong to field reporters. Because of her ratings and the station now moving into the top slot in their market, no one questioned her.

The Bethesda Chief knew it was in his best interest to give the channel 7 team some sort of statement. He knew Gina, and figured that she wouldn't stop until she had something. He moved over to the position that his men had the news camera crew stationed. It was close to three-hundred yards from the Thorpe home and out of range of the shooter. Because of the tree lined street you could not see the home clearly from the position the news crew was assigned.

The Bethesda Police Chief was a veteran of the department. He had been acclaimed by the Governor many times for actions his department had been involved in. Gina saw the chief headed her way and she motioned to the camera team to get ready for a possible interview. "Chief, Gina Warren, Channel 7, can I get a statement?" Gina knew how to get her name and channel call letters into every interview.

"We have a situation that requires our officers to make sure everyone is safe and hopefully this could be solved with the least bit of problem." The chief wanted to give Gina some information without key details being released. He wasn't sure who was held up inside shooting at his men, and if it was Mr. Thorpe, how would it affect the possible murder case at the Medical Center. Defense lawyers were quick to get evidence tossed out because prejudice to a case.

"Chief, do you know who is held up in the home, and why they are shooting at your men?" Gina was hoping to get some answers for her viewers by questioning him.

He hoped to avoid giving her too much information. "Gina, our people were here to gather information from the owner, however we are not sure who is in the home or why they are firing at our people. I plan to get with our command team and if we have any more information I will be glad to share it with your viewers." The chief was back off toward the bank of vehicles that had been set-up along the perimeter of the driveway of the Thorpe home.

Gina and her film crew panned back toward the Thorpe home as she continued to give the viewers a recap of what was happening. The house was tucked into the trees from her vantage point but she did the best she could with limited view. Although she only had little more information than when she started, Gina Warren tried to give her viewers a thorough picture of the events. She opened with the following description. "We are positioned outside of a residence here in Bethesda on Elm Street. The Bethesda and State police have come under fire from someone inside and have surrounded the home, hoping to get the person to surrender. We aren't sure if it's a hostage situation, but we will keep you aware of the action. We also know there was an incident at the Bethesda Medical Center that may be related." The camera team panned toward the home as Gina continued. "Our channel 7 team will stay out here as long as necessary to keep you informed until the situation is resolved; this is Gina Warren, channel 7 news team."

Gina knew that until other stations arrived she had the scoop. It was her interview with the police chief that was first on the scene, and she would remind viewers of that throughout the day. Gina saw some neighbors standing a few feet behind the blockade and she headed toward them, hoping to gather more information.

The neighbors were watching the police who had surrounded the Thorpe home. When Gina and her camera team approached they were thrilled with the prospect of being on television. "Hi, Gina Warren, Channel 7 News," She stated. "I was wondering what you know about the people who live in the house across the street."

Gina hoped that this was a typical neighborhood in the suburbs and everyone knew everybody else's business.

"Oh boy, do we," Answered the first woman. "The Thorpe's moved in a few years ago, and it seems that every week since there has been a police car in their driveway breaking up a fight. We feel that their marriage was destined for disaster." Gina could not have been happier. Now she had enough information to keep her viewers riveted while the action stalled at the house.

The local chief was working with the state troopers on the best way to get the shooter out of the home without incurring more gun fire. The state police had a SWAT team with a mechanical battering ram on the way. They could use that to break down the front door without anyone being in the line of fire. Once they rammed the front door the person inside would see that their options were limited and possibly surrender. The chief ordered his men to move the channel 7 news crew back a few more feet, for their own safety. He also wanted his men to push the road block out around the perimeter. Keeping everyone safe was a main concern of his.

When a large black SUV pulled around the corner on Elm Street the crowd buzzed. It was a very impressive with large lettering announcing the arrival of the State police SWAT unit. The camera team from channel 7 captured the arrival for its viewers and Gina was quick to update the information and make sure she was being filmed with the SWAT vehicle behind her.

The lead State trooper was meeting with the chief and the SWAT team leader. They discussed the option of using the mechanical robot battering ram. The team leader had his men fan out around the home as he ordered the back of the unit to open and unload the robot. The mechanical robot was four feet tall and close to three feet wide. It looked like something from *Star Wars*. Some of the children on the block murmured that it was CP3O from the

Star War's movies. Residents knew that it was getting out of control if SWAT had to be called in.

The chief wanted to make another approach to the person inside the Thorpe home before they made any other decisions. One of his troopers was still in position under a large shrub in the driveway and another of the officers had moved behind the Hummer. He called to the trooper in the driveway. They hoped that could he make contact with the shooter. The trooper responded that they haven't had any communication with the person or persons inside.

The chief got on the bull-horn and called out to the home once again. "This is the police, we have you surrounded and you need to drop your weapon and come out now!" There was no response. He called out once more, but to no avail.

He ordered his men to move closer without putting themselves in the line of fire. As they approached, there was no action coming from inside. The police knew that they had the house completely surrounded and no one could have escaped. It had been a long time since the last gunfire had taken place. The trooper in the driveway started to crawl closer to the porch. He was able to shield himself from the front door and picture window as he moved within ten feet of the home. He was armed with both tear gas and mask. He called back to the chief that he was in position to toss a tear gas bomb into the home.

The chief wanted to get the robot into position before continuing the assault. He gave his orders and passed the information to the rest of the team. The mechanical machine was now in front of the porch and the troopers were ready to make their move. One more call to the person inside and then they would charge. No answer from the house and the plan went into action. The trooper on the ground in front of the home heaved the tear gas devise toward the front picture window and rolled over under the wooden lip of the porch. The front window shattered as the tear gas canister broke through the window pane. The fumes quickly consumed the home and on-lookers could see that smoke was coming out from the front of the home. The robot rammed through the front door and smoke poured out onto the street. There was still no response from inside. A second tear gas bomb was launched into the house.

They wanted to end the stand-off before dusk. This had already turned into a nightmare that the officers wanted to end. Getting the person inside to surrender had not worked. The assault on the house was their only option.

The chief ordered his team along with the state troopers to advance. The trooper who had now moved under the lip of the porch was in the best position for the assault. Three officers moved in toward the back of the home, as two more men moved around the side entrance. The plan was to rush the house from all three sides. The robot was their battering ram and the SWAT team moved into the front door to protect the men coming in behind. There had not been a response for close to an hour from inside and with the interior filled with tear gas the officers felt it was time to make their move.

Officers and troopers busted in the side and rear door of the home as four men moved onto the front porch behind the path that the robot took. The robot had smashed in the front door and gave the officers a clear opening into the living room. Tear gas mask had been issued to the men so that they could enter the without ill effects. Gina had her camera team squatting to catch the home assault on film and it would be on the channel 7 news all night. It would be picked up by the network and CNN. They carried the action with Gina telling viewers what was happening. Channel 7 and Gina Warren would be on every channel.

Once inside they found the body of a middle aged man lying on the living room floor with an apparent self-inflicted gunshot wound to the head. He was lying on his left side. Blood was spattered all over the living room wall. The officers proceeded with caution. No one was sure how many people had been in the home. One of the officers moved close to the body and rolled him over. His face was pale, almost transparent; his eyes were glazed and wide opened. The men didn't disturb the body further until the chief arrived.

The report went out to the Bethesda Chief that one person inside was found dead. The television camera crew had focused its lenses on the front of the home, as Gina continued to update her viewers on the action that was taking place. The chief moved from his position to the driveway of the home. He ordered some of the men to retreat and inspect the perimeter of the home for any additional evidence.

The house was a small three bedroom bungalow. There were a week's worth of newspapers and take-out wrappers scattered all over the floor. It looked like someone hadn't cleaned for weeks. Neighbors had said that Mrs. Thorpe had moved out two weeks ago. The officers searched the remaining rooms for any other suspects or if the shooter had a hostage. None were found. The chief entered the home along with the lead trooper. It was now clear that the suspect that was on the floor was the one that had been shooting at them.

The front living room glass had been broken out and the tear gas had been defused with the flow of fresh air that entered the home. The man on the floor looked to be around thirty-five years old and there were two rifles near the front door and a handgun at his side. It appeared that he shot himself sometime before the tear gas had been catapulted into his home. The gunshot wound was from under his chin to the back of the skull. Blood was on the wall opposite from him and his hand still held the handgun. It looked like a 9 mm. The chief bent down to search the man's pockets for any identification. His wallet was located in his left rear pocket. He opened it and read the name on the driver's license, Ryan Thorpe. The dead man and the picture on the license confirmed that it was Mr. Thorpe. Part of his skull had been torn off from the bullet when he shot himself.

The chief ordered everyone out of the home so that a CSI team could gather any evidence necessary to close the case. Although they did not know for sure, it appeared that Mr. Thorpe might have killed his ex-wife who was recovering at the Bethesda Medical Center, then killed himself once the police came to question him.

The State trooper called the details into his chief who was still at the Medical Center. Chief Moss nodded when he heard the information and headed into the Medical Center to update the FBI with the news. He knew they would be watching the special report that was covering the action. It was hard these days to keep anything quiet with 24/7 news teams and people that had Smart Phones to capture and send images immediately to news organizations. It was a technical world and the police had to deal with it.

Four

Chief Moss headed back into the Medical Center. This time he had key information to give to the FBI that hadn't been on the news. He stopped to talk to his team that had kept the area corded off until the forensics team had completed their investigation. After talking to the head of his CSI team he walked toward the Medical Center and got into the elevator. He was again met at the on the fifth floor by an FBI agent. "I need to see Mr. Jackson," He stated. So much had happened in such a short time.

The agent remembered the chief and directed him down the hall toward Blair's room where Andy had been talking to Blair and Robert. The agent called ahead to Robert to make him aware that Chief Moss was headed down the hall.

Robert opened the door of Blair's room and waited for him to enter. "We're in here chief," He called out. Moss continued walking toward room 505 and Andy Jackson told Robert he would talk to the chief in the hallway. Blair already knew too much, and he felt it was better to find out what the chief had to say first.

"Andy, I have information that you'll want to know. It appears that we have wrapped-up our case here at the Center. Our men headed to question Ryan Thorpe about his wife's death. Upon their arrival, someone inside the Thorpe's home started shooting at them. After a few hours of a standoff, they rushed the house only to find that Mr. Thorpe had taken his own life. It's pretty clear now that Mr. Thorpe was here late last night and killed his wife. We know they had been going through a nasty divorce, and once our team headed to his home to question him, he had no way out, so he killed himself. Our CSI team also found Mr. Thorpe's fingerprint in room 405."

The news was good for the FBI.

He continued. "Once our CSI team found Mr. Thorpe's fingerprints in his wife's room and on the chair next to her window we were sure that he committed the crime. He wasn't a very smart man."

Andy was relieved to hear the details. He was pleased that Dan was personally delivering them. Maybe that's all it was, a domestic dispute. The FBI investigation had found that Mrs. Thorpe had been admitted through the ER department. She had been in the emergency room for an apparent assault by her ex-husband. She was first put in another room on the 4th floor before being moved to room 405. The move to 405 was about six p.m. last night. There was no guard on her room because Mr. Thorpe had been arrested and was in jail for the assault. They didn't know that he had posted bail earlier. With the CSI team finding Mr. Thorpe's fingerprints in her room, it was confirmed that he had been on the scene.

Andy planned to call the new information in to the director after he met with his team, and now he could complete his report. He had kept John Martin aware of the events and he was glad that everything was over. Jackson couldn't believe that it was just a coincidence that a woman resembling Blair was killed in the same area of the Medical Center as Blair. Her room had been just below Blair's. Andy thanked the chief and walked with him back to the elevator.

"If we could be of any assistance to you in the future don't hesitate to call," Andy told him.

The two men shook hands and nodded. Chief Moss was surprised that everything had gone so well with the FBI and that the murder at the Medical Center might be wrapped up so quickly.

"I've got to ask you one more thing!" Moss asked.

"Sure," Andy answered.

"Hope this doesn't seem like a dumb question. With your name and all, are you related to former President Andrew Jackson, by any chance?"

Andy laughed. "I get that a lot, especially from people that are history buffs. No, not related, just parents that were had a weird sense of humor. My father was a history professor at Georgetown University. I never got too many questions until moving to the Capitol."

Both men had a chuckle and headed off in opposite directions.

When Blair got the news from Andy, she understood the aspects of the domestic issue and how it exploded into the murder. It was a sad situation but at least it was nothing that involved her being at the Medical Center. She wished that these sorts of things didn't happen but it was part of life today. It was nice to know that she had been at the Medical Center for such a long time without an incident. Robert was relieved with the news. He dreaded that something had happened on his watch. He normally was off duty at noon but stayed until the situation was resolved. The twelve hour shifts at the Medical Center had gone so smooth for months and the news that Blair was being released in a few days had him on edge. Now that everything had been cleared-up he could go home.

Jackson contacted the director and finalized his report. John Martin said he had been watching CNN and realized that the action wasn't related to his team. He was glad that the local police hadn't revealed that the Bureau had been on the scene too. Blair would soon be headed home to California in two days and her protective duty would be the assignment of the Los Angeles Bureau Chief.

Andy told Blair that his team would still be in place and stationed outside in the hall if she needed anything. "You shouldn't be bothered after this. I hope you will call us once you're settled in back home."

"You know I will," Blair answered. She expressed her appreciation for all the time and effort that his team had devoted to her. "I wish you didn't have to be here, but it has been nice to have your people around. Maybe once the director sees that no one is after me after all, he'll call off the protective duty."

Blair's thoughts again would be on packing for her trip home to California. She would need to find a new apartment and get her furniture out of storage. Her parents said that they planned on coming out to help get her settled in. Blair was looking forward to seeing them. Her mom had been at the Medical Center constantly until she knew that Blair was fully recovered. Going home to California and being back with her friends had been on her mind since arriving at Bethesda.

Blair smiled at Robert. "Bet you're pleased that this is almost over."

"You bet." Just then Robert got a call from one of his men downstairs.

"I've got a television reporter down here asking questions about why we're at the Medical Center."

Robert shrugged and said he would come down to talk to them. He headed toward the elevators and traveled down to the first floor. As the doors opened up on the main floor he could see an attractive lady and her camera team at the end of the hallway. Robert's first thought was what a looker. He moved over to where the young woman was standing. Gina Warren was indeed a looker. Her long dark hair flowed to the right side of her face and she was wearing a tan skirt with colorful scarf. Her matching jacket was buttoned but you could see the top of her pink blouse peeking through. She was talking to the men stationed near the entrance. She had drawn a crowd, and Robert was sure it had everything to do with her looks. He strolled toward the reporter.

"Hello, what can I do for you?"

"Gina Warren, Channel 7 news team!" she said. Gina was the consummate professional. Cameras were rolling and Robert hoped that it wasn't being sent live. He had been able to thwart off other reporters before so he was confident that he could do it again.

"Yes, Ms. Warren," He said. Robert did not plan on telling Ms. Warren his name. Better leave that off, he thought.

"Our viewers have been aware that there was a shoot out at a home in suburban Bethesda, and it may be related to an FBI situation here at the Medical Center."

Gina was a real news hound, and if there was a story to be had, she would dig it up. Gina had done a story on Blair Adams last fall when Blair was still at the Arlington Hospital. Although Arlington was not in their normal news coverage area, Gina knew that the story in Northern Virginia was big. Gina had won an Associated Press award for that coverage and it helped propel channel 7 into the top slot in the market. Time had passed, and the FBI had moved Blair so the story fell out of the headlines.

"This problem was a local issue Ms. Warren and the FBI was here as a courtesy to the Bethesda and state police. There are many military personnel here at the Medical Center we were called in to consult on the action here. We were here as guest of the state police, that's it," Robert stated.

He hoped that he could deflect her questions and by referring to the Medical Center as home for recent Iraq war veterans that sustained injuries, he thought it would give a solid reason for the FBI involvement.

Gina was not buying his answer. She probed further but Robert offered nothing more. She would try to get information another way.

"If this is over why are you still here at the Medical Center?"

Robert said they were completing paperwork and would be leaving once the state police wrapped everything up.

"Thank you, what did you say your name was Agent?"

"I didn't say." Robert headed back up to Blair's room to say goodbye. He figured that she probably needed to rest. He knew he sure did.

"I'll see you in a few hours," he told her. Robert was finally able to head home. He made sure the rest of the team was aware of the news crew downstairs. He told them that they needed to keep the fifth floor access off from visitors. Robert headed back downstairs and to his vehicle.

Gina and her camera team were out filming the side of the Bethesda Medical Center. They were capturing the 4th floor window where Mrs. Thorpe had been thrown out. Gina of course was in front of the camera as she gave her viewers the picture of events at the center that led to the confrontation at Mr. Thorpe's home. It was clear that she was not going to give up on why the FBI was there too. She was now able to give her audience the full picture. The events at the Thorpe home were now tied together with the previous events and Sandy Thorpe's death at Bethesda Medical was complete.

Robert made sure that Gina saw him getting into his vehicle. That should help his story that he had given her. As Robert pulled away he took one more glance at Gina. Pretty hot, he thought. Bet she gets a lot of information from men.

Gina had moved toward the team of Security Guards from the Medical Center that still had the area barricaded off. It was the only assignment that they had been allowed to do. She would try another angle to find out how the FBI was involved. This time Gina told the camera crew to hang back. Gina hiked her skirt up a little and opened her jacket. She was wearing a bright pink silk blouse and showing enough cleavage to entice any man. She moved over to one of the security guys that were standing near the barricade.

"What happened here?"

When he turned around you could see that his eyes took her all in. It must have taken him five minutes to answer her. His eyes danced over her beauty as he stumbled for words to say.

"Miss, someone was killed here during the night." The man was definitely looking directly at her bulging chest as he answered. She made sure that enough cleavage was showing to get his attention.

Gina had a live one. "Killed, how terrible! How did it happen?"

This was great he thought. He could keep this pretty thing around for a long time giving her the whole story.

"Me and my partner found her body. It seems that her husband snuck into her room and tossed her out of the window. We got him though. You never can get away from us." He was feeling pretty proud of himself. He hoped his buddies saw who he was talking to.

"Did you catch him here at the Medical Center?" Gina was probing for more information.

"No, we got him at his house. The dumb shit killed himself once we showed up."

Gina was set for the kill.

"Are you with the state police or the FBI?"

He shook his head. "Neither one. We are the security team here at the Medical Center. Them FBI guys didn't do nothing." His chest was pushed out as he boasted about the role he played in all the action.

"Why were the FBI guys even here?" She inquired as she moved closer to the officer.

Gina could hear him breathing hard, they were so close. He leaned down to whisper to her.

"Seems they have some real special person here that they were all worried about. Our boss just told them to say the hell out of our way."

Gina had the information she hoped for. She planned to head back into the Medical Center and find out what the FBI was really up to. "Thanks so much," she told the security guard. "I'm glad we have people like you to protect us."

"Names Bobby, Bobby Conway. If I can help you just let me

know." He was very proud.

Gina waved as she strolled away and smiled. She motioned for the camera crew to follow. She headed to the main office. Last year there had been a story at the Medical Center. She ended up with an exclusive story regarding the deplorable conditions that the soldiers returning from Iraq had when being treated. Her contact was a doctor that fed her information to break the story wide open. Gina hoped to use him again. When Gina and the camera crew made it to the entrance, the lady stationed there figured that it was related to all the action near the west wing.

"Yes, can I help you?"

"I'm here to see Doctor Kelly."

Doctor Kelly had been an Army physician stationed at Bethesda for the past five years. He tried to bring some changes to the conditions that enlisted men had in the wing designated for them at the Medical Center. After several failures he contacted Gina, knowing that she might be able to bring attention to their plight. He was a good Doctor and cared for his patients.

"Doctor Kelly isn't on duty today," The receptionist answered. "He won't be back at the Center until Friday. His rotation is four days on and three days off."

Gina was stumped. She needed someone on the inside to get her into the west wing, or get the information she needed. She didn't want to give-up but it was getting late and she could still get back to the station to be on air and cover her big story. Doctor Kelly would be her Friday mission. Gina knew she had one story in the bag and another one in the bush.

"Let's get back to the truck," she told her team. She would view the footage they had in the truck and see if they could put it together on the trip back to the station.

Gina had the scoop on the story of the day, maybe the story of the week. She had footage of the standoff at the Thorpe home, and the material from the Medical Center to put the whole story together. Of course she was the only reporter to get an interview with the State police before the shoot-out.

Her camera team had some great film when the police stormed the Thorpe home, and they also had some footage of Mr. Thorpe's body being taken from the home. This was a neat little package. She planned to be back at the station and be on air to detail the whole thing. Gina smiled as she entered the station.

"Great Job," The station manager said as he saw her enter the front door.

"Thanks, Boss," Just doing my job.

Gina knew she had the station manager wrapped around her little finger. After all she put their ratings in first place.

She hoped that she could get more information about the person at the Medical Center but now was the time to air what she had. Gina always made a great impression on viewers. Of course she was very good looking and always seemed to have critical stories that caught everyone's attention. The lights were on and cameras were rolling as Gina stood in the limelight and spun the story for the viewers.

The story would be in the headlines for days.

Five

Blair was happy with her choice of where to live. The move back to California had gone well. She had been in the apartment two weeks now and getting used to everything. Her parents helped get her settled in and had gone back to Alabama a few days ago. Although she had lived in Santa Monica for six years, Marina del Rey was where she found her new apartment. It was within a-half-mile walk to the beach and she could ride her bike to Santa Monica to visit friends. It was another beautiful day in Southern California and she planned to walk to the beach.

The events at Bethesda Memorial were just a blur and she was grateful for all the great friends she made while recuperating there. Robert Sampson was able to keep Gina Warren and the channel 7 News crew from finding out that she was the one recovering at the Center. It was lucky that she was only there two days after the events of the murder on the floor below her. She made sure that the director knew how super Robert Sampson and Andy Jackson had been during the two plus months stay. She never told her parents about the murder the last week she was still there. No sense giving them something else to worry about, she thought.

Andy Jackson was aware of Gina and channel 7 and they would continue their quest for a story but his team was able to cover the details of Blair's stay at the center. Blair had called to thank him once she got back to California.

Blair checked her mailbox before heading down the staircase. There was the usual junk mail and an official looking letter. She looked at the return address. It was from FBI headquarters, and the return address was the J. Edgar Hoover Building in Washington. Maybe this was her new assignment. She opened the letter immediately as she stopped on the stairway. She had been waiting to get some information on her assignment. At least now she might finally find out what she would be doing. She stood on the landing and opened it.

Dear Blair,

I hope your new apartment is working out well and the move went smooth. I'm sure you kept up with the trial for El Yawer. We were pleased that he was sentenced to life without parole. He is in a maximum security prison in Kansas.

It is hard to believe that he had escaped from New York and was able to track you and Allisa down. Your team did a great job capturing him at the motel in Virginia. I know you will be safe now.

I talked to Allisa's mother the other day and she mentioned that you call her often. I know that Allisa would have appreciated that. We will never forget her.

I want to meet you in Los Angeles at the FBI field office and introduce you to Steve Orrison, your new Bureau Chief as soon as you're ready. I'll talk about your assignment then. Steve will be contacting you soon.

Sincerely,

J. F. Martin

John Franklin Martin
Director, Federal Bureau of Investigation
Washington D. C.

Blair read the letter over again to see if she missed anything. She wished that the director gave her more information on her assignment. She often talked about her first assignment with Allisa when she was in training. Guess all new agents start off doing research and background checking, she was told. It was hard to believe that Allisa was dead. Blair blamed herself for the events of the abduction. She was determined to be a good an agent.

She put the letter in her windbreaker pocket and headed toward the beach. The walk would be good she thought. She had seen a notice that there was going to be a sailboat race today from the channel. Blair hoped to catch a glimpse of the boats heading out to the ocean.

The cool breeze along the Marina helped the fleet of sail boats that were maneuvering into the channel. It was the annual regatta, and residents of Marina del Rey lined both sides of the channel. Each year the regatta seemed to grow. The estimate for this year's race was close to fifty boats, and they were moving from the channel to the opening to the Pacific Ocean. The channel was almost three miles long, and the wall of rocks at the end protected the fleet from the oceans waves. There were walkways along both sides of the channel and you could see people walking their dogs, bicycling and jogging along the path. Marina del Rey was home to North America's largest man-made small craft harbor with more than five-thousand-three hundred pleasure craft.

It was a normal June day in Southern California. The sun was starting to rise and a slither of pink sky had appeared on the eastern horizon. The wind off the Pacific Ocean had greeted tourist walking along the boardwalk. Blair stood alongside the edge of the channel and watched the fleet. Their sails were engulfed by the breeze, as they opened to show their beautiful colors and designs.

She moved closer to the edge of the shoreline as she watched the fleet assemble in the channel. Blair was finally home. It had been over a year since she had been on the beach.

People would often stop and stare at her. She had the looks of a Hollywood starlet. Tourists were always on the lookout for someone famous. She often wore a baseball cap when out of the beach to ward people off.

Blair and Hunter had moved to California so she could pursue a career in acting. Her career was like many other hopeful's that traveled to southern California. She appeared in some commercials and magazine ads, but like so many; it took part time jobs to keep her dream alive. She found a job working as a bartender in Santa Monica. It was a great place to work. Two other bartenders were also pursuing careers in acting and they all helped cover shifts if an audition came up. Although she was only five foot four inches tall, she had strong features and lovely short blond hair. Her deep blue eyes reflected the pools of water washing ashore from the Pacific Ocean. Her features reminded people of a young Sharon Stone. Like so many young hopeful women who headed to Hollywood, Blair was beautiful. She had worked at The Pub in Santa Monica, along the promenade, with her new friends Ashley and Meagan, who were also pursuing acting careers.

Blair and Hunter enjoyed the grand life that California offered. She had grown up in Georgia and Alabama, and her parents were supportive of her move to California. When Blair and Hunter moved into their apartment they had to make sure they could afford it on his military pay and her part time bartending job. The Pub was located on the promenade and it was the perfect location. She could walk to work and take the bus to Culver City, where many of the studios were located. Although she and Hunter had a vehicle, most people used mass transportation in the Los Angeles area. Parking was a nightmare and the cost to rent a parking space made it prohibitive for them to have two vehicles. The freeways were always crowded, and for someone new to the area, they could be confusing. Hunter was often away on missions with the United States Army's Special Forces and being close to everything was important to her.

Blair watched the fleet now making its way through the opening from the channel into the Pacific Ocean. Their sails were fully opened and the collage of colors was breathtaking. The palm trees that lined the channel bent gently in the oceans breeze. It had been a long time since she was able to enjoy a simple pleasure like this. Her new apartment was along the edge of the channel, and she could stroll from her building to the channels path that led to the strand of beaches. She walked toward the beach as she continued to watch the regatta moving into position. She was armed with her digital camera that her dad had bought for her. She hoped to get a few good pictures to send to her parents. The beach was just about a half-a-mile from her apartment building.

She slipped her sandals off when she hit the beach. The grains of sand between her toes felt great. The sun had raising high over the ocean as she continued along the path. She could see the sailboats lining up in formation as they prepared for the race from the Marina Harbor to Catalina Island. She had been to Catalina

Island with Hunter, the last time he was home. It was close to fifty miles off the coast and offered both day trips and impressive overnight stays. She loved hiking and Catalina was great for that.

Large waves came crashing to shore as she made her way down the beach. The white surf was bubbly as it came rushing to the shoreline. The waves cascaded over the rocks that protected the harbor. The beach was dotted with beautiful homes that faced a million dollar view to the west. The opening from the marina to the ocean had a wall of rocks that kept the channel protected from the crashing waves. Surfers were paddled into the ocean, hoping to catch a great ride on the white rush of water. She continued to watch the line of sailboats as she walked along the strand of beach. You could see all the way to the mountains of Malibu from the shoreline. The view was striking. She made her way along the sand toward Venice Beach.

She was lucky to find her new apartment in Marina del Rey. Most of the places she had looked at were out of her price range, but the Mariners Village offered a great location at a price that she could handle. New FBI agents didn't make that much, and if she planned to continue in that career she would have to make sure that she could afford the rent. She was always concerned about being safe, and the Mariners Village had a full time guard that was stationed at the entrance, near the parking structure.

Her apartment was on the second floor and she could see the channel from the deck. On the other side of the channel you could see the planes taking off from the Los Angeles airport. The runways from LAX sent the planes out over the Pacific Ocean and they curled back over land to head to their destinations. Her mom and dad had helped her move in and they would sit out on the deck in the morning and have a cup of coffee and talk. Blair's dad was always up early and would make a pot of coffee for himself and read the L.A. Times on the deck. Pretty relaxing, he would say. Blair appreciated their help, and felt that they had a special relationship. Her furniture had been in storage and getting it settled in took help. Her mom was good at that sort of thing and they enjoyed doing it together.

Once her parents had left, Blair tried to put some of her personal thing away. They were things that she had been putting off since coming home. There were two small boxes stacked in the corner of her bedroom next to a small marble table. She had avoided looking in them but felt that she needed to handle the contents. The top box was the first one to draw her attention. When she opened it, one set of Hunter's uniform was on the top. Dress blues neatly pressed and folded. A shoe shine kit and a Smokey the Bear Hat were just under the uniform. It was clear that Hunter had packed the box. Everything was neat and folded in a military fashion. He was always careful with his army uniform and military equipment.

Hunter never talked about the war. On occasion, if they were walking on the beach at night, he would mention some aspect of his time in the service. These were heavily guarded moments and you could see that they were hard for him to discuss. Tears ran down Blair's face as she ran her hands along the creases of the uniform. She had a solemn look on her face as she neatly packed everything back in the box. She decided to put the two boxes in her closet for now. It was harder than she thought. The box was put back in the corner on top of the second one that was still unopened.

Blair needed time, and now time was all she had. Her sadness was normal for someone so young to lose a spouse. The war in Iraq had left thousands of family members wondering why, why such a price they paid and how it seemed for naught. She knew Hunter loved the military and was proud to be a soldier. She was proud to be his wife and everything he had done.

The director promised Blair that she could take as much time as she needed to get settled in. He was hoping to capitalize on her fame and Hollywood connections to help recruit other women to the agency. The FBI knew that with the recent turmoil in the world that it would need more agents and women offered them a great new opportunity. Many were college graduates and had bi-lingual skills that were in high demand. Using her in commercials and personal appearances would help him with his plan.

His plan was to have her work with the new Los Angeles Bureau Chief, Steve Orrison, once she was ready. Steve had been appointed to L.A. Bureau chief from Seattle. He was instrumental in helping uncover a major drug ring that was operating along the Canadian border. The director knew that Steve would be able to utilize Blair's fame and intelligence to help the agency grow its ranks.

It was a perfect day to walk along the shoreline. Blair knew her dad loved the walk to the beach. She wished they could have stayed longer. The sun was high overhead and the temperature was hovering around the mid-seventies. There wasn't a cloud in the sky. The panoramic view along the coast looked like a postcard. It was the type of California day that you heard about in songs from *The Beach Boys*. So many people had moved to the state in the 1960's through the 1980's, with their own California dreaming, that the influx almost tripled the population during that time period.

The beach was crowed and tourist had gathered to watch the start of the Catalina sailboat race. She didn't realize that there was a race today when she first left her apartment. She had been working all week to get settled in and needed to take a break. She figured the walk would be just the thing she needed. As she passed the group of sailboats and headed north along the beach she spotted a group of young men carrying their surf boards. She always wished that she had the nerve to try surfing. Her fear of the ocean kept her from trying. Hunter had attempted to teach her but she never could get passed the fear of the crashing waves and what the ocean life held. As a kid her parents would take her to the beaches in Florida but she usually stayed close to the shore or in the pool.

A group of young men were waxing their boards as she approached. One of them looked up and smiled at her. She returned the smile and continued along the path. Don't look back she told herself. He was cute! There were so many cute guys and each one of them seemed to have the same look. It wasn't hard to miss that California look, bronze bodies, well built and blond streaks in their hair. She had gone about fifty feet past the guys and slowly turned back to catch another glimpse of the surfer. He was entering the water, and just then seemed to be watching her. Blair felt a rush of emotion that she hadn't felt in a long time. She smiled to herself and continued along her walk.

Marina del Rey was just south of Venice Beach. If you were looking at a map, you would see the coastline dotted with Malibu to the northern edge followed by Santa Monica and Venice Beach. Many movies had been made along that strand of coastline. You could close your eyes and see the Beach Boys in your mind, singing Surfing USA, or Annette Funicello and Frank Avalon running into the surf.

Blair heard that MTV was filming last night on the corner of Washington Avenue and Venice Beach. It seemed that there was always something happening. There were roller bladders, bike riders and joggers that occupied the walkways that connected the cities along the beach route.

She planned to walk to the pier that was about two miles from the channel. The breeze was warm and the sun was in her face as she continued along. She had taken a few pictures of the sailing regatta when she first got to the beach and looked at them in her view finder. My mom will love these she thought. Blair remembered that whenever they traveled anywhere her dad would always take a thousand pictures. She was happy that he had taken so many pictures of her and Hunter, when they traveled out to see them. Her mom had a special album made for her with many of those pictures.

Her mother and father had been very supportive through all her turmoil. They had been in Arlington for the FBI graduation ceremony and with her when she was in the hospital recovering from the bomb blast. Her parents accepted the award from the president and director, recognizing Blair for her heroism. She promised herself that she would keep in touch with Allisa's mother in New York. She thought about Allisa and Hunter as she walked along the shoreline.

The Marina del Rey pier was just a few feet away and she was surprised how quickly she walked there. It was the first time she had walked all the way to it and from the edge of the channel it didn't look this long. It jotted out about five-hundred feet into the ocean and seemed to have a small building at the end. She moved onto the pier and saw that there were benches along the sides about every twenty feet. Men were fishing off the sides and families seemed to gather near a spot a few feet ahead of her. She stopped to see what they were looking at. There was a school of dolphins that were playing around the pier's edge. Blair could see that children were tossing food to them and every once in a while one of the dolphin would jump out of the water to retrieve the treat. Everyone was snapping pictures and the children were laughing with glee as the dolphin continued to amuse the crowd. She smiled at a little boy who was standing next to her. He was so cute and seemed to be having the time of his life, she thought.

It was now clear that the building at the end of the pier was a small snack bar. As she got closer she could see a window where you could order food. The sign above the window announced the menu's fare. They had ice cream, soft drinks, snacks and sandwiches. There were chips and cookies hanging in packets near the opening. The small sign on the window announced the daily specials. Today's special was ham and cheese sandwiches or grilled burgers. The building was rectangular in shape and you could walk around the back side and watch the water as it crashed into the end of the pier. There were some small picnic tables built into the side of the pier for guest to eat the food that was purchased.

Blair stood at the end of the pier watching the sailing regatta as the lead boats disappeared from her view. The race to Catalina Island was around fifty miles long and the southern breeze offered a great start for the sailboats. The majesty of their sails with the multitude of colors was almost mesmerizing. She set the focus on her camera to telescopic and was able to bring the colors into view. She snapped a few pictures and was pleased with what she was able to capture. The brilliant yellow's, reds and blues of the sails puffed out in full grandeur, dotting the ocean for as far as you could see. She turned toward the small pier restaurant and decided to get a drink.

"Can I help you?" The voice from the window stated.

"Yes, I'd like a bottle of water please."

"That will be two dollars."

She put her hand into the pocket of her beach jacket and pulled out a five dollar bill. She gave it to the young man and took the bottle of water. He handed her the change and she moved back down the pier toward one of the benches along the sides. Blair sipped her water and focused her attention on the surfers that she had spotted on her walk. They were riding the waves that came crashing to the shore. She could see the young man that she had smiled at, and he was now standing on his board, maneuvering the white cap that carried him to the shore. "Wow, he's really good", she said, as she drank her water. The walk made her thirsty. Two children ran past her yelling back to their parents.

"You need to hurry, there are dolphins in the water," They were telling their parents.

Blair laughed as she watched them bubbling with excitement at their discovery. She could remember doing the same thing when her parents took her to Florida. It seemed like just yesterday when she first saw a dolphin off the pier in Destin, Florida. It was exciting then and still is. She got up and started walking back toward the beach. Guess I need to finish putting my clothes away, she thought, as she got to the sand. The walk back was refreshing as the sun was at her back and the breeze cooled her. She was approaching the area where the surfers were just coming back to shore.

Blair tried not to stare at the young man that had smiled at her. He was picking up his surfboard. Just then he turned and caught her eye.

"How are you doing?" He was unhooking his wet suit and smiling at her.

"Pretty good," She answered.

The surfer was even better looking up close than she first thought. He was maybe five foot ten and had a little stubble on his face. His blond hair was short and it was easy to see that he was in great shape. His body was evenly tanned and he appeared to be very muscular. He laid his surf board down and moved closer to her. His wet suit was unhooked over the left shoulder, and he was releasing it on the right side. He grabbed a towel off a small blanket that was about three feet from her. "Do you surf?" he asked.

"No, I love watching, but never gave it a try." Blair looked down at the sand as she answered. She didn't realize that she was avoiding eye contact.

"My name is Connor," He stated. He extended his hand out to her.

"Hi!." She didn't want to give him her name. He had a great smile that was inviting and his muscular build was a plus.

He continued to dry himself off with the towel and said, "I'd be happy to teach you. "I've been surfing for quite a few years and it is really a lot of fun."

"I'm sure it is, but I have a lot to do this afternoon and I was just taking a break."

"Do you live close by?" He questioned.

"Not too far away," she answered. "I hope you enjoy your surfing," She continued, "I'm on my way to meet some friends."

Blair was always careful and didn't want to let him know that she was alone on the beach. She had promised the director that she would be careful. He was still worried that someone might be after her, but she was sure that he was wrong. She learned that when Hunter was on a mission, letting people know that you were alone would be a mistake. Her FBI training had also made her suspicious of strangers. You never know what someone may want.

"Have a great time with your friends," He said. "I'm out here every day about the same time. If you're ever interested I'd be happy to teach you to surf."

It all seemed very innocent; after all she was staring at him. Blair thanked him and continued toward the walkway along the channel. She knew that she shouldn't turn back to check him out. She made it all the way to the walkway and leaned down to slip her sandals on. She peeked back while sliding them on, and saw that he was getting his surf board and clothes together. It appeared that he was also leaving the beach. She sighed and started walking down Via Marina Street toward her apartment in the Mariner Village.

The apartments were located along Via Marina about a block off the beach. The street stretched along the strand of beaches toward Lincoln Boulevard. It was a peaceful area that was home to some of the best surfing in Los Angeles County.

It didn't take too long to leave the sand and head down the path back to her apartment.

Six

The stroll along the beach was great and the scenery was awesome. She kind of chuckled to herself as she strolled back along the path inside the gated area. The last of the sailing regatta was near the end of the channel and she watched the crew hoisting the final series of sails. How beautiful she thought as people waved at the crew. She wished that she had a chance to experience the gliding of a sail boat along the oceans waters. Her friend Tommy at the Pub had often invited her but she had this fear of the ocean. That was something she planned to conquer.

The final few yards of her walk led to the main gate of the Village. Many of the streets along Via Marina were named after islands in the Pacific Ocean. The names conjured up images of palm trees blowing in the breeze. Bora Bora Way and Tahiti Way crossed Via Marina just past her apartment complex. To the south, the Marina opened up to one of the largest fleets of privately owned sailboats on the west coast. Via Marina winded through a maze of flowering trees and beautiful landscaped shrubs. Tall palm trees dotted the entrance to her apartment complex just past a huge waterfall. The entrance was always dotted with flowers freshly planted each season.

The guard at the entrance smiled at her as she flashed her residence pass. He was tanned and wore a khaki uniform complete with safari hat. She was sure he had been in the sun way too long because his face had a leathery look and heavy lines across his forehead. The small guard shack had a post that blocked the entrance until the guard raised it allowing you to enter. If you were walking you entered through a path that was lined with beautiful flowering shrubs that ran next to the guards shack.

The management made sure that only residents and guest were allowed in. With three swimming pools, Jacuzzi's and the amenities offered at the Village, they wanted to keep non-residents out. With the close proximately of the beach it was important to keep a guard on duty 24/7. Her vehicle was parked in the complex garage that was tucked under the buildings.

She took the note from the director out of her windbreaker pocket and read it again. She was hoping that she missed something that would give her a clue to her new position. Blair wanted to be involved in some real work not just be behind a desk in the L.A. Bureau office.

Blair headed up to her apartment to take a shower and planned on going to Ralph's. Ralph's was the closest grocery store to her apartment. It was located on Admiralty Way about a mile past the Cheesecake Factory. She had walked to the Cheesecake Factory with her parents the last night they were in town. Her dad loved cheesecake and her mom loved the salads there. Marina del Rey had a lot of specialty shops around the marina, as well as three or four nice grocery stores. She loved the bakery and seafood shop at Ralph's. Although her favorite place to shop for food was the new Whole Foods on Lincoln Avenue near Santa Monica. When she went there with her mom, her mom loved to go to the .99 cent store next door to Whole Foods.

Steve Orrison was sitting at his desk in the new FBI field office, located in downtown Los Angeles. The Bureau's office on the corner of Wilshire Boulevard was just off California Highway 110. It was strategically located, and made it easy to be in contact with local officials. You could walk down the street to the Los Angeles Civic Center and City Hall. The Justice building was next to the new headquarters and Los Angeles police department was just one block to the west. The FBI building was at 11000 Wilshire Avenue, and housed one of the largest FBI field office in the country. There were ten satellite offices in California counties surrounding Los Angeles. Steve had been appointed the L.A. Bureau chief in March after fifteen years in Seattle.

The Los Angeles office often coordinates efforts with other law enforcement agencies and helped establish the Joint Terrorist Task Force. They recently made the news with its chemical explosion dog, Disco. Disco is a yellow Labrador Retriever. Disco has been seen at such prominent events like the Academy Awards, the Super Bowl and the Golden Globes. Steve had a special team of handlers that works with Disco and the Joint Terrorist Task Force assigned to him. The exposure he had in the Los Angeles Bureau was much greater than that of the Seattle office.

Steve was having a hard time getting use to sunshine every day. Los Angeles was so different than Seattle. In Seattle the absence of the sun from the sky was a daily ritual. You would rarely see rain in Los Angeles versus rain being an everyday event in Seattle. It was funny not to see an umbrella rack in the office. It was a normal part of every office decor in Seattle. His office was located on the twenty second floor of the FBI building. He could see all the way to Dodger Stadium from his desk. He told one of the women in his office that the view alone was worth the move to L.A.

The Federal Bureau of Investigation knew that the growth of the population in Southern California would make the LA Bureau critical in law enforcement. The Los Angeles Bureau's office was staffed with over five hundred and fifty agents, and an enormous support staff. The Los Angeles FBI office had the third highest number of field agents in the Bureau. The office covered the geographic area south from the United States border with Mexico, and north to San Luis Opispo, California.

The San Francisco Bureau covered the Northern part of California to the Oregon state line. Steve was working in consort with his counterpart in the San Francisco Bureau. He also coordinated efforts with the Phoenix Bureau. The Western part of the United States continued to have large growing population issues, and with that comes more crimes. Drug traffic was always an important issue, and all the agencies made sure that they alerted each other to possible problems along their borders. Steve's experience with drug trafficking along the Canadian border helped in his new appointment.

The Los Angeles Bureau had been working on a very important case with the bureau's office in Las Vegas and the agents there. It seemed that a group of businessmen from Atlantic City had purchased the old Frontier Hotel and Casino's property. This group had also recently opened a new casino in downtown Detroit and was rumored to be looking at other locations. The Casino in Detroit was the fourth new casino that downtown Detroit had built. Together with Caesars of Windsor, the Metro Detroit area had five casinos.

Downtown Detroit had undergone some dramatic changes to its landscape. Along with the new casino's, there was two new sports stadiums, and the Renaissance Center which was the home of General Motors. The Renaissance Center was composed of five tall skyscrapers that lined the waterfront and offered a centerpiece for the revitalization of the area. Many prominent people had been involved in the project to rebuild the Detroit waterfront including former Pittsburgh Steelers Super Bowl star Jerome Bettis. The city had been suffering with the current recession and the projects along the waterfront were a great shot in the arm.

Recently the two local sports teams, the Lions and Tigers were doing well and their success on the field meant more visitors to downtown. With more visitors came more money in the casinos coffers. All the casinos now had hotels to go along with the gaming property and often had full occupancy especially on game days.

One of the brothers, Omar Ellis had a suite in the Marriott hotel that was located in the Renaissance Center. He stayed there during the opening of his new casino. The local FBI Special Agents, Brian Sikorski and Frank Lemke, had run information for the director that might become useful in the pending investigation. Omar Ellis had now moved back to Atlantic City but would still return to Detroit every now and then to keep an eye on the new operation. The Ellis brothers were originally from Canada and the Provincial authorities were cooperating in the investigation.

The FBI had the two proposed owners for the new Vegas casino under surveillance for years. Omar and Salem Ellis were originally residents of Toronto, Canada before moving to the United States. There were suspicions that the men were financially supporting a prominent Senator. There were also rumors that a senate investigation was in the works. Efforts to uncover information and key documents or leads had been futile. If there was a tie-in to a corrupt politician the bureau hadn't released that information as of yet. There was big money in legalized gambling and having a key vote when measures that supported gambling came up was critical to the growth of that industry.

The Justice department along with the FBI had been investigating the organization's including some new casino's in Phoenix, Arizona. Possible implications of a Supreme Court Justice and Senator being involved caused concerns all the way to the White House.

The Nevada Gaming Commission didn't have enough evidence to stop the sale of the Hotel and Casino to the two businessmen. Steve Orrison knew the importance of working with other bureau offices. When he was the bureau chief in Seattle, he worked with the Canadian authorities in thwarting drugs from being distributed across the US and Canadian border. Together with Vancouver authorities, his office was able to infiltrate the drug underground, and made the largest arrest and confiscation of drugs ever along the border. The director knew that Steve was the right person for the L.A. Bureau and problems that the office faced.

Steve was in his early fifties, and he had been with the bureau for close to twenty five years. His record was outstanding, and he had been successful in every position that he had been appointed to. Steve was married for close to fifteen years, and had two daughters. He grew up in Flint, Michigan and joined the Bureau after graduating from the University of Michigan. Steve's first appointment was in the Washington Bureau's headquarters as liaison with the Justice Department. His degree in Criminal Justice made his appointment an easy choice. The FBI Director at that time took many suggestions from Steve, and his rise in the bureau followed. The appointment to bureau chief in Los Angeles was one that Steve had earned, and the president was pleased to have Steve in that position.

Steve was happy that his family had finally moved into their new home in the Los Angeles area. They settled in the hills, east of Los Angeles, near Pasadena. His wife wanted to make sure that their two daughters would be able to attend the same type of school's they had in Seattle. Steve's wife, Sue was a stay-at-home-mom. Steve had to do a lot of traveling, so Sue felt it best for her to be with the kids. Steve liked it that Sue was always with the girls. The girls seemed to be enjoying their new surroundings. Pasadena was a well established area and all the places they had in Seattle were available in their new neighborhood.

It was understood that the Los Angeles Bureau would have to handle some public relation issues due to the proximately of Hollywood and its efforts to depict the Bureau in some movies. The appointment of Blair Adams to the L.A Bureau seemed to be the sort of thing that would help in these efforts, Steve figured. Steve knew that the director planned to assign Blair to his office, and that she was going to be involved in a special mission to help the Bureau recruit prominent women to join the FBI. He had not met her yet, but knew of her involvement in two highly prominent cases. She had made headlines in both the case in New York as well as the events in Michigan. Steve hoped that she would not be a distraction to his team's main goals.

The director told Steve, that once Blair was settled in her new home that he would get them together. Steve was also to make sure that Blair had 24/7 security at her home. Steve arranged to have the Mariners Village allow his team to use a vacant area as a satellite office. They could guard Blair and continue normal operations along the coast. The men assigned to protect her would also handle other duties from that site. Blair was not aware of this special protection assignment. Steve hoped she would not find out. The director hoped this special assignment would be a temporary thing.

The plan was to introduce Blair back into the Hollywood community. If the director could get her on the afternoon television talk-show-circuit, bringing-up the opportunities that the FBI offered, maybe the bureau's recruitment numbers will pick up. The hope was to bring both more educated women and bi-lingual people into the organization. Blair's fame and good looks made her the best candidate for the job.

The director knew that Blair had been through a lot in the past year, and he wanted to make sure she had enough time to address her personal needs. He never gave her an overview of what her assignment would be, just that she would be back in Southern California. That was her request when she agreed to the FBI training program.

Blair liked her new apartment. It was close to shopping and the beach, two things she loved. Her old apartment in Santa

Monica was on the Promenade, and she could walk to many restaurants and shops within a few blocks. The Mariner Village was virtually on the beach, with a few restaurants within walking distance. You could also walk to other small places near the marina. There was a small store in the complex and it had a great deli. Blair had met the owners and loved the sandwiches and specialty pizza they made.

Blair headed down to the parking garage to her car. Hunter had bought her a VW Beatle convertible and she sold it when she came home. It had been sitting in the storage for almost eight months and just reminded her too much of Hunter, and made her sad. It was time to move on she thought. She found a cute two seat convertible that she fell in love with when her parents had visited last month.

"You know it can be hard with a two seat vehicle when you have friends visiting," Her dad had said.

"Yes, but your MG is a two seat vehicle, isn't it?" She had him there.

"I know, but we also have a Jeep to use when you come to visit or were moving large items." He was back peddling and soon gave in to her choice.

Her dad was probably right, but that little two seat convertible was just calling her. Anyway, how often did more than one person ever come out to see her? She didn't admit to him that it was a real pain while moving. Either you had the top down and a few boxes on the passenger seat, or some items in the trunk with a lamp on the seat next to you. It was silver with red and gray leather seats. It was the perfect California car for a single woman.

She planned on heading to Ralph's for some groceries after visiting with some friends. She pulled out of the garage and headed toward the gate. Blair waved to the guard at the entrance and turned onto the road in front of the Mariner Village. She slowed at the stop sign and saw a young man putting a surf board on the roof of his car. She watched and saw that it was Connor, the guy she talked to on the beach. She smiled to herself as she pulled off toward Ralph's. He sure is cute she thought, and then she laughed as she headed toward the store.

She turned right on Admiralty Way and headed into Ralph's parking lot on the north side of the street. She wanted to purchase a bottle of wine to take to Linda's house. Linda had been so great during her move, and Blair appreciated all her help. Linda had let Blair stay at her apartment while her furniture was being delivered, and with it being only a few blocks to Linda's from the Mariners Village, it was easy to walk back and fourth if needed.

Linda was her good friend and the two would do anything for each other.

Seven

The events at Bethesda Memorial were still fresh in the news when the story began to break about an investigation regarding one of the more prominent U.S. Senators. The evening Washington Post had released some information that was leaked to them. Every news team would be in the Capitol tomorrow to cover the story. Channel 7 and Gina Warren would be there too.

The Washington Monument stood out like a beacon of truth in the foreground as the press waited for the Senator to make his way to the hastily called press conference. It was a series of leaks that had them now waiting for the Senator to make his appearance. It was already one-thirty and he was over a half-an-hour late. The pending story was too big for the press to give up. Albertson's press secretary had told them that he would be holding the press conference at one p.m. In the past it had been unusual for the Senator to be late, but lately it seemed that all his appearances were late. With the current investigation by the Senate sub-committee on finances underway, rumors were escalating and Senator Albertson was now main the focus of the investigation. There was also an investigation into other public officials relating to Albertson's case.

Channel 7 news team was also on the scene. The station manager had sent his best reporter, Gina Warren to the Capitol, to see if she could land the lead story for the six pm news cast. She had covered stories from Northern Virginia to the suburbs surrounding the Capitol. Gina was the stations star reporter. Her addition to the news team brought their ratings to number one in the market. Gina and her camera team had been waiting in front of the Senators office for close to an hour and hoped to get some inside information. Her news chief knew that she had many male friends in the Senate chamber and could use those relationships to get an exclusive.

Albertson's aide had told her that he would try to get her an interview in return for some favorable press. She knew the aide, Corey Hart, from interviews in the past and he always tried to get her in to see his boss. She had always been fair, but never swayed from the facts. If there was a story she was determined to get it. She had done a nice piece on the Senator last year after his re-election, and his aide had hoped to piggyback on some of the facts from that interview. He had given Gina a few questions that he hoped she would use them along with any that she wanted to ask. She thought there was an unusual relationship between Corey and the Senator but almost everything in Washington politics was unusual.

Albertson sat behind his dark mahogany desk. His office walls were covered with plaques and awards from his years in the senate. A pen set, gift from former President Bush, adorned the center of his desk. He was talking to his attorney and best friend. He was obviously agitated as his attorney explained the process of the pending investigation. His face was flush and he lit another cigarette. He was in his early sixties and had receding gray hair. Even as a young man he was never in great shape. He was a large man, close to six foot two inches tall and slightly overweight as well as a heavy smoker. His eyes had bags and dark circles under them and he looked like he hadn't gotten a good night's sleep in a long time. Albertson wore a dark gray suit and the usual blue striped tie. His white shirt looked a little like it had been slept in and Gina could see from the outer office that he somehow seemed different.

"Senator, we need to go out there," His aide warned. "We're already late, and if we have any hope of early favorable press we need to go out there and talk to them." Albertson's aide was very close to him. They had been together for a long time and he wanted what was best for his boss.

The Senator knew Corey was right. The press in Washington had pissed him off lately and they always were quick to jump on rumors. He wanted to tell his side, or at least the side he wanted people to believe. He also hoped that he could get the press off of him and onto something else. If he could get his side of the story out sooner than the six o'clock news, maybe he could sway public opinion his way. His aide had planted some information earlier that showed that the Senator was working with the special committee and was actually helping the case. His aide had placed details hoping to deflect the news that was in the Washington Post article yesterday. That article tied the Senator to the gambling investigation that covered both the Arizona and Nevada Casino's in question.

"Senator, I have Ms. Warren from channel 7 in the outer office. She can help us by spreading the story of your involvement in the case as a material witness, not as a suspect." The senator's aide was working every possible angle to protect his boss.

"Okay, I'll meet with her then get out there and face the pack of wolves. You're sure she'll use some of the questions you gave her?" Albertson wasn't sure that she would be sympatric to his situation. Although the Senator knew Gina and liked her, the pressing case left him doubting that he would get any fair treatment by the press. He trusted his aide and his role in helping him. Gina had interviewed him in the past, and now he needed all the positive press possible. Albertson put his suit coat on and headed out of his office. How he hated this.

"Gina, how nice to see you," and he reached out and grasped her hand with both of his. Gina was pleasant on your eyes and always got great responses from members on Capitol Hill. She wore a black suit that revealed a little cleavage, and always made sure her interviewee got a glimpse of what she had to offer.

The Senator's eyes darted back and forth from Gina's cleavage to her beautiful blue eyes. He smiled and opened the discussion. "Gina, I want you to be the first one to know the whole story. Our committee has been working on an internal audit and although I'm not an official committee member, Senator Baker asked me to be involved. How this story came out that I'm being investigated is completely inaccurate."

Gina was surprised by Albertson's statements and her camera team ran their equipment as she waited for an opening. She thought that he looked unusually rough and she could see that the veins in his face seemed more pronounced than normal. "Sir, our viewers are wondering how your involvement with the committee can be viewed as anything but being under suspicion." Her informant had obviously linked the Albertson to the investigation.

Albertson voice was gravelly, and he quickly answered her.

"My involvement is as a courtesy to Senator Baker, not that of being under investigation. I understand that right now it is hard for the general public to see what is actually going on, but once the committee has gathered all the facts, you'll see that I will be exonerated of any wrong doing." Albertson smiled as the cameras kept recording the interview. He hoped that a smile would tell the viewers that he was innocent.

Gina sensed that he was slightly irritated and that if she pressed any further that he would just storm off. She had interviewed him before but knew today was different. She asked him one of the questions that his aide had given her regarding the party's leadership of the Senate. Albertson then tried to tell her that he was looking into special committee activities and deciding who from his party would be involved, especially in the stimulus plan the President had pushed through the Senate. Albertson was pleased that the question his aide had given to Gina was used. He could relax now, he thought.

Gina leaned forward and thanked him, and said, "I have just one more question."

"Anything for you, Gina," He said. Albertson's eyes again darted toward her supple breast as Gina smiled into the camera.

"Senator, with the pending investigation of your possible involvement with illegal gambling, do you really think that you're going to be involved in any Committee leadership plans?"

Albertson gave her a stern look. "I will always be involved in Senate leadership plans." He was irritated and started to push his way down the hallway. As Albertson stormed off Gina turned to the cameras to close the interview.

Gina planned to tell the channel 7 viewers what Albertson had stated, and that he was going to be asked to appear in front of the Senate committee tomorrow and it was his opinion that he would be vindicate of any wrong doing. She had some good footage of the Senator when he was talking to her outside his office that the station could piece into her coverage. She then headed down to the news conference to make sure nothing new developed before sending her story in to the station.

Gina noted that Albertson was starting his fourth term in the Senate and was now the ranking United States Senator. He had first won election in Arizona eighteen years ago. He had always run on a conservative platform and had been touted as a possible leader of his party. He was never married but early in his career was referred to as one of the more eligible bachelors in Washington, although he had never been linked to anyone in the past. He was also a very close personal friend of one of the members of the Supreme Court. They would often be seen dining at local Washington establishments. The Washington Post once questioned this relationship, but Albertson and Justice Leonard grew up a few miles from each other in Arizona and their friendship, although unusual, seemed to be that of two guys just getting together to eat. It all appeared normal.

During the last election, Albertson painted his female opponent as an extremist and questioned money that she received from a group lobbying for casino rights in Arizona. Albertson had always positioned himself as against gambling. Now with five new gambling places in Phoenix, some of his constitutes wondered how they got established without the Senators support.

Gina's information was that the Senate committee on financial affairs had received some information a few months back questioning Albertson's campaign money coming from groups that supported legalized gambling. The amounts discussed drew a red flag. If these allegations were true they had no choice but to investigate him. The Senator had recently built a new home on the edge of the Colorado River south of Lake Havasu City. The home was over four-thousand square feet and had a great view of the London Bridge. The bridge had been purchased by a group of local investors and used as a tourist attraction. The house he built had to cost well over five million dollars.

Senator Baker who had headed the ethics committee on the investigation did not want any of this to leak out to the press. How it did, meant that there was someone on the inside who was giving details out. Senator Baker was attempting to find out who had leaked the information to the media outlets. The committee was conflicted on the possible investigation of a Supreme Court Justice as well as Albertson. If they needed to go in that direction they plan to get the chairman of the judicial department involved.

Gina stood in the rotunda and watched as the Senator addressed the group gathered in the press area. She wondered if Albertson could hold it together. Just her few questions seemed to set him off. Albertson gave the group the same story that he had told Gina, that he was helping Senator Baker with the possible investigation. He made sure he was stern and again voiced his position of being a champion of the good people of Arizona. "I will always be there for our citizens," he told them. He was just finishing his speech when the reporter from the New York Times pushed his hand up.

"Yes, Sam, what can I do for you," The Senator had a big smile on his face. He felt it was going good.

"Senator, I have a reliable source that states you will be indicted by the Senate committee on internal affairs tomorrow for corruption in office. Do you have any comment?"

Gina kept her eyes on Albertson as he squirmed at the podium. Everyone thought he looked extremely rough when he first took the podium. She could see a vein bulging across his forehead as he looked intently at the audience. The crowd of reporters pushed closer and the Senator shifted from one side to the other and cleared his throat. The Senator's aide had pushed through the mob and was now just behind him.

Hands jotted in the air and reporters started barking out questions in unisons.

"Sir, any comment?" The questions could be heard from all around the room. From the back of the room came a yell, "Senator, Senator?" But Albertson was no longer looking at the group.

Gina could see that he was trying to gather his composure but the throng of reporters was circling him like vultures over their prey. His face was flushed, and Gina made sure her camera man moved as close as possible to capture the events. Corey tried to move in and get him off the podium, but his efforts were futile. Albertson raised both his hands and tried to get control of the group but they were all tossing questions at him. He tried to clear his throat again and started to cough. Gina saw him push back from the podium and turned to move away from the crowd when it appeared that the he slumped. His aide was now close to his side when the Senator turned and fell face first on the floor of the conference room.

"Give us some room," Yelled Corey. "Is there a doctor here?" He called out. You could hear the sound of feet running as reports pushed closer. There was confusion in the crowd as Albertson lay on the floor. Gina didn't know if he fell or passed out.

The aide rolled the Senator over on his back and two security guards pushed through the crowd to assist his efforts. Another guard had grabbed the defibrillator that was on the wall behind the presentation area.

"Let me through!" he hollered.

The reporters pushed back but most of them kept their cameras rolling. She made sure her camera team pushed ahead to see if they could get a view of the Albertson on the floor. Gina planned to get her scoop regardless of the Senator's condition. She could piggy-back this with her interview earlier and ties it together in a neat little package for her television audience.

Two more members of the senate medical response team came running up and shoved their way through the throng of reporters. Lights from cameras filled the area and the security team tried to push the media members back.

The aide stood next to his boss that lay helplessly on the floor. He was sobbing as the paramedics continued to work on him. They ripped his shirt open and one of them had made a tracheotomy insertion into his neck. The second paramedic continued to perform CPR and the reporters could hear sounds of gurgling coming from Albertson. A team of men carrying a stretcher and life saving equipment came rushing through the crowd. It didn't look good. The two Capitol paramedics shook their heads as they moved away to let the team load the Senator on the gurney.

The news was breaking on the air reporting that it a fatal heart attack took the Senator's life. Gina would add details of the pending investigation by the special committee. Of course every station had the events on Capitol Hill as their lead story. But only Gina had the Albertson interview on tape giving her his side of the story. It would be in the news for days as the details of the investigation into Senator Albertson involvement continued. Channel 7 had the scoop and Gina was again the star reporter.

News of Senator Albertsons sudden death spread across the Capitol from both chambers to the White House. Senator Baker's committee had to deal with this as they planned to continue their investigation. Their information had Albertson linked with a group that owned casino's in many states including one in Atlantic City and the another one in Detroit. There was also a connection to a new casino that was being constructed in Las Vegas. This was the same group headed by the Ellis brothers, and questions remained about their involvement.

The evidence from the Senate committee investigation was pretty solid. They also knew Albertson may have been involved with other government figures. That information wasn't detailed enough and they needed to tie Albertson to his co-conspirators. They hoped to get more information to help their case. Now they would have to follow other leads without having the Senator to question.

Senator Baker had requested the FBI to check into Justice Leonard's financial information. Because Leonard and Albertson were together a lot, it was only natural to check out the Chief Justice. It was unusual for a Supreme Court Justice to be close to any Senator or House Representatives individuals, although they knew each other for many years before either were in their present position. Neither man was married, nor did it seem unnatural for them to get together, especially for dinner. Baker tried to keep the investigation quiet but leaks had gotten out.

The Director of the FBI, John Franklin Martin had given the lead on the casino investigation in Arizona and Vegas to Steve Orrison, and the Los Angeles Bureau team. He suggested that Steve plan a meeting in the Los Angeles office to put the combined efforts of the FBI into action. The death of Albertson and the public news of the senate investigation would accelerate that process.

John Martin was confident in his people. He wanted Steve to put a team together as soon as possible. Steve called his counterparts in Las Vegas and Phoenix and set up the meeting for Friday morning in his office with the director. Martin also told Steve to contact Blair to see if they could meet Thursday afternoon before the Friday conference. He told Steve that he had sent her a note regarding her new position in the L.A. Bureau. She might not have gotten it yet but he figured that it didn't make sense to make two trips to the west coast. John could introduce Blair to her new bureau chief and get her started in her new assignment.

There was no plan to involve Blair in any on-going cases.

John Martin's plan had been to use Blair to help improve and promote the image of the FBI. The events of her injuries in the motel bombing had him concerned about her future assignments. He wanted to make sure she was healthy before putting her in any assignment that may involve a lot of physical activity.

Blair had other ideas.

Eight

The meeting at the Los Angeles Bureau had been set-up. The bureau chiefs from Phoenix and Las Vegas were planned to arrive early on Thursday morning. The director was taking the red-eye from Washington's Dulles airport and planned to have Blair meet him. He hadn't told Steve his plans yet. His private jet would arrive in L.A. around ten a.m. Martin wanted to spend a little time with her before going to the bureau's office. He hadn't seen her since she left the Medical Center at Bethesda. He hoped to give her an idea of her new assignment so that the conversation with her new bureau chief would go smooth. He knew that Blair could be a little hard headed and in the past had taken measures on her own that might endanger her.

Blair liked the director. He had always been honest with her, and she hoped that she could convince him to let her get involved in a case as soon as possible. She had pretty much had her stuff unpacked and the move had gone well. She was happy to be back in Southern California. Maybe now her life could get back to normal.

Blair's trip to the grocery store was short. She just purchased a bottle of Chardonnay to take over to Linda's house. Blair and Linda became friends when they both worked at a local restaurant on the Promenade in Santa Monica. Their lives crossed paths so many times the past seven years and they had so much in common. She planned to take the bottle of wine and a dessert that she made to Linda and Raffi's.

Linda was a classy looking brunette who always dressed very stylish. She reminded Blair of a Hollywood star because of her style and air of class. Linda was always dressed smartly and her long dark hair was styled in Jackie Kennedy fashion. Raffi, her husband, was Lebanese and had always been smart when it came to business opportunities. He had great foresight and purchased a small store on the Santa Monica Promenade when they were just closing the street off to car traffic. Raffi thought that the area could become a great tourist attraction. He opened his jewelry store, Rafinity, on the Promenade twenty years ago and it has grown into a Hollywood legend. His designs would be seen on many starlets at the Oscar's, Academy Awards and at many elite parties. He always made sure that Linda had the finest jewels on when they went out together. Blair loved to visit their store. It was like a trip to Disneyland but better. Guess you had to be a girl that loved diamonds to understand it, she would say.

Their house was located along the channel and Linda liked to sit on the patio in the morning and watch the sailboats making the way in and out of the Marina. Today they planned to watch the return of the sailing regatta that had raced along the coast line to Newport. Linda became a real fan of sailing after watching crews making their way in and out the channel. Linda met one of the owners at a Hollywood party once and they soon became friends. She introduced Raffi to Bill Starr and knew they all enjoyed the same things. Although Raffi was Lebanese, he also spoke fluent French. Bill enjoyed having someone to talk to in French.

Starr was a veteran sailor that had sailed all over the world. He was originally from Canada but lived a great deal of his life in Sidney, Australia. Bill had many adventures and Linda found his stories fascinating. Linda and Raffi had sailed with Bill to the Mexican coast a few months ago. It was a great trip. She planned to introduce Bill to Blair with the hope that they would become friends too.

Bills' boat was a forty foot sailboat that raced weekends along the Southern California Coast and to Catalina Island. It was a French built Beneteau 40.7' Polars and usually ran with a crew of ten sailors when racing. Bill had taken Linda and Raffi on a sailing voyage after they first met to Newport Beach, and they had a marvelous time. Linda knew Blair loved Catalina and hoped that Bill would be willing to take all four of them on a trip there. Linda was hoping that by introducing him to Blair that they would hit it off. Never know what might happen, she thought. Blair hated it when one of her friends set her up with a date, but Linda was special. If she thought that Bill would be someone Blair would like, Blair was willing to at least meet him. Drinks and dessert at

Linda's would be a safe.

The ride back to the Mariners Village gave Blair time to decide how to handle meeting Bill Starr. It hadn't been that long since Hunter's death and Blair had no interest in dating. She was just getting settled back in California and hadn't even met her new bureau chief. Too many things going on to even think about dating she thought, as she pulled into the parking garage. The guard at the gate was surprised to see her returning so quickly. It seemed that she had just left. She was always surprised when the guards seemed to be aware of the tenant's travels.

Her parking spot was under the Mariner Village apartment building. She loved her new car. It wasn't really new, but it was new to her. The Mercedes two seat convertible was the perfect car for a single girl in Los Angeles. It was deep silver. It handled great in traffic and LA was all about traffic. She would have to take Highway 90 to the 405 North then east on Highway 10 into downtown when going to the Federal Building. Her car was pretty good on gas and easy to park. She planned on calling the director on Monday to set up a meeting in the bureau office downtown next week. She was pretty much settled into her apartment and ready to get to work. It was kind of exciting to think about working, especially after being off for so long after her hospital stay.

The bag that had the bottle of Chardonnay was on the passenger seat. She also had picked up some appetizers so that she could make a Mezza dish for Raffi. Mezza was a Lebanese tradition when having guest over or just to set out to snack on. Raffi would tell his friends that Mezza in Lebanon is to eat a feast. In doing so, it evokes a sense of a celebration. The idea is to share with friends. He loved to have a little Mezza plate when he came home from the store. Blair had some Kibby, Greek olives, feta cheese, humus, tabouleh, vegetables and pita bread. Blair's mom had given her a plate with sections that would be perfect for the Mezza tray. Blair was familiar with the tradition because her dad's parents always set out a similar tray when they came to visit. Mediterranean food had grown in popularity, and many guests at Linda and Raffi's enjoyed the traditional meal. Blair was happy to be allowed to make it for today's guest.

She loved ethnic traditions. Many of her new friends were from other countries and learning about their traditions and customs was always fun. Her friend, Jennifer, was from Normandy, France. She met Jennifer while moving into her new apartment. Jennifer's apartment was on the floor below Blair's, and they seemed to be at the elevator at the same time every day. Blair's mom made dinner for the both of them a few times while she was still there helping Blair move in.

Jennifer was the marketing manager of a famous French surf shop that had expanded into California. She lived in the Village apartments for about a year and was teaching Blair French. Jennifer said that she hadn't found any American food that she liked. Blair had taken her to some of her favorite places and Jennifer had finally found some things that she felt good about. There was a Cuban restaurant on Venice Boulevard that they both liked and of course Bay City Italian Deli on Lincoln was a big hit. They both loved Sushi and there was a great little place, Hama, in Venice Beach off of Main Street and Windward Circle.

She had called Linda to ask if it was okay to bring Jennifer along. Linda told her that was fine. Linda had met Jennifer before at Blair's apartment, and she knew that the two women had become good friends.

They planned to walk to Linda's from their apartment. Linda and Raffi lived about a mile away down the channel. It was easier to walk than to try to find a parking spot. She put the wine; dessert and Mezza try in a carryall bag and headed down the stairway. Jennifer met her at the first floor elevator and they headed out of the building together.

The walk along the channel was invigorating. It was close to 75 degrees and a light wind from the west had the tall palm trees swaying. The flowers that lined the channel were in full bloom. The brilliant colors of rose, pink and yellow filled the shrubs along the gated entrance to Linda's place. Blair stopped to take a picture of both of them with her new camera. It had a great timer that allowed you to get into your shots. The two smiled as the flash went off. "I'll email you a copy," she told her friend.

As they walked along she told Jennifer about the letter from her director. She was hoping that she would be able to meet her new boss soon. She had kept in touch with her friends from the FBI training and they had told her that there was an investigation in Washington regarding some political figures and gambling money. It looked like the LA Bureau would be involved. If there was a way she could help, she hoped Steve Orrison would consider using her.

The Washington Post headlines reported that Senator Albertson was a key figure in a possible scandal regarding gambling money and campaign financing. They also reported that a special committee was looking into other government figures involved in the scandal. The director of the FBI was furious over the leaks to the press. He ordered a full investigation into the senate probe and what they were planning. He had to stop the leaks so it would not compromise the case.

Senator Baker had a meeting with John Martin in the morning before the director had planned to head to the White House to meet with the president. The two men hoped to get a handle on the investigation and reel in the press leak as soon as possible. The president was perturbed about the leaks, and needed to be brought up to speed on the investigation since Albertson's death.

The Senate Judicial committee wanted to bury as much as possible due to Albertson's position in the party. The committee had two prominent Senator's in high places and they were meeting at the same time the FBI was meeting with Senator Baker.

One of the committee members expressed his concerns. "Christ, we have to get this shit off the front page as soon as possible. We can't have Justice Leonard involved in all this crap."

The former president had appointed Leonard and they were good friends.

Who knows where all this could go?

Leading members of the committee were frazzled. You could tell they were grasping at straws.

Steve Orrison planned on calling Blair to give her the details of the pending meeting in the Los Angeles office on Thursday evening with the director. Blair had just gotten to Linda's place and she excused herself to take the call.

"Hello Blair, Steve Orrison here. I'm looking forward to meeting you and putting your assignment in place. Do you know how to get to our office?" Steve hadn't talked to her before.

"Thank you, Mr. Orrison," Blair answered. "I'm very familiar with downtown and know right where the Federal building is located. What day and time should I meet you?"

"The director is planning to arrive on Thursday afternoon the sixteenth. My team will pick him up and bring him to the building. Guess if you got here around three p.m. we could meet and go out to dinner."

"Why don't I pick him up for you sir? I'm just ten minutes from LAX and I know the Director. We could head to your office from there." It became obvious to Steve that Blair was a take charge type of person.

"I will get back with you on that. I'll contact the director and get his flight plans and ask about your request. Maybe it might make sense if I send an agent to travel with you. I know the director doesn't like fanfare but I want to make sure your both safe." Steve wasn't sure about having Blair pick-up John Martin, but he would run it by him before giving her final confirmation.

"Tell the person to call me on my cell and we can meet before going to pick-up Mr. Martin. I don't have a land line just the number you called."

Steve agreed and said he would get back with her later in the day.

Blair headed back into Linda's and apologized for the interruption. "That was my new boss here in LA wanting to set up a meeting later this week," She told her friends.

Jennifer and Linda knew that she was anxious to start working. They also knew she would try to take on too much too soon. She was aggressive and very confidant.

Linda told them that Bill Starr was going to be a little late. Seemed he had to go to the Marina to check on his sailboat for an upcoming race to Newport Beach. That sounds pretty cool they said.

Raffi was walking in the front door when Linda had just placed the tray that Blair had brought next to his overstuffed chair.

"Blair, how good to see you," He said, and kissed her on the cheek.

"Raffi, this is my friend Jennifer. She lives in my apartment building." Blair knew that he would be impressed with Jennifer.

Raffi spoke French as well as Arabic and he and Jennifer would have fun talking to each other. She hadn't met too many people in California that spoke French. Most everyone spoke Spanish if they spoke another language.

"How nice to meet you," Raffi said, and took Jennifer's hand and smiled at her. She greeted him in French and his face lit up. They were both speaking so fast that Linda and Blair just looked at each other.

"Guess they don't need us anymore," Blair laughed

Jennifer and Raffi looked embarrassed but smiled at both of them.

The four of them had a glass of the Chardonnay and sat and talked. Blair thought how nice it was to have friends that had so much in common. The Mezza tray was a big hit and they all dug in without remembering that Bill Starr was still on his way.

"We better save something for Bill," Linda told them. Just then the bell rang and she got up to answer it. "Bill, glad you could make it," Linda said.

She guided him into the room and introduced Bill to her guests. Bill smiled and took a seat after greeting the girls and shaking Raffi's hand. He liked Linda and Raffi and enjoyed their company. Bill had been in the states for about four years. He knew a lot of French and he, Jennifer and Raffi had fun talking to each other. Linda and Blair asked if they wanted to be alone, and everyone laughed.

"Sorry."

"No, it's not your fault. Before you arrived Raffi and Jennifer were having a meeting of the United Nations. It appeared that the French had taken over Marina del Rey."

Everyone had a big laugh, and Raffi poured Bill a glass of wine. He picked up the remainder of the Mezza tray and they all moved to the patio that faced the channel and watched the rest of the fleet that had been returning from the morning's regatta. Bill told them interesting details about some of the vessels that were in the Marina and they all had a great time watching the boats and visiting.

"One day, I need to take you all out on my boat," He stated to Blair and Jennifer. "It's comfortable for a small group and we could sail to Catalina, if you would like." They all agreed that it would be very nice. "A weekend trip, maybe a Sunday morning would be perfect for everyone's schedule."

Bill fit in to the group very well and they all enjoyed the conversation, wine and appetizers. Blair was glad that she brought Jennifer along. The five of them sat on the patio until it got dark.
She made Linda promise not to tell Bill that she was in the FBI. Too many questions arose when you told people that you were an agent she would say.

"Guess we should go," Blair told them. "I've still got things to unpack and after the walk on the beach today I'm tired. The fresh air really gets to you."

Bill stood up and reached out to shake her and Jennifer's hand. "Very nice to meet both of you," He said. He then spoke to Jennifer in French and they smiled at each other. "I told her that it was nice to meet a beautiful French lady."

The two women headed across to the walking path along the Marina. Blair turned and waved to Linda as they rounded the bend. "I think he likes you."

Jennifer just laughed and they headed back to the Mariners Village.

Nine

The meeting with the director and her new bureau chief was all Blair could think about. She waited for the call with details on where and when to meet him. She knew that he would be traveling via private jet to LAX but she had never been to that area of the airport. She had pressed her blue suit after coming back from Linda's last night and thought that she would wear it with a white blouse. She wanted to make sure she made a good first impression on Mr. Orrison.

She was watching CNN. Robin Meade was recapping the events of the death of Senator Albertson and the rumors of a pending investigation regarding one of the Supreme Court Justices. The news was big, never had there been a Supreme Court Justice under this kind of investigation. CNN stated that the FBI was manning the probe of the senator and justice. The story went on to disclose a link to possible gambling and casino's interest in Detroit, Phoenix and Las Vegas. With Detroit's involvement and recent scandals with the ex-mayor, who knew what else could come about? Blair was happy that her bureau would be involved in the case.

Even if she was relegated to a desk job, maybe she could be doing background work on this. She planned on telling Mr. Orrison that she had some solid working knowledge of the Washington D.C. area since her weeks of FBI training there. She spent over two months in the Bethesda Medical Center and watched news cast. That helped her understand the cities that made-up the Capitol. Her two friends from training, Michele Kennedy and Bruce Sawdon had assignments in the Capitol. They were involved in cases and using the training that they all received. Now she hoped to be finally involved in some real investigative work.

Her phone rang and she grabbed it from her purse to catch the call. It was from her new chief. "Hello Sir."

"Good evening Blair, hope I'm not calling too late?" "No Sir, I'm watching the news."

"I'm going to have agent Booth give you a call to work out the logistics of picking up the director. He lives near you and I've set-up a code name for your assignment. I don't want to have any problems with either yours or the director's safety."

Steve knew that the director had been very protective of Blair since the events of Allisa's abduction and Blair's injuries in the motel bombing. Plus the FBI had often used code names for key personnel arrivals.

Blair was amused at the prospect of his reference to a code name for picking up the director.

"Yes Sir, I'm ready for the information."

Steve gave her the arrival details and agent Booth's phone number just in case. He then gave her the code name for the assignment. "Blair, the assignment will be classified as, Falcon."

She loved it. Now she really felt like an FBI agent. "I've got it, Sir. I'll wait for Booth to contact me. I'm looking forward to our meeting on the sixteenth."

Steve's first impression was good. Blair was all business and following his lead. Not a lot of explaining or questions to answer. Just the way he liked it. "See you on the sixteenth."

The LA office was teaming with anticipation. They were preparing for key meetings in two days with other bureau chiefs and the director. Steve had planned to bring in some of his seasoned agents for the meeting and had extra staff ready for security detail. He knew that the director would be arriving downtown via helicopter and landing on the helix-pad on the roof. Booth would fill Blair in on the mode of transportation once they got together. Can't have them driving through LA in the crazy traffic.

Blair hung her suit in the closet and planned on taking a stroll to the beach. She grabbed her windbreaker and headed to the door when her phone rang again. She thought that she hadn't had this many calls in a long time. "Hello."

"Hello Blair, Special Agent Brandon Booth here. Mr. Orrison told me to give you a call. I want to go over the details for Falcon's visit."

Blair was surprised at his opening. She answered quickly,

"I've got some of the information from the chief but he said you'd fill me in." Blair didn't want to appear that she was in the dark. Make the other person think that you know something and they often give you credit for knowing even more she figured.

"Good," Booth said. "Then as you know the director is arriving via private jet at ten-twenty-five a.m. I'll pick you up at your place at nine. I've looked up your location from the address that Steve gave me. I see that your complex is across the channel from LAX!"

"Yes, just down Lincoln, maybe ten minutes away."

"We'll park my car in the airport lot and after meeting the director ride the helicopter with him to the bureau's office."

Blair thought for a minute. *Did he say helicopter?* Thought we'd be driving. She didn't let on that she was surprised about the travel plans.

"That makes sense. I'll meet you downstairs outside my building. I'll let the guard know that you will be coming so that he will let you in the lot. Make sure you pull in the second entrance because it is closer to my place."

Booth was good with the plan. "Once we're done someone will get us back home," he finished.

Blair kept it all business. She wanted to find out where Booth lived and how long he had been in the bureau, but there will be time for that. After all, she was the new person on the block. She knew rookies were treated with mostly grunt work and chasing information to help seasoned agents with their cases. Maybe if she didn't act like a rookie, they wouldn't treat her like one. They said goodbye.

Just then CNN aired a special report. She forgot that she left the television on. After not having a TV for years, it was hard getting used to having one. Have to keep up with all the latest news from every source possible she figured.

The report was detailing that an unknown source had revealed that photo's of Senator Albertson had surfaced in a compromising pose with another man. The other person in the photos wasn't identifiable, but the source said they had other pictures that they would release later.

Holy shit! What a turn in the events. Who was the other man in the photos? She had been glued to the television. They were replaying the press conference that showed Albertson having his heart attack. The reporter, a local Capitol person, Gina Warren, had stated that the Senator wasn't married. She inferred that the Senator was close friends with Supreme Court Justice Leonard, also unmarried. Blair decided to call her friend, Michele Kennedy in the D.C. office to see what she knew. *This thing is getting very interesting.*

Michele was working in the District of Columbia's. office when her cell phone rang. *Who was calling her at work on her cell*, she thought. She took it from her purse and was happy to see Blair's number on the screen. "What's up?"

"My number one source, fellow agent Kennedy," Blair chuckled.

Both women laughed. They had formed a special bond during their FBI training. Michele helped capture the man who killed Allisa and blew-up the motel injuring Blair.

"How's it going?" Michele asked.

"My bureau is involved on this end in the casino investigation after Albertson's death. I'd like to be up to all the detail possible so that I can be part of the team."

Michele knew Blair was very competitive. They once raced for three miles with neither girl giving in. "How do you figure that I'm your number one source?"

"The way I hear it, Albertson and Leonard may be a couple, and if so, they might both have been involved in bribes from the casino lobbyist."

"I know you haven't been in the office yet. Are you watching television?"

"If the news is true, doesn't it stand to reason that Leonard would have known about the money from the casino guys?"

Michele thought that she could be right. "Okay, what do you need?"

"Fax me anything you can on Justice Leonard and his ties with Albertson. If I can bring something to the meeting on the sixteenth, I'll be able to show how I can help the investigation."

"I'll see what I can get to you. Just be careful and don't get me involved. I'm still the rookie in this office."

"You know I'll take care of you. I'm going to search the net for anything I can find. I'll call you if I come up with something from this end."

"Cool, maybe this investigation will help both of us. Take care, I'll send what I can."

Morning would come fast and this new information would be useful.

Blair grabbed her laptop and started doing research on any subject that might connect Albertson, Leonard and the casinos. She ate a bagel while running news articles. She found that the Ellis brothers had been adding new casinos to their gambling group over the past few years. It seemed that the brothers were moving faster than most new casinos usually were approved. She checked every web site to bring herself up to speed on the issue.

Steve had his team working on new information that had just come in. The Washington Bureau had sent him a packet with pictures linking Albertson and Leonard in more than a friendship relationship. The pictures had been found on Albertson's computer. Why someone would keep something like that, he wondered. Did Albertson and Leonard have a falling out? What else was going on? He hated all these new questions.

Booth walked in Steve's office. "I just got off the phone with Blair, Sir. Everything is set for Falcon's arrival."

"Good. Wish she was here now. We could use all the researchers possible."

"Do you want me to call her back?"

"No, I'm going to do it." Steve knew that he could use Blair, and maybe getting her involved early in a case will help her adjust. He spun around and dialed her number. The sun was high in the sky and he took a deep breath. He thought that maybe he should send Booth to pick her up.

Blair grabbed her cell phone and looked puzzled at the number on the screen. The number showed it was coming from downtown LA. She let it ring another time before picking it up.

"Hello."

"Blair Steve Orrison here, sorry to bother you again."

"No problem, I was just on the computer doing some work."

"If its okay, I was thinking about having Booth pick you up, we could use you in the office today. Your help doing some research with the rest of the team would be appreciated. We'll still have you and Booth pick-up Falcon tomorrow."

Blair was excited when she heard the request. "Absolutely! I'm ready now. He doesn't have to come all the way out here, I'll drive on in."

No, I don't want to upset the director's plans. Let's play it safe and let Booth come get you in about two hours. Should he call you first?"

"No, just remind him come into the second entrance of my complex. I'll be waiting for him."

Steve went out and found Booth. "Take a ride out to Marina del Rey and pick her up. She will be outside of her apartment waiting for you. Make sure you use the second entrance. I told her that you'd be there in two hours."

Blair jumped in the shower. Her heart was beating fast and she was thrilled with the prospect of finally being involved as a real FBI agent. Now her biggest decision was what to wear.

Booth had a picture of Blair from an official FBI personnel site. He headed down to the garage to get a vehicle from the motor pool. The trip to Marina del Rey would take about an hour this time of day. Steve also wanted him to drive by the airport to make sure he was familiar with where the director would be coming in. It was just a few miles past where Blair lived.

Blair wore her black suit and a white blouse. She planned to save the blue suit for tomorrow. She wanted to look professional but not stand out. She went down to the parking area near her apartment. Checking her watch, Booth should be there in a few minutes.

Booth found the complex easily and made sure he drove in the second entrance. The guard opened the gate once he identified himself. He drove to the second building and saw a young blond talking to two men. *Must be her*, he thought. He pulled the black SUV into an open parking spot and got out.

Blair saw the vehicle and knew it must be him. She nodded to the two guys she was talking too and headed toward the SUV. Booth walked around to the passenger side and held out his hand.

"Brandon Booth, nice to meet you." He had opened the passenger door for her.

"Thanks for picking me up. I was willing to drive in because now someone will have to bring me back. I hate to put people out."

"Not a problem. I live pretty close by."

They got in the vehicle and Booth smiled. Blair had a small attaché case on her lap. She wanted to be viewed as a professional and the black leather case helped paint that picture.

"This is a pretty nice place. I'm live further in near the Santa Monica airport."

"My friend Ashley lives at the top of the hill about three blocks from there. Nice neighborhood. Good schools nearby. Do you have kids?" Blair was probing for details.

"No! Not married. Got a great deal when the market went to hell."

"That's cool."

Blair found out quite a bit already. She hoped that by the time they got downtown she could get the answers to the rest of her questions.

Ten

Washington was still a buzz with the news of Albertson's death. The photos of Senator Albertson and another male in what appeared to be a very compromising position had sparked all kinds of rumors. Three pictures had surfaced so far, and now they were being sent over wire services and the internet. Everyone was trying to blow them up to see the other person who was in the photos with Albertson. The CSI team in Federal One Plaza was studying every angle but the second man had his back to the lens and only his left shoulder was visible.

The local news was all over the investigation. Gina Warren who had the exclusive the day of the tragedy continued to research any event that might be related to the death of the Senator. She wouldn't go away and the bureau knew it. With all her Washington contacts the office of the director hoped to derail her efforts.

Michele Kennedy made her way down to the forensic lab in the Capitol where they were working on the photos. Her friend Bruce Sawdon was working on the source that had sent the pictures. They were coming from a server that was sending them through several layers of internet protocol that appeared to be coming from Europe. Cyber criminals could bounce their signal off of several servers on many Continents. She hoped that he could get her some information to pass along to Blair in Los Angeles.

The director was waiting and hoping that his teams could help identify the other man in the photos. Although they had the latest equipment, they had not been able to come up with any answers. How could someone have sent these photos and his investigators were not able to trace them down? The FBI had the newest equipment and every available technician working on cracking the case. Cyber crime had gotten pretty sophisticated. Criminals had been able to hide their location through a variety of routers and servers. Just when you thought you knew their location, poof they were gone.

"Bruce, can I bother you for a minute?"

"I'm really pressed for time right now. John Martin has everyone on this project," He said. "Everyone in Langley, Virginia was dedicated to this project."

"I just need a minute; you can keep working while I ask you what I need to know." Michele was hoping she could get some answers for Blair.

Bruce nodded and Michele grabbed a stool nearby. They talked as he continued to punch information into a series of computer terminals in front of him.

Blair and Special Agent Booth arrived at the Federal Building on 11000 Wilshire Boulevard. The trip allowed her time to ask him some personal questions without Booth realizing what she was doing. She got information on some of the agents in her new field office and Booth's initial opinion of the new boss, Steve Orrison. She wanted to come into the office with a little background information. It was always hard being the newest member of a team. She felt having a little information would even the playing field.

Booth informed her that Steve was a matter-of-fact guy. He made sure everyone on the team had all the material and information necessary on every case that they were working. The more details each agent had, the better the possibility of success. Blair hoped to hit the ground running. She had been waiting for this moment and now it was here. This is how all the training would pay off.

They parked in the lower level. Blair was impressed with the security in the garage. Booth accessed the garage from Wilshire Boulevard and inserted his key card to open the gate. Once inside they proceeded down the ramp where a uniformed guard approached. Booth had to produce another set of identification to pull into a second gated area. They parked the car and headed toward an elevator along the east wall.

Booth was telling her that ever since 9/11 security in the building had been raised to that of the highest levels. He said some of the agents had told him that at one time anyone could park in the lower level of the Federal Building. "Guess that is probably the case everywhere now," he stated. They pushed the up button and got in once the elevator arrived. He had to insert his key card to activate the elevator. He pushed the button for the seventeenth floor. The whirl of the elevator rising quickly up through the shaft seemed almost weird. It was like it was announcing their arrival to those above.

The doors opened and Booth waited for Blair to exit before he followed. He motioned for her to follow him. The corridor led to the right and they passed a series of offices and cubicles as he turned and told her that Mr. Orrison's office was just ahead on the far corner of the floor.

"I know that he will want to show you around," Booth was saying as a man approached.

"Hello Blair, I hope everything went okay when Booth picked you up?"

"Hello Mr. Orrison, I'm glad to finally meet you. Yes, everything went smooth and I'm ready to get started."

"I would like to show you around, but first come into my office. I'll have one of our tech people create a set of identification badges and get you a key card for the parking lot and elevator."

Blair followed Steve as he headed toward his office. Steve was talking as he motioned for Blair to have a seat. The view from his office was unbelievable. She could see all the way to Dodgers Stadium and The Getty Museum north of downtown. His desk was close to seven feet long with a glass top and chrome legs. There was a gray wood credenza behind the desk with pictures of a woman and two young girls. She figured that the picture were of his family. Her FBI training taught her to be observant of minor details. You never knew when they would be important.

"I talked to the director a little while ago," Steve was saying, as he swung around in his high backed leather chair facing the gray credenza. He had a key in his right hand and unlocked a drawer. He pulled open the drawer in the lower left hand side and grabbed a manila folder. She could see that her name was on the top of the file folder. Steve turned around now facing her.

"I have all my agents' files close by. I received yours from the Washington last week. I gave your data to my identification clerk, but he will need to take your picture for the badge. He should be up here in a few minutes."

Blair never saw anyone make a call to get the technician guy to come to Steve's office. Soon there was a knock at the door and a young lady walked into the office. She had some equipment with her. They planned on taking Blair's picture in Steve' office right then. Blair was surprised but complied with the clerk's request. They took a series of pictures and had Blair choose the one she liked the best.

Steve chuckled, "I always want my agents to be happy with their picture or we have to redo it. Thank God for digital." They all laughed.

The clerk said she would have the badge in about ten minutes. Blair thanked her and Steve said, "Let's take that tour."

The Los Angeles FBI Bureau controlled seven floors of the Federal Building. Steve told Blair that she would be located on the seventeenth floor. He introduced her to the group of agents that she would be working with her in a group of cubicles located along the west glass wall of the floor. She had heard most of their names from Booth on the ride from Marina del Rey, and now she would be able to put a face along with the name. Two men in dark suits approached and motioned for Steve to join them.

"I'll leave you with Kathy; she'll fill you in on our investigation so far." Steve headed off with the two men.

Kathy O'Connor showed Blair to her desk and said she would bring in the files that they were working on. Blair sat in her chair and spun around. This was pretty cool, she thought. Kathy reappeared holding a stack of folders. A young man followed her. Blair this is Chris Kawiecki, he will be working with us on this project. "We just call him Quicki!" She laughed and he looked at her with a scowl. "Gee Thanks," he said.

Chris had a stack of files in his hands. He put them on Blair's desk.

"Can I get you something to drink?" He asked.

"No, Thank you, I'm good."

"We'll show you where the lounge and bathrooms are," Kathy added.

Blair was happy to be accepted so quickly and tossed into an investigation. She knew they were busy with the new case and she only wanted to be part of the action.

They pulled chairs up to Blair's desk and started to fill her in on the case. Blair took in all the information and asked questions when appropriate. She didn't want them to know that she had been gathering information from her friend, Michele Kennedy in the Washington Bureau. The more she knew the better chance she would have to become involved in the case.

Hours passed as the three agents continued their discussion. Blair had received her identification badge and parking pass from the clerk that had taken her picture and made sure she placed it on her jacket as instructed. After a little while Kathy had walked with her to the lounge and they grabbed a bottle of water from the fridge. She pointed out where the restrooms and storage areas were on the way back. Kathy O'Connor had been in the L.A. bureau for over ten years and was the lead agent in the office on this case. Blair knew that Booth had a lot of respect for her. He said she was top notch investigator and knew her job. Brandon had been assigned to the L.A. office from Chicago when Steve Orrison was made the bureau chief. No one knew much about him and because he worked with Orrison before everyone figured he had an inside track to the boss.

Blair's cell phone rang and she excused herself from the discussion. It was Michele calling and maybe she had something. Kathy and Chris were going through some documents and Blair stood near the glass windows talking low.

"Yes, I hope you have some information for me!"

"What? No hello! Just slam bam thank you Ma'am!" Michele laughed.

"Sorry, I'm with my new team and don't want them to wonder why I'm taking a call at work."

"Shit, I'm sure they get calls all day long."

"I'm sure they do, but not on their first day."

"Okay, well Bruce is tracking down a lead on the photo's coming across the internet. He has traced them to the DC area. Guess it appears that they are coming from overseas but the FBI tracer has followed the routing and they are now concentrating on the two key states around here. It makes sense that they would be coming from Virginia or Maryland. It also appears that whoever sent the first one out, is asking for money to get the rest of the pictures."

"It must be someone close to either Albertson or the guy in the photo with him," Blair surmised.

"That's what they are thinking here."

"Can I use any of this?" Blair was hoping to impress her colleagues with an update.

"Bruce said give him ten minutes and the information will be updated on the FBI files. It will be released on the internal web site. You can say you pulled it off the internet. At least you'll be one of the first in the office to have the information."

"Great! I really appreciate your help. I'll call you later."

Blair set her I-Phone on the FBI internal site so that it would beep when the news hit. She walked toward her desk in her office and Kathy and Chris looked up. "Sorry guys, my landlord wanted to let me know that he handled a problem at my apartment."

Kathy nodded, and Chris said that apartments always came with issues. Blair placed her I-Phone on the corner of her desk. She sat back down and seconds later her phone chirped. The message was quick and she was surprised that it came though so soon.

"Hey, here's an update coming through," she said. "Looks like the Washington Bureau has a lead on who is sending the photos with Albertson. The person is asking for money up front to see the rest of the pictures."

Both Chris and Kathy were amazed. They usually checked the main FBI site on their computer but they hadn't set their phone to the site. This was big news. Kathy reached over and turned Blair's flat screen so that all could see it. She punched in her code and the information came up confirming what Blair had just told them.

"We need to tell Steve, Kathy said. Blair come with me, you're the one that picked up the news."

"That's okay, you can tell him, and I'll just stay here with Chris and see if we can come up with more details."

Kathy headed to Orrison's office. She gave him the update and he spun around and pulled up the web site. There it was everything she was telling him. "Great job Kathy."

"Not me boss, Blair found it. She has the site on her phone and checked for updates and it just come through."

"Well she must have picked it up instantly because it says that the release time was just two minutes ago."

"We were meeting when her phone beeped and she was

reading the message to us. I think she's going to be a great addition, Sir. New agents have all the technical savvy that some of us are still getting used to."

Kathy headed back to the meeting in the cubical. Blair and Chris were looking over some of the documents.

"The boss was pleased with your information, Blair."

"I was just lucky that I saw it coming through."

Brandon told Kathy that Blair had pointed out that one of the pictures seemed to have a mirror placed across the room. Maybe they could get the analyst downstairs in the lab to see if there was an image in the mirror of the person with Albertson. Good idea. The team was working together well and all three felt at ease with each other. Blair was thankful that Bruce had given her that clue. He would probably have it done before the LA office started but now she had a new idea for her team. She was happy that she could be involved and not just be the new person on the block.

They must have been working for quite some time because it was getting dark and the skyline was beaming with lights from all around the building. Blair looked out and could see the stadium lights in Dodger Stadium from a distance appear like a beacon in the night sky. She had been there a few times with her dad. Her dad was a big baseball fan and whenever he came to town he would try to take in a game. He often wanted to go see the Angels or Padres but if the Braves were coming to LA then he had to be at Dodger stadium. She wondered who the Dodgers were playing.

Chris looked at Blair and asked, "What are you looking at?"

"Oh! Just the stadium lights off in the distance. My dad loves baseball, whenever he's in town I try to get tickets for the Dodgers, Angels or we head down to San Diego for a game. He's been to almost every major league park."

"That's pretty cool," He answered.

Kathy said they would call down to the lab to see if they can get a view of anyone from the mirror in the picture they had been studying. "I bet the Washington lab is on this right now," she said.

Blair smiled and thought of her friend Bruce in the D.C. lab and that he was working on the same case. Bet he's having the time of his life. How Bruce loved doing that sort of thing. She wished that she could call him, but knew that it wasn't a good idea. She was sure that Bruce solved the mirror image by now. He was great in the tech area. She planned to text Michele as soon as possible. The Washington lab would be working on it with every piece of equipment. Guess two labs working on the same thing wouldn't hurt.

Booth walked into Blair's office and saw the three agents with documents scattered all over her desk. "Guess you will be at it for a while longer," he said.

Blair looked up and remembered that Booth had driven her into the bureau office. "I forgot that we came in together." I'm not sure how long this will take, but I can always get a ride.

"Not a problem," he answered. "I've got a project that I'm working on for the chief, and figured that you would all be ordering something to eat soon."

Kathy checked her watch and was surprised to see that it was close to seven-thirty. No wonder it was dark outside. "Let's call and get something to eat," she said. They all agreed. She headed to her office to grab some menus. Booth smiled at Blair and asked how it was going. Before she could answer Chris said that she had already helped them get a clue into the investigation of the photo's that were on the internet.

Booth knew there was something special about Blair. He could see it in her eyes and hear it in her voice. He knew she was famous for events in Arlington and that she helped break the case of weapons in Iraq. Like a good investigator he checked her Bio and was impressed. He hoped to get to know her a lot better. He was glad that she was working with Kathy and Quicki. They were a good training team.

Eleven

The investigation in the Washington Bureau was moving at a fever pace. Bruce and his group were busy blowing up the image seen in the mirror. They all had been studying the photos for a clue and the mirror was the best shot. They knew the original was the back of a man's head but if they could get close enough maybe they could still get identification. The FBI would not get into a bidding war for the rest of the photos and they knew news media all over would be jumping on the wagon to get the pictures first. The news of Albertson's death brought out many speculations about the Senator's life. How could he afford that big new house he built on the Colorado River? Was he involved with casino gambling interest? How did all of his votes on critical reform affect the outcome of those issues? His sexual orientation however brought out the most bazaar questions. His possible sexual involvement with the Chief Justice of the Supreme Court or someone else was becoming a big question. Newspapers from New York to Los Angles carried stories and pictures of his life. Photos of him and the Chief Justice were prominently displayed on the front page of the New York Times, Washington Post and other big city papers. Editors were digging through file photos everywhere to put their spin on the story.

Gina Warren and her channel 7 news team were no different. They continued checking out related people and updated their viewers about the investigation. They had Gina travel to the former senator's new home and interviewed people who had seen the Chief Justice with Albertson in Arizona. The director was sure that this story would not die until all the answers were revealed.

The information and pictures that the FBI had gathered from Albertson's home computer brought a further link between the Chief Justice and Albertson. Justice Leonard had been a conservative voice during the twenty years since he had been seated on the Supreme Court. The first President Bush had appointed him and through retirements and changes he arose to the position of Chief Justice just two years ago. His rulings often favored traditional marriage, against legalized gambling and hard on crime. His possible sexual involvement with Senator Albertson would be the farthest thing from anyone's imagination. Could this all be a mistake? What about the gambling issues? How could the Chief Justice's involvement fit into that scenario? The director had reported everything that the Bureau had uncovered to the president in a late night meeting at the White House. He wanted to make sure that the president wasn't getting miss-information or blindsided by the press.

John Franklin Martin had been considered one of the most respected director's of the FBI by both parties. He made sure that he kept his political opinions to himself and always kept both parties aware of issues that might be important to their positions. He wanted his team to be considered fair and unbiased. He planned to take a red-eye flight to Los Angeles on the department's jet after meeting with the president. He knew that the bureau chief in Los Angeles, Steve Orrison, had Blair come to the office a day early but that she was still going to meet him at the airport with another agent.

Martin hated the flight to LA. The four hour time difference put him out of the loop too long he thought. At least on a private jet he could stay in touch with his lap top and cell phone. Maybe he could catch a few winks while heading out west.

The evening shadows had cast an eerie spell over the buildings downtown. Blair looked out the office windows and told one of the other agents that the shadows took on the shape of creatures from some of the old movies of the 50's and 60's. They agreed and Kathy O'Connor said she really hadn't noticed that before. The team of agents had done all that they could do that evening and Booth was ready to take Blair back to her apartment.

She thanked Kathy and Chris for all their help and that she looked forward to being part of the team. They said they were happy she would be joining them and looked forward to working together. Booth smiled, knowing that she must have made a great first impression. He knew she made a great impression on him. Of course being a cute blond didn't hurt any. Booth figured that he should ask if she wanted to stop off for a drink on the way home.

Blair pulled her jacket off the back of her chair and grabbed a file and shoved it into her briefcase. She looked around and smiled to herself. This was going to be pretty cool she thought. "Booth!" She hollered.

Booth turned around and smiled at her. "Now what do you want?"

"Take me home!" She said, and they both smiled at each other. This was going to be a good relationship. He had grabbed his keys and headed toward the elevator.

"Let me just stop in and say goodnight to the Boss," She said. She peeked into Steve's office and saw that he was on the phone. Blair smiled and waved and Steve waved back. She headed toward the elevator and joined Booth who was waiting for her.

"It's about time you're ready," He said. Booth pushed the button for the garage and they got in. "So how was your first day?"

"Pretty good, I like the group that I'm working with and Mr. Orrison seems pretty cool too." Blair wanted to say more but just keeping it simple. Less said made more sense to her. She was tired but pumped up after her first day in the new office.

They got to the car and he pulled his keys out. "Not quite as nice as the company's SUV," He said. Booth's car was a new model Chevrolet Malibu, dark blue with leather seats.

"I like it. I bet it runs great!"

"It gets about thirty miles a gallon, and has plenty of pep. I got it a few months ago and have been happy with the car so far." Booth didn't want to go on this much but for some reason he was a little nervous. He was okay on the ride to the Federal Building but seemed a little off on the ride home. "Would you like to stop for a cold drink before we head out?" He asked in a nonchalant manner.

"Sure, I could use a drink to relax a little. It has been an exciting day for me and I really appreciate your help." Blair smiled back at him as he headed out of the garage area.

"I know a nice little place along the beach in Santa Monica, if that's okay with you?"

"Sure, I used to live in Santa Monica when I first moved to California. I still have a lot of friends that live there.

Booth listened as he headed down the ramp toward Highway 10, the Santa Monica Freeway. He planned on getting off on Lincoln Avenue and they could head toward the parking structure on the corner of Broadway and Colorado in the new Santa Monica Mall. He wanted to take her to a local spot where he felt they could talk without feeling like they were on a date. It was late, close to midnight, and they both had been working on the Albertson case. He hoped to fill her in on what he was working on and maybe get the information that her group was looking into.

The traffic was light and the ride to Lincoln was smooth. The exit came up on the right and Booth headed off the 10 and North on Lincoln. He turned right on Colorado and then right again on 2nd Street. They pulled into the lot and found a spot on the second floor. Booth said they could walk along the Third Street Promenade to Santa Monica Boulevard. Booth started to tell Blair about the quant English Pub that he really liked and she stopped walking. "What's wrong?"

"The Britannia Pub? Is that where we are going?" She was looking at Booth and he had a puzzled look on his face.

"Yes, is that okay?"

"I worked there when I first moved to California. And I have a lot of friends that always go there. I've only been back in town a few weeks and haven't been able to get in touch with many of them. I don't want to see them like this." She was standing still on Third Street and wasn't moving.

"I didn't know," He said. "Really I didn't know." He felt that he really screwed up.

"It's not a big problem I just don't want to see everyone just yet. I was married to Hunter when I worked there and so many people wouldn't understand if I walked in with you." Blair was turning around and walking back toward the parking lot. Booth rushed behind her and kept apologizing. "Don't worry," She assured him. "It's just not the right time."

He ran the information back in his mind that he knew of her history. He remembered that she was married to a decorated Army Special Forces Officer who was killed in Iraq. There was nothing in the file about her working at a Pub in Santa Monica. How could he be so stupid? What should he do now? He just walked along next to Blair without saying a word.

"Hey Booth, have you ever been to a little Sushi restaurant in Venice? It is pretty famous. Do you like Sushi?"

"Yes, and No, I haven't been there. What's the name?"

"Hama. They have a late night bar on the side that will still be opened. Take Ocean to the Windward Circle in Venice Beach. It is just to the left of the round-a-bout. We might have to walk a ways because parking is tough. I'm glad you like Sushi."

Booth had a feeling of relief as they got back into his Malibu. He hoped that he hadn't screwed up their friendship with the suggestion of going to the Pub in Santa Monica. He followed her directions and they headed toward Venice Beach. Hama was a small cute little Sushi bar on the curve in Venice. The owner, Tony, greeted them as they grabbed a stool at the bar. Booth asked Blair what she wanted, and then ordered a glass of wine for her and a Sapporo beer for himself. They toasted their drinks and Booth let out a sigh of relief. "Blair, I'm really sorry about before."

"How could you know? I love the Britannia Pub, but it just isn't the right time to go there yet. I worked there for a few years whenever I didn't have a modeling or acting gig. There were a few of us in the profession that would take each other's shifts if something cool came along. I want to go there but maybe in a few weeks." Blair turned toward Booth and asked if they could order something to eat. "I didn't want to seem like a pig in the office and just had a small salad."

Booth laughed. "Girls are funny about that. A guy would order half the menu and not think a thing about it."

They both laughed and asked for a menu. After a drink and appetizer they decided to head home. The day had been long and when Booth dropped Blair off at her apartment he reminded her that they had to be at LAX to meet the director early in the morning. "What if I pick you up about eight-thirty?" He asked.

"Works for me," She said. "Thanks again for the ride and sushi. I had a nice time." Blair walked toward her apartment building and he waited until she was inside. He knew that both the director and his bureau chief wanted to make sure that she was safe.

Blair looked into the mirror in her hallway and smiled. This was a good first day, she thought. She planned on getting an outfit together for tomorrow before taking a shower and going to bed.

Looking good the first day was important, but with the director in town it was critical to her. I have to look like an agent, not some Hollywood bimbo, she thought to herself. No matter what John Martin would say to her, she wanted to be an FBI agent, not some spokesperson for the agency. She would have to prove herself but she was confident that she could do it.

Brandon Booth turned off of Lincoln onto Pico and up to his house. He lived just past the golf course on Greenway Street. It was a small two bedroom home not too far from the Santa Monica airport. It needed a lot of work and with his schedule there wasn't a lot of time to do it. He had hired a guy to repaint the entire interior and has a landscape company work on the outside. It was starting to take on a nice appearance, and he hoped that by the fall he could get a few more things done. He parked in front of the home and walked up the path. The front door had a leaded glass panel that reminded him of his parent's home back in Kentucky. Although he was young when they were killed in a car crash, he always remembered walking through that front door. That might have been the final selling point for him. He said it always made him feel at home when he put his key into the lock on that door. Booth was a nice guy.

He was happy that the night ended good with Blair. He hoped to make a good impression on her, and was afraid that he blew it with the suggestion of going to the Pub. He was glad she explained it to him and that they were able to stop sat Hama for a drink. It was really a pretty cool place. I'll have to go back there he figured. It had been a long day and tomorrow looked like it would be more of the same. Booth knew with John Martin coming to town that everyone will be on their best behavior and want to look good in front of him. Booth had met the director once before and he was all business. He was surprised that the bureau chief wanted Blair to come along to pick-up the director. It didn't seem to him that John Martin was one to become personally involved in the life of one of his agents. Blair was obviously special. He thought he should text Blair to re-confirm their meeting time tomorrow before going to bed. Booth was very organized and never left anything to chance. In that area he and Blair had a lot in common.

Blair appreciated the text and sent Booth one back. Let's meet in front of my apartment complex, that way you don't have to spend time at the gate. She figured that it would be better to be an hour early than a second late.

Both Agents knew that LAX was a mad house in the mornings. So many business travelers along with the throng of foreign vacationers made it tough to get around. She wasn't sure where private jets landed, but remembered that Booth had said they might take a helicopter from LAX to the Federal Building. *Looks like tomorrow will be a very interesting day*, she thought. With that Blair climbed into bed and set the alarm on her cell phone as well as her alarm clock.

Twelve

Steve Orrison was glad that he had Blair come to headquarters a day early. He had heard both Chris and Kathy comment on how well they thought she would fit into the group. He had a fear that having someone new that came in with a high profile would disrupt the team. Blair made a good first impression with his people. Steve had touched base with the director before he left the office and clued him in on his team's efforts so far. He also told John Martin that Blair was in the office and working well on research with his team.

The ride home was always a time that Steve used to organize his thoughts and plans for the next day. It bothered his wife when he would come in and go into the den to continue working on bureau business. With a forty-five minute commute it allowed Steve to do that and be a father and husband when he got home. Unfortunately, he often got home so late the girls would be asleep.

The flight from Dulles airport to LAX would take close to five hours. John Martin had brought three files with him to review along with the Albertson case files. The Lear jet had both closed circuit television as well as wireless internet so that government personnel could work while traveling. The seats were more like large lounge chairs and the galley included a nice array of food and drinks. This was not your typical coast to coast flight. There was no problem with other passengers, luggage, getting something to eat or drink, and most of all cramped quarters. No, this was more like a flying hotel room, with 24/7 room service.

He working for the first few hours then hoped to catch a few winks before arriving in Los Angeles. The television was tuned into to CNN when a special report was coming on. The anchor was saying that new pictures had been sent to CNN on the Senator Albertson scandal. *Shit, now it's a scandal*, John thought. He immediately called his office to see if the bureau had the pictures.

The phone rang two times when a very pleasant voice came on.

"Hello, director this is Vanessa." Vanessa was the evening secretary in his office. She was a very bright young woman who had been with the bureau for about five years. The director's office had someone manning the phones around the clock. Patch me though to the crime lab, the director asked. Vanessa put his call through. When the red phone in the lab rang, a light flashed letting them know it was either the director or a key official in the Administration.

"Crime Lab, Drew Jones speaking." John Martin was still watching as the CNN anchor was explaining that the photos were being checked for authenticity before being shown on the air.

"Drew, what's this about the news of more photos being released? Do we have them? What the hell is going on down there? People in the bureau knew that the director would often call with three or four questions before you could answer any of them.

"Sir, our forensic team has the two new photos but they're very grainy and we're not sure either of them is authentic. They came over the wire service to CNN and FOX news a few minutes ago. We are checking the servers to see where they originated from." All FBI personal in the central office tried to answer every question in one breath before being hit with three or four more. It was kind of a machine gun approach, but effective.

"Okay Drew, I'll wait a few minutes for an answer. Patch the photos to my lap top so that I can check them out. I'd like to be able to contact the networks and advise them of the authenticity before their people release the photos to the public."

"I've just sent them there, Sir, just as your call came through." John Martin was pleased with his team's response. He opened his lap top as he continued listening to the CNN anchor's tale of the events over the past few days. Drew was right. The pictures were not the same quality of the earlier pictures. John flipped the channel to FOX news to see what they were reporting. He hated Fox news. They seemed to be more sensational and he feared they would release the photos without checking them. His fears were true. The FOX anchor was explaining the first photo to the television audience. His interpretation was that the figures in the photos proved that Albertson and Leonard were having an affair of sorts. As John looked closer at the television he could make out a little more details then on his 17 inch lap top screen. These were definitely different from the first photo. John's first inclination was that these were from another source. Maybe they were authentic, but not from the person or person's that sent the first ones. He flipped back to CNN and they still had not released the photos. His phone rang.

"Director, we've blown up the photos and our team has traced them to a location out of New York. It appears that neither man in the photo's have the same physical attributes as either Albertson or Leonard. It was probably just someone hoping to capitalize on the events. Sir, we've talked to FOX news and they paid a source thousands of dollars for the photos. If anything, their photo shopped."

"Dumb shit's, they can't wait to get a leg up on the competition. Did CNN also pay the source too?"

"As far as we can gather, their people said they picked them up off a feed from FOX news. Kind of funny FOX paid for them and CNN picked them up for free from FOX. I bet FOX doesn't know that." Drew laughed, and so did the John. Drew also told the director that a local reporter, Gina Warren had been snooping around and called the lab a few times for comments.

"Let me know if we get a lead on the source that sent these. I want them arrested and give the story to Channel 7. Maybe if we throw that local reporter a bone we can get her off the story." John Martin was pleased with his teams work. They were on top of the events that were unfolding and handling everything as it came along. He looked at his watch and decided to set it to Pacific Time. It would still be three hours until he landed in Los Angeles. He left his lap top on and the television set on CNN. He decided to try to catch a few winks while he could.

The sound of her alarm startled Blair. Just when she reached for the clock to turn it off, the alarm on her cell phone went off. *Give me a break already*, she thought. She sat up and saw that it was six-forty-five a.m. Maybe I'll text Booth to let him know that I'm up. She turned on the television and the local station was flashing new pictures they picked up from their affiliate saying that a hoax had been sent to the news stations claiming that they had new photos of Senator Albertson and Justice Leonard. After investigating, both the FBI and the television stations had released a statement saying that the photos were not real and that the FBI had arrested two men in upstate New York in an extortion plot.

Christ, when did all this happen? She decided to text Booth with the information she just saw on the television. Her phone rang a few minutes after sending the text. "Hey Booth, didn't know if you had seen this morning's events?"

"I had just turned on the television when you called. I bet the director is involved in the arrest of the men in New York," He said. "I hear he almost never sleeps, and has everyone reporting to him 24/7."

"I guess that comes with the territory," Blair said. "I'll be ready whenever you want to come over," she told him. "Just let me know and I'll meet you outside the Village apartments."

Booth made some small talk and said he would ring her when he was about a block away.

Blair looked at her cell phone and saw that she had a message from Bruce in the Washington office. She played her voice mail message.

"Blair didn't want to bother you, so I just left you a message. It appears that our team has a good idea of the second man in the first photo. It isn't Leonard. It looks like it could be his aide. You can't use this information. No one knows yet, not even the director. Call me when you're up and I'll fill you in."

Wow, this was big. She grabbed her phone and looked again at the time. It would be almost ten in Washington. She dialed Bruce's cell phone. His voice mail came on. She left him a message and headed to the bathroom. She would start getting ready and hope Bruce calls her back before Booth comes to get her.

John Martin looked at his watch and knew it was nine a.m. Pacific time. He would be landing in an hour and half. He watched as CNN gave the details of the arrest of two men in Albany, New York, who had sent the false photo's to FOX news. The CNN report was from a feed in DC and Gina Warren was giving the details. The men would be arraigned in twelfth circuit court, her report stated on federal extortion crimes. The report also said that

FOX news paid the men ten thousand dollars for the two photo's and that the news director at FOX was being transferred to another position for airing the photo's without checking them out first. John Martin laughed, and nodded with approval. He moved about the cabin and an attendant asked if they could get him something. Just a cup of coffee please, he replied. He planned to change his clothes and shave. One more call to his office before doing that.

"Hello director, Vanessa here, how can I help you?"

"Put me through to the lab, please."

"Hello director, this is Drew."

"Drew, do we have any more details that have come in?"

"Sir, the forensic team has been completing their work on the original photo and a few minutes ago came up with an identification of the second man in the photo with Albertson. I'll put you through to Bruce Sawden who has more details for you." John Martin was again pleased with his team.

"Director, our team has just identified the man in the photo with Albertson. Its Albertson's aide, Corey Hart. We have been studying recent photos of both the aide and Albertson and it looks like this photo may be more then five years old."

"Great job! How long has he had the same aide?"

"He joined the Senators staff three or four years ago, Sir."

"Guess we know how he got the job."

Bruce didn't say anything but smiled when the director made the reference to the possible affair of the aide and Albertson. "Sir, I'll patch this information through to you. We haven't told anyone outside our office of this news."

"Keep it that way!" John Martin had critical information that he wanted to keep close to his vest until he needed it. You did a super job on this, he told him. John headed to the dressing room in the back of the jet.

Blair was almost dressed when her phone rang. It was Bruce calling her. "Thanks for the information," she said.

"I wanted you to know but you cannot tell anyone. I just got off the phone with the director, and he ordered me to keep it a secret until he's ready to reveal it."

"Don't worry, I won't say a thing. I appreciate you keeping me in the loop. I also understand that Mr. Martin knows that you and I are friends, and I won't let on that we've even talked." Blair wanted to protect her friends but keep the inside information coming.

Bruce said he would let her know when the director was going to release the details so that she will be on the fast track with the information. It was great to have friends in key positions.

Blair went downstairs to wait for Booth. She loved her apartment and stood at the entrance next to the waterfall. One of the nicest things about the location of her apartment was the waterfall was just outside her window. She felt it was soothing when she was ready to go to sleep. Just then her cell rang.

"Blair, I just turned onto Admiralty Way. I'll be there in a couple of minutes. I'm on the corner, next to the waterfall. See you in a few."

The ride to LAX should only take ten minutes. Booth came around the corner and pulled up where she was standing. "Going my way sailor." she said laughing.

"Hop in lady," Booth replied. Although they had only met yesterday, there seemed to be a special connection between the two of them. They both had a good sense of humor and liked many of the same things. She told him that it was better to take Via Marina to Admiralty Way, and follow it to where it meets Lincoln. We can avoid the traffic on Washington by doing that she told him.

Good idea, I figure that the director's plane should arrive in about an hour. We will have to park at the terminal where private jets land. I called this morning and got directions to the entrance. Blair reached in her purse and pulled out printed directions and handed them to Booth. Guess great minds think alike, she said. He looked at the print-out from Map Quest. Yeah, I guess great minds do think alike.

The ride south to Lincoln was quick. Signs for LAX appeared on the right side and Booth followed the entrance to the airport. He saw the signs for a variety of airline carriers coming up. "One of the things I like about coming here is all the different airline carries. I grew up in Kentucky and we only had the major US carriers. Here you have so many planes landing and taking off from all over the world." Booth was still talking when Blair interrupted him.

"Where in Kentucky did you grow up?"

"Why?" He asked.

"Because, I was born in Louisville and my dad is a big University of Kentucky fan."

"Christ, you're kidding! I love the Cats! I bleed blue." Booth almost forgot to watch the road.

"Shit, look out," Blair yelled. "You almost hit the Volvo in front of us."

"Sorry, I get carried away when talking about UK." Booth hoped she didn't think he was a poor driver.

"Oh! I understand. I can't tell you how many times my dad would be watching a basketball game screaming at the top of his lungs and my mom and I would just be looking at each other. Every game seemed to be life or death to him, especially if it was an SEC game. If we were going out to eat, they had to have the Kentucky game on or we couldn't go there. It's kind of funny my dad always says I bleed Blue too!"

Booth was amazed to hear that Blair was from Kentucky, and especially glad to hear that her dad loved the Wildcats. *Guess that's something else we have in common,* Booth thought.

The turn into the private jets area was coming up on the right. Booth pulled over into the right lane and slowly approached the gated area. A guard was in the booth as they approached.

"Yes, who are you here for?"

Booth showed the guard his FBI badge and said that they were there to pick-up a special guest from Washington. The guard opened the gate and gave him a card to put on his dash. He told him that it must be on the dash of his vehicle and to park in a designated area for arriving guest. You can go into the terminal but cannot go to the gate area, he told them.

He put the parking pass on his dash and informed the guard that his car might be left there over night.

"I understand," the guard said. "Whenever we get someone from the Capitol being picked-up there is usually a vehicle or two left behind. That is why I gave you the blue parking pass. It signifies that your vehicle has been approved for overnight parking."

Booth pulled away from the gated area and pulled into one of the spots marked overnight guest parking on the far right of the lot. They both got out of the car and Blair grabbed her jacket out of the back. She had her small leather briefcase in her right hand and followed him inside.

"I've been to LAX a thousand times," She said, "But I've never noticed this terminal."

"First time for me too!"

They were greeted by a young lady who inquired what plane they were there to meet. When Booth told her, she pointed them to an area that also had a sign with the picture of a Helicopter. They figured that their flight to the Federal Building would also leave from the same terminal.

"John Martin's flight should arrive soon," Booth said. "Do you want anything while we wait?"

"No, I'm good."

The blue and white striped jet bearing the flag of the United States on both sides made a wide bank to the right on its final approach to LAX. The director looked at his watch and saw they were running a few minutes early. Good he thought. John Martin was looking forward to seeing Blair again. He was pleased that she had recovered well from her injuries and that she had settled back in Southern California. Steve Orrison said that he was sending Brandon Booth along with Blair to meet him. John remembered Booth from a previous trip to the Los Angeles office last year. John grabbed his briefcase as they landed on the western runway and made their approach to the private jet terminal. He planned to be back in Washington early the next day. Meetings, organizing the task force here and dinner, then back home he figured.

They stood at the ramp waiting for the director to appear. Blair was happy to see John Martin again, Booth was anxious.

Thirteen

The team of agents in the forensic lab in Washington had sent the pictures that they had uncovered identifying the man with Albertson to the director's cell phone and computer. They wanted to make sure that he could see how they came up with the answer's they did. Once he cleared their findings it would be released to other bureau offices. Bruce also sent Blair the picture to her cell phone. He added the note to please make sure no one ever saw it.

The staff in the Federal Building in Los Angeles was making final preparations for the director's arrival. Steve Orrison was making sure the people on the roof knew that the director would be arriving by helicopter about eleven-thirty. It wasn't unusual for business people in LA to use a helicopter service. With traffic always so congested it helped make it to appointments especially downtown. Steve hadn't told his staff that John Martin was planning an undercover assignment in Vegas to help flush out key information on the gambling connection between Albertsons and any possible mob ties. It had been years since anyone suspected mob ties with the casino industry. It had become big business and major players came from all areas including the likes of Donald Trump. Many of the casino's were being purchased by conglomerates like Harrah's Entertainment who now owned over fifty major casino's all over the United States and six key locations in Vegas, including Caesar's Palace, Paris, Rio Suites and the Flamingo. The MGM-Mirage group had other great landmarks along the strip in Vegas. They even had a new location in downtown Detroit and had been expanding across the country.

The plan would be finalized with the director and the two bureau chiefs who would be meeting in the LA office with Steve that afternoon. The chiefs from Las Vegas and Phoenix should arrive around the same time the director does. Steve knew that some of his people would be involved with the Vegas bureau's staff. He was thinking of having Booth and maybe Kathy join the undercover assignment. The final decision would be made by the director.

The sliding doors opened to the terminal with a screeching sound that caused everyone to turn and look at the person who was coming through. John Franklin Martin was a good looking man and always dressed very sharp. He was holding a black leather case in his right hand and Booth jumped up when he saw him. Blair was standing a little behind Booth and smiled at John when he saw them. The director was pleased that he made sure Orrison had her come to the airport to meet him. There was a bond between Blair and the director. With the previous events they shared John felt as though Blair was like a daughter to him.

Booth extended his hand and John reached out and shook it. "Brandon nice to see you again." He was surprised that the director remembered his first name. They had only met once before.

"Welcome to Los Angeles, director. Ms. Adams and I will go with you to the LA office. I have confirmed our helicopter and it is standing by at gate eight." Booth was nervous and he hoped that it didn't show.

"Good job," John answered. He turned and smiled at her. "Let me look at you," he said. "How are you feeling? Is everyone treating you okay? Fill me in on your apartment!" Just like always a machine gun approach of questions before you could answer the first one.

Blair extended her hand and John grasped it with both his right and left hand. "I'm great," She said. "Everyone has been super and I love my new team."

John was proud of her accomplishments. "You're looking very classy as always."

"Sir, we need to move to the gate to grab that chopper," Blair said. She wanted to be professional and the director picked up on it.

"Absolutely!"

They all headed toward gate eight. Booth wasn't surprised that the director seemed to know so much about Blair. They both had their briefcases and moved alongside the director. Booth addressed the person at the chopper desk and gave him his identification. They moved outside toward the whirling noise of the chopper blades. Blair had never been on a helicopter, but she was always ready for something new. He turned toward her and said, "Make sure you duck when getting closer." They went up the two hanging steps and Booth and John sat in the rear. She moved in and was motioned to sit up front. This was going to be very cool. Flying over the tall buildings of downtown LA would be a treat. She turned toward the director and informed him that her first day in the office was very informative. She got to meet with the two agents that she would be working with and they were great. John Martin said, "I understand you were able to give them some key information that was released on the agency site before they had it!"

Blair felt a little sheepish and was surprised that he knew about that. "It wasn't anything special they would have seen it too!"

"Yes, but keeping your cell on the site was good planning." John knew that she had good friends in Washington and that they would probably be helping feed her key information. He was good with that. Using your sources is critical for good agents to succeed. Booth kind of felt like a third wheel in the discussion. He knew the director had been close to Blair from previous events but didn't realize that he followed her so closely.

The helicopter was banking low over the Pacific Ocean as it left the helipad at the airport. All flights went west from the airport before making their turns in. Blair could see her apartment complex as they made the loop over the Marina. Booth and the director had their headphones on so that they could talk and hear each other. Booth was trying to tell Blair that he could see her apartment building but she didn't have her headset on. He tapped her on the shoulder and pointed to the headset he was wearing. She gave him the heads up signal but didn't put them on. Guys just didn't realize what those things did to your hair style. Booth was confused but sat back. He and the director conversed about the Albertson case as the ride took them over Venice Beach and up over Highway 10 to downtown. Although the noise from the choppers blades was loud Blair seemed to be enjoying herself. Booth didn't realize that she had ear buds in and the noise wasn't a problem. The trip downtown took less than fifteen minutes. It would have taken close to an hour and you never knew if an accident would cause you a bigger delay. They banked over the Veterans Building in Westwood and turned to land on the roof of the Federal Building. Blair looked down as the chopper spun in its decent. The roof had a large circle that resembled a target. That was the designated landing spot. It was a soft landing which surprised her. The door slid open and Booth jumped out followed by the director. Blair popped open the front door and thanked the helicopter pilot. He smiled and was happy that the cute girl sat upfront with him. Steve Orrison was standing on the roof waiting to greet his guest.

Steve Orrison knew that the director wanted to spend some time with Blair discussing her position in the bureaus office. Now that she has been assigned to a team it might be a little harder to tell her what his plans were. John Martin shook Steve's hand and Booth and Blair followed them down the stairway from the helipad. When they got down to the next level they grabbed an elevator and went to the 17th floor. John Martin told Blair that he would like to talk to her once they got downstairs. "I'd like to have some time with my team first if that's okay with you Sir?" Blair wanted the director to know she wasn't window dressing.

"Sure, no problem, I plan to get with Mr. Orrison anyway." Steve told John that the bureau chief's from Las Vegas and Phoenix had arrived a few minutes before the chopper landed. The director knew it was important to get with all three of his chief's first. "Blair, I'll come find you," he told her.

Booth moved down the hallway to his office and Blair turned right and headed toward her cubical. Kathy and Chris were pouring their eyes over some new documents that had just come in. "Morning guys," She said. They turned and instantly asked about the chopper ride. Blair smiled. First time and flying over all the building was really cool. Kathy and Chris wondered why she was sent along to get the director, but it wasn't their place to ask. "I'm glad that I got to go with Booth to pick him up," She said. "I got to meet the director a few times in Washington and I guess Mr. Orrison knew that." She figured giving her team members an explanation was better than them guessing why she was sent. "So anything new," she asked. Kathy said the forensic lab in D.C. was sending over the photo's that were released by FOX news last night. We're not sure what they have but we also got this release just a few minutes ago. Chris handed it to Blair. It was a statement from the Judicial Committee that Justice Leonard was not under suspicion of any wrong doing and not a suspect in any case by the FBI. "I bet they have the identification of the guy in the photos with Albertson, and it's not Leonard," Blair said. She went on wondering out loud if there was any connection to Albertson and his aide before the aide started working for the Senator.

Kathy and Chris looked at each other. Nothing says we can't track that down. "Blair that might be an angle no one has looking at?"

Blair knew she had to use the information carefully that Bruce had given her, without revealing too much. Chris grabbed his keyboard and punched in the name of Albertson's aide. He started reading aloud to the two women. "Attended college in Phoenix and started working for the local newspaper. He was a beat reporter for a year and landed a position with the Albertson staff as a researcher during his last campaign. From that he seemed to progress to position in the office in Phoenix. Three years ago he moved to D.C. as Albertson key office aide." Kathy asked if the aide had any family ties or a wife or girlfriend.

Blair suggested checking to see if he had a social network page. So many people do today and we could get some insight into the aide's personal life if he has one. Great idea! Chris ran a check of facebook and myspace and sure enough, there it was. The aide has a facebook page with photo's and information that might help them.

"Do either of you have a facebook page?" Blair asked. Chris didn't but Kathy did. "I do too," She said. "Let's request to be his friend and maybe we can get more information."

"That would let us see his pictures and information," Kathy said. "Mine won't help because I say what kind of job I have. Besides that, Blair, he would be more likely to add you because guys always want good looking girls as friends so they can brag to their buddies." After saying that Kathy felt she may have been out of line. "I'm sorry Blair, didn't mean anything by that."

"Don't worry, I appreciate the complement." She sent the Senator's aide a message along with her friend request. She posted a picture from a magazine that she had done a few years ago. Chris was watching and asked. "Where's the photo from?" "I did a shoot for a local chain of hair salons. They did your hair in different cuts for their prospective customers to look at before people had their own hair styled."

"Yeah, I like that look," he said. Kathy gave him a strange look and Blair said they can obviously do anything with photo touch-ups. They all laughed, and went back to the aide's face book site.

There were a lot of photos of various Washington personalities posted on his page. They must have gone through five-hundred photo's when all of a sudden, Chris froze. The picture on the screen was of Albertson, the aide and Leonard. It didn't look like an official government function photo like the rest of them. This looked to be in someone's house or apartment. They wondered if there could be more. What else will they find?

"We need to get this to the boss," Chris said. Kathy suggested they ring Steve and see if he was in his office. The call went through and Steve answered. "Boss, I don't mean to bother you but we have a photo that you might want to see. I'll send it to you." Steve said put it though. A few minutes later, Steve, the director and two other men were moving toward Chris's cubical.

"Where did you get this picture?" The director was staring at Chris. He felt a rush of blood drain from his face and his nerves tumbled as he looked up at the group. His face was getting red and Kathy looked down at the table. All four men now seemed to hover over Chris in the small area.

Blair jumped in. "Sir, we saw the memo from the Judicial Committee and figured that if Justice Leonard wasn't involved who would be the most logical suspect. I guess our only person was Albertson's aide. We started checking social network sites and found this posted on his face book account. We didn't want to go any further before you saw what we had."

"Crap, why didn't someone else think of checking this. Great job!"

"Actually," Chris said, "Blair suggested that we check social network site's for personal information into the aide's life. We also sent him a facebook request to see if he reacts." Chris was feeling a little more confident after John Martin's remarks.

"Who sent him a request?"

"Well Sir, we felt that Blair should do it because her facebook site didn't have any reference to the bureau and maybe he would respond because she is, um, like, um."

"Shit son, spit it out!"

"She's pretty good looking Sir." Chris was now back to feeling nervous and his face was now red as a beet.

The director nodded and said good thinking. "You're doing a good job guys and we might want the three of you join us in a meeting in a few minutes. Let us know if he responds to Blair's request."

The men walked down the hallway and Kathy could hear one of them ask who Blair was. It made sense to them since she had only been in the office for a day and both Chief's from Vegas and Phoenix wouldn't know anyone in the LA office. Just then Blair's I-Phone beeped. She looked at it and it was Bruce telling her that the information had been released to all FBI offices on the identification of the person in the first photo. She figured that the director had told the bureau chiefs about the aide first before it was released and the picture they found really fit the puzzle. Before she could put her phone down it beeped again.

"You're pretty popular today." Kathy said.

"It's a message on my facebook account."

Kathy said, "Log on to Chris's computer so we can see if it's Albertson's aide." Blair was concerned that it might be a message from Bruce, but she couldn't stop now, since this was all her idea. She moved over the keyboard and there it was. Senator Albertson's aide had not only accepted her friend's request, but he added a note.

"What did he say?" Both Kathy and Chris were now hovering over Blair.

"He wants to know how I know him. I'll answer him back." The aide's name popped up in an instant message box because he was on-line. Blair looked at her two partners and asked what should she do? Let's get the boss back in here, they suggested. A second call went to Steve.

Steve and the director came back down the hall and Kathy explained what was happening. John Martin suggested, "You'll need to come up with a good answer, maybe that you saw him at a Washington function."

Blair suggested that she could say they met in Vegas, at one of the new casino's grand openings.

"How do you know if he's been to one?"

"One of his face book pictures was at the opening last year of the new casino in the City Center." Blair was confident that she could pull this off.

"Go for it," John Martin said.

She started typing. We met last year during the opening of the New City Center. His answer back came quickly.

The texting back and forth was quick. "I don't remember you?"

"I guess in your position you meet a lot of people," she was typing, "but your boss was telling me about you. She knew it would make him curious."

"So, what did he have to say?"

"He told me that you were special to him, and that you both had been together for a long time." There was no answer for a long time. They all were starring at the screen. It seemed like ten minutes passed before the response came back.

"Yes, we've been together for about four years, I miss him very much."

The director was amazed. Blair was making inroads that no one expected. Getting the aide to respond to the questions of a personal nature was great. He hoped that she could get something they could use. See if you can set up a meeting, Martin told her.

Everyone in the office was curious as to what was happening. There was the director, their chief and now the two visiting chief's, all hovering around Chris's cubical. Booth came down the hallway and stood wondering like everyone else what was going on?

Blair didn't ask for any directions but kept the conversation angle going. She responded to the aide with an open invitation. "I understand how you must feel. I experienced a loss like that and have had a hard time dealing with it. Why don't we try to meet, maybe we can help each other." She watched as the texting went back and forth.

His answer was quick. "I've got a lot to deal with, but would love to get together."

Blair looked up and asked, "How much leeway do I have?"

"Whatever it will take Blair," John Martin said.

She punched in her response. "I have some time off. We can meet when it's convenient for you." She knew that any hope of getting more personal information had to be face-to-face. She sent the next message. "I can get you a comp room at one of the nice casino's in Vegas where I work if you want?" The hook was there. Minutes went by, and then came the answer they hoped for.

"I have a lot of contacts in Vegas, too! Maybe we can get together next Monday after my friends funeral. I'll catch a flight to Vegas and send you my information." Blair smiled as she finished reading his answer. She started typing back.

"Sounds great, just send me your information and I'll pick you up at the airport. I'm so glad that we can get together. I feel like I've know you for a long time already. After losing my girlfriend a few years ago, I tried everything. I'm sure we have much in common." The girlfriend note would cause him to assume that she might be gay. There might be safety in that for him.

The confirmation came back agreeing to the timetable and he requested her cell phone number. Blair looked up at the director.

"Hold on a second." He motioned for Steve to grab an office throw-away cell phone. The director read the number off to Blair. Blair punched it in, and the meeting was all set.

Steve quickly called one of his tech people and they set the phone up for Blair's use. We have these for undercover situations he told her. You can add a personal message on it now. She did as told. Everyone in the bureau jumped to make plans and identification information to assist with the undercover operation.

All of this changed the director's original plans. He wasn't sure how bringing Blair in to help now turned into her going undercover but now she was key in the case.

"We need to get everyone together to plan this out. The three of you need to meet us in the conference room," Steve directed them. Kathy and Chris were amazed. Blair had been in the office only a day and a half, and now she was in the middle of their investigation. The director told them that his team in Washington had confirmed that the image in the photo was that of the Senator's aide. He also said that the aide did not look like he was fully dressed. "We are releasing the identification to all the offices but not any of the news services. You are not to tell anyone, even your family what you know." They all nodded and Chris logged off his computer before they headed to the conference room.

Fourteen

The director and Steve were surprised that Blair had made so many inroads. They couldn't have guessed that the Senator's aide would respond to so many personal questions, especially over the internet. John Martin was sure that the aide would be checking Blair's face book site before going any further.

He suggested that Blair immediately edit her account so that there wasn't any reference to the FBI, her family and the events of the past two years. "That's not going to be a problem. I stopped using my facebook account after Hunter died. There were too many creeps sending me trash messages."

He was relieved with that information. "We need to log on to your account and go through it together." She nodded. They asked her to log on in the conference room. Her picture was from a photo shoot when she was in a play performed in Birmingham. Nice picture, they said. The profile read, single and living Alabama. There were about five photo albums on the site and all of them were modeling pictures.

"He's going to ask why it says you live in Alabama."

"Although we carried on an instant message conversation, he can't log on to my information until I confirm him as a friend. We have time to edit this,"

"How do you do that," asked the Vegas Chief.

"I can go to my own email account and transfer pictures from there to my face book. It will take about five minutes." They agreed that she needed to work on that right away. While she was editing her face book account, the men discussed how they would use Blair in the investigation. Steve paged Brandon Booth to the conference room to join them.

Booth came into the room only to see Blair on a computer, Chris and Kathy taking notes, and the John Martin and the three bureau chiefs discussing something. "Booth sit down, we need to involve you in our plans." The director looked at Booth. He didn't answer but just took a seat. Just about then, Blair announced that she had completed her updates.

"Could you put it up on our screen," Steve asked her.

She projected the computer image to the large overhead screen in the conference room. The photo that showed on her facebook account was one that her friend had taken in Vegas. You could see that it now referred to eight photo albums. She brought up the first one and it showed her in front of Caesar's Palace in Vegas. The caption under it read my new job. This was followed by five other pictures in and around Vegas. Another album showed her in an apartment. The caption read my new home. The sequence would be a good cover if the aide was searching through her baggage.

"Blair, I contacted my staff in Washington and they have created a full background listing you as a resident of Clark County, Nevada. It shows you living in Vegas and we will have you a new driver's license with photo. It will be sent here within a few hours. They are also making sure that your cover will be complete with some information we have planted." The director had the Vegas Bureau Chief make sure that she would show as an employee at Caesar's Palace, and that records would reflect that she had been working there for a couple of years. This was all done through the magic of the FBI creating a phony identification for undercover personal.

Booth looked confused but didn't say anything. "Booth," Steve said, "We're going to send you to Vegas. Your cover will be as a Pit Boss at Caesar's Palace. Along with two members of the Vegas FBI branch, you, Blair and the Vegas team will try to uncover any activity that might have a bearing on this investigation. We feel that if Albertson's aide can say that he has contacts in Vegas, the contacts were probably Albertson's. Maybe they can lead us to who else is involved."

This had all happened so fast. Booth agreed that it would be a good plan and he looked at Blair. She was right in the middle of everything. How did that happen he thought? He had just met her yesterday, and now they would be in an undercover operation in Vegas together.

"You both will need to be in Vegas tonight," Steve said. "Go home and pack, I have flights being worked on right now. Your new identifications will be here by the time you get back so that everything will be set."

"Sir, my car is at the airport," Booth said.

"Yes, I know. The helicopter will be here in about thirty minutes to take you both back to get it. Get your clothes together. If you need you can buy things in Vegas. The local team there will make sure you have everything you need. The Vegas FBI will have apartments for you both in your new names. You are to report to the Vegas FBI during your work there and they will let you know how to communicate with them. Don't blow your cover. This should only be for about a week."

Blair thanked the director and Steve for having confidence in her for this assignment. "You earned it. Just don't try to do it all by yourself. Booth and the Vegas team are there to help pull this off." Steve wasn't sure that this was a good idea and after the meeting with the Senator's aide his two people would be sent back to LA. The director knew Blair, and he was worried that she would try to make too much of this chance. "Blair," he again stated, "Work with and through the Vegas team and Booth. We just need you to get whatever you can from the Senator's aide. We will do the rest."

"Yes Sir, I understand. I'm just the face that got put in front of him. I will get you whatever I can."

They headed to their offices and grabbed their briefcases to go up to the roof and catch their ride to the airport. After they left, Steve asked John Martin. "Are we expecting too much from her?"

John Martin said, "She seems to have an inside track on things. She fooled my men in New York a couple of years ago, and brought me critical information that no one expected to find. Last year while attending the academy, she was stalked by a terrorist who ended up abducting one of our agents. Blair helped lead us to him, although she was severely hurt in a bomb blast. She is one tough cookie." It was obvious that John Martin had a lot of respect for her.

The helicopter ride to the airport was smooth, and they talked about the plans as they headed to his vehicle. "I'll drop you off and swing back to get you."

"I only need a few minutes," she said. "Why don't you come up while I pack and we can head to your place? Why should you have to double back to get me?"

"Okay." They headed down Lincoln Avenue and turned onto Admiralty Way. "I'll wait for you in the car."

"Don't be silly. Come on up. I'd like you to see my place." Blair's apartment was on the first floor, but appeared to be higher because the garage ran underneath the building. They went up the elevator and she let Booth in. He was surprised on how organized it all was. "How long have you been here?"

"Moved in a couple of weeks ago, why?"

He shook his head. Booth thought about his house. He had been in it for a year and there were still boxes all over. She had this great leather couch and beautiful tall dining room table. Her apartment was pretty cool, he thought. She was in the bedroom and asked if he thought she would need any real dress up things. "If you do, I'm sure the bureau will buy it. We'll be working at the casino in some sort of position. Guess I'm a Pit Boss. What did they say you will be doing?"

Blair stood still in her bedroom. No one ever said, she thought. "Hell, I don't know," she hollered to Booth. She came out of the bedroom pulling a medium size suitcase. "All set."

Booth was surprised that she did it so fast. "That's all you're taking?"

"I'm good, just mostly make-up and some casual clothes. If I need anything else I get them in Vegas."

Booth didn't know many women that could get ready that fast, let alone pack so quickly and light. They headed downstairs' to his car. Booth apologized for his place before they were even out of Blair's apartment.

"Hey, if you could have seen some of the places I had in college you would puke. I had a lot of help from my parent's when I moved in this time."

They rode up Lincoln to Pico and then turned toward Booth's house. Once inside he offered her a drink as he grabbed some suits and shirts. He knew a Pit Boss would be wearing suits for work. "Better grab some jeans for evenings," Blair suggested. Good idea he thought. They jumped back into the car and Booth stopped. "Hey, if we're flying to Vegas, why do we have to head back downtown?"

"I guess we need our documents," she said.

He called the office and asked for Steve. "Boss, we're all

ready and only about fifteen minutes from LAX. Do we need to come back to the office, or can someone bring the documents to us? Steve thought for a minute. "I'll put one of the guys on the road to bring everything to you. Your flight leaves in two hours. We have plenty of time to get the things to you. Once you have everything, call me and we will go over it one more time. Tomorrow you both are to report to the Vegas Bureau office. They will get you set up in your apartments and they have and introduce you to your contacts at Caesar's. We'll have a couple of room for you tonight at Caesar's. Put them on the company credit card. Booth, that does not include gambling money."

Booth laughed. "Sure Boss. If I'm working at Caesar's I can't gamble there anyway."

They headed to LAX and Booth figured he would park in the lot at the special terminal from earlier this morning. He still had the long term parking pass they had given him. If necessary he could have someone from the office come out and get his car. When you left it over night or longer, you had to leave your keys with the guard.

Booth and Blair knew they wouldn't actually be working in the casino. It would just be a cover. Both of them had been to Vegas a number of times, so they knew the lay of the land. Blair said that she really didn't like gambling. "I never could afford to lose any money. I do like the shows and the hotels are great." She didn't know that Booth had a gambling problem a few years ago. He just nodded when she told him that gambling seemed dumb. He knew she was right.

They were at LAX and called back to the office. Steve said their contact would be at the Alaska Airlines desk to meet them with their packet. There would be new drivers licenses complete with photo ID's showing them as employees of Harrah's Entertainment. They used their FBI photo so the pictures were recent. They grabbed the shuttle and headed to the Alaska Airline desk in the terminal. Booth wanted to get to know how this all happened. He was curious how Blair was chosen to be part of the undercover team.

"So, as I understand it, you talked to Albertson's aide?"

"No, not really talked. Somehow when Kathy, Chris and I were searching the web, we found a way to contact him. Chris and

Kathy wanted me to be the go-between, so I sent him an instant message on facebook. He replied and that is how I got involved."

Booth smiled. He was thinking, if you sent me an instant message, I'd reply to you too!

"He said, "I guess he has a thing for the ladies."

"No, we're kind of thinking he might be gay. I'm not sure why he replied but I'm glad he did."

"Blair, maybe he goes both ways. He could have been using Albertson to further his own career. He wouldn't be the first to do it."

She knew he was right. Just then one of the guy's from the Los Angeles Bureau came into the terminal. Booth hollered to him. They all sat down and looked through the material that he brought. He had identification's for both of them, and a listing of the contacts that they would be working with. Booth knew one of the girls on the list. She had been in the LA Bureau for a few years before moving to the Vegas office. That would be cool he thought.

Blair was surprised that they put this all together so fast. The driver's license and Caesar's identification's were perfect. She saw they included a map with the location of the apartments that they would be using. She knew she had a lot of studying to do on the short flight to make sure she didn't slip up. Their new ID's used their real first names so that would help. She figured that she better start calling Booth by his first name. "Brandon," She said. "Does it say anything about a car?"

He was surprised to hear her use his first name. "No, it doesn't, but we'll just use shuttles and a taxi service, I guess."

"We need to work on our details," She told him. He realized that this was her first case and was probably nervous. That would only be normal. "Good idea. We can do it together tonight after we get settled in. Don't worry, I'll help you."

Blair smiled at him. "Thanks."

The flight from LAX to Vegas was only thirty minutes. It seemed that by the time you got to normal flying altitude you started you're decent into Vegas. It had been quite a day. Blair was happy that the director and her new bureau chief allowed her to be part of this operation. She planned to make sure that she only kept to the script that they gave her. She was there just to probe into the relationship of the aide to Albertson and possibly Justice Leonard.

Booth was supposed to find out about the gambling connection that Albertson may have had in Vegas.

McCarran International airport in Vegas was always busy. There were so many tourist and business travelers arriving and departing daily. It seemed that it was never slow. They grabbed their bags and headed out to the taxi stand. There was a line of people waiting, but it was moving fast. The plan was to head to Caesar's and get checked in. Booth had told Blair on the flight that they would make contact with their counterparts in Vegas in the morning. They could settle in and grab some dinner. That sounded good to her.

They were next in the taxi line. A bright yellow cab pulled up and they jumped in. "Caesar's Palace," Booth said. The ride was quick and Booth handed the cab driver a twenty. "Keep the change," he told the driver. They were in the giant circle that had been built along Flamingo Boulevard. They heading into the lobby and Booth said they each needed to check into the hotel separately. They had rooms reserved in their new names by the Vegas team.

She moved to the counter and Booth was in line behind her. It all made her think of the commercials. Beside in Vegas no one at a front desk really cared what you were doing or why. What happens in Vegas, Stays in Vegas? They both checked in and walked toward the bank of elevators. The one on the far left opened and a group of young men piled out. One of them checked her out and almost walked into the large vase of flowers in the middle of the hallway. Booth laughed and his friends gave him a rough time.

Once in the elevator Booth pushed the button for the 16th floor. "I'm on sixteen," Booth said.

"Me too," Blair answered.

As they rode up the elevator Booth asked Blair when they should meet for dinner. Give me about an hour to settle in and I'll call your room. Blair wanted to change clothes and just review all the events of the day. Booth was good with that. "Call when you're ready," He said, as Blair put her room key card into 1636.

"I'm in 1645," Booth told her.

Blair went in the room and put her suitcase on the metal stand that was in the closet. She looked in the large mirror in the bathroom and smiled. She felt that she was really an agent now.

Fifteen

Dinner was the last thing that Blair was thinking about. She needed more information from Booth and her new contacts in Vegas. She wanted to get all the details so that she would be the best agent possible. Blair had her lap top and she saw that Caesar's Palace had Wireless Internet throughout the hotel. She logged on to search for any information on Senator Albertson and his aide. The more she knew the better it would be to probe the aide for details. She knew that a key piece of information they were looking for would be any ties between the Senator, Justice Leonard and organized gambling.

Booth looked out of the window and he could see the Flamingo Hotel across the street. He knew the Flamingo was big in Vegas history. He had read a book the hotel left in his room detailing Vegas history. The Flamingo was built by one of Las Vegas original settlers Charles 'Pops Squirles' in 1944. In late 1945, mobster Bugsy Siegel and his "partners" came to Las Vegas. It was finally opened as the Pink Flamingo Hotel on December 26, 1946. It was the first luxury hotel on the Vegas strip. Booth knew the history of Vegas and loved reading about how legalized gambling changed the face of the desert town. He loved the glimmering lights and action. He needed to make sure the lights didn't interrupt his mission. Booth was sure he had his gambling problem under control, but does anyone every get their demons under control. He continued to stare out the window when the phone rang.

"Okay, I'm looking out the window and can't think about anything except what if I screw this up." Blair was panicking.

"Take it easy," He said. "I'm coming down the hall to your room now."

Booth had a new problem. How could Blair who seemed so confident and all of a sudden start falling apart. He knocked on her door and it seemed like minutes went by without an answer. He looked at the room number to make sure he was in the right place. 1636, yeah, that was the right room. He knocked again. "Give me a second," was the answer.

She opened the door and Booth could see that she had been crying. "Hey good looking, you okay," He tried to make it lighthearted.

"You know," She said, "When Hunter was killed I fell apart a few times but knew he wanted me to stay strong. Guess I'm just nervous, but I'm going to be okay. I want to do a good job." She smiled.

Booth was happy that she seemed to be okay now. "You ready for dinner?"

"You better be buying, buddy," she said, pulling her door shut behind her.

They headed downstairs and Blair asked him where they were going to go. He shrugged his shoulders and asked what she was in the mood for? They looked at each other and both almost at the same time said, "Pizza." This was going to be a problem. She liked mushrooms on her pizza with a variety of cheeses and other exotic toppings. Booth was an all meat lover guy. The more pepperoni, sausage and ham the better for him. "I know this little place between Harrah's and the Flamingo that has bands, cold beer and pizza," he told her.

"I'm in," she answered.

They moved through the casino and she marveled at the people, money, lights and action everywhere. Booth directed Blair to the moving walkway that traveled through the new sports book. The walls of televisions screens yelling out scores, plays and sporting action from horse racing, baseball and women's basketball to the finals of the World Cup in Soccer. The moving walkway made a low humming noise like that of a child's toy running on a hard surface. The light at the end of the walkway was like looking toward the last leg of a tunnel. It was bright and calling you to the outside world.

The evening had cast a bright glare on the face of the massive buildings that stood along the strip. The windows of the Flamingo Hotel reflected the mountain view off to the west. The sun was descending near the top of the jagged mountain landscape west of

Vegas. It would soon be evening and the lights of the strip were starting to glow in the shadows. Booth pulled Blair by the hand and told her that they needed to move toward the Mirage Hotel and cross the street. Traffic was bumper to bumper. License plates came from all over the country.

The place he had told her about was an outdoor restaurant with an avant garde stage in the middle. The bartenders performed for the customers as they prepared their drinks. One of them had just been juggling three bottles of liquor and another was stacking glasses about five feet high. Like everything else in Vegas, it was all about the presentation. Drinks were good, but the show brought in the customers. They grabbed a seat on the right side under the canopy that covered the entire area.

"What can I get for you?" Booth looked up. The waitress was tall, blond and a knockout. Uh, guess we should order a drink? Blair smiled at the girl. "I'll have a glass of white wine, how about you honey." Booth knew he had been had. Blair was smiling and tried not to laugh. "Bud Lite," He answered. She left them a menu and headed off to the bar. Once the blond left they both laughed out loud. "Pretty cute," Blair said. He just looked down at the menu. He didn't have a comeback. Blair could see a large stage at the far end of the canopy. "I guess that's where the bands play?"

Booth nodded. He was watching the bartender who was now doing a hand stand on the bar while pouring their drinks. "Guess you have to be a circus performer to work here," he said. Kind of cool, they both thought. The waitress brought their drinks and they said they would wait to order something to eat. A band was starting to set-up on the stage and the place was getting pretty crowded. Glad we got here when we did they said.

Vegas were teaming with night life. Harrah's Casino and Hotel was just to the left of the restaurant and the opening was wide so that people sitting outside could see gamblers putting their luck to the test. Like a lot of casinos in Vegas, there weren't any doors. The clanging noise of slot machines rang out calling patrons in to try their luck. Vegas was a 24/7 town. Nothing closed and there was always action to be found.

John Martin had completed the process of assigning the

investigation to his three bureau chiefs. Chris had been assigned to go with him back to the airport and bring Booth's car to the Federal Building. "Make sure they all know how critical this is," He told his people. They knew the director expected to be kept in the loop on everything they uncovered. The helicopter arrived at the Federal Building and Chris and the director climbed in.

Steve Orrison went over the details again with his counterparts. The investigation would be led by the Vegas Bureau with Booth and Blair responsible for meeting the Senator's aide and getting whatever they could from him. It was a simple task. Somehow Steve knew it wasn't going to go that way. It never does, he thought.

Senator Albertson's aide was completing the inventory of documents, books and furniture in the Senator's office. It would all be put into storage until a new Senator would be appointed to fill his seat. The Governor of Arizona had the task of appointing a replacement and the seat would be up for re-election next year. It would more than likely be filled by another person from the same party. Both Senator Albertson and the Governor were long time friends.

Because Senator Albertson wasn't married, his aide would be the person most likely to be involved in handling closing the office and helping set-up arrangements for the Senator's funeral. Corey Hart was twenty-nine years old and a graduate of Arizona State University. Although he was a law student, he never went to take the bar exam. He moved around and didn't have many friends. He was kind of a loaner. It was when he worked as a reporter on a local newspaper where he first met the Senator. The immediately became friends and Albertson appointed him to his staff. Once Corey became his aide he just didn't think he wanted to practice law. What would he do now? He had nowhere to go and very few friends in Washington. All his acquaintances were because of the Senator. Now that he was gone they would soon forget him. The office was very quiet. Everyone was gone and Corey was alone in the Senator's office.

He sat behind the Senator's desk and scrolled through the computer files, backing them up on his flash drive. There were many things the Senator had been working on and now maybe the aide could use them. One file was very big, it was titled, The Vegas Connection. The aide seemed to spend a great deal of time reading material as it was being copied on his flash drive. He had a thirty-two MG flash drive and he hoped it would all be compressed to fit.

Once that was completed he erased the file from the computer hard drive. This would be his information now. It would be his ticket for the future. The flash drive was placed on his key ring. No one would think to check out something that is so obviously in the open. He could easily get through security with it.

Senator Albertson had many friends and well wishers who were sending messages of sorrow to the office. The two secretaries had made sure they extended thanks on behalf of the Senator's family.

Albertson had one brother. His brother was a successful attorney in Phoenix. He ran a large legal firm that handled corporate mergers and real estate transactions. The firm employed a staff of eight attorneys and many legal aides. They were certified to practice in Arizona, Nevada and California. Albertson's brother had talked to the aide and requested that the aide handle affairs in Washington for him. He said that his company was in the middle of a major case and he couldn't get away until the funeral. People didn't think it was unusual because Albertson and his brother seemed to have very little contact over the last few years. Rumors were that there was a falling out after the last re-election campaign. The Senator who had run on a very conservative platform failed to come out strongly against the new casino's being built in Arizona during the primary. That upset many people especially his brother. His brothers firm had fought the new casinos because one of his largest clients owned a string of Bingo Parlors in Tucson and Phoenix. The new casinos would put his client out of business.

During the election, Albertson's brother's firm did not endorse either candidate. There was some talk about it, but the Senator had other strong backing and with it being his fourth term it was impossible to get any negative coverage from the Arizona press. The story was buried the back pages of the newspaper. Although Albertson always said in his speeches that he was against the expansion of legalized gambling in Arizona, he didn't introduce any measures that would have stopped or slowed them down. It was also suspicious that soon after winning his re-election, Albertson started to build his new home on the Colorado River. People never asked why he needed a five thousand square foot home, or why was it built it in that location. One of the new casino's was just across the river maybe within ten miles of the Senator's home.

The Senator's aide locked the office. Corey left some papers out on the large desk so that if anyone asked he could tell them that he was sorting items out for the records. The office staff thought that Corey was a weird little guy. They figured he was very bright, why else would Albertson have him on the team. It did seem to them that the aide had a little more authority than any previous aide for the Senator. Albertson's staff was very small. He kept many things to himself and very seldom used staff to handle anything other than paperwork and press releases. It was unusual for a Senator like himself not to have a head chief of staff, but Albertson didn't want one.

Corey lived just a few blocks from the Capitol off of K Street toward Georgetown. He had a four room apartment in an old brown stone building. It was very neat and well kept. When he got home he took out his flash drive and loaded the last file from Albertson's office computer on his own lap top. Once that was complete he thought he would check on the girl in Vegas that he had made plans to meet. She sounded very interesting he thought. What was that she had said? Yes, she understood loosing someone close. She had lost a girlfriend not too long ago. Maybe they both had a lot in common. He needed a friend and protection. Maybe she could help him solve his problems.

He checked his email messages then logged onto facebook. Yes, there she was, added as a friend earlier. He went to her main page and checked her profile. There was that picture again of a cute, blond and slightly built. Her face seemed familiar he thought, but from where? Guess she was right. Maybe they had met in Vegas with the Senator. He knew that he had seen her somewhere, but where was it. He opened one of her photo albums and it contained pictures of her in and around various landmarks in Vegas. He checked another one and she had her arm around another very cute girl. The picture was in front of Caesars Place.

He wondered if that was her friend she told him about. Her profile stated that she was single, living in Clark County, Nevada and enjoyed music and the theater. Those were two things he also liked. He was happy that she had made contact with him. Maybe she could help him get something out of those Vegas contacts that Albertson had, he thought. He needed someone who knew Vegas but not too smart. Blair could be his ticket.

Booth and Blair finished their pizza and watched the performers on the stage. The band was pretty good and the young girl singing was excellent. "It is hard to see how someone so talented hadn't made it big," Booth said.

"Problem is there are so many talented people and without a break making it in the movies, music or modeling it is very tough." Blair knew what she was talking about. She had been in Los Angeles for two years before she had her first modeling job. The competition is tough. There are so many talented people and getting discovered is the key. "That is why shows like *'American Idol'* and *'America's Got Talent'* have so many contestants," she said. There is very little difference between Carrie Underwood and Elsa Johnson that you can hardly tell them apart."

Booth looked at her and asked, "Who in the hell is Elsa Johnson?"

Blair laughed. "She didn't win *American Idol*, but sings as well. You can see her in the lounge of the Wynn in Vegas, but she doesn't have any hit records. She hasn't been discovered yet."

Booth nodded his head. "I see what you mean. Guess I've never looked at it that way."

It was totally dark now and the lights of the strip were gleaming brightly. Signs flashed the likes of *'Penn & Teller'* at the Mirage, *'Cher'* at Caesar's and *'Wayne Newton'* a Las Vegas legend at MGM. Smaller casinos just north of Harrah had flashing lights and billboards announcing 98% return on their slot machines. It was always exciting in Vegas. Booth felt a twinge as they crossed the street and headed back to Caesar's. He knew that he would love to put a few bucks into play on the dice table. Can't stop at a few, he knew it.

Traffic had clogged up Las Vegas Boulevard. It was bumper

to bumper and nothing was moving. It seemed that every other vehicle was a taxi carrying its fares to and from some of the hottest night spots in the world. People from all over the world came to Vegas. They traveled along the street to the moving walkway. They passed statues of Roman figures that could have graced the Coliseum in Rome. It was obvious to everyone that each casino tried to outdo the others. The Mirage had that Volcano that erupted daily from six p.m. to midnight. Treasure Island had the Pirate fight with two large Pirate ships in a lagoon with both male and female pirates fighting every evening for tourist to watch from the street level. The Bellagio had the dancing waterfall and of course New York, New York had the roller coaster that went through the hotel, around the Statue of Liberty and appeared to go underground only to arise to the highest levels of the hotel. Yes, Vegas is a one-of-a-kind place.

Booth reminded Blair that she should keep all receipts. "Anything you purchase is able to go on an expense account. If you need a dress, make-up or anything while we are here just hold on to the receipts." She appreciated the advice. It was good to have someone who knew all the inside information.

The trip back through the casino only found more people crowded at the tables and slots. The noise of the slots playing music from popular shows like, *I Dream of Jennie*, and *The Beverly Hillbillies* rang out as people were playing bonus rounds. The casinos had the right thing going. Bring in color, music, free drinks and sexy staff so people can't resist any of it. Blair liked to play blackjack if she was going to play anything. She felt it gave her the best odds of winning. Her dad had taught her how to play. They even had played a few times when they went to Vegas together a few years ago.

Booth felt a strong desire to hit the tables just for a few minutes. He knew it was a bad idea. How was he going to make it the whole time here would be another story? Their trip back took them through the fringe of the main lobby and to the bank of elevators on the north end. Blair could see that Booth was starring at the gaming tables as they walked through the casino. "I'm going up," She told him, "But if you want to stay down here and play some, go ahead."

He had the look of a kid in a toy store. Booth took a deep

breath and shook his head. "Better not, not today anyway. Besides, we can't play here. If we're employees we can't play in any Harrah's casino. We'll have to be up early and meet with our team from the Vegas office."

The doors to the elevator opened and they both got in. The sixteenth floor came up fast and they walked down the hallway. Blair stopped at her door, "This is my stop," she said. "What time should we meet tomorrow?"

"How about eight," Booth suggested.

"Sounds like a plan. Thanks for tonight. I feel better about everything." Blair opened her door and said goodnight. She saw that there was a message on her phone. A voice mail was left. The person identified themselves with the Vegas office and said they should plan to meet tomorrow at seven a.m. to go over the plans. Guess I'll call Booth and change our time to meet she thought. Before she could reach for the phone, it rang.

"Blair, we got a message from our contacts here."

"Yes, I got one too."

"Let's meet at six-thirty tomorrow and head downstairs. My message said to meet in the Coliseum café for breakfast."

They agreed and hung up. The plans were made and tomorrow would be the start of their operation.

Sixteen

The day of Senator Albertson's funeral started out like any other for his staff. They met in the Senator's office and had coffee, fruit and Danish. His office secretary always made sure there was a nice array of breakfast items for the Senator's staff. They all had their assignments for the day. Albertson's brother was arriving about eight-forty-five a.m. from Phoenix. Corey had arranged a service to pick them up. Corey told them that he was handling arrangements at the church. Albertson would lie in state tomorrow morning from nine a.m. to noon, with the funeral planned for one pm the next day. They could all head to the church together at eight-forty-five.

The two secretaries wondered once they cleared up Albertson's paperwork if they would have a position with the new appointee. The staff lady that took care of the office knew she was out of a job. They would all have to fend for themselves once a new Senator is appointed. Once in a while the new appointee would keep a secretarial staff member because they could ease the transition for them.

Albertson was a member of a large Baptist Church in Georgetown and all the plans were made with the Minister that he had for the past twelve years. It would be a quiet event with dignitaries from both the House and Senate making appearances. The Vice-President was scheduled to make a speech and they didn't know if Albertson's brother wanted to say something. The burial was going to be at a small cemetery off of Maryland Parkway about ten miles from the Capitol. Some people were surprised that he wasn't going to be buried in Arizona. Most senators and Washington officials were buried back in their home state. It was the brother who said that Albertson had wished to be buried in the Nation's Capitol. He already had a plot and arrangements were made. Everything was scheduled to end at around four p.m. Corey said he had planned a private dinner for the staff and Albertson's family members after the burial. We shouldn't be too late he told them.

Everyone was be dressed in traditional dark suits and one of the secretaries who had been with the Senator for close to ten years planned to bring a dozen of roses. She said that she hoped they would all put one on the Senator's casket. Of course everyone nodded and smiled at her. She was moved to tears as the others comforted her.

Dulles Airport was always busy with many people coming and going especially early in the afternoon. The flight from Phoenix was shown to be on time. The Senator's brother and wife were traveling alone. They had left their children back in Phoenix. Although the Senator was their only uncle neither of them really spent any time with him. Early in his career, his brother brought the kids to Washington, and Albertson made sure he showed them all around the Capitol. Now it was a man from the staff waiting to greet the family members. The man waiting for the Albertson's held a sign so that he could be recognized. He was to take them to their hotel and then the church and stand by to escort them wherever they needed to go for the day.

Senator Albertson's aide talked to the Minister at the church and hoped to make sure everything was set. The church was very large and had a congregation of close to three thousand people. The Secret Service was already in place and made sure that everything was secure and that only those who were invited would be allowed in the church's front area. The last dozen rows were roped off for the general public. The Vice-President would arrive close to noon and planned to enter from a side entrance that the Secret Service had arranged for him. The Speaker of the House along with distinguished members of the Senate and House would also use the same entrance. This would be the third time the same church was to hold a memorial service for a Washington member of the Senate or House in the last year.

There was no mention of any of the Justices of the Supreme Court attending yet. Everyone was sure that his friend, Justice Leonard, would be planning to attend. With so much speculation about him and Albertson it wasn't sure what he planned to do. They were very good friends, everyone knew that, and his absence would be worse than his attendance. If any last minute plans were made only the Secret Service would be aware of them.

Brandon Booth woke up early and marveled at the sun as it rose in the east along the mountains that surrounded the Henderson Valley area. The site of the sun rise in the desert was always something special. Booth felt that the mountains cast shadows along the ridges that took the shape of figures from old western cowboy movies. As a little kid he always watched old westerns with his dad. It was something they both enjoyed. One summer his father took him to Arches National Park in Utah. The landscape was like that of no other. The earth's rugged mountains had formed many arches that appeared like windows looking out into the vast wilderness. Booth kept an old picture of his dad standing between the openings of the massive double window arch. It always made him smile when he looked at it. It wasn't long after that trip that his parents were killed in an auto accident. Booth went from one foster home to another over the rest of his childhood.

His watch said five-thirty and he planned on a quick shower and getting dressed. The meeting was set for six-thirty with the team from the Las Vegas FBI office. Booth knew Blair would be ready so he just jumped into the shower. Blair's alarm had just gone off and she couldn't believe it was morning already. She slept sound and felt pretty good. A hot shower and Red Bull drink was all she needed. She loved those little cans of Red Bull and how the caffeine jolt it delivered brought her to life. She planned on calling Booth after taking her shower. They were to meet with the Vegas team in a little out-of-the-way café near the Flamingo Hotel. It would take them maybe five minutes to walk there.

People started arriving at the First Street Baptist church and the security team from the Secret Service was handling checking identifications if necessary. Many of the dignitaries' were easily recognized by the security team. Instructions were clear. All key members attending were to enter the church from the side entrance off of Thirty-First Street. The front entrance was to be used by the general public.

The events of the previous day went very well. The public viewing was covered by the local and national press. One of the local reporters was Gina Warren. She was the last person to interview the Senator and had the follow-up story that was carried by all the news agencies. She had a keen aspect of the events and she was invited to cover the funeral from the Senator's staff.

Corey was in the vestibule talking to the pastor. He wanted to make sure that the schedule speakers were going to be allowed plenty of time to eulogize his boss. He seemed pre-occupied, the pastor thought. As they talked, the aide would often be looking off into space. The pastor figured he was still suffering over the loss of such a close friend and mentor.

The back of the church had filled up very fast. They had originally roped off the last twelve rows for the public but now were thinking about adding four more rows of seating for them. The church was large, and it could accommodate a large crowd. Some of the Washington's guest started to arrive and they were greeted by the Senator's office staff. The aide along with other staff members thanked them for their attendance. They were happy that although there was a cloud of allegations still hovering around the Senator, that his colleagues still came out of respect. Many Senator's had served with Albertson for years in the Senate and on special committees. He was once a very powerful man in the Senate. The Party Chairman had just arrived with the Speaker of the House and their wives. The Vice-President was expected in a few minutes. The stage was set for a final farewell to a long time representative of the people.

People in front of the church noticed that Chief Justice Anthony Leonard was not yet present. It was expected that not only would he attend but that he would say a few words at the funeral for his long time friend. The implications of him being involved with Albertson in both a scandal and possibly a sexual affair weren't known to many of those attending. The FBI had kept most of their investigation quiet. Although some leaks had linked the Chief Justice as being investigated by the bureau, none of them linked him with Albertson or his corruption case.

Albertson's career started like many politicians. He graduated from Arizona State University and attended law school at Stanford.

He found a comfortable group with the young republican's at Stanford. They often discussed important legislation that was pending and all admired then President Ronald Regan. When he went back home to Arizona he got involved in local politics and ran for a seat in the Arizona state house. His first attempt went badly and did not muster more than two percent of the vote in the primaries. That is when he met Anthony Leonard. He and Leonard soon became very close friends. Leonard was a sitting Judge in Phoenix handling small cases, however, he was very close with the leader of the Arizona Republican party. Leonard introduced Albertson to his friends and they all seemed to have many of the same opinions. Leonard was recognized after he had handled an important case that ended up in his courtroom. It involved a suspect in a serial murder in Phoenix. It was the first time DNA evidence had been used to link a suspect to a string of murders. Leonard's ruling had been appealed all the way to the Supreme Court only to be upheld by the nation's highest court. The then Chief Justice wrote in his opinion why Leonard's decisions were both accurate and opened the way for DNA evidence to be used in similar cases.

As time went on Leonard career rose to the position of Justice in Arizona's Supreme Court, and as he rose, Albertson's career rose with him. The two were often seen together at parties and because of their political relationship there was never any inference of them being gay. Even as they both assumed positions of power in Washington no one ever linked them in any way other than friends.

The Baptist church was crowded and the Vice-President was taking the podium to speak. Many people were now aware that Justice Leonard was not in attendance. People were murmuring about his absence. They were wondering if he was sick or away because of some case in the court.

The Vice-President covered Albertson's career and the many accomplishment he had during his time in the Senate. People nodded with approval as he detailed important legislation that Albertson had spearheaded through the Senate. The leader of the House had also spoke before the Vice-President and honored Albertson for his work in passing key bills. Albertson's brother was to be the last speaker. He requested to be last and out of respect for family everyone agreed. His aide and office staff wished they could go over what he planned to say, but his brother wanted to handle it all himself.

When Albertson's brother took the podium everyone was very silent. His speech was a retrospective look back into their childhood and how their parents had always taught them right from wrong. He talked about family values and this played well with the republican constituents there. When he looked down at the casket in the center of the alter he slowed his speech. "My brother had some great ideas and always was concerned about the people of Arizona and those of this great country. Recently, we've had some differences. In Washington many of us have differences but that shouldn't change the fact that he was a great man serving our country."

Both the Senator's aide and office staff were holding their breath as his brother mentioned their differences.

His brother finished with a tearful memory of him and the Senator as young children going on vacation with their parent's to Washington. "Never in our lives did either of us expect to be in this position today. From my family, I thank you, for all the kindness and support you have given to our family."

Everyone was moved by his remarks. Families always have differences, but it was nice to know that there was still love for one another. Would the events that unfold over the next few days change that? Will the bureau try to soften the blow of the Senator's involvement and life style? These were questions that only time would tell.

The funeral ended with a private burial as requested in Albertson's will. He had made The plans to always be in Washington and his burial place was within a few miles of where the church service was held.

When the service was over many in attendance went out to grab a bite to eat. The discussion was centered on the fact that Justice Leonard wasn't there. People wondered why. It was a known fact in Washington circles that Albertson and Leonard were very close friends from a long time ago in Arizona. They often were seen together at concerts and plays. Why wasn't Leonard there? No one could answer that question.

Gina and the channel 7 news team had run their coverage

through the funeral all the way to the procession leaving Georgetown to the cemetery. Gina ended the coverage by telling viewers who was in attendance and highlighted the Chief Justice being absent. Her staff had file photos of the two of them being together at major events and that they were both from Arizona. She planned on finding out more once this segment was aired.

The meeting with the two members of the Vegas FBI team went very well. They were able to answer all the questions that Blair and Booth had, and brought the keys to the apartments and a car for their use. Blair's cover was that of a dancer in a review that was appearing on weekends in the lounge. Booth's cover was that of a pit boss in the high limits area. Neither of them was expected to actually fill those rolls. The brochures for the lounge act did not have a group picture on it. Blair would be introduced to the group later in the day and they will understand that she would be a stand-in, a reserve in case of someone getting hurt. Her former Hollywood credentials would help pull that off.

Booth on the other hand would be given a tour of the high limit area by the supervisor. They will tell the other employees that Booth is with Caesar's Entertainment accounting offices and will have access to all the areas in the casino that have high limit betting. He would need to wear a dark suit, as he expected, each day. He would only have to show up once in a while to keep the cover intact. Booth was there to support Blair in case the meeting with Albertson's aide went bad. He would be able to shadow her and her plans were to keep Corey on Caesar's property.

All of this made sense. The Vegas team was working undercover looking into improper activities with the Nevada Gaming Commission by two of the new smaller casino's that had opened recently. It is these two casinos that also had locations now in Arizona and Michigan that were at the center of the gambling probe. If Albertson's aide gave Blair any gambling information she was to get it to the Vegas unit.

Senator Albertson's aide seemed distant to those of the staff after the burial. He was somewhat occupied they felt with another matter. What could it be? He left the dinner after the funeral service early. The rest of the office staff planned things with Albertson's brother.

Corey told them that he had some important things left to do.

Albertson's brother never liked Corey. He was more than happy to excuse him from the event. He felt that Albertson gave the aide too much power. He felt Corey compromised his own position with his brother.

Corey got in his car and headed off to Georgetown. He had made several calls after the burial and it seemed that whoever he was calling wasn't answering. One of the secretaries said she heard him leaving a very curt message. It was as if he expected someone and they were avoiding him. "Strange little man," She said to her friend.

The ride to Georgetown only took about twenty-five minutes. Georgetown had many beautiful brownstone homes that lined the main street. There was also a cluster of shops and restaurants that ran from Wisconsin Avenue to the river. The University was in the center of downtown along with the main hospital and renowned research center.

Corey parked his car along the meters on Wisconsin and walked a few blocks past a small deli. He was on a mission. He turned off of Wisconsin onto Biltmore Avenue and continued walking down the street. He stopped in front of 23433 Biltmore. It was a two story brownstone building with a beautiful porch that wound around the front. The stark white pillars on the porch were a vivid contrast to the rest of the building. They had been refreshed by sandblasting last year, along with the eleven steps that led up to the front door.

This was Chief Justice Anthony Leonard's home. He had been here many times with Senator Albertson. He had talked to the Chief Justice just yesterday, and it was confirmed that he planned to attend the funeral. Leonard had told Corey that he would give a short speech. The aide thought that the Chief Justice had been unusually solemn since Albertson's death. The three of them were close and often shared personal feelings, but Leonard was remote and did not seem to want to talk to him. Once he was asked about the funeral plans he hemmed and hawed before agreeing to speak at his friend's funeral.

The climb up the eleven cement steps was quick. Corey rang the bell and waited for an answer. None was to be heard. He decided to knock on the front door in case the bell was out of order. There still wasn't a response. How he wished that he had a key to the Justice's home. He knew that Albertson had a key, but he wasn't aware where he kept it. He had to find out why the Chief Justice wasn't at the funeral. The three of them had shared so much the past few years. He loved the Senator and knew that Leonard did too. What should he do now? How should he handle this without causing a scene? He descended the steps and went around to the side door. Leonard's brownstone was an end unit and it had a side entrance. At one time, the aide was sure it was used by maids or milk delivery.

There were two smaller steps and the door at the side entrance had an oval leaded glass window at the top. It was too high for him to peek in. He pulled his cell phone out and rang Leonard's home number again. He could hear the phone ringing from inside the unit. There still wasn't an answer. Now what, he thought. Just then a squad car pulled up in front of the Justice's home. Two officers got out and saw the man at the side entrance. They had a call from a neighbor across the street saying that someone was trying to break into the Chief Justice's home.

One of them stood near the car as the first officer approached. "Hey! You there, Stop!" He hollered. Corey looked up and started moving toward the officer.

"Yes Sir, I'm here trying to see Justice Leonard. I've been calling and knocking but he isn't answering.

"Son, you need to make an appointment with his office," The officer told him.

"No, you don't understand. I'm Senator Albertson's aide and today was his funeral. The Justice was supposed to be there."

The officer could see that the young man was out of breath and seemed emotionally shaken. "Son, come over here and sit down. You don't look too good." He was concerned that if the young man was telling the truth, that he should call it in to the Secret Service team that had the duty to cover the Justice's home. He wondered where they were.

Just then a black Chevrolet Suburban pulled up. Two men in dark suits came over to the squad car. "What's going on here?"

They asked. Corey had been at the Chief Justice's home for close to five minutes now.

The first officer said, "We have this young man saying that he's trying to get the Chief Justice to answer his door." They recognized the young man. "You're Albertson's aide," He said.

"Yes, I am Sir."

"I thought you would be at the funeral?"

"I was, it was over a little bit ago, but the Chief Justice was supposed to be there. He never showed." Corey didn't want all this commotion but now he had a squad car and the Secret Service asking him question. He was breathing hard and looked flushed.

The two Secret Service agents looked at each other. "Okay, I'll call his office to see if he showed up there." They talked to one of the law clerks who said that the Chief Justice wasn't in. The clerk said that Leonard had planned on attending a funeral for Senator Albertson. The Secret Service agents talked to his partner and they went up the stairs. They knocked and rang the bell. There wasn't an answer. One of the men pulled out a set of keys and looked down to the two local police officers. You both stay here with this young man while we check inside. Because of the police call and the action outside of the Chief Justice home news crews were alerted to the breaking events.

A few minutes later a channel 7 news team van pulled up in front of the brown stone. Gina and her camera man got out and the men standing with Corey wondered why they were there. She was moving toward the group when noise from down the street caught everyone's attention.

All of a sudden sirens could be heard coming up the street. The two officers looked at each other in dismay. The ambulance slid to a stop in front of the home. Two men in white jackets and carrying an emergency case ran up the stairs. It was silent for a while and one of the agents came back out and talked to one of the officers. They nodded and told the aide that he would have to come to headquarters with them.

"Why, what the hell is going on?" Corey demanded to know.

The men looked at each other before telling him anything. We will fill you in once we're at headquarters.

"I want to know now what is going on!"

Gina had cameras rolling and captured everything that was

happening. She knew the Senator's aide very well and had been with him the morning before the Senator's heart attack. She was positioned near the front of the house with the ambulance in the background. The officers were still standing with the aide and she could tell that they were arguing about something.

Just then one of the paramedics came out and talked to a Secret Service agent. They had the officer that was talking to Corey come over to them. They all had huddled and the officer headed back toward Corey. Gina was trying to get closer but the team of police on the scene now kept her crew back from the action. She kept the film footage running and was giving viewers live details as the action picked up behind her. How did Channel 7 know there was something going on? Who called them? Was Gina following Corey after the funeral?

The officer moved toward Corey as he was still arguing with the other men that he needed to know what was happening. He looked at him and stated. "Okay I'm going to fill you in on everything but you're going downtown with us." Corey seemed to calm down a bit and waited for the news. "We found the Chief Justice in his study." The officer told him. "It appears that he hung himself."

Fear came over the Corey's face. "What! Hung! No, that can't be!" Tears welled up in his eyes and he slumped to the ground.

The two officers tried to help him but he cried uncontrollable and crumbled onto the grass. The men just starred at each other. They felt helpless.

Gina was catching it all with her cameraman filming everything. She heard the officer tell Corey that the Chief Justice was dead, looks like he hung himself. This had been an unusual turn of events and the Capitol would be flooded with reporters from all over. Again Gina and her team were on the scene that would be bringing the news to the world.

Seventeen

The events of the past few days had rocked the Nation's Capitol. They were almost unthinkable for the members of Congress. First there was the possible investigation of one of their highest ranking members, then his sudden death. Now the news that the Chief Justice of the Supreme Court, Anthony Leonard had killed himself! The White House was concerned for many reasons. With only three months before the upcoming election, the president didn't need any more scandals to hurt his party's chance of keeping them in power. Recent political poles had shown almost an even race between the two men running for the presidency. How will these events change the race? Only time would tell!

The press was having a field day with events on so many fronts. Gina Warren was on every night with a recap for the viewers in the Nation's Capitol. Her stock was climbing and her coverage was being carried by all the networks. Thousands of television markets had the story from Washington, all from Gina's perspective.

The Secret Service had started a thorough investigation into the death of the Chief Justice. Although he was found hanging from the beam in his library, there wasn't a note, which is always unusual. The forensic team from the Washington FBI was working the case for them. John Martin wasn't sure how these pieces were fitting together, but he knew something was wrong with this picture. Albertson's death was of natural causes. Stress and the pending investigation combined with a man out of shape, all of that had made sense. But this suicide didn't fit. The Chief Justice had just received the support of his colleagues in a recent press conference. He also couldn't know that the FBI was looking into his relationship with Albertson. Now how does the picture of Albertson's aide in a possible compromising position with the former Senator and now the same aide at the Chief Justice home fit together? There seemed to be more questions than answers.

The Secret Service agents made sure that Albertson's aide was okay. Although they had him taken to the Georgetown police station, it was only a formality. They realized from his reactions that he couldn't be involved in Leonard's death. They made sure he got home safely. One of the Georgetown police officers drove Corey's vehicle to his apartment. It was just a few blocks from Justice Leonard's home. They were concerned that the aide might need medical attention, but he gathered his composure and just wanted to go home. He continued to say that he was afraid and needed protection. When they questioned him he just said that he was worried that someone might be after him too. What did he mean by that?

When that was reported back to the head of their unit he just said the little guy is just paranoid since the two deaths. Gina Warren tried to contact Corey but he didn't return any of her calls. He suspected that the Chief Justice did not commit suicide but he couldn't tell anyone. Corey wanted to get out of town as soon as possible. The contact with Blair on facebook would be perfect he thought.

John Martin contacted his three western bureau chiefs to inform them of new events in the on-going case. He thought that Albertson's aide probably won't be going to Vegas now. The undercover operation that Booth and Blair were involved in might be called off. Steve Orrison suggested that they keep things going for a few days to see if the Corey contacted Blair. The director was good with that. Maybe Booth could help the Vegas team with their work in checking out the implications of Albertson being involved with two casino figures that may have mob ties. The director also contacted his New York and Detroit teams to continue their investigation into the casino's that were operated by the same two men.

When Booth got the call from Steve he covered the new events with Blair. They were both wondering how much longer they would be in Vegas with these changes. Blair made sure she checked her facebook account in case the Corey contacted her. There was nothing there yet. She planned on reporting to Caesar's employee lounge and wanted to make sure that she was seen around the area. Although her cover was that of a back-up dancer, she knew they would be practicing. Why not take the opportunity for a workout, she thought. How many times do you get to be a Vegas showgirl? She chuckled to herself as she got ready. She would at least be around so that if asked, other dancers would say that they knew her. It had been years since she had any dance lessons and the last time she did anything physical was a Roller Derby show at the Hilton Hotel and Casino a few years back. Most all her recent promotional jobs had been as a model.

The head of the lounge show was given a story that would help cover Blair's roll. The local office had told him that she was doing a cover story on showgirls. He also wanted to help with her cover. He didn't know her real reason for being there. He planned to have her watch the routines and maybe practice with her after the other dancers left. This would help her story he thought and maybe get him a mention in it. They had not met yet.

Blair was dressed in her leotards and carried a change of clothes in a duffle bag that said Caesars Palace. She wore a silver top and short black skirt over the leotards. She had planned to meet the shows director a few minutes before the other dancers arrived. She wore her Caesars identification badge that was attached to a plastic holder with a clip on the end. As she walked through the casino to the lounge area she could see that not too many players were gambling at that time of the day. It seemed that the early gamblers were mostly older people, often pulling their oxygen carts or wheel chairs around with them. The casino crowd changed dramatically from the morning to the evening. Older gamblers liked the low limit slots. The nickel and penny slots were popular with that crowd. They came for the cheap buffets, free lounge acts and entertainment. The evening crowd was younger, dressed better, liked to drink and gambled big time.

Blair entered the lounge and could see that it was roped off from the general public. Everything was dark. As she moved toward the stage area she heard a person call out to her. "Miss, you can't be in here." It was a security guard. He approached and saw she had a badge and was obviously dress like a dancer. "I'm sorry," He said. "You're here pretty early. Most of the dancers don't get here until ten-thirty."

"Yeah, I would rather be sleeping too, but I hurt my ankle last week and hope to give it a try out today. I'm meeting with Jacob this morning." She thought by using the show director's first name it would look normal.

"Hope your ankle is okay." As the guard strolled away he slowly turned back to take another look at her. He shook his head and thought, so many pretty girls here, wonder where they all come from?

She moved onto the stage and saw a light off to the right side of the curtains. She approached and a voice called out. "Can I help you?" It was Jacob, the shows director.

"Good morning, I'm Blair."

Jacob was surprised to see her so early. He had planned to get her the background details of his show so she would have the information needed for her article. He hadn't met a writer before. He had been told that she had some dancing experience so that would help. He extended his hand and said, "I see you're dressed and ready to go."

"I hope that I don't cause you any problems. It's been a long time since I had been in any dance reviews. I'm in pretty good shape so hopefully I can keep up."

He smiled at her. "Okay, let me assign you a locker for your things and when the other dancers arrive I'll introduce you. There shouldn't be a problem, especially because you'll be a back-up dancer. Everyone is always worried about someone taking their job. I will give you whatever information you want for the article."

Blair grabbed her duffle bag and headed back stage with Jacob. The dressing room was small and she could see that it would be very crowded at show time. He had told her that they performed Wednesday's through Sunday nights with two shows each evening. One was at seven p.m. and the second one was at ten p.m. Each show lasted about ninety minutes. "We're here to entertain and keep everyone in the casino. Don't need them going somewhere else. We have everything here for them."

There was a beautiful mahogany bar that stretched from the left side of the stage to the far corner. The lounge had small tables that had three chairs placed at each of them. The ceiling was sparkling with silver stars hanging down from the rafters. The room was larger than she expected. She bet it could hold close to one-hundred-fifty people easily. There was a glass wall in the back of the room so that it could draw the attention of anyone walking by. Often gambler's that weren't doing well would come in and watch the show and catch a few drinks.

"After you put your things away, come back to the right side of the stage."

She was nervous. Maybe she could do a couple routines with Jacob and get the feel for what was expected.

"Blair," He said. "There is a warm up bar against the back wall. I don't want you to pull something."

She had taken ballet lessons as a kid and knew how to use the bar. Her gym also had a similar bar that she would use before exercising. She started to warm up and Jacob was doing something on a small desk near the end of the backstage entrance. He turned and watched her for a few minutes. "Well maybe not so bad," he said to himself. She was moving slowly in a dance motion that he recognized. Now he turned his total attention to her. Blair was on her toes doing a normal ballet warm-up routine. Jacob was pleasantly surprised. "You didn't tell me that you were a ballet dancer," He said.

"It's been years. I took ballet as a kid and then again when I got a roll in a play a few years ago, I went back to ballet for strength and conditioning. Most people don't realize how tough dancing is."

Jacob was impressed. His fears were that he would never be able to let the other performers see her dancing. He also appreciated her understanding the profession. Not many people did. He was surprised but happy that if she was doing a story it helped that she appreciated the career of showgirls. "Do you feel like doing a few routines?"

She was pleased and said, "Sure."

He moved to the right side of the stage and told her to watch him. He was maybe in his early thirties and looked to be in great shape. He moved gracefully as she watched him twirl around. "This is how we open the show," He said. All the dancers would move from the right curtain area and spin out onto the stage. Their choreographed routine was designed to grab the audience's attention. He knew that most lounge acts had to compete with the clanging of slots machines, waiters serving drinks and loud conversation. He hoped that his show was one that would get the crowd's attention and that the performance kept them watching. His dancers and singers were electrifying. Their costumes were like many those in Vegas, skimpy and sexy. The singers had been in his show for the past three months and their music was contemporary. Most nights his show received a lot of positive reaction and applause. It had been touted by the local Vegas Insider Magazine as a great show.

Blair followed his moves and seemed to be doing okay. It was obvious that she was rusty but had great potential. Jacob was pleased. They had two days before the first show and he felt that Blair could step right in if needed. He had to remind himself that she was just there to write an article. "Christ I could use her," he said.

The morning went well and Blair made sure she was visible to as many people as she could. In case Corey did come to Vegas, maybe she could cement her cover by bringing him to the lounge. She had been working with Jacob for close to two hours when a few more dancers started showing up. Blair heard the voices from behind the curtain. He said he would introduce her. "You just need to watch them. I have another back-up dancer, Julie that will be here soon. The two of you should sit off to the side and watch the routines." He knew that women were catty, and there would be naturally some concern about a new dancer. He planned to tell them that Blair would be a back-up with the show until he was ready to send her to the Flamingo for a new show he was producing. Jacob had been with Caesars Entertainment for about ten years. He started as a dancer then progressed to his current position. He was well respected by the Vegas entertainment community.

Blair enjoyed the morning and smiled when Jacob introduced her around to the girls that were arriving. Many of them were Vegas regulars. So many dancers and entertainers made the circuit around Vegas. With most casino's having multiple shows both in their lounge and main theater acts that there was always a spot where you could get a job. She was well received, especially with the news that she wouldn't be staying long. Many of them were not very confident, so a new face might be a problem. They loved working for Caesars Entertainment. With so many casinos under their control you could always get a position in one of their shows. A few of the girls had been in the show at Paris, and the show at Caesars was easier they felt.

Blair sat with the other back-up dancer and watched the rehearsal.

Booth arrived at the casino and was being escorted around by the head of security. He would be introduced as an internal Caesars Entertainment employee checking on the operation at the Palace. He looked sharp in his black and gray pinstripe suit. Booth played the role well. He kept a stern look on his face as he was shown around. His identification tag just stated Caesars Entertainment Central office. The main office was downtown Las Vegas off of Fremont Street. That was one of the original locations of the founder's first hotels. Now Fremont Street was the main drag through downtown.

A few years back the Las Vegas Convention Bureau decided that they should enclose Fremont Street with a canopy and close it off to traffic. This made it a great tourist walking area with restaurants, gift shops and casinos dotting the landscape. The Union Plaza Hotel and Casino was at the end of the street and he Golden Nugget and 4 Queens Hotels and casinos anchored the center of the new strip. The Fremont Street Experience is a covered area of Downtown where local casinos have been connected to the street and to each other in a unique visual manner. With more than two million lights and a state-of-the-art sound system, the Fremont Street Experience brings nightly shows through the world's largest audio-video system.

Las Vegas had branched out so much in the past ten years with the Boulder Highway now having four major casinos and hotels along with the new venues of The Red Rock and Green River Hotels and Casinos out about ten miles from the main drag. Both of these new locations boasted of a city within their properties. They had condos and malls built to support their guest staying on the property. All of this had grown greatly until the recession hit in late 2008. Now Nevada had the nation's highest unemployment and led the country in foreclosures. Many people that had purchased a second home there now had defaulted.

Booth hoped to spend about two hours at Caesars Palace and then meet with the two agents from the Vegas office to go over their plans on the investigation of the two casino owners. He knew that the Nevada Gaming Commission had researched the two men thoroughly without finding anything.

The group that these men headed also other locations and now the Old Frontier Hotel and Casino property was on their radar. A connection with east coast mob could not be proved, however the money trail always seemed to get fuzzy. It appeared to come from an off-shore group in the Bahamas. This group also owned a large casino in Freeport on Grand Bahamas Island. How this all fit together along with the investigation to Albertson was what the FBI wanted to know. The director had assigned another team checking things out in Freeport. The answer had to lie somewhere, and he planned on finding it.

The Phoenix team was doing background investigation into the purchase of the house on the Colorado River by Senator Albertson. Albertson, like many politicians, had other financial venues. He often was a guest speaker in and around the Capitol: as well as, in Arizona. However, none of them offered the amount of monetary return to make a purchase of this magnitude. He had put down seventy percent of the cost in cash. Many questions remained on the purchase of the home. Why build it there? Why would a single man in his late sixty's want such a large home? How long had he owned the property? All these questions were being checked into by the Phoenix Bureau office.

Blair had completed her time with Jacob and watched the girls perform their routine. It was pretty interesting. They had choreographed the entire routine to highlight the current NFL football season. The songs were hits to honor the various teams and cities in the National Football League. With so many tourists in Vegas it was very popular with them. Often times when they heard a song depicting their team and city cheers would go out. They rehearsed every Monday and Tuesday and shows were on Thursday's through Sunday. With the events that just happened in Washington, Blair figured she would be gone by Thursday.

Jacob wanted to make sure Blair had everything necessary to write a great review of his show. He used the practice session with extra workouts so that he could showcase the routines for her. No one had told him how long she would be shadowing the show but he wanted to take advantage of every moment.

She made sure before leaving that she congratulated him on the performance. "I can't wait to see the real thing in lights and with costumes." Jacob smiled and was pleased with the events of the morning. He handed her a costume and she thanked him. Sweet Jesus, she thought. *I hope I don't have to wear this thing.* She could tell that it was cut very low in the front and extremely high on the hips. Booth would roar if he saw her in this.

Eighteen

Blair arrived back to the apartment that the Vegas Bureau set up for her. She decided to check her facebook account before going down to the pool. Might as well take advantage of the great amenities the place had, she figured. There it was! The Senator's aide had posted a message on her wall. She read it and dialed Booth's cell phone. This was critical.

Booth was on the strip and was just leaving Caesars Palace. He was having a hard time not going into another casino and placing a few wagers. Just a few hands of Blackjack, that couldn't hurt anyone he thought. He started to walk into the Mirage Casino entrance. You could hear the sound of slot machines playing the sound of people winning from a hundred yards away. Booth smiled like a kid heading into the ice cream parlor. Just then his cell phone went off. He saw it was Blair calling. "Crap, What does she want now?"

"Booth, I got a weird message from Albertson's aide. He said he's catching a flight tonight and wants to get together as soon as possible. The weird part is if we thought he was gay, he kind of wanted to stay with me at my place." Booth could tell that Blair was breathing hard and might be freaking out a little.

"What happened to his contacts here?" Booth remembered that the aide said he didn't need help with a room. He knew Blair was starting to panic. "Maybe you can say that you have a friend staying with you but you can get him a room." Booth was thinking how to help her.

"I've got a great idea! I could tell him my sister came in and surprised me. Maybe one of the agents in the Vegas team could pose as my sister?"

"I'm heading to the car right now. Go ahead and answer him back and see what his reaction is. I'll contact the Vegas office." Blair's call probably kept Booth from doing something he shouldn't do. It was hard to play just a few hands of blackjack, but for a gambler, it would be impossible. Booth never told his boss about the gambling problem. It had been a few years and he was sure he could handle it now.

Blair decided to send the reply from her I-Phone. She wanted to make him think that she was working. He might wonder why she was in her apartment or near a computer at three in the afternoon. Her message was clear and short.

"I'm looking forward to meeting you. I would be more than happy to have you stay at my apartment but my sister came in to surprise me. I can get you a comp room at Caesars?"

She held her phone waiting for a reply. It seemed like an eternity. Just then the sound of a message chimed. She hit the key to retrieve it.

She read it aloud although she was alone. Thanks that would be great! I just don't want to be alone. Could you put the room in your name? I don't want anyone to know where I am right now.

Blair sent the reply without calling Booth. "No Problem, Can I pick you up at the airport?"

The answer came back quick, Yes, that will be nice I'll send you the details when I have them.

Blair called Booth to give him the update. He told her that she needed to get his flight information. Washington has three carriers that fly to Vegas and quite a few flights each day. You also need to set up a meeting place. I'll call the Vegas office to get rooms set up. Booth was thinking two steps ahead.

"Booth, he has my picture from facebook and I have his. Hey! I'm getting another message from him."

The message answered all of Booth's concerns. I will be on flight number 2312, Delta Airlines arriving at eight-thirty-five p.m. I have your picture and will meet you at the baggage area.

Blair sent back an approval. She also said she made dinner reservations and told him not to grab some junk at the airport. He sent a thank you back and was looking forward to meeting her.

She updated Booth. By now he was just around the corner from the apartment. "Hey, I'll be there in a minute. Are you at your apartment?"

She laughed, where else would she be. "Yes, I was going to use the pool until I got his message."

Booth got to her apartment and they called Steve back in Los Angeles. They gave him a complete update and said they were going to contact the Vegas team to set up everything they needed. Steve said he would call the director and Vegas Bureau Chief before they called it in to them. The Vegas team was happy to help and set up a room at Caesars for Corey in Blair's name. Both bureau chiefs wondered why the aide didn't want anyone to know where he was. He had previously said he had contacts, and a room wasn't a problem. When the director contacted the D.C. Bureau they told him that their agents reported that Corey was skittish when they took him back home after the events at the Chief Justice home. He stated that he was afraid. The director was pissed that no one thought to report that to him. He chewed out everyone in ear shot.

Booth relayed the message to Blair and said that Steve said to make sure he was following close by. Who knows what's going on with the aide? He seemed unstable.

Flights from D.C. to Vegas were about four and a half hours long. Blair planned on using the car that the Vegas team left for her and Booth. Booth suggested that maybe she could take a team member from the Vegas office and introduce her as the sister that was visiting. Blair felt it would be too much. If she was supposed to gain the aides trust and get anything from him, she needed to do it alone. Booth knew she was right and agreed. They set her up in a junior suite. It was listed under her name but it would be the one Corey would be using. The Vegas office put a tracer on the phone in the room and a camera in one of the vents.

The evening of the flight showed to be on time as Blair found the baggage area. One cool thing in Vegas was that they always posted arrivals early in the appropriate baggage carrousel so you knew where the bags would come to. She felt she could just stand around and watch for Corey to come get his bags. Booth got a second vehicle from the motor pool in Vegas and stood at the next baggage carrousel that Blair was waiting at. He had parked in the row behind Blair in the parking deck and brought an empty suitcase to pull as he followed them to her car. He wanted to make sure everything was going as planned and that if needed he would be right there to help her. If only Booth realized that Blair was a martial arts expert. She could take care of herself if necessary.

She had been waiting about twenty-five minutes when she saw Corey coming into the baggage area. He was looking around a lot and seemed to be acting strange. Blair waited, and when she had made eye contact, he started to approach her. She moved closer as he put his carry-on on the floor and opened his arms. Blair hugged him and she felt that he was trembling. "Are you okay?" She said sympathetically.

He kept holding onto her and whispered, "I'm hoping no one is following me."

Blair was not quite sure what he meant, but played along. "It wouldn't look suspicious if we just kept holding each other for a little bit. That's kind on normal in airports." Corey was scanning the area as he continued to hold Blair.

Corey was happy that he came and felt comfortable in her arms. Booth was watching from the next baggage area and wondered what in the hell was going on. They've never met before, and now a five minute love-in. He wanted so badly to go over there but just stood and watched.

"Are you feeling better?" Blair asked.

"Yes! Do you think anyone is watching us?"

"I don't see anyone paying attention to us. Why do you think someone is following you?"

"I'll tell you in the car. So many strange things have happened." He grabbed his bag. It was plain, blue about twenty-six inches and larger than if you were going somewhere for an overnight. She directed him toward the south doors and said she was parked in the short term lot.

"I made the reservation as you requested," She told him. "You know I feel stupid, we haven't been formally introduced." She was definitely making him feel comfortable.

The aide looked at her and smiled, "Corey Hart, and your Blair Andrews." Blair had made sure that her facebook account didn't show her real last name. Someone from Washington might put it together after the events from last year. The FBI never released her picture to the press so the cover with a different name would be fine. She knew that a local reporter had tried to find out who the bureau had been protecting at Bethesda Medical Center but never found out who it was. By the time the reporter got access to the Medical Center Blair had been released.

They walked together toward her car. Blair popped the trunk and Corey put his bag in. "When was the last time you were here," Blair asked.

"I've actually been here many times, as recent as three weeks ago."

"Corey, I hope it's okay that you can't stay at my place but I have a nice room for you at Caesars."

"I understand. Tell me about yourself?" He asked.

Blair was on now. How well she handled these first few questions would tell if she could get Corey to open up to her.

"Its pretty much a dull story. I grew up in the south and kind of moved around a lot. I always wanted to be on the stage. I came to Vegas, against my parents wished a few years ago. I've been lucky and had a few shows that I've been in." She turned out of the airport drive onto Flamingo Boulevard. They headed west on Flamingo and it was only a few blocks to Caesars. Corey hadn't responded yet so she kept on talking. "After the first year I met a very good friend. We were in a few shows and soon moved in together. I thought it would be forever, but a month ago she left. She never said anything to me. I came home and saw that she just took her belongings and left." Blair decided to start to cry and Corey put his hand on her shoulder.

"I understand, more than you might know," he said. "I too had a similar experience." Corey took a deep breath, and turned around to look out the back window. "Do you think that blue car is following us," He asked. Blair acted cool.

"What blue car?"

"That one, he's about two cars behind you. I saw him pulling out of the lot and he has been following us every since."

"Corey, this is the main drag to the strip. It is probably a tourist just going to check into his hotel." As Corey kept his attention on the blue car, she tried to text Booth to fall off the trail. She had been so good with the I-Phone that she could text one handed. She held her phone in her left hand, along the side of the driver's seat, so he wouldn't see what she was doing. "Corey, tell me about your loss?"

He turned around and looked down at the floor of the front seat. "Well it's actually losses. I want to tell you but hope you understand it is all too fresh, maybe tomorrow." Corey turned back to watch for the blue car only to see it making a right hand turn on Maryland Avenue. Blair was watching from her rear view mirror and waited for Corey to say something.

"I guess you were right. He turned off."

"Who turned off?" She said. Making sure that he thought she wasn't even thinking about the blue car.

"I'm just paranoid, I guess. After yesterday, I don't know what to think." Corey was nervous, and Blair could tell that the last thing she needed to do was probe into what happened. Just let him open up when he was ready. They pulled into the check-in area for Caesars Palace. It was located off of Flamingo just past the front entrance on the Las Vegas Strip. She told the attendant they were checking in and would valet the car. He inquired if they needed help with luggage but she said no thank you. "The room isn't in my name is it?" Corey asked.

"No, I put it in my name. That was better anyway because I get a few comp rooms every month and hardly ever use them."

"I'm surprised your sister didn't want to stay here?"

Blair had to think fast. "We were never close growing up. I was kind of the bad kid and she always followed whatever my parents wanted. We just got back together a few years ago, and when she learned that Jenny left me, she wanted to come to make sure I was okay."

Corey was impressed. "It's important to have someone to talk to. Blair, I just knew from your facebook responses you were a kind person. I don't have anyone like your sister to confide in."

"Then I'm glad we got together. Maybe I can be that special person for you."

Corey had tears well up in his eyes and Blair stopped talking and held his hand. He was sobbing and she wasn't sure what to do. "Let's move off to the side, do you need to use the restroom?" He nodded and she said she would get him checked in. "Corey, I can list a second person because I did tell them a room for two just in case you decided to bring someone."

"There's no one left for me, I'm all alone."

Blair felt sorry for him and knew he truly was lost. Corey headed to the men's room and she headed for the front desk. When she saw he had entered the restroom she sent Booth a text. He's really broken up and crying. Also paranoid that someone is following him. I'm checking in and will text you his room number. Be careful he is scared of something. She checked him in under her name and told them that they would be staying at least two days. The desk clerk saw it was comp from the Hotel Manager with an open ending departure date. He could not have been nicer, she thought. Anything else you need please call the front desk he told her. She got two keys just in case and could always pass one off to Booth if he wanted to check Corey's bag. Corey came out of the restroom and saw Blair at the end of the front desk. He waited until she left the desk and moved down the hallway toward the elevators. She saw that he was watching and nodded to him. Corey followed her down the hallway. She figured that he didn't want to be seen. He smiled at her and appreciated her helping him. She really understood, he thought.

The room was on the fourteenth floor and the hallway was long and curved as they made their way toward 1422. She handed Corey his key. He inserted it and the light turned green. He turned the handle and they went in. Corey was pulling his bag along and Blair went over to the windows and opened the curtain. Great view, I didn't expect a suite. He pulled the suitcase stand out of the closet and placed his case on it. "I need to get these things out or they will all have to be ironed." He was fussing over his clothes and Blair felt at ease. Corey was acting just like one of her girlfriends. He pulled a small black leather bag out of the suitcase and took it into the bathroom. She could see that he was taking shaving cream and other toiletries out and placing them on the counter. Corey came back into the room and Blair was sitting on a very lovely half rounded chair. It was across from the desk in the corner of the room.

"Now, tell me how I can help," Blair asked. She figured he could go anywhere or nowhere with that opening. It was important that he had confidence in her. She was relaxed and holding a room service menu. "I kind of thought we could go out to this little out-of-the-way place that I like, if it's okay with you., or we can order in." She had done everything they had taught her at FBI training. Make sure your contact doesn't have any idea that you are undercover and let them take the lead. If you push, you will only get resistance.

"I don't know where to start. Tell me more about your friend

Jenny," He asked. "You said she hurt you so much, and I understand." Blair knew she had more to do. She had to make him comfortable about saying he was gay.

"It is still kind of hard to talk about. I told you we were in the same show together and I've had boyfriends before and always felt I was straight. Something just seemed to trigger with Jenny. We had the same interest and felt the same about many things. Then it just happened. I loved her and thought she loved me. We were together for two years and everything was going great. Jenny was married before and her ex-husband lived in Iowa. He started contacting her a few months ago and she didn't want to talk about it. Then out of nowhere, she packed and left. I haven't really been the same." Blair let the tears flow and put her head down. Corey came over and knelt in front of her. He held her hand and cried with her. She just held on to his hand.

Her acting skills were coming in handy. She hoped that this story would get him to open up about his relationship with the Senator. She wasn't sure what else might come up but this was a good start.

Minutes passed and he said, "I know how you feel." He was wiping his tears away and grabbed some Kleenex. "I always knew I was different. Even in college I tried dating but it never seemed to work out. I tried to get involved in different things and eventually found an interest in politics. That is where I met my special person. The last week has been terrible for me. I not only lost him but yesterday lost someone else that meant so much to both of us. Blair, it's been so hard and now I'm afraid someone is trying to kill me."

What, she screamed in her mind. Where did this come from? Who was trying to kill him? What does she say now? She took a deep breath. "Corey, why would you think that?"

"How familiar are you with politics?" He asked.

"I can name the president and that's about it." Maybe she needed to play the role of dumb blond for him to open up more.

"Yesterday the Chief Justice of the United States Supreme Court was murdered! They say he killed himself, but I know it had to be murder. He knew too much, and so do I."

Blair wanted to yell for Booth at that very moment. What should she ask? How much should she pretend to know?

Nineteen

Booth was pacing in the lobby of the hotel waiting for Blair to call or text him. He knew she had made some progress with the Senator's aide that he didn't know what else he could do. He figured they would be coming down to get something to eat soon. That was the plan. Get Corey out and probe him a little more for answers. He wanted to go upstairs and sit near the room in case she needed him. He felt helpless.

Blair was still holding his hand after he told her that he thought someone was trying to kill him. The suggestion that the Chief Justice had been murdered tossed a curve at her. Her original plan was to get more information about the aide's relationship with Albertson, but now she was getting critical details that might shed light on other aspects of this case. Getting in touch with Booth and not let Corey know was a concern. She slid out of the chair and put her arms around Corey who was still kneeling on the floor in front of her. "Corey, I feel so bad. My problems seem so minor compared to yours. I want to help but don't know what to do." She thought that she could get to the bathroom to alert Booth of what Corey had just told her.

Corey looked at her. "When you sent me the facebook message I thought we might have a lot in common. Once I found out about the Chief Justice, I knew I was in danger. That is where I hoped you could come in. I figured I would be safe with someone no one knew. I needed a place to think. I didn't know what to do next. That was all before yesterday's events. Now I'm terrified. I'm sure they'll be coming for me next. I might know too much and need to hide. I can't let anyone know where I am. Could you hide me, please?"

She could tell that he was truly desperate. Corey was still shaking and it was now Blair's move. She knew that she could say yes to his request. How long would it be before the Bureau would want to take Corey into custody would be the next question. Could she get more information on why he thinks that Anthony Leonard was murdered and didn't commit suicide? They were both kneeling on the floor and she tried getting up with him. "Let's sit on the bed. My back is killing me!" He moved with her and they moved to the bed that sat in the center of the spacious room. "Corey, I will do anything to help you. I'm sure I can get this room for as long as you need. We can come up with a plan to hide you. I just need to make an excuse to cover my time."

He was feeling better. It was good to get this information out, especially to someone who didn't know any of the players. She was safe, he figured. Christ, she didn't know anything about politics or any of the people. He was sure she didn't even know what the Supreme Court was. He was happy with his decision to come to meet her.

"Let me get a wash cloth for you." Blair let go of Corey's hand and headed toward the bathroom. "I need to go to the bathroom anyway," She said, and Corey nodded. Blair came right back out and handed him a damp wash cloth. She wiped his face with it and he slumped on the bed. "I'll just be a moment, you understand, a girl thing." He looked at her and had a blank stare on his face. She headed back to the bathroom. With the water running she felt that she could text Booth quickly and not cause any concern for him. Her text took just a minute and she flushed the toilet and brought another damp cloth out. He was curled up in the bed in a fetal position. Blair went over to him and held him. He was sweating and she thought he needed to calm down some. "Corey, if I'm going to help you, you have to help yourself a little. You can't get sick." She was right. He understood and realized she was making sense. His heart was beating too fast and he needed to calm down.

Booth read the text over again. Holy Shit! This is more than we expected. He had to call his bureau chief right away. The story that Corey had told Blair made more sense now. They all wondered why he was so willing to meet with someone he just met on facebook. He's scared! There was no known reason the Chief Justice would have committed suicide. No final letter, which you find at almost every suicide. Who had murdered him? Was this gambling related? How did the two brothers who the FBI had been investigating in the casino deal fit in? Booth's call went through to Steve. Booth relayed all the information that Blair had sent to him. The facts were starting to fit together. He revealed that he had an affair ongoing with someone in politics. The bureau already had suspected that. The fact that the Chief Justice may have been murdered meant that the director would have to put a full court press with his forensic team at Justice Leonard's home. What evidence could they find that collaborates this accusation? How about the request to hide Corey? Should Blair keep him in the hotel room at Caesars, hoping to get more details? The case was moving faster than anyone could have hoped. Blair was getting more information at a quicker pace than most agents could. The role of a jilted lover was working for her.

Booth wanted to text Blair back but was afraid that Corey might get wise. He wished that he had set something up, like maybe a code word, just in case they needed to talk to each other. Just then his cell phone went off. He looked at the screen and it was Blair calling. Booth clicked it on and waited for her to speak.

"Hi Sis, looks like I going to be spending the night with a friend. There is food in the fridge if you're hungry."

Booth just listened knowing that Blair was trying to send him a message.

"No, I'll be home early in the morning, you know I have rehearsal." Blair was trying to give Booth some direction so he could ask questions.

He thought for a minute and asked, "Do you need anything?"

"Don't worry, Sis, we're having a great time catching up and will probably order room service." Blair was letting Booth know everything was okay and that she wouldn't be leaving the room. Now he needed to figure out what he should do next. Her safety was critical, but the information from Corey was more important. Maybe he could get a room near hers'. He called his contact in the Vegas office and soon she made her way to the lobby to meet Booth.

"We have a team that will monitor the floor Blair and the aide are on," She stated. "We've got cameras and surveillance inside the room plus a tap on the phone. I also have a room for you that is across the hall, two rooms down from the room she is in. When they place their room service order one of our people will take it upstairs." She had everything covered. Booth felt okay with the plan and took the room key card that she delivered. He knew Blair was resourceful because she had been able to text him both while driving and in the room with Corey. There was nothing to do until she sent him another message. He moved toward the bank of elevators and went upstairs. The room was large and he kicked off his shoes. Looking out of the window he could see down the strip toward Paris and Bally's. They were now calling this area of Vegas the Miracle Mile. Lights from the signs brightened the sky as only the lights of Vegas could. There were hundreds of people walking down the street heading out to the evening's late entertainment venues. The fountains at the Bellagio were going off and Booth could see thousands watching from the street. He couldn't do anything now but wait. He looked at his watch and it was close to ten-thirty. A call came to his room. He answered, not knowing who would be calling his room.

"Booth, they just placed an order for food. I've got someone headed down to the catering area right now." He wanted to be the one to deliver the food but knew that wasn't a good idea. If he blew his cover now he couldn't help out later if needed. Sitting waiting sucks, he thought.

The order was ready and a member of the Vegas team had it on a cart to deliver to Blair's room. The tray had two turkey sandwiches on whole wheat, a fruit plate and Chamomile Tea for two. Not the typical Vegas late night spread. This was more of an order for someone who actually cared about their health. Blair and Corey were now sitting on the bed quietly talking. "Corey, what do we need to do to make sure someone isn't following you?" She hoped to re-open the subject so she could probe further.

"Blair, I know these people here in Vegas. They will do anything to keep their plans a secret. They aren't the nicest people to know. Once, my friend and I were here in Vegas meeting with them. My friend came back to our room really concerned. He said that if he didn't do exactly what they wanted that there would be serious repercussions." Corey was very animated in his conversation. He was flinging his arms around and at one point held his hands around his neck in a strangling motion. "My friend held his hands like this when he came back from talking to them. They are very forceful. The big mistake that we made was helping them the first time, not knowing the requests would never end." Corey slumped back into the bed and laid his head on the pillows.

"Okay, I've got it. I've been here long enough to know of those types. They make you an offer you can't refuse." She hoped using a term that was attributed to the mob would get his attention and that she was dialed in. "I can tell you that when they come into a showroom everyone falls all over to give them the best seats, finest liquor and food."

Corey was in tune with her. There was a knock on the door. He jumped. Blair told him to go into the bathroom and she would answer it. He didn't want to be seen, so he hurried and got up to follow her advice. The attendant wheeled a service cart into the room and looked around. "Room service Miss." He signaled to inquire, where was Corey? She pointed to the bathroom and made an okay sign.

"Thank you very much, could you just leave the cart?"

"Of course, I'll leave it outside your room and collect it later." He handed her a note and she quickly read it. Once she did that she handed it back to him. She didn't want it around for Corey to find.

"Corey, it's all clear."

Corey came out of the bathroom and had undone his shirt. "You were right, my shirt collar was wet. I need to change into something dry. Guess I am hungry too, what time is it?" Although he had only been in Vegas a couple of hours he felt as though he knew Blair for a much longer. They did have so much in common and he felt safe for the first time in the past two days. He needed a plan and someone to help pull it off. Maybe she was the right person to do it.

The director was in his office late hoping to get an update from Vegas before going home. It was twelve-forty-five a.m. in Washington and nothing could be done until the morning. He already had a top notch forensic team that was going to be at Justice Leonard's home at six a.m. and he planned to meet them there. A couple hours of sleep are all he needed. John Martin knew that his teams in Vegas and Los Angeles were on top of the situation. Blair had made great inroads with the Senator's aide and Booth along with the Vegas Bureau would be on top of any information she got.

Steve Orrison left a text message for Kathy O'Connor and Chris to be ready if needed to head to Vegas. You both might be able to help the Vegas unit with research once we get a little more information. They both were surprised at how fast the case was moving. A little trip to Vegas was okay with both of them.

Blair pulled a chair over from the desk and she sat on the bed. "Hope turkey on wheat bread was okay with you." He approved and sat down across from her. They started to eat and Blair said she needed to get a change of clothes if she was spending the night. There is a little clothes shop next to the gift shop that I can get everything I need for tonight. He understood. After all she was there helping him. "After we eat, I'll run down and get some things from the little gift shop. Do you need anything?" He said that he had everything he needed. "I guess I can get one of those tacky T shirts to sleep in," She told him. Corey hadn't thought about her needed a change of clothes or something to sleep in but it made sense and he was feeling safer now. They finished their sandwich and she left him eating fruit. "I'll be thirty minutes at the most. When I come back, I'll tap on the door three times so that you know it's me." She left the room and Corey pulled the tray closer to the bed. He wanted to turn on the news to see if CNN had any update on Justice Leonard. He watched for a few minutes when they switched to a special report from Washington regarding the investigation into the death of the Chief Justice. There she was again. Gina Warren was standing in front of the brown stone that Leonard lived in. She reported that the FBI was involved in the investigation and that a key person in the case was now missing. She went on to state that the aide to Senator Albertson who was seen at Chief Justice Leonard's home hadn't been seen for close to twenty-four hours and the FBI and local authorities had questions for him. Corey was sure that he was in trouble.

Blair shut the door and tapped lightly on Booth's door. He opened it and she went in. "What are you doing here?"

"Listen, I told him I needed a change of clothes and toiletries. I'm sure by morning I can get more information from him."

"Be careful, we're not too sure how he's involved in all of this." Booth was right. Corey knew a lot about the coming and goings of Albertson and had been to Vegas with him. He also had some kind of relationship with Justice Leonard, but they didn't know what it was yet.

"I'm okay. Going downstairs, just watch the room to make sure he doesn't leave." Blair headed down the hallway once she made sure the coast was clear. She just needed something to sleep in and a toothbrush and toothpaste. She was glad that the agent from the Vegas team gave her a note with Booth's room number. She knew he would be there to help in an emergency if needed.

The trip downstairs was quick. She got everything she needed and picked up some gum and a bottle of spring water. Everything was charged to her room number. The elevator ride back upstairs was filled with people that had just left the early Cher show. They were all talking about her costumes and their favorite songs. Blair smiled at a young man that was standing at the back of the elevator. He winked back at her. When she got off the elevator he got off with her. She started down the hallway and he said, "Blair, wait, I have a message for you." She turned and he held his badge out for her to see. "We will have a man posted down the hallway all night if you need. Here is my cell number, call with an update if possible." She nodded and headed back to her room.

When he heard the door open Corey jumped. "Who is it?" He yelled. Corey felt a sense of relief when he saw Blair. Didn't you hear the three knocks before I opened the door? "I'm glad your back. Guess I was hoping that you weren't going to leave me here."

"Why would you think that?"

"Well, I tossed a lot of shit at you, and I couldn't blame you if you just wanted to run off." Corey couldn't tell Blair about the news flash that CNN carried. Not yet, at least.

"Corey, I said I would help you. If I'm going to do that you need to tell me everything so that we can figure out what to do." Blair was playing, I'm the only friend you have card. Corey felt that she was on the up and up. After all she picked him up at the airport, set him up in a room, stayed with him and comforted him during his story, and then came back after going downstairs. She could have easily copped out even after he just asked for her to hide him. Although they had just met, he felt safe with her.

She put the bag on the desk and said she was going to wheel the food cart out in the hallway. There was a large mirror at the end of the hallway and she could see the agent that she met on the elevator sitting in a chair. She nodded at him and he signaled back an okay sign. Once she was back in the room she turned to Corey and said, "Okay let's take it from the top. Who do you think killed your friend?"

"Well, my friend was a Senator in Washington, Senator Albertson, have you heard of him?"

Blair shook her head no. "Not sure, where is he from?"

"Guess that's not important, Corey continued. The last Senate race was very tight. Although he had been the Senator for three terms because of pressure from democrats he needed to raise more money for re-election. One of his friends introduced him to this guy from New York who was willing to help."

"How would they help him?" Blair continued to play into the story without Corey becoming suspicious.

"Money! Plenty of Money! Do you know how many votes you can buy with loads of cash? Well, we went ahead in the polls and won by a respectable margin. The only thing they asked for was the Senator's vote on a gambling issue back home. There were already a few casinos in Phoenix, so he figured one more wouldn't hurt."

"That makes sense to me too."

"The problem was it was just the first of many favors. They wanted more and more and some of the things were out of the Senator's control. He had a good friend who could help."

"What about the Justice guy you talked about?"

"Yes, they had been friends for years and Justice Leonard pulled a few favors back home in Arizona to get the measures they wanted passed. When they were questioned and it went to the courts, Justice Leonard had the people in place to make sure everything went through smoothly."

Blair had it all. The relationship of Leonard and Albertson was about one friend helping another in a tight jam. They both were involved in helping a gambling syndicate. Now did the aide know who they were helping? "Why do you think these people killed that Justice guy?"

"When my friend died last week of a heart attack, only the Chief Justice and I knew about the arrangement. I had talked to the Chief Justice and he was planning on attending the funeral and making a speech. When he didn't show up, I was afraid something happened to him. I went to his house and he was found dead."

"How did he die?"

"They said he hung himself. He would have never done that. Justice Leonard was a good man. His only mistake was helping a friend. Now he's dead and I'm sure I'm next."

"Okay, I've got it, but hiding isn't going to solve anything. If these people are as bad as you think they will find you. We've got to think of another way." Blair was hoping Corey would reveal what his plan was. Maybe she could find out more about the gambling syndicate too.

"I don't know anybody in the FBI, but maybe if I could get them the details they might let me off and put me in witness protection." Corey had just said the magic words. He wanted to become a states witness and help put the gambling syndicate away.

"Corey, are you sure about this?"

"Yes, it's the only hope I have. At first thought that I could get someone in Washington to help me, but Blair, I'm involved too. I took money, favors and had this relationship with the Senator. They might never let me free. Coming to Vegas was the perfect idea. When I saw your post on face book, I had to reply to you. You live where I needed to get to, and maybe you would be someone to help me. I hoped you could be trusted."

It was obvious that Corey was relieved after telling Blair the whole story. He smiled for the first time. "Blair, I hope you're okay with this?"

"I'm fine, we can work this out together. I think we will have an opportunity to look at this better in the morning. I have a friend that can help us." Blair didn't think it was a good idea to tell Corey she was with the bureau. He put a lot of trust in her and she could get him to Booth in the morning and he could take him in. "Corey, do you know who these mob guys are?"

"Yes, I do. The weird part about it is I have a tape recording that the Senator made the last time we were here in Vegas. He was concerned that he could never get out of doing those favors. He promised to do one more favor and in return they built a big new home for him. He planned to retire before anyone found out what he had done. Unfortunately, a committee started looking into things and I think he realized the jig was up."

They continued to talk for a while and she said she was going into the bathroom to change. "I have this great night shirt that you just have to see to believe."

He laughed, and said he was going to change while she was in the bathroom.

"At least you have some real clothes to change into."

"I have a feeling you'd look good in anything you put on."

"Thanks." Blair went in the bathroom to change and sent Booth a text with all the details. He couldn't believe his eyes. "Christ! She got him to tell the whole story and now is willing to turn himself in to us." Booth was amazed. Who is this Blair Adams? And wow, is she good. He couldn't wait to send the information to Steve Orrison and his Vegas contacts.

Twenty

The information Booth sent caught everyone in the bureau by total surprise. So many scenarios were discussed, but none of them had Corey wanting to get help from the FBI in return for witness protection. How did this all happen? They were scrambling on how to handle this departure in their plan.

John Martin hoped that with this new information Corey would help them with their investigation of the two Ellis brothers and possible connections with the mob. He also wondered who else might be involved. Will there be other political figures that would fall in the investigation? It was now two a.m. in Washington and Martin couldn't sleep. There were too many things to work out. He didn't plan to update the White House of the events until he had more information. Hopefully his forensic team will find some key evidence when they searched Justice Leonard's home in the morning.

He instructed the LA bureau to hold off on offering too much to the aide unless he could give the names and places that he and Albertson had meet the men bribing the Senator. Hard evidence was the key. The director also made sure his best men were on the investigation at Justice Leonard's house. It was all coming together but he wanted to make sure they had facts. The last thing they needed was having it all blow up in their face.

Morning came faster than Blair expected that it would. She had been talking to Corey as they laid in the king size bed until almost three a.m. He was telling her about the Senator and their relationship. Yes, they were involved. How did it start? He said that he could just tell that Albertson was interested. Soon they were together. Albertson was lonely and Corey filled that void. No one would know. It just seemed normal for them always being together. The job Albertson gave him meant they had to travel together and meeting all the time. His background in law school and then the journalistic field was a perfect fit for the position. Many politicians got into trouble with their staff members but no one thought anything about a man having another man as a close aide. Just look at recent events surrounding other politicians. No one suspected Corey and Albertson was a couple.

She had so much information floating in her head that she thought she would never fall asleep. Now the bright sun glared through the windows of the room waking them both. She had never closed the curtains and sun rose over the Las Vegas Mountain Range to the east turning its glare into beacons of light. The sun in the desert came on bright and strong. She looked across the room as the sun shined like a beam from a lighthouse. Corey was still fast asleep. He was lying on his right side facing away from the window. She eased out of bed and quietly pulled the curtains shut. Blair grabbed her cell phone and saw that it was five-forty-five a.m. Christ, why am I up so early, she wondered? It was the glare of the sun and all the information floating in her head that woke her up. She had to get in touch with Booth.

The hotel room was very large and she loved the overstuffed chair in the corner near the windows. It was in that chair that she sat last night when Corey held her hand and revealed the triangle of information regarding the Senator, Chief Justice and himself. It wasn't exactly what she had expected but it all made sense now. He told her of his panic when the Chief Justice didn't show up at the funeral. Why he wanted to get out of Washington and meet her in Vegas and the fear of being the next target. Now the request for a room not in his name made sense. Corey was on the run. He had to find a safe hiding spot until he could get protection and a guarantee that he would not go to jail. Blair was the key. He could find safety while hiding in one of the busiest spots on earth. If she provided what he needed then all would be well.

Could she get more information from him this morning before she brought Booth and the Vegas team into the investigation? How should she continue with Corey and not spook him? She was aware that the Vegas team had surveillance equipment monitoring the action in her room. They had the detail but not their witness yet. It was up to her to make that last step.

She moved toward the bathroom as she kept an eye on Corey who was still in a deep sleep. The bathroom was becoming her office, a place to transmit information to her team on the investigation. It helped being a girl she thought. He wouldn't suspect anything if she was in there for a long time. After all, all men felt women spent too much time in the bathroom. She started to text all the updated information to Booth and copied Steve and her contact from the Vegas team. Her I-Phone had so many neat features. She had loaded all of their email addresses in her contact file and it only took a few seconds to add them to the text. Her closing lines were that Corey had opened up about everything except the names of key people in the gambling connection. She didn't want anyone else involved until she had a chance to try to get that information.

Booth also had a hard time sleeping. What happened if he changed his mind? What if he hurt Blair? What if he left the room during the night? Too many things could go wrong, he thought. He had pulled the large leather chair near the door and kicked off his shoes. Sleep came in short naps. It seemed that every time he dozed off, something would wake him. Maybe it was a couple coming down the hall talking too loud, or people laughing on their way in or out of their rooms. After all it was Vegas. Time didn't matter in Las Vegas. Everything was open and operating 24/7 and Booth wanted to make sure his part of the investigation didn't fall apart. When his cell phone vibrated and beeped he jumped out of the chair. It was Blair. What time is it? The message was long. He could see that she sent it to everyone involved. Details were clear. The relationship with the Senator and his aide were just as they had thought. The key addition was places that the aide had told Blair that they visited, including Atlantic City. The contributions to the Senators campaign helped them understand how he got involved and once the mob had you, you were theirs forever. Corey had told Blair that he had been with the Senator to Vegas numerous times, driving sometimes from Phoenix. They drove so that there wasn't a trail for someone to follow. They couldn't fly or else a reporter would start checking why a Senator who had positioned himself against gambling interest was going to sin city. Corey's reasoning on the murder verses suicide of the Chief Justice made sense.

Blair was getting so much information from Corey that Booth

couldn't wait to interrogate him. They still wanted to find out more about the Vegas connection. Who else was involved and where do they go next? Booth wanted Blair to turn the rest of the investigation over to him. She shouldn't take any more chances. His cell phone signaled that he had another message. He looked and it was from Steve, back in Los Angeles. As he was reading it the phone beeped again. "Shit, it's six a.m. and my phone is going nuts!" He hollered at it. "Let me read the damn messages before you go off again." Booth wasn't used to being on the fringe of an investigation. He was always in the middle of the action. He didn't like this at all.

Steve was thrilled with Blair's progress and agreed that Booth needed to keep a watch on the two of them but wanted to let her have more time. If she could get some names from Corey it would speed the process of the investigation. The third text was from his Vegas contact. We're ready whenever you want us to move in, it said. Booth was sending Blair a message back when his cell beeped again. He had a disgusted look on his face, as he tried to complete the text to Blair. The new message was from the director. It was already nine a.m. back in Washington and Steve had forwarded Blair's text to John Martin.

The Washington forensic team had been in the Chief Justice home for three hours and found many clues to his death, and concluded that it was indeed a murder. Finger prints had been discovered on a window near the side entrance of the brown stone building. The window had been jimmied with a sharp object and there were paint chips on the pavement below the window sill. The chair that was under the Chief Justice that everyone figured he kicked out after applying the noose around his neck also had the same finger prints on it. It appears that the Chief Justice was murdered about an hour before he would have left for the Senators funeral. Now they were searching the FBI data base for an identification of the persons who left the finger prints.

John Martin wanted Blair to continue to probe Corey for more information. The connection to the gambling syndicate was critical in the investigation. Booth knew they were all moving in the right direction. He just wanted to be more involved. Steve had also told Booth that Kathy and Chris from their office were on their way to Vegas to help. They would be reporting to the Vegas Bureau Chief and assist in any way possible. He wanted as many members of his team involved.

Blair figured if she had any hope of getting more information she had to keep her cover. It might also be important for Booth to stay under cover too. She had passed on all the information she had. Now she wanted to see if she could get Corey to reveal details about the Vegas contact. She moved back into the bedroom and pulled the curtain open about two inches. The glare of the sun almost hurt her eyes. She was looking out when she felt a hand on her shoulder, she jumped.

"I'm sorry I didn't mean to startle you!" Corey said.

"Christ you scared the hell out of me!" She turned and was breathing hard. Good thing she didn't knock him to the ground. That would have messed it all up. "I was kind of daydreaming and forgot where I was. It was like an old horror movie, the girl is watching out the front window and boom, the attacker was behind her. You need to be careful when sneaking up on a girl."

He was very apologetic, but started. "I really didn't mean to scare you! I don't think I've ever scared someone like that before."

They were both standing at the front window and Corey was telling her that he felt great after a real sleep. "I slept great for the first time in days." He seemed much more relaxed than at any time yesterday. She was sure that she had made in-roads with him yesterday and that he felt secure with her.

Blair didn't want to press him for more information, but thought she should let him lead her to what he wanted to do next. "I know we ate late, but I'm hungry, how about you?"

"Sounds good to me, what do you have in mind?"

"Well we could eat in our room again if you want, or I know this little place near my apartment." Blair had seen a mom and pop place around the corner from her apartment complex, just off of Sahara Avenue. She still wanted Corey to feel that he was in charge.

Corey was doing much better this morning. He was talkative and calm. "I'm not too sure about getting out, I'm afraid that someone is going to be searching for me."

"Corey, I'm a little confused, tell me more about this Judge guy who you think was murdered?"

He moved back toward the center of the room. He looked

down at the carpet, and turned toward the door. "I pretty sure that no one knows where I am. I covered it real well. I packed my things in an old blue suitcase and took a cab. First I went to the bus station and then grabbed another cab to the airport. Blair, these guys are for real. Maybe we better stay here."

"Okay, let's figure you're right. They had the Judge killed. Why would they do that?"

"It is like I was telling you last night. The Senator needed help in his campaign and his friend, the Chief Justice, hooked him up with someone. Neither the Judge, nor the Senator knew they had mob connections. Once the Senator won re-election, he was stuck. Blair, they kept asking for more favors. He knew we were in trouble. The Senator tried to get help from his friend the Chief Justice, but they were both locked in. Even the Chief Justice felt he was being compromised."

"Corey, did you ever see them threat the Senator or Justice?"

"It was when we were here last time. I told you that I came with the Senator three weeks ago. The Senator wanted to meet with them and wanted off the hook. They gave him one more request, or at least they said it was the last request. They wanted him to do this one more thing. He didn't want too, but they promised that if he did, he would be off the hook. That is when they also gave him a bag with a lot of money in it."

"How much money was in there?"

"A lot! He was scared when we left. He told me that they would never let him off the hook. He never let me know how much money was in there, but I could tell that it must have been big time."

"Was that the first time they gave him money?" Blair was working the questions based on the information Corey was revealing.

"No, I told you about a year before that, they took care of the money he needed to build that big home. And before that they helped him win re-election. Man that home on the river was something. You know, he never moved in." Corey looked down and stopped talking. Blair moved closer to him and put her hand on his shoulder. She hoped that he would continue and she could get to the names of the contacts.

"Corey, do you think you could pick these guys out of a line-up?" This was the first direct police type of a question that she asked. He turned toward her.

"Yes, I know who they are! That's why I'm scared. Blair, they are right here in Vegas. I figured if the FBI got involved here, I'd have a better chance of getting off without going to jail." Corey was giving Blair everything she needed. She just needed names.

"Remember, I told you that my sister is visiting. She used to date a FBI guy that works here in Vegas. I can call her and she could give us his name." Corey perked up.

"Okay, but don't give her any information yet. I've got to be sure that I'm safe and not going to be charged with any crime. Blair there is also this reporter in Washington that seems to be on the case and on CNN tonight it appeared that she was saying I had something to do with the Chief Justice murder."

"Don't worry Corey we will get people to help you." Blair moved toward the middle of the room and looked for her purse. "I can try to get the number first then we can discuss our next move." She was wondering if she should call her Vegas contact or Booth. Hopefully he would catch on. She pulled her phone out of her purse and walked toward Corey. "Do you think this is a good plan?" She had to have him thinking he was still in total control.

"Great, but remember just get a name, we'll talk about it."

She thought before dialing. What if Corey wanted to talk to the person? He would want to hear a female voice. After all Blair was supposed to be calling her sister. She decided to contact her Vegas contact instead of Booth.

Blair dialed. "Hello Julie, this is Blair. Hey sis. Sorry that I got tied up. Did you find everything okay at the apartment?" She wanted to give her contact as much information so that she knew what she was doing. "I need a number from you. Remember that guy you met last year here. Well I have this friend who has a thing for G-men types. Do you still have the number of that FBI guy you dated? Yes, I know he ended up being kind of a jerk, but she is looking for a date for a special event." Her contact just listened and Blair was handling the whole conversation. "Okay, call me back with his number. Call my cell?"

Blair turned to Corey and told him that Julie would call back with the number. She told Corey that her sister, Julie, said that the guy was all business, all the time. That is why Julie didn't get along with him. She said one time they were on a date and the guy broke up a robbery and left Julie at the restaurant when he took the guy in. Julie liked the fact that he was with the FBI, but wanted to be number one. With this guy the job came first regardless what he was doing.

"Sound like the type of guy I need." Corey bought the whole thing.

The Vegas contact called Booth. "Looks like Blair wanted the number of an FBI guy. Maybe the aide is ready to turn himself in!"

Booth cautioned her. "Let's only do what she is asking. Who do you have in mind?"

"My chief wants to be the guy to handle this." The Vegas team felt like they were on the outside with the two Agents from LA clearly doing the work.

"I can understand that. This is pretty important. I'm really in the best position across the hall, plus I know my partner. Call and stall her but give her my number and one of your guys. Let the chief's decide. Meanwhile we need to keep monitoring this. I'll report it in to my chief." Booth hoped this was his chance to take to the stage.

Blair's phone rang. "Yeah, Julie thanks for calling back so soon. Sure I got a pen." The contact was now asking Blair a series of questions. She wanted to make sure everything was okay. Was Corey ready to turn himself in? Blair was giving her yes and no answers and threw in a, I'll be home soon. Once she had the phone numbers she said that she was busy right now but might be able to get home a little later on. The contact knew that it was close but not quite there yet. Blair needed more time, and once she made contact with the Vegas Chief they would know where the investigation was and who to contact.

She turned toward Corey and said, "Well we've got a number. You have to just let me know when you want to call, or I can do it for you."

"Once I'm sure, I'll want you to make the initial call. We can't tell him too much until I have assurance that I will get everything I need, especially protection."

Blair decided to change course a little. "Are you ready for that breakfast?"

Corey had forgotten about their discussion about eating.

"Guess you're hungry? Let's call room service."

Blair jumped on the bed. I shouldn't be this hungry but I am. She grabbed the menu and asked him what he wanted.

"How are you so thin eating like this," He asked.

"You can come downstairs after and watch our rehearsal. You'll see why I eat so much." This was a clear move to cement her cover.

"Yeah, I'd love that, but right now I can't leave the room. What time do you have to be down there?"

"Well, I need to be there from 10 a.m. to about one. It's three hours of a tough workout."

"Maybe once this is all over, I can see you perform."

"I'd love that," She said. Blair didn't bring up the FBI contact again. She wanted Corey to make up his mind and still hoped to get the names of the Vegas contacts.

"Okay, what do you want?" She asked, bouncing on the bed like a little kid. Corey smiled and said, "Give me that menu."

Twenty-One

The director was busy reading the report from the DC crime lab. They had the identification of the person whose fingerprints were left at the Judge's home. He wondered who was Assad Jacoby? How does he fit into the events in the Nation's Capitol? The report showed that he was a resident of Las Vegas, Nevada. He had a list of prior's, and had done time at Leavenworth Prison for assault and battery. Assad was a bad guy, breaking and entering, armed robbery and a juvenile record for drugs also filled out the report. But nothing like this was in his history. Usually hit men were not from this type of background. Looks like Assad might have moved up to the big leagues. His last known address was in Henderson, Nevada. John Martin called his bureau chief in Vegas. They needed to find Assad as soon as possible. A fax was on the way to every agency in the country. Dangerous, needs to be captured alive! The only picture they had was from time served at Leavenworth.

Assad was a stout individual with a scare on his left cheek. He had a dark completion, black hair and brown eyes. He stood five foot nine inches tall and weighed two-hundred pounds. The picture would be sent to all agents across the nation.

Booth continued to pace around his room. He had the new information from the Vegas contact that Blair was getting closer to having Corey willing to turn himself in. He knew that a team of agents started to search for Assad Jacoby, the man who possibly killed the Chief Justice of the United States. The only thing he could do was sitting and waiting. This was killing him. He called Steve. "Boss, I've got to get out of here and help some way?"

Steve liked Booth and respected him. He knew that his main investigator was flipping out. "You're very important in this whole thing. You're Blair's protection and I bet she's counting on you being there. Remember this is her first case in an undercover assignment," Steve needed both of his people on this.

Booth knew he was right. "Okay, boss, but once this breaks, promise me I'll be involved."

Steve needed to make sure his special agent knew how important he was. "Booth, I wouldn't have it any other way." Steve wanted his number one investigator involved.

Booth hung up and moved toward the window when his phone rang. It was one of the Vegas agents asking if he wanted to take the breakfast that Blair had ordered to her room. "Hell yes!" He hollered. He opened the door and moved down the hallway. He was met by a man wheeling a room service cart. He handed Booth a white jacket and the breakfast order form. They went over the plan and he pushed the cart toward Blair's room. He knocked on the door and announced room service!

The answer from inside said just a minute. Blair was letting Corey have enough time to go into the bathroom and hide. Once he was safely inside she opened the door, and moved back when she saw it was Booth who delivered the tray. "Just push it near the bed, please," She said. "I want to make sure you got it right. I ordered two egg white omelets with spinach and mushrooms. Also wheat toast, crispy bacon and croissants."

"Yes, Miss, it's all here. I need you to sign this, please." He had written her a note. She took it from him and wrote down answers to his questions. He quickly looked it over.

It read Everything was going as planned. Corey was in the bathroom and really afraid. She wanted to get the name of the Senator's contact before she put him in touch with the FBI team. Booth nodded and motioned her to come closer. He whispered in her ear. "Be careful, call if you need help, I'm just across the hall."

He backed out of the room and closed the door. He signaled to his contact down the hallway. They talked for a few minutes at the end of the hallway and then he headed back to his room. Booth felt a lot better after being able to do something. He shook his head up and down and pumped his fist as he went back into his room. He was happy to have at least been in the room with Blair and saw that everything was good.

The Vegas team was now bringing Kathy and Chris from the

Los Angeles office up to date on the investigation. They had just arrived from LA and reported to the bureau chief who assigned them to his investigative team. They were now tracing the where-a-bouts of Assad Jacoby. One team went to his last know residence but he wasn't there. The neighbors didn't have any help for them. No one was really familiar with Assad. He kept to himself and seemed to be a quiet person. Neighbors said he often had visitors, but they think he lived there alone. One neighbor said she saw him loading his car with two suitcases a few days ago. She was able to give them a description of the car. No, he was by himself she told them.

No one in the neighborhood seemed to have any connection to Assad. A forensic team arrived and started a search for fingerprints. Agents started to canvas the strip mall around the corner to see if anyone remembered seeing him. His picture was carried by agents to all the airports, bus station and car rental locations in and around Vegas. So far nothing helped. It was as if he had vanished either just before or after the Chief Justice was found dead. It had only been a few days since the body had been found. The time frame of Assad moving out matched the time of the murder. The agents from both Los Angeles and Vegas were working the area around Assad's last known location.

Booth sat near the door of his room at Caesar's Palace wishing Blair would call him. He wanted to take Corey into custody and get everything he knew about the gambling syndicate and the Senator's involvement.

It had been more than an hour since he delivered the breakfast tray to Blair's room. He knew she was working Corey for answers but what if the aide didn't have any more information. Just then his cell phone rang. He almost jumped out of the chair.

"Hello!"

It was Steve. "Booth it looks like Blair has gotten all the information she can from the Senator's aide. We need to move in, but I want to keep her identity a secret. Never know if we can use her again to talk to him. Take it easy Booth we don't want to spook him. Blair might want to come in with him, as a friend."

"Sure boss," He answered. "Does the suspect know we're coming?"

"From her text, Blair stated that she told him she had a friend that could help. He seemed open to that. She also told him that she knew the guy from her sister. The background story is the guy dated her sister a while back, so follow that lead."

Booth nodded to himself, this made sense, better than having her hold up in that room trying to work it all out. Safer too! He was proud of his partners work on this assignment. She was going to be a great agent he thought.

Booth grabbed his jacket and moved down the hallway. The knock at the door was crisp and announced his arrival. Just a minute came the answer from inside. A few minutes passed and Blair opened the door.

"Brandon, I glad you made it here so quickly. I hope it was okay that I got your number from Julie?"

He followed her lead. "You know you can call me anytime. What's up?"

"I have a friend that needs help. This is pretty big and I'm not sure what to do but I know you can help me."

He walked inside and the room was empty.

"It is very important that you understand what he tells you. He will only give you the information if you can assure him that he will have protection and not be charged."

Booth smiled. What now, has Blair had become this guy's attorney. She was negotiating a deal for him.

"I can't promise to much but I can assure you he will have all the protection he needs."

"Guess that will work but unless we can get him out of the loop of being charged with something he might not want to give you the information he has. This all has to be off the record."

"Okay, I understand. Where is this friend of yours?"

She turned toward the bathroom door and called out. "Corey, it's okay! My friend I told you about was working downstairs in the Casino." Booth realized that he should have waited a few more minutes. Blair was covering for his quick arrival.

The bathroom door opened slightly and the aide moved into the room. He stayed close to the doorway as Blair continued to talk. "Booth, this is my friend Corey. He needs our help and you're the only one that I know can help us. Corey, Booth is an old friend that dated my sister. He promised that this is all off the record. So you can tell him what you need and if you change your mind he will honor that."

The aide moved closer and Booth extended his hand. "Any friend of Blair's is a friend of mine. What can I do to help?" Corey looked a lot more relaxed now. He shook Booth's hand and smiled at Blair.

"Your right," He told her. "He does seem very nice."

They all moved to the small table in the corner of the room and Blair asked Booth if he wanted something to drink. "Sure what do you have?" He wanted to play it cool and not jump into questions about what Corey wanted.

"Is Diet Coke okay?"

"Great!" He took the drink and started to tell them that he had been following a lead on a fugitive that had been on their radar. The guy was spotted at Caesars and they caught him downstairs playing blackjack. Booth laughed. "Crooks are dumb. There are cameras all over casinos and he had the nerve to come here and was playing cards. He was up close to ten thousand when we grabbed him. The guy should have quit, but no one knows when to quit in Vegas."

"What kind of scam was he running?" Corey was asking.

"Guess I can tell you as long as you promise not to tell anyone else. He had swindled people on this false land ownership scheme. He was selling land in Arizona that belonged to the Federal Government. We only found out when people traveled there and saw the fences and signs stating that it was government property. We had been tracking him for months."

Things were going good. Booth was taking it cool and Corey was warming up to him. Blair started telling Booth the story. "What if someone knew that there was a bribe of an important political person but never reported it?"

He thought before giving an answer, "We'll as long as you are not the person bribing them or involved in paying off, you would only be witness or at the most a minor defendant."

Corey jumped in. "What do you mean by minor defendant? Would I go to jail?"

"Remember I'm not with the DA's office. But if it involves a politician it would be a Federal issue and you wouldn't have to worry about the local guys. In most cases you would actually be a witness for the state to put the guy or guys doing the bribing in jail."

"How would I be protected if I was a witness? Would I get into the witness protection program?" Corey was rattling off questions and Booth could tell why Blair was being so cautious.

"Absolutely, especially if these guys are as dangerous as you say. It happens more than you would care to think about. I've never lost a witness."

Corey let out a breath of relief. He nodded to Blair. She knew he was cool with giving Booth all the details. They both started filling him in on what had happened and that the aide was sure that the Chief Justice had been murdered. He feared that he would be next. He was the last person that knew what Albertson had done, and now that Chief Justice Leonard was dead he was sure they would come after him. Booth was writing the facts down and only asked questions when Corey stopped or left a gap in the events. When the aide had finished, he looked at Blair and said he felt a heavy burden had been taken off his shoulders. She went over and hugged him. "You're safe now," She told him.

Booth smiled and looked over his notes. He already had the same information from Blair but Corey added places, times and a few more names including one of the suspected Vegas insiders that were buying the old Frontier Hotel and Casino. When the aide named Salem Ellis, Booth had everything to do so as not to jump with joy. That was a big step forward. "How about I call this information in, without using your name yet?" He asked. Corey was thrilled with that approach. "I'm going to call it in to some of our staff and get a protective detail up here. We'll have someone outside the door for you." He moved toward the west windows and took his cell phone out.

The call went to Steve, and he could make it a three way call by patching in the Vegas Bureau Chief. They discussed all the information that the aide had given them and confirmed a protective detail coming up to the floor. The news about one of the brothers involved in from the Frontier Hotel deal was what the Vegas team needed. Now they could stop that deal from happening. They would get the Nevada Gaming Commissioner on the case right away.

It had been suspected that the two brothers were involved in something big with the acquisition of Casino's in Detroit, Atlantic

City and now the old Frontier property. No one was able to turn anything up on them. This information puts them right in the middle of bribing Senator Albertson and maybe ordering the murder of the Chief Justice. The case was coming together fast. Now they needed to find Assad and put him in the hot seat for the murder. He might give up the two Ellis brothers who were likely involvement in the plot. That would seal their fate.

Teams of agents from Vegas and across the nation had an all points bulletin out for Assad Jacoby. His picture had been sent to each agency including local police departments and Interpol. With a three day head start he might have left the country. Once everyone had been notified the FAA would put Assad's name on the no fly list. John Martin made sure that every airline that had overseas connections searched their previous passenger list to make sure he hadn't already fled the states.

Booth turned to them and updated them on the protection team that was going to be stationed outside the room. No one is going to get down this wing of the floor without one of our people seeing them. We will make sure you both are safe. He was thanking Blair for all her help. He looked at Booth and had tears in his eyes. Sir, you have been everything that I was told. I can never thank you enough for what you have done. Booth looked at him and nodded, "I would do anything to help Julie's sister or one of her friends."

He walked to the door and checked with the two men standing in the hallway. "Don't let anyone in or out."

The two men had been involved in the detail from the start. They had been guarding the floor when Blair and Corey were in the room. Booth had been communicating with them before he had moved to the room across from Blair. He needed to bring them up to date on what had transpired over the past hour in the meeting with Corey.

The Vegas teams, along with agents from the Los Angeles office were putting together the search teams to find Assad. Another group had started to investigate the actions of the two brothers and the details on purchasing the old Frontier property. The director would be mobilizing his bureau's in Detroit, Atlantic City and Arizona. The information was setting action in motion all around the country.

The two of them continued their conversation with Booth once he returned. He assured them that they would handle everything. Booth protected Blair's cover story and she was able to keep her identity from Corey. Never know when she would be needed again in that role.

Twenty-Two

John Martin was elated with the quick results from Las Vegas. Steve's team had put together critical information from the Senator's aide and his teams were now moving in on an organized gambling ring that might cover three states. The Detroit Bureau was getting a search warrant for the apartment of one of the two brothers that operated the new Casino in downtown. This was the fourth Detroit Casino to open in the past ten years and now questions arose about someone in the Michigan that may have been on the take to approve the license for it. Casinos had been springing up all over the country and the FBI had been involved in several cases checking out the prospective owners.

The second brother that was being investigated was living large in Vegas. His headquarters were in the newly built City Center in Las Vegas and his residence would soon be among those being searched. If more evidence could be found linking the two brothers with the bribing or hopefully the murder of the Chief Justice it would cement the case. Charges could start with the extortion of Senator Albertson. Hopefully they will also be tied to the murder of the Chief Justice. Assad Jacoby was still on the loose, so the FBI needed him to link the brothers to the murder. Offices would be searched in Atlantic City where the brothers had built their first Casino. It was currently operated by a cousin and he too will be part of the on-going investigation. Omar Ellis still had an apartment there so they hope to find him too.

The search for Assad was in full swing. Nothing had turned up from airport records of anyone who had flown using Jacoby's name in the past four days. The investigators had circled back to his neighborhood to re-question the man who said Assad had moved out a few days earlier. Could he have moved out a week ago instead of a few days ago? If so he might have left from the D.C. area instead of Vegas. If he returned to Vegas after the killing he might have headed to Mexico. With a valid passport he could have easily driven through the border days ago. Assad had a few days head start on the Bureau's investigators. Given the U.S. current relationship with Mexico and their concentration on the drug war, it would be hard to get them to look for a fugitive from the states.

John Martin contacted the NSA for help. He might be able to get our liaison with the State Department to make a plea with the Mexican government. John also approved the relocation of the Senator's aide once the trial was completed. Blair was happy to give Corey the news.

Blair never revealed her role as an FBI agent to Corey. Booth took Corey into custody and the Vegas Bureau placed him in a safe house until there would be a trial. Federal prosecutors would be taking his statements and preparing their motions. They also planned on making a video tape of his statement just in case. There had been another case similar and the key witness was found dead before the trial began. The bureau was going to make sure they had all their bases covered.

Once Corey was in protective custody, Blair was finally able to leave the room at Caesars Palace. She waited for Booth to pick her up in the showroom. The director of the show in the lounge was sad that his new performer wasn't going to be in his show. He really thought Blair had a lot of talent and looked forward to using her, even though she was just supposed to be doing a story. Blair wanted to thank him personally for his help. She told him that she had been given a new assignment.

Booth came into the lounge and saw her with the shows director. "I would have liked to see you in that outfit," Booth said. "I know you've been in other shows here, and I bet you're pretty good."

Blair smiled, "Sure you haven't had a good laugh in a long time."

They both walked toward the lobby. Booth was happy that Steve had assigned Blair as his partner in this case. They got the results they had hoped for and got them pretty fast.

"I talked to Steve and he wants us to hang around here in Vegas until we have a location on Jacoby. He might return here and the boss wants us here just in case. He also feels that you can still be of assistance with Corey. Never know when he might get scared and want to back out."

Blair nodded, and said she just needed a hot shower and a good night's sleep. Booth understood it had been a long night. They walked to the employee parking lot and jumped into the vehicle that the Vegas team had loaned them. The ride to the apartment building near Henderson took about fifty minutes due to so much construction on Highway 15. It appeared that they were adding two new lanes to the interstate through downtown. Vegas had grown so much in the past twenty years. This gambling oasis was now a huge city with a population over a half-a-million people. People who were driving through Vegas were surprised to find an interstate system that was ten lanes wide and had so many interchanges that you better be prepared especially during key traffic times. Highway 15 going from Los Angeles to Salt Lake City ran through the Strip. Although the recession had hit the area hard, the lights and action kept tourist coming.

Booth drove as Blair leaned back in her seat. "I really feel sorry for Corey," she said. "I've never seen anyone so scared. He was sure that they were coming for him. No wonder Albertson had a heart attack. With all the pressure of the investigation and the spot he was in with the casino guys, he was in a tough position. "

Booth looked over at her and nodded. "Corey's probably right. If he is the last one to know what was happening in the blackmail deal, they would have to knock him off."

They took the 215 interchange south of the Vegas airport and headed east toward Henderson. It had been completed a few years back and saved locals a great deal of time going east to west. The highway department had just completed the western stretch of the highway that took you west to Red Rock Canyon. The ride along 215 was similar to any highway in America. You passed Wal-Mart's, shopping centers, and neighborhoods along the way. The occasional Casino sign was the only thing that set it apart from most other cities. The road ended at Highway 95 where it led you directly into Henderson.

Meanwhile, the Vegas Bureau was teaming with action. Agents had a lead from reports that showed that Assad Jacoby had used his credit card for fuel along Highway 15 south heading toward Los Angeles two days ago. They were tracking his movements with every angle possible. It was a short jump from there to Mexico. They did not see any further action on his card since then. Why would he use a credit card if he was escaping? This didn't make sense. Was it to misled authorities? It put more pressure on the FBI team to get assistance from Mexican Authorities. The director waited for an answer from the NSA Director. Would they get help from Mexican border patrol? Would they allow FBI investigators into Mexico to conduct a search? These were all variables that there was no answer to yet.

The bureau hadn't any leads from airport authorities on Assad traveling by plane anywhere. Could the credit card receipt be a miss-direction aimed to throw them off track? What if the two brothers flew Assad out of the country in a private plane? They might have even killed their assassin after he finished the job. There were so many possibilities that the Bureau had their people all over working on the case.

Booth and Blair arrived at the apartment the Vegas office had rented for them. They had only been in Vegas a couple days and most of the time was spent at Caesars Palace working the case. Blair said she needed to clean up and catch a nap. "Let's meet in a few hours and get something to eat and check in with Steve," Booth suggested.

"Sounds like a good plan. How about one-thirty."

"Good," Booth said. I'll let Steve know what our plans are and that we'll check in then."

Blair had taken a few things with her from her apartment to Vegas, and she tossed out a skirt and blouse to change into after a shower and nap. She was going over everything that had happened and questioned in her mind where Assad could have disappeared to. I have to let it go, she thought. I'm sure they will come up with where he is in a day or so. The events were slow moving for so long but now that Corey was in custody and the search for Assad was on-going she kind of wanted to be involved in that part too.

Booth made a bunch of calls before jumping into the shower. He also wanted to be involved in the search for Assad. He thought they should make another trip to the neighborhood he was living. What if the FBI was getting bad information from the neighbors?

What if others were involved that were hiding Assad? He had to let it go. His part was over and the bureau had good people on the search. Booth never liked being told to lie off. He would try to gather information on his own as soon as possible. He could see across the courtyard to Blair's apartment. He couldn't sleep. He looked at her patio and saw her sitting outside with her lap top out. He thought she was going to take a nap? Booth grabbed a change of clothes and headed out to Blair's apartment.

"I thought you were going to take a nap," He said walking toward her patio. "Crap, you scared the hell out of me! Don't you ever call first?"

He laughed. "What are you doing?"

Blair looked down at her screen, she than turned it toward Booth. "The credit card receipt is a bad lead. I don't think he's headed to Mexico. The station isn't just off the highway, but it's over eight miles down Foot Hills Boulevard. Why would you go past a half-a-dozen stations to get gas that far off the highway?"

Booth took the lap top and looked at the information Blair had checked on. Foot Hills Boulevard was a very popular exit near the intersections of Highways 15 and 10. Could Assad know someone in Rancho Cucamonga or the San Bernardino area? The hills of San Bernardino, California could hide someone for years. There were many hidden areas along that stretch of land. Its old Route 66, not many people travel that road now with the interstate.

Booth knew that Blair might be onto something. "We should call Steve with this information." Blair looked up at him. "What if we headed that way to check it out?"

Booth liked her idea. They were thinking alike. He hated sitting on the sidelines anyway. "I'm good with that, but we better check in with the boss. Don't want to get you into trouble so early in your career. I know I've been there before," Booth told her.

"I can be ready in ten minutes," Blair said. "I know the area real well. I've stopped there many times with my parents. There is a new shopping center just west of the Foot Hills exit. We would get off there because there is a Chick-Fill-A restaurant in the shopping center." Booth laughed. "Only you would tell me a story that included a restaurant."

They were becoming good friends and great partners. Booth headed toward his apartment and called in to Steve back in Los

Angeles. He knew he would have to convince the boss to let them do some investigating on their own. Booth had a good rapport with his boss. Steve knew that Booth would use good judgment and had been on many critical cases before.

Blair grabbed some clothes and put it in her bag and followed Booth to his apartment. "What did the boss say?" Booth was surprised to see her so quickly. "He's not happy, but he said he would allow us to start searching around only if we had another team from the office with us."

"Sounds reasonable to me," Blair answered. "Let's go!"

They headed to the car and Booth asked, "So are you going to fill me in on our plans?"

Blair smiled, "It's pretty cool that you are willing to go along with me on this. Once when I was with my parents, my dad thought that he could take a shortcut through the San Bernardino Mountain's and cut off a lot of miles. Of course we got lost for a while, but he found this small road that headed through the mountain pass and down toward Riverside. I thought my mother was about to kill my dad until we saw the pass that headed down the mountains. Most of the ride was through the National Forest and there were tons of small cabins up there. I bet Assad could be holed up in one of those spots."

"Why would he hide there instead of heading to Mexico?"

Traveling to Mexico could be a problem. With all the drug wars and problems, maybe he felt that hiding out here for a while would be safer. He could always escape later when things died down. Maybe he used the credit card to send us tracking him to the border.

Either Blair had lost her mind or they were on to Assad's possible location. Anyway you looked at it Booth was in for the hunt. It was better than sitting in Vegas waiting for something to happen.

Blair reminded Booth that the pass led through Big Morongo Canyon and it had a desert atmosphere and would be very hot and dry. She had grabbed a six pack of bottled water and put a pair of shorts on. Booth grabbed a few snacks for the car and a change of clothes. The ride would take just a little over three hours from Vegas.

The two agents had their plan and were excited to be back in the game instead of on the sidelines waiting for instructions. Booth always wanted to be in the middle of every investigation, he hated waiting around. Blair was new to all of this but she had a tendency to take chances and ever since Hunter's death became more daring. That is how she was able to find the package that Hunter had sent from Iraq. It took a lot of deceptive moves to avoid the agents assigned to watch her but she was able to pull it off. Now she was one of the agents and had to follow protocol. She was glad Booth was willing to take a chance that she was right.

Twenty-Three

The drive south through Nevada to Los Angeles was always boring. They came to the California State line in about forty-five minutes and Blair was telling Booth about her last trip from Vegas to Los Angeles with her parents. He enjoyed hearing about her family. He never told anyone that he had grown up in Foster Homes. His parents had been killed when he was ten and there were no other relatives. He had gone from one foster family to another and being rejected so many times made him quite a loaner. He felt that the FBI was a great opportunity once he finished college. Blair's background was so different than his. She had funny stories about her parents and schools that she attended.

The sign on the side of the highway read one-hundred-ten miles to Barstow. Booth told Blair that he used to head to Vegas almost every weekend when he first moved to Los Angeles. I know this ride all too well. He got real quiet and Blair wanted to ask him more but thought he would tell her when he was ready.

The temp gauge in the car showed that it had reached one-hundred-twelve degrees outside, which was normal this time of year. They were traveling through the Mohave Desert and Highway 15 wound its way through the desert down toward the San Bernardino Mountains. Booth asked Blair to tell him about the ride her dad chose through the mountains. He gave her a map to trace the route so that they could set up a meeting place with the team from the LA office. We'll give them a call once we get to the Apple Valley exit. Booth knew that they were looking for a needle in a haystack, but this beat sitting around.

John Martin was concerned that his people hadn't found any other trace or information about Assad. Where could he be? What about the credit card receipt from California? He called Steve again to see if they had any other information. Steve was expecting to hear from the director. No, he didn't have any more details that he could tell him. Steve had gotten used to John Martin's questions. The director was always hands on, especially in a case with this much magnitude. He was also tracking the information of Salem and Omar Ellis, the casino operators.

Blair filled Booth in on the San Bernardino Mountains from what she remembered. It helped with the map on her lap. She was able to retrace the previous trip she made with her parents. They would have to exit the freeway at Foot Hills Drive and head west for about ten miles before reaching the outer edge of the mountain pass. The exit should be a good meeting place with the other agents. Booth relayed that information to Steve and also found out that there had been a helicopter ordered to make a surveillance trip along the pass. The copter could make it through Big Morongo Canyon before it got dark. Blair hoped that she wasn't sending the Bureau's team on a wild goose chase. Booth told her that they didn't have any other leads and that the FBI had dispatched a team toward the Mexican border in case Assad headed that way.

Booth had just turned off of Highway 15 onto Foot Hills Boulevard and took a left at the bottom of the ramp. He had told the teams coming to meet at the shopping center just a quarter of a mile down the road from the exit. It would be a good spot to put their search plan together with the other units. She looked over at him when they pulled into the lot. Maybe we should grab something to eat it's a long ride through the mountains. He agreed and asked her if she had a preference. "Yes Chick-Fill-A!" The answer seemed way too quick. He laughed. "I hope you didn't come up with this theory just to get a Chick-Fill-A sandwich?" "No, I want nuggets!" They both laughed out loud. Booth checked the parking lot and their contacts hadn't arrived. "Okay, we'll get something to eat."

The Vegas team was working with Corey and he was giving them all the details that he knew regarding the connections with the Senator, Chief Justice and the casino group in Vegas. Yes, he knew that the Chief Justice and Albertson were involved in the gambling ring. No, the Chief Justice and Albertson were just close friends. His information could help them because it also detailed involvement in interstate gambling. The R.I.C.O. unit of the

Bureau was now called in to assist with the investigation. The connections with all the casino's owned by the two brothers completed the picture.

They planned to move in on the brother living in Vegas at his operation before he had a chance to get rid of any evidence. The old Frontier Hotel and Casino was prime property. It was across from the new Trump Hotel on Las Vegas Boulevard. The Vegas Bureau had sent men to both locations that the suspected brother had lived. They had two local addresses on file.

A team of Agents headed to the New City Center area where Salem had a Condo on the twenty-fourth floor. It was the in place to live in Vegas. The businesses, hotels, casinos and apartments were all connected together and the ability to move around the strip from there was perfect. They entered the high rise and headed to the office of the building manager. They explained that they needed to get into the unit owned by the suspect. They showed him their search warrant and said that there might be danger to other tenants. If things looked bad they would have the manager help clear out the other units. He told them that the floor was only half occupied. The unit they were interested in was one of three on that floor.

He accompanied them to the twenty-fourth floor and one of the agents took the key from him. "It would be best if you're not here while we search the residence," he explained. "You never know what we might find and we don't want you to get hurt." The manager was concerned but thanked them and headed down the hallway to the bank of elevators.

The agents knocked on the door. There was no answer. They knocked again and called out, "FBI!" Still there was no answer. They used the key and slowly opened the door. Both men had guns drawn just in case. Again they called out into the opening, "FBI, anyone home!" The doorway was clear and they moved into the room, guns were now lowered. Just then a figure appeared from around the corner in what was possibly the kitchen. They could see that the man had something at his side, could have been a gun, but they weren't sure. "Federal Bureau of Investigation!" they called out a third time. The figure moved back into the kitchen and hollered out. "What do you want?"

The two agents looked at each other and one of them shouted,

"We have a warrant and we're looking for Mr. Ellis."

It was quiet for a minute, and the agents moved back toward the doorway in case the man decided to fire at them. "He's not here!" Came an answer from inside.

"You need to come out into the hallway; we have a search warrant for this property!" The Bureau had also sent two other teams of agents to another residence that Mr. Ellis had been know to own. It seemed like five minutes before something happened.

Shots rang out from inside the apartment. They were too many shots to come from a hand gun. It must have been an automatic, possibly a sub-machine gun. The agents scattered back into the hallway and pushed a wedge under the door so that they would have a view of the action. One of them called back to the office and informed them that they were being shot at and had at least one suspect at the City Center Condo unit shooting at them.

The Vegas FBI office dispatched two other units and called the local Clark County Sherriff to inform him what was happening. There would surely be calls to the police from other residents. It was important to let the local officials know about the shooting on the twenty-fourth floor of the high rise.

No one in the bureau wanted a standoff but that is exactly what had happening. The first goal would be to make sure everyone in the adjacent apartments were safe. One agent moved down the hallway and knocked on the door to the right of Mr. Ellis apartment. There wasn't an answer. Might be the empty unit they told us about. He crawled back toward the opened door and motioned to his partner that no one was at home. There was one other unit to the left side of Ellis' apartment. They decided to keep an eye on the opening while making sure that no one was in that apartment. The agent on the floor called out again while his partner checked on the second apartment. "You need to drop your weapon and come out with your hands up!" This never worked but he was making sure that whoever was inside knew they were still there. More shots rang out from inside the apartment toward the opened doorway.

A call went out to the building manager to have him contact any residents on the floors below and above. The high rise had only three penthouse suites on each of the floors from the 24th through twenty-sisth floor.

A second team of agents had just arrived on the scene and they were accompanied by two members of Clark County Sherriff's office. The agents filled them in on the events and the six men planned their next move. The Clark County Sherriff's men said that they checked with the building manager, and he was aware of the events. He had called all the residence on the floors above and below to clear the building. The standoff and shooting was the last thing they wanted, but that was what they had on their hands.

The agents told the new arrivals that they suspected that there was more than one man inside. Shots were too rapid and seem to come from more than one direction they. The Vegas Bureau Chief was on his way to the twenty-fourth floor and he had the building plans with him. Maybe there was another way into the apartment. He hoped to resolve this as soon as possible. They wanted the man or men inside alive.

The standoff at the high rise was now into the second hour and the Bureau's men had checked the building plans and saw there wasn't another way in or out of the unit. They had hoped that the man or men inside would see that it was hopeless and give up. The Chief decided that they needed to push the envelope and force the guy into the open. He drew up a plan to have two of the agents slide into the opening and then his men in the doorway would start shooting. Maybe they could bring the person into position to get an open shot.

The two agents that were first on the scene at City Center wanted to try to enter the apartment. One of them slid on the floor and saw that there was a short wall that divided the main part of the living room from the rest of the apartment. The other agent pushed himself into the opening and the second man started shooting to cover his partner that moved along the floor to a spot behind the wall. The person inside didn't return fire. The first agent was in place and the second agent had just moved into the doorway when shots rang out from behind around the corner. A volley of bullets rang out across the opening and sprayed the hallway with loud explosions. They weren't normal bullet shots. Much to rapid and sprayed the opening to the hall.

The agent that had made it to the short wall was hit in the shoulder and rolled over toward the wall. His partner returned fire to protect him. The new arrivals heard the shots and crawled toward the action. Blood splattered over the entrance floor and the agent slumped as he lay along the wall. The chief knew they needed to do something, and it had to be now. He motioned for the Clark County guys to use the heavy armor that they had brought with them. One of them grabbed the large barreled gun and positioned himself in the hallway where he had a clear shot into the apartment. He motioned to the two agents inside and they ducked down.

An enormous blast rang out and the noise was almost deafening. The wall between the living room and kitchen ripped opened and they could hear the sound of men inside scrambling for cover. A second blast tore a section of the wall out. There would no longer be a place to hide for the men in the kitchen. The officers now had a view of the doorway all the way into the kitchen. The agent called out again to drop your weapons and come out with your hands up. Nothing happened and there wasn't an answer. The Clark County Sherriff reloaded and fired a third blast into the kitchen area. When he did the chief was able to slide into the doorway and pull the injured agent out into the hallway. This blast brought an answer of bullets and swearing from the men inside.

The injured agent was being administered to as the assault on the apartment continued.

There was no other option but to return a flurry of bullets into the apartment. The Clark County officers had procured a layout of the apartment from the building manager. They knew from reviewing the plans that the kitchen didn't have an exit into the rest of the apartment. The men were cornered, they had no exit and either had to give up or they would be killed. Two more FBI agents were able to get into the apartment and were in position with one of the Clark County Sherriff's men. One more warning went out without an answer. The agents and the Sherriff fired a hail of bullets along with the large blast from the large barreled gun into the kitchen area. They heard one thud and a cry for help. The siege was over.

The agents moved into the kitchen. Walls were crushed and one of the men inside lies dead on the kitchen floor. Blood was splattered all over appliances. The second man was severely wounded. There was a gash in his leg and he was holding his chest.

Neither of them were Mr. Ellis.

As the chief and his men pushed the weapons away from the two suspects they could see a pool of blood under the man closest to the opening to the apartment hallway. One of the blasts had apparently made a direct hit on him. The second man way lying against the counter and kept yelling for help. "I've been shot twice, I need help!" The chief smiled and told his men to call for a medic, but first make sure the agent was taken care of. "I need some answers first," he told the man on the kitchen floor. "Where the hell is Mr. Ellis?"

"I don't know a Mr. Ellis," was the answer.

"Okay," said the chief. He then leaned over the man and stepped on the leg that was bleeding. "Shit, my leg, get off my leg!"

"Now again, where is Mr. Ellis?"

"He's not here," cried the man.

"Wow," said the chief. "You're really helping yourself with that crap. If you expect me to give you medical assistance you better have a better answer for me." The chief pressed harder on the injured leg.

"Help, you can't do that. I know police can't hurt you when you're arrested, I have rights too. I'll have your ass in a law suit!"

"Who said we were the police, and who do you think will be your witnesses? Now, for a last time before I step on your balls, where is Mr. Ellis?"

The man looked up with tears running down his face. He left yesterday but didn't tell us where he was going.

"Now you're doing better," the chief said. "Give us a number how to reach him!" With that the chief took his left foot and pressed it against the man's crotch. The two local Clark County guys watched and laughed. Wish we could do that they thought.

"It's 902-555-8686. Please get off of me now!"

"Just a few more things," the chief said, still pressing on his nuts. "Is that his cell number?"

"Christ sakes, yes!" The man was in dire pain as blood oozed out of his leg. He was holding his hands on his chest and the chief could see that he was just grazed on the right side of his rib cage.

"You're getting closer to being taken care of, but first what are you doing in this apartment?" The bureau chief wasn't giving him any help until he had everything he needed.

"Mr. Ellis told us to watch the place for him. I need help before I bleed to death."

The chief told his men to call in the phone number to their office. Let's see if we can get confirmation of the cell owner he was saying. Once they had the number they could track it via GPS. "You're going to be okay," he told the guy on the floor, "But only if your information checks out."

One of the paramedics moved into the kitchen and asked if they needed him to start working on the guy on the floor. "Not yet," said the chief. The man was crying as the chief kept his foot on the left leg and pressed down with his heel. "You better be telling me the correct information or you'll need the morgue, not the medical staff." Blood started to puddle under the man as the paramedic looked on. The information came back that the cell number was registered to a corporation owned by Mr. Ellis and his brother. "Okay," said the chief. "Let's bandage him up and we'll take him in."

"I need to go to the hospital," the man yelled.

"You should have thought about that before you and your buddy started shooting at my men. You're lucky we don't finish you off." The chief walked toward the County guys. "You didn't see shit, got it!" They nodded and moved back into the hallway. Both of them appreciated the measures the FBI used and only wished they could get away with them.

Now they had a lead and planned on tracing the cell number. With GPS they could get a possible location and hopefully Mr. Ellis was still in possession of the cell phone.

Twenty-Four

Hours had passed since the siege on the twenty-fourth floor at City Center. Steve called Booth telling him that the Vegas guys had a lead on Mr. Ellis and his possible where-a-bouts. They were tracing his cell phone number and maybe they can get a lead from it. It was looking up to find Salem and now it was up to Booth's team to find Assad. The bureau would continue to search Detroit and Atlantic City for Salem's brother Omar. The two brothers were the focus for the bribing of Senator Albertson and the possible murder of the Chief Justice.

Booth was waiting for the second team to meet them at the Foot Hills exit and he and Blair had pulled their vehicle into the middle of the parking lot so they could easily be seen. He filled Steve in on what they knew, which wasn't much. "They should be here any minute," he told Blair.

She had just finished her Chick-fill-A nuggets, and Booth was still teasing her about the stop at the restaurant. She laughed and then asked if he liked them. "Well I hate to admit it but the sandwich was great." Just then they looked up and saw a black suburban pulling into the lot. Booth flashed his lights and it pulled next to them. They all got out and Booth pulled his map out. Blair had highlighted the road through the pass. They placed the map on the hood. The route through the mountains was narrow and there was only one way in and out. The plan was that when they got to a fork in the road, one of the two cars would circle through the area just in case there was a sign of the fugitive. There were only three spots where someone would hold up Booth told the second team of agents. Blair had them marked on the map.

Booth reminded the team that many residents didn't like the government. Guess some of them retreated here after the sixty's and we better be careful not to identify ourselves as agents. It would be better to keep undercover, just looking for a friend. They all agreed. The second team updated Booth on plans that the bureau had made. They were sending a chopper to circle the area. It was agreed that they would get going before it got dark. The ride from Foot Hills Boulevard to the narrow pass was only about ten minutes. Booth was leading the two car caravan and Blair was navigating them with the map on her lap. She also was using her cell phone app for directions and road information. Because of the terrain, there could be many problems driving through the narrow pass.

Steve was getting updated information from the Vegas Bureau chief on the search for Salem. They also discussed the details that Martin had given them on the possible arrest of Ellis' brother, Omar in Atlantic City. John said that the bureau's team had a location on the brother and an arrest was imminent. Once they had the two brothers in custody the details that Corey had given them could be put into place. The bureau had times, places and names. Now all they needed were the accomplices and some collaborating evidence. Corey had brought bank account materials with him to Vegas. These were being checked out by the Bureau. The picture was coming together.

Booth knew finding the suspected killer was critical to the murder indictment on the brothers. If they could find Assad and bring him in alive it would help seal the case. He might turn state's witness against the Ellis brothers for special consideration. It was up to the two teams to see if the search of the mountains held their man.

The ride along the narrow pass toward the San Gabriel Wilderness and Sheep Mountain was steep. The ridge had a metal railing that had many marks where a vehicle must have veered off the road. Booth kept his eyes on the cliffs to the left as he listened for directions from Blair. She told him that they would be coming to an opening with a circle drive. It would be the first spot the two teams would split up and check out the cabins. They were near the Cloudburst Summit with an elevation of over seven thousand feet. Booth could see all the way down the mountain side to Pasadena. If it wasn't for the search he wished he could have stopped to take in the view.

"Christ, how far it is to Pasadena?"

"I'm not sure but my father said it was the coolest view of

eastern Los Angeles that he had ever seen. I forgot how beautiful this was."

They passed an old pick-up on the side of the road. It had a bumper sticker on the back. Booth pointed it out to his partners. It read, "Thanks for visiting, now get the hell out!" They all nodded when they passed the vehicle. It wasn't unusual to see trucks up here with gun racks on the back window. It was almost as if you were in the deep south. He motioned to the second team to take the turn to the right as he and Blair would take the circle to the left. The area would have both tourist and long time residents. They planned to check all the houses. There was only about five or six cabins so it shouldn't take too long. The cabins were in two clusters with three cabins sharing one road in a small circle. Booth and Blair pulled into the first drive and got out of the vehicle. Let's stay together he suggested. They would knock on the door of the first cabin because it had two SUV's in front and fishing equipment on the porch. It looked like best place to start and appeared to be normal tourist on vacation. When Booth knocked on the door Blair stood off to the left. They both were dressed very casual and would use the cover of looking for a friend that should have just arrived.

A lady came to the door holding a small child. "Yes, can I help you?" The little boy was squirming and wanted down. As soon as his feet touched the ground he was off. "Billy, come back here," she yelled.

"Sorry we didn't mean to cause you a problem." Blair and the lady chased down the child. "Your pretty quick," Blair laughed as she held him for his mother. Booth knew they needed to keep their cover. They didn't want to alert the area's residents to a possible man hunt. "Sorry, we're looking for friends who should have just checked in the past few days. I lost the number of their cabin."

The lady held her son's hand as she headed back to the front porch of the cabin. She put the child down but kept holding his hand. "We've been here all week and haven't seen anyone in the other two units. My husband and his buddy are down by the lake fishing and maybe they can help you."

Booth thanked her and asked for directions to the lake. She pointed him in the direction down the road and cautioned that they needed to be careful because it was a steep grade down. "You could walk from here if you want."

"Thanks," Booth said, as they moved off the porch. He turned and waved as the lady went back in the cabin. He turned to Blair and told her that they should check the other two cabins out. She agreed and he called the second team to inform him what they hadn't found anything. The second team was just pulling into the drive where two small cabins sat next to each other. They said there wasn't any sign of a vehicle or tire tracks. They would check the cabins out and meet back at the fork in the road.

The cabins that they checked were empty and you could see clearly into both of them. The drapes were wide open and each had large picture windows in front. A call came from the second team that their search came up empty. Booth told them to wait at the fork because he was going to stroll down to the lake to check with two men that were fishing. Maybe they had seen a vehicle driving through the area.

The walk down the lane toward the lake was as steep as the lady had told him. Blair waited at the vehicle and checked the map for the next spot where cabins were located. As she stood at the front of the vehicle she heard noise from behind the cabins. It sounded like a small engine coming through the woods. She turned her attention to the woods and the noise. It grew louder and she realized that whatever it was, it was coming closer. She immediately called Booth. She moved behind their vehicle and ducked down as she talked on her phone to him. He said he was headed back toward her position.

"Booth, I'm not sure what it is. I can handle the situation here."

"I'm sure you can," he said. "I'd rather be there just in case."

Just then the noise stopped. She decided to move near the front of the vehicle while keeping an eye on the area behind the cabins where she heard the noise. Just as she got to the front she spotted a young boy coming from behind one of the cabins. He headed toward the cabin where they had talked to the lady on the porch. He appeared to be a teenager and had a helmet in his hand. The lady came back out of the cabin and waved to the young man as he approached.

She called out to him. "How was the ride?"

"Pretty cool mom. I wanted to go down the path to the falls

but there was a guy down there and he told me that I had to turn back."

"Why?" asked the woman.

"I'm not sure but he didn't look very friendly. I decided that I would wait until dad came back from fishing. Maybe he could ride down there with me."

"That's a good idea."

Blair waved at the boy and he waved back. "Hello," she called out.

"Hi," he said. It was clear by the look on his face that he saw she was cute and moved toward her. Booth had just come into the clearing and stood back as he watched Blair moving toward the boy.

"How far is it to the falls?"

"Not too far. It is a lot closer if you go through the woods, but you can get there from the road. It's about five miles, and you have to go down the hillside to the left. You have to walk the rest of the way."

"My husband and I are supposed to meet a friend and he might be down there. Did you say the path to the falls was closed?"

"No, but there was a man was down there and did not appear to be very friendly. He told me to turn back."

She continued to move toward the young man. "What did he look like?"

"Kind of tall with dark hair but he wasn't dressed right for being out in the woods."

"I bet that's my friend," she said. "He's kind of a geek, always involved in his science experiments."

The young man nodded. "He had a beard and didn't act very friendly. He had a rifle with him, so I'm not sure what kind of experiment you would need a gun for."

"I'm sorry if he scared you. I'm sure he was just making sure that he didn't meet up with a bear or wolf." That made sense to the young man since so many bear attacks had taken place across the country.

Booth walked toward her and the young man. "Honey, there wasn't a sign of Jim down by the lake." She was now standing with the teen and introduced Booth. "This is my husband did I hear your mom call you Tim?"

"Yes." The young man was obviously disappointed to meet a husband. *Too bad* he thought *this chick was pretty cute.*

"Babe," she said to Booth, and putting her arm around him, "Tim might have run into Jim down by the falls. He is doing one of those experiments and you know how he can be."

Booth looked over are her and nodded his head. He asked Tim the same questions that she had asked. Tim again gave Booth the directions to the falls. He said by riding the four wheeler it made the trip a lot easier and allowed him to get to the falls quicker. Booth said that he wished they had one available. The lady from the cabin had now come down to where her son was talking to the couple. A little tyke was following her carrying a small stuffed bunny.

Blair bent down and started to talk to the little child. "What is that you're carrying?"

He ran behind his mother and hid between her legs. "He's so cute," she told the mom.

"Thanks," she said. "Billy, tell the lady what you have." He stayed behind his mother and peeked out toward Blair.

"Guess we need to head toward the falls she said aloud to Booth. Looks like Jim might be down there according to your son." He agreed and they thanked the lady and her two sons for their help. Booth told the teen that he would talk to Jim and make sure that Tim could come back down to the falls tomorrow after Jim finished his experiments.

They got back in their vehicle and contacted the second team with the information about the man at the falls. They all figured that there was a good chance that it was Assad. It was certainly suspicious. They would head down the road and pull off in a spot and walk to the falls. Maybe their search would be close to over. Booth called in to the office so that the helicopter would not enter the area. They did not want the copter to spook the man if it was Assad.

The two vehicles met at the fork in the road and reviewed the map of the area. There was a pick-up in the clearing that was nosed into its spot. The truck didn't have a plate on it and was a later model Ford.

They could see from the map that the falls were about a mile or two off the road. The grade was steep and the terrain was rugged. The plan was set. They would head down the road toward the bend and pull off into a spot to hide their vehicles and continue on foot. It was suggested that they split up. It made sense in case it was Assad. Although it didn't make sense that he would camp out. He wouldn't have to be seen if he was camping. The map did not show any cabins in the area of the falls.

The two teams arrived at the spot they picked about half way down the path and coordinated their plans. They headed down the main path and the second team moved around the right side. Just in case Assad had left the falls and was coming back toward the main road they would block the retreat. Booth made sure everyone was clued in to the fact that they needed to take Assad alive. They nodded as they made their way into the thick wooded path. The main trail was steep and the brush was getting thicker. They separated so that they had the area around the falls covered. He didn't like that idea. He was concerned that if they separated something could go wrong. The second team would have the path covered to the right so moving along the trail made sense. He could hear the rush of water as they neared the falls. He motioned to Blair that they needed to get off the trail. They moved into the thicket and proceeded slowly. He grabbed his cell and made sure it was on vibrate. He waved to her and pointed to his cell phone. She understood and put her phone on vibrate too. He hoped that the second team was nearing the ridge of the falls. They would have the area covered and there would be no path of escape. Just then a blast rang out. Both Agents hit the ground. A second blast rang out and they could tell it was from the wooded area just north of the falls.

They moved together, guns drawn, toward the area of gun shots. It was definitely a shot gun blast that they heard. She looked at him as he motioned her to move closer. It was about thirty seconds since the second blast. Booth didn't want to alert whoever it was shooting that they were on the path. They could now hear the sound of water running over rocks and the falls must have been close.

He made a circle motion with his right hand in the air and she moved around to his side. They stooped down and he drew something in the dirt. She could see that he was drawing plans for them as they got into the clearing. She nodded that she understood.

Now a third blast rang out and a voice hollered out, "FBI, drop the gun and come on out."

The chase was on.

_____Twenty Five

Shots again rang out and this time they were closer. The noise sounded like a cannon. The echo of the blast told the agents that the person shooting was near an opening. Could there have been a cave nearby? The team of agents continued moving cautiously toward their prey. Another flurry of shots seemed to be coming from close to their position. There wasn't any return fire. Booth figured that the second team of agents was moving in and the person shooting was being flushed out in their direction. This was a smart maneuver. The suspect would know that there were men coming from one direction but unaware of being surrounded. It was important that they hold their position. They were about fifteen feet into the thicket and could see a ridge in front of them. If the man shooting truly was coming their way they would have the drop on him. The ridge would box him in.

Booth crouched down behind a clump of dead tree branches that were stacked up about four feet high. It looked like someone had intentionally stacked them that way. He saw what appeared to be brown material pushed into the side of the logs. He pointed it out to her as she stooped down. It could be a rolled up sleeping bag. He motioned to her to circle around to the side of the logs as he crawled ten feet forward. If they could catch their suspect between them they had a better chance of disarming him.

She checked out the sleeping bag and saw that there weren't any weapons rolled up in it. It made sense to move a little further into the thicket. Blair continued moving until she felt that the person was close. She had positioned herself about forty five feet to Booths right, and could hear the sound of a tree branch breaking. Someone was near. She tried to motion to him but he was too far away. She was lying low along the tree line. Just then she heard footsteps that seemed to be in front of her. A man's leg appeared almost stepping on her right arm. Before she realized what had happened she was on the ground. The contact from a tree limb caught her on the side of her head. Blood trickled from her temple as she was being dragged into the thicket. It all happened so quickly. She couldn't think. What had happened? Her arms were flailing about as branches scratched at her face and legs.

Booth heard commotion to his right. He knew the two of them were close and maybe the suspect had been grabbed by Blair. He radioed her but no answer. He started to move through the underlying brush to the right hoping not to alert the man they were trapping. His calls again went without an answer. Where was his partner? Why didn't she respond? He could see the clump of stacked branches where they had last been close together. There was no sight of Blair. He continued to survey the area and saw marks on the ground. Looks like someone or something had been dragged through the brush.

He had her! And now she was his prisoner. How did he get the drop on her? She was being tied to a tree. A gag was stuffed into her mouth. She could hear her radio with Booth calling her. She needed to warn him. The man was behind her. She still hadn't seen him. He grabbed the radio and smashed it against a rock. It now seemed like an hour had passed. She had been left against the tree, tied up and gagged. She would be no help to anyone now.

The second team of agents arrived to the location that Booth had radioed them. He showed them the drag marks and that Blair was not answering his calls. The update told them his suspicions and that his partner was gone, maybe captured. It was quiet now. The only thing that the teams had to go on was the direction that the last sounds came from. The three members were now working together. How did the fugitive escape their trap? They thought that they had him between them. He obviously knew the wooded area very good. Now they had two missions. Capturing the suspect and to find out what happened to Blair.

Booth was working with the other team members planning to encircle the location where she had been. They worked closely together hoping to make sure their suspect didn't get away. He was worried about her. Was she okay? Where was she? They could all follow the marks in the woods where someone had been dragged, but needed to be careful. Now it seemed that the hunted had become the hunter. It was decided to split up and Booth would follow the marks on the ground.

Blair continued to struggle against the stump and was biting at her gag. If she could only get it out of her mouth she could warn her partner. She was disorientated and bleeding. There was a gash on the right side of her head. Her hair was matted with dried blood and mud. The gag was getting loose and she kept biting the edge and turning her head right and left to pull it out of her mouth. She had to yell for help. Her hands were tightly bound behind her and the tree rose about twenty feet high. No way to stand up and get free. Short branches jutted out above her head. She was helpless.

The three agents had made their way down the path. It was close to where they saw the dragged marks on the ground. There was nothing but silence ahead. This was not good. Booth felt they should stay together. Whoever they were chasing was clearly aware of the area and had a head start on them. The main object now was to find his partner.

Blair continued to struggle and was able to pull the gag from her mouth with her teeth. By biting at it and thrashing around it finally came loose. Just then Booth heard her gasping. "Over here! I'm over here!" Blair's heart was beating a thousand times a minute. Was this the right thing to do? Should she be yelling out? She needed to warn her team, not worry about being set free. The suspect could be near.

He was glad to hear her voice. He started to run toward it. "I'm okay, be careful, I don't see anyone but he's probably still around." She was warning them but Booth was just glad that she was alive. He slowed down and realized that she was right. Be careful, it could be a trap to capture him too. His first reaction was to call back to her but that would give his position away. He didn't know what to think at first when she was missing but now he was back in command. He radioed the other team members to his position and that they needed to cover the area. He had the other agents circle the perimeter where her voice was coming from.

She continued to try to get free. Her hands were bound behind the tree and she was unable to stand up. She felt the pain on the side of her head as she tried to get loose. How could she help? She wanted to do something to help. She curled her legs to the right and started rotating her arms in an upward motion hoping to move the rope further up the tree. If she could get her legs under her she could stand and maybe help with her rescue.

There was no sound coming from the area around where her voice was coming from. He probably left her and headed down the raven she thought. There might be an escape route that they were unaware of. She called out to Booth once again. "I'm okay, don't worry about me. He might be headed down the cliff." She was now able to kneel. The ropes were slowly moving up the tree trunk as she kept rotating from right to left. If only she could stand up.

All of a sudden a loud crash happened from somewhere behind her. She could hear struggling and thrashing. Booth leaped into action. He sprang up from his position tackling the man bringing him to the ground. A gun shot from the rifle rang out sending a blast straight up into the air as the suspect was sent sprawling to the surface. Booth jumped on the man and pushed the rifle away from him. Blair could hear the action but couldn't see what was happening. It was all behind her. She called out hoping that whoever it was in the struggle that the rest of the team would come to their aid. Now all three agents were together and had secured the man on the ground.

They had their suspect. He was able to subdue the captured suspect and handcuffed him. Booth was headed to the tree and now to free his partner. Two agents had the man under control and were handcuffing him. Booth scrambled to free her. He hurried to release her. "Are you okay? She was now standing up and Booth was checking her out. He saw the gash on her right side and the matted blood. "We need to get you taken care of."

"I'm okay, go find out who the hell he is!" She was mad at herself for being captured. "I want to club the S.O.B. myself!" She saw the captured man. He was about six foot tall and had a straggly beard. It didn't look like any of the pictures they had of Assad. Who was he?

The agents had hoped that they found Assad hiding in the deep forest, it didn't pan out. Guess that would have been too easy. It was not the man they were looking for, but who was he? Booth took the handcuffed captive and pulled him up. "What's your name?" The man just stared at them. He had no reaction and sneered at the questions they were asking. "It will go a lot better for you if you talk to us," Booth stated.

He spit at them and tried to pull free. Finally he said, "Damn feds." They held him tight and pulled their captive toward the edge of the path. Booth told the team to help Blair and we need to take the man to their truck. She was up now and one of agents was helping her. What happened, they asked? "He got the jump on me, but I'm okay." She felt ashamed that she had been captured.

"Hey, don't worry, we got him. It could have happened to any of us." They were glad that she was up and seemed okay. Blair knew they were trying to make her feel better. One of them ran back to their vehicle to get a first aid kit. The other agent said that they had a fingerprint scanner in their car. I'll go get it and we can see who we have. Booth knew that was a great idea. He pulled the man with him and they started toward their vehicle. "This would go a lot better for you if you talked now." He hadn't said anything since his remark about them being feds. The agents traveled back to the location of their vehicles and hoped to find out who they had.

She was now sitting on the front seat of the suburban and one of the agents was administering to her injury. The gash looked worse than first suspected. Her wound was a few inches long but the cut wasn't deep. Most of it appeared to be surface scratches. Any cuts to your face always seemed to bleed a lot. They applied an antiseptic to the wound and placed a gauze pad over it. She wasn't happy that he got the drop on her. She wanted to get back to Booth who was checking his identification out.

The agents were now all together planning their moves. Booth was holding his captive as they waited for results from the fingerprint analysis. Although they knew that not all people had their fingerprints on file, it was possible that someone carrying a shotgun in the woods was on file. Sure enough the results came back. They had the identification of their man. He was an escaped prisoner from a northern California prison. The man had been on the run for close to two years and had been convicted of armed robbery. He was wanted in both California and Nevada for bank robbery. At least they had a fugitive to turn in for their efforts.

Let's call it in to the chopper and have them take him off while we head further down the path. They all agreed and the chopper pilot said there was a clearing about a mile up the road that he could land in. The second team said they would meet the chopper and Booth wanted to make sure his partner was really okay. He knew she was tough but it looked like a nasty cut. Any ordeal of being captured is tough, be this might be especially rough on her. He didn't know all that she had been through before. She had experienced much worse.

The search for Assad had been delayed due to the false lead by the falls but now would continue. The two teams would meet at the clearing and head along the narrow path. Blair assured Booth that she was fine. Just her pride a little hurt she told him. "Don't let that bother you, if you knew how many times I got my head handed to me, you'd be surprised." It made her feel a little better as they headed to the meet area.

The sound of the chopper taking back off was just in front of them. The agents would again scout out the area ahead and search for Assad.

Agents from the Vegas bureau had been canvassing the last known neighborhood that Assad lived at. They broadened their search to the two blocks around his last known address. They were concentrating on any lead that developed from the area. Unfortunately, it turned up zilch! They were reporting back to their bureau chief's, but none of them had any real information. It looked like Assad had vanished into thin air. The Vegas bureau chief was busy with the suspects he had in custody from the siege at the apartment in the City Center. He had a new lead and he had dispatched some agents to check out. The GPS trace showed that someone using the cell phone of their suspected casino owner was still in the Vegas area. They had the location on the far west side of the city near The Red Rock Valley. Teams of agents were making their way to the search area and the chief had his suspect from the apartment siege put into a holding area. He was still bleeding and yelling police brutality. A medic had patched him up but the man claimed that he was in severe pain. The chief told him that either you need to cooperate or we will have to report that you died in the siege too. The man knew he was in trouble. He had to cooperate.

The FBI had the identification of both their captive as well as the dead man from the apartment. They were all long time small crooks. They were more the enforcer types. The arrest records showed that one of the men once lived in Atlantic City. That was very interesting because the suspected brothers had owned a Casino along the boardwalk there.

They were still tracking the names of the men that Corey had given them during the time he was in the bureau's office being questioned. Some of them were being rounded up in Atlantic City and Detroit, but as of yet the brothers had not been found. Both brothers were on the run and the FBI had an all points bulletin for their apprehension.

Booth hoped that his teams could come up with some new information. He was very proud of his record and wanted to be instrumental in the case. Knowing now that Blair was okay, they could continue the search through the pass. She sat in the passenger seat checking out the map on her lap. The gauze and bandage on the right side of her head was bothering her. "I'm taking this off," she said.

He gave her a stern look. "You need to keep that on at least until the blood has stopped."

She knew he was right but didn't want to look like a victim. They studied the map and saw that there were two areas that held cabins ahead. Let's stay together and hit each area. They were in agreement. The winding road ahead held many dangerous curves. The path at times was nothing more than crushed rocks and you had to be careful not to take those over five miles an hour. It was a tedious ride and you had to watch each turn. At some points it was only wide enough for one vehicle at a time. They wondered who in the hell thought this was a good idea. Booth asked Blair if she remembered this part of the road when she made the trip with her parents.

"Oh yeah, my mom screamed the whole time. She was never too good with any type of curvy road but this one was the worst. I will never forget that panic look on her face."

He laughed as she told her story. How he wished he could have that type of memories from his life. All of his memories were dashed when his parent's were killed by that drunk driver. He turned to his partner but just smiled. They continued slowly through the treacherous path and soon came to the next search area.

Twenty-Six

The search for Assad continued through the rough terrain of the San Gabriel Wilderness. The path led the team of agents to Twin Peaks with an elevation of over seven-thousand-two-hundred feet. The California Department of Highways had given the road the identification of California Highway 2. When you followed it on the map you could see that it ran all the way down to the Los Angeles National Forest. The ridge overlooked Pasadena and Arcadia. The area at the bottom of the path had become the place to live for so many affluent residents of the Los Angeles area. Many people had built beautiful homes along the base of the San Gabriel peaks.

The next opening that came into view was wider than the other spots they had searched. Booth asked her to give him a map update. She told him that they were nearing an area called Red Box Gap, and it was a popular spot for cabins because of the large lake below. People loved fishing that spot because the water pooled from the falls above. The agents were now well below the area where they had captured the escaped man from the California prison. The view was gorgeous. Nature had a way to create beauty that was breath taking. The pine and elm trees dotted the landscape to the right and giant California Spruce trees ran along the ridge to the left. The sun was starting to set and the glimmer of sunshine off the lake below was almost blinding. The lake appeared to be a giant mirror on the ground reflecting nature's beauty on its shore. Booth pulled over into a wide area off the right side of the road and waited for the second team to catch up. They had taken the captured suspect to meet the chopper and were just a few minutes behind. "We need a plan," he said. "Time is running out. The sun will be down and we will have to stop our search in just an hour or two."

He could see the vehicle pulling up behind their position and he motioned to them. All four agents got out and gathered around the map. Blair pointed to the area that they would search next. It was much more populated than the other spot they checked out. It would take them a while to complete the task. Booth said they needed to start at each end and meet in the middle. All four members agreed and the search started.

The cabins that lined the thin winding road had large porches that overlooked the bluffs below. It was obvious that the people that rented or owned then could have one of the best views of the L.A. basin. Blair had laid the map between them and secured her weapon in the holster on her right hip. She pulled the sweatshirt that she had just put on over the handle so as not to have the gun exposed as they moved through the residents. There was no need to alert or scare anyone. It was important to keep their mission as close to the vest as possible. Booth made sure his gun was loaded and also secured out of sight. He turned to his partner and asked, "Sure your okay?"

She knew he just was doing his job and cared but she hated the fact that the escaped fugitive got the drop on her. "I'm fine, now let's forget about that and find this guy." He nodded and smiled at her. "Good deal, I'm on it," he answered.

The second team of agents had pulled their vehicle into a clearing at the far left side of the first cabin. It looked like it was set up for as many as five vehicles to be parked there. The vehicle in the first spot closest to theirs was a yellow Hummer with oversized tires and a huge roof rack with flood lights attached to it. The vehicle next to it was an old Jeep Wrangler with the door removed and a gun rack across the back. They would start their search with the two parked vehicles.

Booth and Blair moved along the path after parking their vehicle and checked out the Toyota Rav 4 ahead of them. It was pretty muddy which would be normal for this terrain. The Rav 4 had been lifted and equipped with oversized tires that made it stand out much taller than normal. It was parked in front of the first cabin they came to. Both agents agreed they would follow the same cover they used during the last search. They were a couple looking for a friend's place and lost the directions. Blair was good with that idea. Booth suggested that if anyone asked she should say she slipped on the path and that was why she had a bandage. The parked Toyota checked out okay and they moved to the porch of the cabin. As they approached a man stepped out and called out to them.

"Can I help you?" Booth waved and hollered that they we're looking for a friend. The man was dressed in jeans and a camouflaged shirt came off the porch and headed toward them. "What was that you said?"

"We're looking for our friend that rented a cabin up here but lost the number," Booth answered. The man nodded and said that he had just gotten to his cabin earlier in the day and hadn't really been out. Booth told him his cell phone doesn't have a signal and they were hoping that they would be able to find his cabin before it got dark.

"What kind of car or truck is he driving?" The man asked.

Booth stop for a second and Blair quickly answered. "He has two trucks and we're not sure which one he is driving. Maybe we just need to drive along looking for one of his vehicles."

"That's probably your best bet," the man said. Your buddy own or rent? Booth said he was renting a place. "Most of the places along here are owned and not rental units, but about a quarter mile down the road there is a group of four units that are vacation rentals. This time of year they are not very popular but in the fall hunting season that are always booked up."

The two agents thanked the man and went back to their vehicle. They checked the map and saw the wide curve in the road that the man had referred to. It would make sense that if Assad was hiding out in this area he would choose a place that was off the path and empty. Booth checked his cell phone and saw that he still did not have a signal. He said they would drive toward the area suggested and hope to meet up with the second team. As they drove through the tree lined path they checked out the cabins along the way. Most were pretty nice with huge porches that overlooked the bluff. It was surprising that everyone had at least one vehicle parked in front and in some cases more than one. It was now dusk and lights from the cabins told the agents that people were getting ready for dinner. Assad wouldn't have lights on and would be keeping a very low profile.

John Martin had the FBI team in Atlantic City searching for more information from one of the captured suspects from the raid in Vegas at City Center. They also had an all points bulletin out for the second Ellis brother. Omar Ellis had been operating the Atlantic City Casino and had a suite in the casino's hotel on the top floor, overlooking the boardwalk. A team of agents staked out the casino's exits and another group headed up the elevator. They were accompanied by hotel security staff that had refused the first request until a warranty had been delivered for the search. The top two floors were secured from the rest of the hotel with special key cards to activate the access to those floors. The seasoned agents made sure that the hotel security staff did not communicate to anyone before the search. The lead agent took the cell phones and any other devise they had away from them immediately after issuing the search warrant.

The elevator ran up a glass shaft so that the passengers had a glorious view of the boardwalk and ocean that met the mile and half of sand along the shoreline. There was only one elevator that went to the top floors they were told. It also had an express button that could take the rider both up or down without any other stops. The ride was quick and one agent made sure he kept the two security men in front of him. They were told that the elevator opened up to a short hallway and there were two doors that opened up to the executive suite. Omar's apartment was on the twenty-eighth floor and his brother would use the one on the twenty-seventh floor when he was in town. Neither security guard had seen Omar Ellis that day. They weren't sure if he was even in town. Once the agents had moved into the hallway they stationed one man at the door on the left side of the hall and the men along with the two security guys knocked on the entrance on the right side of the hall. After knocking for a few minutes they demanded access to the suite. One of the security guys handed over his keys. They unlocked the door and again called out with no response from inside.

The four men moved into the suite and one of the agents again called out, "Mr. Ellis, FBI we have a few questions for you." Just then the door at the far end of the interior hallway opened and a female voice called back. "Omar is that you baby?" The woman moved into view and the agents stepped back. She had long blond hair that fell off one shoulder and was wearing a shear night gown. She was gorgeous about five foot ten, a real model type with milky white skin and beautiful hazel eyes, although the men weren't looking at her eyes.

"What do you want?" She hollered. "Get the hell out of here. Wait until I tell Mr. Ellis that you broke into his place."

"Take it easy sister," one of the agents said.

"I'm not your sister; I said get the hell out of here now!" She raised one arm over her left breast to partially cover up but the sight of her long legs and ample breast filled the imagination of all the men standing there.

"We're here looking for Mr. Ellis," the agent in charge stated. "Do you know where he is?"

"No! Now get out!"

Without answering her, the agent again asked if she knew where he went. The woman didn't respond. She just starred at them and in a defiant move put both hands on her hips, without regard to her voluptuous body showing through the sheer nightgown. "I said get the hell out!" She yelled at the two hotel security men that they knew better than to allow these men up to the suite and Mr. Ellis will have them fired as soon as he got back.

"Lady, go put some clothes on you're coming with us." The agent moved toward the woman and pointed to a room with the opened door. "Don't try anything silly and I'm coming with you." He was now only a few feet away from her.

She didn't move. "I'm not going anywhere unless Omar tells me."

"Fine," he said. "I'll just have to gag and handcuff you to the bed until he gets back." He grabbed her right arm and spun her around and turned her toward the open doorway. "Grab those two security guys and bring them along. Until we get a solid answer we'll cuff all three of them." The agents looked at each other and smiled. Wait till the office gets a look at our suspect they thought. The first agent held the woman's arm as she squirmed and tried to get loose. "If you follow my orders I'll let you go," he told her. Maybe now she would be willing to listen.

"I haven't done anything you need to let me go." The agent removed his hand from her arm. She turned toward them and slapped him across the face.

He stood there for a second without a reaction.

She asked questions in rapid succession. "Why are you here? What did Omar do? You need to leave us alone. We haven't done anything. Mr. Ellis will have your jobs once he finds out that you broke into his place!"

The two security guys were now being escorted into a back room of the suite and one of the agents was asking them questions about Mr. Ellis and the last time they had seen him. The first agent again told the woman that she needed to get dressed and they were taking her to headquarters. She was out of questions and now submissive to the request. "I need to have some privacy," she told him.

"Lady, you know where Mr. Ellis is and I'm not letting you alone to warn him." Just then two more agents entered the suite. "Hey Jimmy," a young female agent said. "I guess you need me to help here?" He turned and smiled at her. "Yes, this woman needs to get dressed so we can take her in." She looked at the blond and saw what she was wearing. "Okay lady, let's move now! You can put those tits aware too. They don't impress me." The female agent grabbed the blond and moved her toward a back room. The other agents laughed at her statement.

"Wait, my clothes are in the other room over there," she pointed to what appeared to be another bedroom. They turned and headed into the room. Jimmy called out, "Make sure she doesn't get near a phone."

The search through the cabins hadn't turned up a thing. The two teams were moving about at the same pace searching both occupied and un-occupied cabins. Most of them had vehicles parked out in the open in front or on the side of the units. Some cabins were very elaborate with large wrap around porches that offered a great view of the valley below. Some were smaller and were probably just hunting cabins. The path that they followed led them in a semi-circle with a winding curve ahead near the middle of the trail. Booth could now see the second team as all four agents came to the area that was described as rental units by the resident that they had talked to earlier. There were four units tucked in to the cove and with the sun dipping behind the large pine trees it was getting dark and hard to see. None of the units had any light coming from them. There wasn't any vehicle present and the two teams decided to search each unit together. Booth figured it would be quicker if two agents check out the back of the places while he and Blair moved through the front of each one. It was now quarter to eight and they had only about a half-an-hour of daylight left. It was easier to check the front of the units because the sunlight streamed through the tall pines so that you see. The back was a different story. The second team had a rougher time because the forest was dense and thicket ran up pretty close to some of the units. They agreed if anything looked suspicious they would stop and advise each other before going forward.

Booth moved to the first unit on the right side of the inlet and saw the second team moving into the thicket that was closely-packed with small bushes and tall weeds. Blair was to stay back near the front of the porch in case she spotted someone moving inside once he knocked on the doors. The second unit would be at the back of each unit in case someone tried to escape from the rear. The two teams planned to search each unit together so that they wouldn't have a similar situation like the one near the lake earlier with the escaped convict. The search of the cabin was quick. There wasn't any sign of anyone having been there in a while. There was a sign in the front window with rental information with a phone number. Blair wrote it down for future reference. The two teams planned to move together to the next cabin. Booth signaled to them as they moved to the left side of the first unit. They would keep the same process on the second cabin too. This cabin was set back further into the cove and the brush had been cleared away from the rear of the unit. There was a path cut into the wooded area leading up the hill. It appeared to have been recently cleared and the agents moving to the rear could see tire tracks. They were maybe six inches wide, similar to that of a four-wheeler. They contacted Booth to let him know that they might need to follow that path after checking the cabin out.

They checked out the second cabin with no results and the sign in the front window had the same rental information as the first cabin. The two teams decided to meet on the side of the second cabin before heading to check out the next one. Maybe we should split up and check out the other two cabins and the path at the same time, one of the agents suggested. Booth didn't like the idea. What if they ran into trouble? "Let's check the other two units real quick then we can check the path out." They were in agreement and headed to the next cabin. It was now 8:00 o'clock and the sun had dipped further into the pine trees. The angle of the rays glimmered off the lake below. The third unit was the largest of the four. It had a wraparound porch with two rocking chairs at one end. The agents that were moving into the back yard could see the same tire tracks that had been one the path of the second cabin. There was a small shed tucked into the wooded area with a metal ramp in front. They traced the tire tracks to the front of the shed and saw that there was fresh mud on the metal ramp. The mud had dried on the edges but was still damp in the center. Someone had used the four-wheeler recently. They weren't sure if it had been returned to the shed or still out in the woods. This was important and he needed to know. One of the agents headed around to the front of the cabin to tell Booth as the other one stood guard near the back door. As he approached the front he heard the sound of an engine gunning in the woods. All four agents were now aware that someone was coming down the path. They headed to the sides of the cabin to get in position to see who it was. The agent at the rear of the unit slouched down along the left side out of sight. The engine noise was louder and would soon be in the clearing. Booth motioned to draw weapons in case it was Assad.

All of a sudden two four-wheel vehicles appeared charging out of the path. A man wearing a dark green jacket and goggles was driving the first one. He was followed by a man who appeared to have a gun rack on the back of his ride. They were moving at a rapid pace and one of them was yelling something that the agents could not make out. The second man brought his four-wheeler to a spinning stop at the entrance of the path as the first rider pulled into the opening. The second man reached back and pulled a rifle out of the rack. He called out to the first man in what sounded like an Arabic dialect. The four agents were now crouched down and had their weapons drawn. They had to make sure they had the path covered to eliminate any retreat back into the woods by the two riders. The man with the rifle was about six foot tall and had a camouflaged jacket and side arm tucked into his belt. These men were not hunters, not this time of the year and hunters never carried handguns. Booth was afraid that the agent at the rear of the cabin might be exposed and wanted to make sure he wasn't in the line of fire. He made a motion with his left hand to Blair and the second agent to crawl into the shrubs that lined the side of the cabins. She was between the second and third cabin and the second agent was along the side of the unit. Booth had moved closer between the units and had a clear view of the two men.

Both men were still talking in Arabic to each other as the first rider was pointing to the last cabin. The team of FBI agents hadn't checked it out yet. Could there be more men in that unit? What exposure would the agents have from the front of the units if they were encircled? Booth was concerned that they might be greatly outnumbered. He wanted to make sure they got their man but didn't lose anyone in the process.

The search at the Atlantic City Casino hadn't found Omar Ellis. The agents had what might be his girlfriend and two security guards in custody. They had radioed to their chief what they had going on and were told to have someone bring in the girl to headquarters. They needed to grill the two security guys and see if they could help in the search for Mr. Ellis. The blond was handcuffed and being led out of the suite by the female agent. She was still running her mouth and telling them Mr. Ellis will have their ass once he finds out. The team went through the suite to see if they could turn up anything leading them to the where-a-bouts of Omar Ellis. Nothing was found. They hoped to find something, maybe a plane ticket or travel information that would assist their search. It was clear that the blond wasn't going to be any help. The two security guys were questioned but either didn't know anything. Probably just muscle to keep people away from the suites at the top of the casino. The Atlantic City FBI teams were working with some information on other locations Omar Ellis had been known to frequent. The city wide search was on going and all the information was being sent back to the director.

Twenty-Seven

The FBI had completed searches both residences of Omar and Salem Ellis and left men staking out their places in case either brother returned. The Atlantic City suite did offer few clues. Because Omar's girlfriend had been brought in for questioning they at least had someone who could offer possible information. With intensive questioning it was possible that she might be able to give the agents a clue to Omar's where-a-bouts. Mr. Ellis's brother Salem hadn't been seen in Vegas since the search of his place at City Center. Agents were continuing to watch the residence along with following up on other possible locations that he may have escaped to.

The search for Assad through the foothills of the San Bernardino National Forest was still ongoing with Booth and Blair leading the team through the narrow pass. There were now three man hunts across the United States and the Bureau had sent pictures and details to Interpol in case any of the men tried to escape from the country. The director had his teams reporting every move so that they could coordinate the efforts in case any leads were discovered. He knew that Blair and Booth had searched the entire area of the mountain pass and were at the very last place that Assad might have tried to hide at. The Mexican government had offered very little help when his request with pictures of Assad arrived at their headquarters in Mexico City. It was clear that if he had made it across the border it would be close to impossible to find him. With all the problems with the drug wars and cartels in Mexico it was understandable that the United States request for one fugitive would fall to the bottom of their list.

The Atlantic City bureau was continuing to question Omar's girlfriend. The only thing she had told them was that her name was Thunder. They finally got her true identification confirmed after getting her fingerprints came in. It was a battle getting them and it took two guys to hold her down. She managed to kick the crap out of the forensic guy who first tried to take hold of her hands. It seemed like a simple thing, she was cuffed and sitting in a chair when he came into the room. He had a scanner that the bureau was now using that would take just a few minutes. One of the female agents stood nearby and everything was going smooth until he reached for her hands. Thunder brought her right leg up and caught him right in the crotch. He went down with a thud and she proceeded to kick him while he was on the ground until the other agent was able to pull her off. It took two other men to help subdue her before they could get her fingerprints taken. Her name was Sally Worth from Austin, Texas. She was once an exotic dancer in the Trump Hotel and Casino in Atlantic City and that is where she and Omar met. Sally went by her stage name of Thunder. One of the agents who brought her in said that he knew she was trouble because it was almost impossible to get her to put any clothes on. He still had a red mark on his face where she slapped him. The female agent from their office had to just about dress her. Thunder was a storm waiting to strike.

The agents in the mountains were watching the men that came out of the wood. They got off their rides and heading into the last of the four cabins. Blair had been able to slide closer to the rear of the unit and tried to make out what the men were saying. She also hoped to find out if there were more men inside. Booth watched her and hoped that she wasn't too close and would be seen. The shrubs were thick and created an umbrella cover over the top of her as she move into position. She could hear the men talking to someone inside. They were all talking in the same Arabic dialect. The other agents were all waiting for direction from Booth on their next move. He was waiting for whatever information Blair brought back. He wanted them all to be on the same page before their next move. The rear door of the cabin was now closed and Blair retreated back to her previous position. He wanted all of them to be together so he signaled the team to come back to his location. It was important that they stayed low in case the men inside were watching out the windows. She could see the windows in the back all had the drapes pulled shut. It was easier to move around the back of the cabin and not be seen. Was this their suspect? If not, why did these men have guns? Booth felt being cautious and assuming that these men were part of the escape that Assad was using was their best move.

He wanted to alert the team of agents from the Los Angeles Bureau that they had a possible sighting of persons of interest. The closest team of agents would be returning from taking the captured prisoner in the helicopter and could head back to the mountain pass. Their chopper had found a landing spot in the clearing near the end of the pass. It was only about a mile and half from the cabins they were searching. He hoped that they could get back soon. More help would make the situation a lot easier.

It was now getting dark and shadows covered the entire area behind the cabins. The trees cast an eerie shape as the agents stooped to peek into the cabin. The call came back from the agents in the chopper that it was too dark to land in the pass. The team thought that it might make more sense to wait until sunrise. It would also give them the advantage of a surprise attack. They all agreed but someone had to stand guard in case the men decided to leave during the night. They would take turns. Booth said they would take the first watch and then they would switch at midnight. Four hour surveillance periods would make sure everyone stayed fresh. The second team from LA had camping equipment in their vehicle that both teams could use. The biggest problem was neither team had brought food. It would be a long night but it was all agreed that they would surround the cabin at five-thirty am when the sun was just coming up. The team from LA could land the chopper in the pass and Steve planned on sending another unit from the office. That unit would come up the pass from the Pasadena bluff and could be there by three am. They would also bring provisions for the group.

Lights came on in the back of the cabin but everything from the front side was dark. It appeared that the men had put heavy tarps over the front windows so that no one would tell that anyone was inside. Booth made sure that he had a clear view of the rear of the cabin and Blair was positioned near the front corner. She was glad that her idea might pan out. If they could catch Assad it would be a real coup for them. There wasn't any movement from the cabin and soon all the lights went out. The two teams switched at midnight and the plan was that at four am they would gather with the group that was coming from the LA office. The final assault would be planned out then.

The team of agents from Vegas had an all points bulletin out for Salem Ellis with no results. It was becoming clear that the two brothers might have gone into hiding. There had been no trace of either Omar or Salem Ellis for close to twenty-four hours now. The director had sent the two teams in Vegas and Atlantic City a detailed message that they may have a lead on Assad in the mountain pass. Once they had him in custody they might be able to get some information on the where-a-bouts of the Ellis brothers. Vegas was teaming with action. The City Center was the new home of the Aria Hotel and Casino along with many spectacular shops and apartments. There were many exclusive shops and outstanding restaurants that lined the walkways and terraces. The fountain in the middle was a gathering place for tourist who often stood around with their drinks and bags of purchases. The glass structure captured a mirror image of the mountains to the west of the strip. The chief's from Vegas and Atlantic City had the same task. Find the Ellis brothers and bring them in alive. It was critical to the investigation that if the bureau was to solve the case of bribery and murder in Washington they had to have the Ellis brothers stand trial. They already had Corey, the Senator's assistant, as a key witness and if Booth's team could capture Assad Jacoby all the pieces would come together. The director made sure all his people knew this case was their top priority.

Steve Orrison had his teams in the San Bernardino Mountains in constant communication with him until they would make a move on the suspicious cabin. The three teams were now planning the assault on the cabin. Booth was to head up the planning. The team from the LA office had been brought up to date along with the three members of the chopper group. Because helicopters often caused so much noise, people would come outside to see what was happening. The plan was that the chopper should hover low over the cabin and hopefully the men inside would come out to see what was going on. That would allow the teams on the ground the opportunity to surround them and overtake them without gun fire. It still hadn't been determined that Assad was in this group or even if these men were related to the events in Vegas or Washington. The fact that they were all speaking in Arabic and acting reclusive was their best bet for now. In any circumstance the men had weapons and acted strangely, so as Booth said, "When there is smoke, there was probably fire." Everyone had their assignments. Blair took one group to the back of the cabin as Booth and his group went to the front. The teams had secured the cabins around the unit to make sure no one else was around. Didn't want any innocent bystanders hurt in the action. Watches were synchronized and the assault was planned for five-thirty am.

They went over the layout of the cabin. All four in the cove had the same floor plans and the team had gained entrance to two of the other units and drew out the description so that if it came down to an attack in the cabin the agents would know how the rooms were set up. You could never have too much planning. Blair had drawn a landscape layout of the rear of the cabin including the path that led into the wooded area where the men had ridden the four-wheelers from. Blair's team had moved around the back of the cabin about thirty minutes before the chopper was to create the commotion. Her plan was to immobilize the four-wheelers that had been parked at the rear of the unit. Blair pulled a few spark plugs from each four-wheeler. That was a trick her dad had taught her when she moved to her first apartment. It wasn't in a very good area, and car theft was high. No one will ever steal a car that doesn't start her dad would say. She always pulled a plug from the front cylinder when she parked overnight. It was easy to remove and put back. Booth laughed when she told him her plan. "Never expected that from a girl," he said. She gave him a look that made him retreat from that remark. He shook his head and just said, "Sorry."

Everyone was in place. The sun was starting to rise and beams of orange spears shot through the darkness. Blair's team was placed strategically around the rear of the cabin all in protected spots in case the men came out firing. Booth and three other agents moved into position around the front of the cabin with two men on the porch and he and the other agent at the side of the front door. They could grab the men if they came running out the front of the unit. The chopper was now hovering about a mile from the row of cabins. The bureau had informed the state and local police what they were planning and both offices had their men positioned along the winding mountain side path in case anyone escaped from the cabin.

The noise was loud as the chopper moved above the cabin and flashes of lights could be seen coming on from the back of the unit. At first there wasn't any movement but all of a sudden a man in a heavy camouflaged jacket came running out of the back toward the four-wheelers. He was yelling very loud in Arabic back at the men in the cabin. "بهاذلك مجاهد نحنو ، انرما." None of the agents spoke Arabic so they we not sure what he was yelling. It was clear that it was something urgent. The man was moving at a fast clip and had turned toward the cabin when he reached the four-wheeler. By this time Booth and his team had busted through the front door and called out, "FBI everyone put your hands up and drop your weapons!"

The man in the camouflaged jacket tried starting the four-wheeled vehicle but nothing happened. He was now hollering something different and yelling at the vehicle when Blair dove over the top and pulled him tumbling to the ground. Two other agents moved to grab him. Just then another man appeared from the back of the unit. He held a machine gun firing rounds across the wooded area. He must have used an entire clip firing into the woods carving up saplings and hit one of the agents that had circled out from behind cover to help Blair with the man on the ground. The agent went down in a clump of bushes with blood gushing from his right side. They could hear more gun fire coming from inside the cabin. The chopper overhead had now pulled off from the roof top and was checking the scene from about thirty feet above to track any movement from the cabin.

A loud crash came from the right side of the unit as a man catapulted out of a window rolling on the ground and now was running toward the wooded area along the side of the cabin. Booth appeared behind the man flying through the same window, rolled twice and took off at full gallop chasing the man into the thick underbrush. Two agents were soon following. Gun fire was still coming from the rear of the cabin as the man with the machine gun had re-loaded and now taking aim at Blair and the other agents on the ground. Blair had pulled her captive in front of her as shots tore through the ground in front of them. All of a sudden the man at the rear came slumping down in a flurry of gun fire from shots behind him. Blood splattered all over the rear of the porch as he fell forward. One of the agents from Booth's team appeared at the rear of the cabin and hollered that he had secured the inside and all was clear.

Blair and another agent held the captured man on the ground that had been shot by his partner's wild gun fire. The wounds were clearly not life threatening. He was bleeding from his leg and still yelling as she rolled him over and cuffed him. She had her knee in the middle of his back and stayed on top of him. She contained the captured man as agents headed over to the other agent that had been wounded during the exchange of bullets. He was lying in the brush bleeding profusely from the chest area and it didn't look good. They pulled his head up and tried to comfort him but his breathing was labored and he was losing consciousness. "Tom, Tom," one of his friends called out as he held his head. "Stay with me Tom, we'll get you some help." It was clear to the others that it was probably too late. Tom's eyes closed and his head drifted to the side.

Booth was charging ahead as he chased the escaped fugitive from the cabin through the wooded area. The low thick ground cover made running harder but he was in great shape and the suspect had a head start that he had to overcome. Two agents that followed had spread out in case the man doubled back. The underbrush tore at his legs as he gained on the man in front of him. Take them alive was all he could think of as he chased the man down. The terrain was rough and Booth was gaining on him. He thought he had him when all of a sudden the ground seemed to give way under both of them. They rolled down a steep hill as thorns ripped at exposed skin on both of them. Booth bounced up spun around and saw his man lying in front of him. The man started to crawl forward and was now up on all fours. He had a pistol in his right hand. He grabbed the suspect and pushed him face first into the ground. He now had the man's arms pulled back and cuffed him. The other agents caught up to the chase and saw that Booth was kneeling on top of his captive, out of breath while keeping the man at bay. They rolled him over and Booth smiled. "Well Assad, nice to finally meet you!"

Twenty Eight

The fugitive that had eluded the FBI for three days and created a massive man-hunt had now been captured. Booth was dragging Assad through the woods back to the cabin. The agents trailing them had marveled how fast the two had been running. Blair had relayed a call for medical assistance for the fallen agent that had been shot during the firefight. The chopper had circled back and hovered over the open area in front of the cabin. Although they feared that it was too late, they needed to make every effort to save Tom. Two agents carried Tom to the chopper that had dropped a stretcher from the opened door. They place him on the stretcher and the chopper pulled him up and took off to the medical center in Pasadena.

The other agents checked the man at the rear of the cabin that had been shot. He was the one that had used the machine gun. He was dead, as they figured, and there was a pistol tucked into his belt beside the machine gun that lay on the porch in front of him. Blair and the remaining agents searched the cabin for any critical material that could be used in the case. They found a small soft sided brief case that was tucked into the side of one of the beds. When they saw it one of the agents cautioned everyone and put on a pair of gloves before touching it. It had a leather strap that went through the handles. The case wasn't heavy but bulged out on one side. When they opened it the first thing they saw was a silver snub nosed 45 caliber pistol. There were papers that were stapled together and all in Arabic. It was going to take an FBI analyst to figure them out. Hopefully there was information that could be used in the case against the Ellis brothers.

Booth arrived with Assad and the other two agents. The call went back to Steve in the Los Angeles bureau with the news of Assad's capture. Cheers went up in the office when Steve announced the news to the staff. He in turn called the information to the director and bureau chief in Vegas. The search teams in California and Nevada were called off. Now they had to put the case together and capture the remaining Ellis brothers.

Booth smiled at Blair. "Sure glad you wanted that Chick-fill-A sandwich," he laughed.

"No! Chicken Fingers," she answered. Booth pointed at her and they chuckled. They nodded to each other as the other agents looked on with queer expressions. They were definitely a good team.

John Franklin Martin had a key fugitive. Assad Jacoby in custody and he was pleased that his new agent had been critical in the search to find him. He was also glad that he approved that Steve got her involved in the case. He had no way of knowing that she would become so crucial in the capture of a key suspect. His Los Angeles team had now solved two pieces of the puzzle. They had Corey Hart the assistant to Senator Albertson in Vegas filling the bureau in on the tie in with the Senator and Chief Justice with the gambling syndicate. The main suspect in the murder of Chief Justice Leonard, Assad Jacoby was now captured and he might be able to fill in the missing piece of how the Ellis brothers planned the murder. The last piece was to find the two Ellis brothers. The FBI had cut off their money supply and neither one could return home. It would only be a matter of time until they would be tracked down and captured.

The director kept pressure on his teams to find the Ellis brothers and bring them in alive. The capture of Assad was important. Bringing in suspects alive often meant that they would fill in the missing details needed to close a case.

The Atlantic City bureau had questioned Sally, Thunder as she was known to the people in the Atlantic City Casino. She was reluctant to give them any information about Omar Ellis at first but when the FBI legal team explained to her that she would be tried as an accomplice in the murder of Chief Justice Leonard she was more than willing to tell everything that she knew. During questioning it came out that Omar had a large yacht that was docked off the coast at a nearby harbor. Thunder told the agents that the dock was somewhat secluded from the shoreline and the first time she went there you couldn't even see the water from the road. The yacht flew the flags of Canadian registry something she found to be very curious. When she asked Omar about it he said that his brother had purchased the yacht in New Brunswick and that they left it registered in the original owner's information for tax purposes. She never thought anything else about it.

The bureau had sent a chopper to head off the coast searching for the yacht and a team of Cigarette boats started combing the shoreline. Now that they had a possible lead on Omar, the bureau was concentrating their attention on his capture and bringing him to justice. The team that had Thunder in interrogation found her to be somewhat elusive at first but with her true identity and the threat of jail time she gave them a great deal of critical information. She provided the agents with a list of phone contacts and locations that she and Omar had used in the year she was with him. They planned to round up many individuals that might be related to the illegal activity the brother were involved in. It was no surprise that some of the names provided were local and state officials from New Jersey, Michigan and Nevada as well as two United States Representatives. There would be many trials across the country on organized crime and gambling syndicates operating in those states.

Blair Adams had been successful in her first case as an FBI agent. This was something that came faster than she or anyone could have expected. Her new Los Angeles team realized how important she had been and they were knew that she would become a key member of their organization. She was just glad that her suggestion had materialized in the capture of Assad. Booth and her were solid teammates and had a great deal in common. The ride down the winding pass into Pasadena was a time for the two of them to review the events of the past few days. If there was a way they could help with the search for the Ellis brother would be icing on the cake. They ran the information found in the briefcase of the cabin back and forth hoping that it would lead to his location. The identification of the men with Assad was also a consideration in possible leads to Salem Ellis' where-a-bouts. They had one captured guy that would be questioned with possible help in their quest.

Steve Orrison wanted Booth and Blair to go home and rest up after the siege and ordeal at the cabin. They of course had other ideas. Booth suggested that they clean up and head back to the chase for Salem Ellis. The briefcase had a map with three significant areas highlighted. One was the cabin in the mountain pass where they captured Assad Jacoby. Another detailed a marina along the Santa Barbara coast. Under the yellow highlighted circle was the name Jasmine. What did that mean? Blair had already been on the internet searching the directories in California and Nevada for anyone with the first name of Jasmine. There were a total of seventy five Jasmine's in California and thirty three in Nevada. Only six lived in the Santa Barbara area and nine in Vegas. She sent the list to the Vegas Bureau of the nine in Vegas and she and Booth decided to check out the ones in the Santa Barbara area. When Booth told Steve their plan he bulked but Booth agreed to have another team from the office work with them on the search. It might not materialize to anything but it was better than sitting around. Steve agreed but only after they had time to come to the office and fill in the rest of the team.

It was now late afternoon on the east coast and the team from the Atlantic City office had dispatched teams on both the air and water to search for Omar Ellis who might be escaping by water. The helicopters were able to cover a lot of the ocean coast line while the search boats plowed through the currents checking most every boat that resembled the description that Thunder had given the agents. The yacht she told them about had distinctive small sails that she said stood out. They were very colorful and one of them had a large red Maple Leaf on a solid white border. It was clear that it was the Canadian flag to the team although Thunder had no idea what the flag meant. She did say that the brothers purchased the yacht in New Brunswick. A request went out to the Canadian government for records of sale on large boats in the Province. Hopefully the records would show them the exact identification and help in the search. The information that came back showed that a forty-five foot yacht was sold to a Salem Ellis from a group in Saint John, New Brunswick on September of last year. Saint John was located on the Bay of Fundy between Nova Scotia and New Brunswick. It was just about a hundred miles north of Maine and a possible hiding spot for Omar Ellis. If he and his brother had contacts in the area it would be almost impossible to find them especially if he made it into the Gulf of St. Lawrence. The Canadian Maritime Islands off the coast of Quebec were vast and some uninhabited. It was critical that the Bureau find the yacht before it got that far.

    The director made a call to the Provincial Governor in Montreal and received the assurance that they would put teams in both the air and water to help with the search. It was now dusk and when the call came in that a yacht matching the description was seen off the shoreline of Yarmouth, Nova Scotia. Both teams from the Canadian and United States government descended upon the vessel. It continued to elude the team from the air but it soon was surrounded by three boats. One was Canadian and two were United States Coast Guard ships. The United States Coast Guard boarded the yacht and took the men in custody. There were three men on board and one matched the description of Omar Ellis. They would all be brought back to New York to the main FBI east coast office. The last piece of the puzzle was now to apprehend Salem Ellis.

Twenty-Nine

Steve Orrison made sure that his agents understood their orders; proceed with caution the goal is to capturing Salem Ellis alive. Steve sent details of the ensuing operation to his counterpart in the San Francisco office in case Mr. Ellis headed their way. Although he knew that the director had notified every office about the situation Steve wanted to make sure that he personally sent out the information to the San Francisco office. It was his way. Steve was a team player and you never knew when you would need each other's help in the future.

Santa Barbara was just south of Point Conception and the islands that the United States Navy used as training grounds. The California coastline was dotted with channels and small islands, many that weren't even on a map. John Martin had notified the Navy and Coast guard of the plans that the Bureau had made to scout out the area from Santa Barbara north in case they could find evidence of Mr. Ellis trying to escape via the Pacific.

While they were riding up the coast from Los Angeles, Blair kept on searching the name Jasmine for any possible lead on Salem Ellis. The bureau had already sent agents to the homes of the nine people named Jasmine in Las Vegas and other cities in Nevada. Six people with that name in Santa Barbara were being contacted. Although it wasn't a common name there were fifteen persons altogether in the region that could have a tie in to Mr. Ellis and they had to track every possible lead. All of a sudden the screen on Blair's I-Phone lit up with the name Jasmine, a forty foot sail boat moored at the Ventura Marina. The owner listed was Mr. Salem Ellis of Atlantic City.

"Booth, I found it! Jasmine is the name of Ellis' boat."

He turned toward her and gritted his teeth. "Shit, why didn't I think of that. He's taken off in that boat and has a huge head start. The last time anyone saw him in was in Vegas days ago." Booth was right. The information they found while searching the suite in the City Center was that Mr. Ellis had left for an unknown location four days ago. It was confirmed during the interrogation of the men captured during the shoot-out. They revealed that he drove off in his Corvette but he didn't tell them where he was headed. Blair called the information back to Steve in Los Angeles and hoped that the director could get the Coast Guard involved in the search. Once Steve had the new information he told Blair that they needed to continue to Ventura and check out the marina. Steve was right. Just because Ellis had a boat didn't mean he took off in it. If he did, it would be like looking for a needle in a haystack.

The trip up the coast took two hours and although the marina wasn't that far north of the city, the ride up the Pacific Coast Highway was tedious. So many people were driving along the road sightseeing and taking pictures that Booth was ready to scream. He wanted to get to the marina and make sure they knew exactly what the situation was. Was Mr. Ellis' boat still there? If not, will they have a record of his departure? Any information would be critical in the search for the escaped man.

"There's nothing we can do until we check it out," Blair told him. "Let's just wait until we get to the marina before you go off and shoot someone." She smiled at him as he turned toward her. "I know you're not going to be happy until you get to plug somebody." Blair was laughing now.

Booth started laugh. "You better be careful or I'm going to shoot you!" They both took a deep breath and just then a lane opened up on the right that allowed him to swing around a line of cars slowing down to enter the beach ahead. "Damn about time I got a break," Booth hollered. He gunned the engine and raced around the line of eight or more cars up the highway and was now cruising at sixty-five miles an hour. "We should be there in five minutes," he said. Up ahead was the sign on the right hand side of the road announcing the Ventura marina two-hundred feet ahead! Booth moved into the left lane and made a sharp turn into the marina while looking for the sign showing the location of the office. He was rambling along while driving, "They should have the records on what slip the boat was moored in and if anyone saw Mr. Ellis pulling the boat out. Possibly they might even have the date and time. We could help the Coast Guard track the distance the boat could have traveled in that amount of time."

He was correct. A forty foot boat with two inboard engines could get a speed of about twenty knots per hour. With a four or five day head start they would have to circle a very large area that the boat might have reached in that time frame. The only thing that might make it easier will be the coastline of California will give the Coast Guard a flat line base that they could use when plotting the distance from the marina. They knew a boat could only travel in three directions. It eliminated any eastern travel spots even if they skirted the coast and headed south to Mexico or north to Canada.

He saw the sign for the marina's office. It was off to the left and Booth pulled up to the parking slot in front. He and Blair piled out of the vehicle and went inside. There was a nice looking young lady maybe about thirty-five years old behind a desk. It that was cluttered with all sorts of nautical items. On the front of her desk was mounted what appeared to be a wheel from a large sailboat. On both sides were models of sailboats with other novelties. The office wasn't very big and there was a door in the right corner that was closed. Booth figured that it was the Harbor Master's office.

"Good afternoon miss," Booth said he was followed by Blair into the room. "I need some information regarding one of your customers that has a sailboat here."

She looked up and smiled back at Booth. "Oh! You do huh! Well what kind of information are you looking for good looking?"

Blair looked at Booth wondering what the, you do huh, meant. She got the good looking part. Was she going to be uncooperative? He just smiled back at the lady and gave her the information of the boat owned by Salem Ellis.

"Well let me look it up for you hon. Let's see, Mr. Ellis has slip seventy-three on the eastern bend about seven slips off shore. It is easy to get to and I can give you a map." She was getting up and pulling a pad of paper that had a drawing of the entire marina. She placed it on her desk and motioned for Booth to come around the side of her desk so she could pin point the spot to slip seventy-three. As Booth bent down to see the line she was drawing, she moved extremely close to him. He felt a little awkward but she was helping so he just stood there. She was telling Booth about the marina and how to get to the slip while rubbing her hip against his.

Blair watched and was smiling. Booth knew he would pay for this.

"Do you know if his boat is there?" He asked.

"I'm not sure but the Harbor Master is out on one of the docks and he could tell you for sure. Should I page him?

"That would be helpful."

If you need anything else, come on back. I can be very helpful."

"Thanks," Booth said. "You already have been. We appreciate your help. When you page the Harbor Master ask him to meet us at the slip. In the meantime we'll head out there."

The marina at Ventura was pretty big. It's the largest marina north of Los Angeles but not as big as the two at Long Beach and Newport Beach to the south. Booth was glad that Jasmine was moored north and not south of LA. It would be a disaster trying to find a boat in either of those two marinas.

The two agents walked out of the office and got into their car. Blair had been holding her laughter until they reached the vehicle. "She's sweet on you. You have a honey now."

Booth just gave her a stare. "Not what I wanted."

She kept teasing him as they headed toward the slip area. The dock on the eastern end of the marina was about a half mile down the way and Booth pulled up to an open spot. Once they got out and looked around there wasn't a sign of Salem's yellow Corvette in front of the dock. They started toward the dock when a man maybe in his forty's wearing tan slacks and bright yellow golf shirt headed their way. "Can I help you?"

Blair called back, "Hello," and asked, "Are you the Harbor Master.

"Yes, I'm Kevin Brown, and who are you?"

"Agents Blair Adams and Brandon Booth of the FBI, we need access to slip seventy-three and any information on Salem Ellis. We need to know if his boat is still in the slip and if not when it left." Blair was quick to the point. If Ellis' boat was gone then the search would continue with the Coast Guard. If not then the bureau would continue to comb the country for him.

Mr. Brown was now in front of them and had taken out some keys to open the gate to the dock. "Can I see some identification," He asked. They both took out their badges and he nodded. "I know the boat left here a few days ago but I would have to go to the office to get the full details. Do you still want to check out the slip?"

"Might as well since we're here," Booth stated. "Where would Mr. Ellis park his car because we didn't see it?"

"Oh, Mr. Ellis didn't take the boat out. He called me and said that he was sending two men to take it out and gave me their description. They had the required permission from Mr. Ellis when they got here and the Suburban in spot sixteen is theirs. I made sure that I had everything in order before letting them take the boat out."

Blair suggested that Booth check the slip out and she would check out the Suburban. As he walked down the dock she turned around and headed toward the vehicle that Kevin pointed out. Of course it was locked but she took out a tool from her purse and slid it into the door jamb. It was about four inches long and when she pulled on one end it telescoped to a foot long. She continued to move it up and down the jamb until the door lock popped open. Blair slipped on a pair of thin gloves and opened the passenger door. The first thing she checked was the glove box. There were a lot of papers and she rummaged through them hoping that some names or addresses were going to give them a clue as to the owners. She found the registration among them. The information showed that the vehicle was registered to Isaac Ellis at 17640 Henderson Circle drive, Las Vegas, Nevada. Must be a relative of Salem's she figured. She went through the other papers and none of them gave her any more information. There was repair records from the Chevrolet dealer in Vegas dated from last month and a couple of owner manuals along with a gas receipt.

Booth was walking back with the Harbor Master and he signaled to Blair. He shook hands with Kevin and headed to the Suburban. "Find anything," he asked. "A vehicle registration with the name of Isaac Ellis and his address is in here, but that's about all. I called it in to the Vegas office and they will send someone to check out the residence."

Booth agreed that it was their only move right now. He said they would call the details from the marina in to Steve back in Los Angeles and suggested that they head up the coast to see if the men met Mr. Ellis at another marina. The Harbor Master had given Booth the location of the next three marinas to the north. that they could check. They were all within sixty miles of Ventura. He also told Booth that the boat was taken out late yesterday and that meant that the men couldn't have gotten too far. At a speed of twenty knots even moving 24/7 they would have only traveled about a couple hundred miles.

Once they called the information in to Steve they planned to check out the other locations. Steve told them that the San Francisco Bureau would be checking from their location south. Now the Coast Guard would have a little more to go on along with the exact description of the boat. There was an APB out on the boat as well as Mr. Ellis' Corvette. Local authorities were alerted to the description and license plate of the Corvette and the Coast Guard had the details on the sailboat.

As they were pulling out of the marina parking lot Blair told Booth to stop.

"Why?"

"Don't you want to say goodbye to your sweetie?"

He gave her a look and reminder her that he still hadn't shot anyone yet but she could be next. He gunned the engine and squealed the tires pulling out on the Pacific Coast Highway. Blair grabbed the Oh Shit Handle on the vehicle as they hit the black top and headed north.

The Vegas team was at the residence of Isaac Ellis on Henderson Circle Drive. It was a large sprawling ranch house with a circular driveway in front. Two agents headed to the front door. The house had a rounded front porch with three steps that led to a gorgeous leaded glass front door. They rang the bell and a beautiful young lady came to the door. She opened it and inquired what they wanted. The two men flashed their badges and ask the where-a-bouts of Isaac Ellis. She didn't know. They asked when the last time she saw him. She again stated that she wasn't sure and only a girlfriend. One of the agents said they needed to look around.

"Do you have a warrant?" she asked.

They didn't, just hoped she wasn't going to ask them. They told her the warrant was on the way and she needed to cooperate.

"Not a problem," she answered. "Once you have your warrant,

you're more than welcome to search the house."

They thanked her and moved off the porch. "Do you think she's hiding something," they asked each other. Probably been schooled by Ellis not to allow anyone in without a warrant they figured. The call went in to the office and a warrant would be issued. They were instructed to keep an eye on the house until it got there. One of the men proceeded to walk around toward the side of the house hoping to see if there was any action in back. There was a six foot tall stone wall that boarded the yard. He could see a fountain over the top of the wall. He figured that a pool was back there, not unusual for Vegas. He couldn't see anything else so he headed back to the car to wait for the warrant. This was an easy stake out; they just turned on the air-conditioning in the car and sat back.

They had no sooner settled in when one of the three garage doors started to open and a bright yellow Corvette pulled out into the circular drive. It peeled out from the front of the house heading toward the winding road that merged into Highway 15. The two agents looked at each other and jumped into action. They were about six car lengths behind the Vette when it accelerated through the stop sign at the end of the road and slid to the right hand lane and entered Highway 15 south. The agents following had called the chase into the office and one team was dispatched to the house and another team to help in the chase. They also informed the local Clark County Sheriff about the pursuit. There would soon be cars from both offices following the yellow Vette.

New questions continued to crop up in the investigation. Who was in the Yellow Corvette? Was Salem Ellis hiding at the house right under their nose all the time? What was the deal with the sailboat? The Vegas Bureau called the information into Steve in LA and the director in D.C. that they had a suspect in a car chase. Could this be a break in catching Salem Ellis?

Thirty

Blair and Booth were still driving north up the Pacific Coast Highway when they got the call about the results from the search of Isaac Ellis' residence. They wondered if Salem Ellis had an elaborate plan that had him hiding at his relative's house in Vegas until it calmed down and then he could make his escape. Could the simple search of the Suburban and finding the address of the house of Isaac solve the search? Why would he hang around Vegas when he had a huge head start? They continued the ride up the PCH to the next marina while waiting for follow-up details from Steve. The sign ahead announced that the entrance to the Santa Barbara marina was five-hundred feet ahead. Booth moved into the left lane and slowed down to show his credentials to the guard at the gate. They were now one hundred miles north of Ventura and felt out of the loop from all the action. The marina was just south of the city and a little smaller than the one at Ventura. The guard at the entrance questioned Booth about what they were looking for. He was out of patience and told him just open the damn gate! Blair was surprised at his statement but it was understandable. They had been on the case for a few days straight and now it seemed that they were left out of real action. Once they entered the marina Booth pulled up to the marina office.

"Why don't you let me go in and ask about any recent activities that may be what we're looking for?" Blair wanted Booth to calm down and maybe it was just a useless act but it still had to be done. She knew it was getting late and they had been on the road for more than five hours. "You could call back to the office and see if the Frisco bureau would check the rest of the marina's north of here."

He liked the suggestion. This would be their third marina without any action, although the information found in the glove box at the Ventura marina might have been the key to finding

Salem Ellis. She got out of their vehicle and headed into the office. An older gentleman sat at a horseshoe desk piled up with maps and large manila folders. "Good afternoon," she said. "I'm with the Los Angeles Bureau of Investigation and need some information."

"Guess you're with the guy that threatened my gate guard?"

"Sorry about that but this is critical to National Security and we've been on the case for days." She felt the National Security issue would get his attention. "We need some details about activity in the past two days here." The man seemed to appreciate her explanation and asked what they needed?

Meanwhile the chase up Highway 15 grew in scope. The local sheriff's office had dispatched five cars to the ramps that were in front of the location that the FBI had reported the vehicle to be traveling. They planned to clear the road ahead and set up a road block. They also positioned cars at each exit so if the car tried to get off the highway it would be trapped. It was difficult to clear the road but at least the exits were south of the city and rush hour was over. As the local guys cleared the highway it caused so much attention that a local news crew's helicopter reported the action. It was now being carried live on channel 8 in Vegas. It would be their high speed version of the O.J. car chase years ago in Los Angeles. Soon CNN picked up the feed and it was being telecast to the entire nation. The director wasn't happy with the attention to his case, but here it was, millions of people turned in across the nation wondering what was going on and who was the person that was being followed? Of course it would be prime-time on the Eastern seaboard and in cities like New York, Philadelphia, Atlanta and Washington people would be in restaurants and bars watching and wondering. How will the bureau spin the details?

The Corvette was now traveling in excess of one hundred and twenty miles an hour and picking up speed. The bureau's men had fallen way behind and if it wasn't for the local sheriff involved in the chase of the suspect's vehicle it would have gotten away from them. It wasn't clear who they were chasing but the license plate confirmed that it was Salem Ellis' car. Could they have the last suspect trapped? The Vegas Bureau was hoping that they would be able to end the case with this last flurry of action. The next three exits had been secured by the local sheriff and the road block was now secured. Three cars were side-by-side overlapping in case the Corvette tried to ram through. It wouldn't make much sense with a fiberglass vehicle to try that but who knows what the driver was thinking.

The yellow vehicle was nearing the Silverbell exit where the road block was set up. The vehicle was now going close to one hundred and forty miles-an-hour now and had to see the police cars ahead. The officers were positioned behind and to the side of the vehicles blocking the highway with guns drawn. The sports car was about three-hundred feet from the sheriff's vehicles when the officer's saw it swerve to the right and attempt to drive up the grass in front of the road block. As it charged up the hillside the rear of the vehicle spun to the left on the wet grass, caught traction and all of a sudden went airborne. The action was all caught by the channel 8 helicopter that was following the chase. The driver must have slammed on the brakes causing a loud screeching noise and leaped the chain-link fence, spun around caught dry pavement and charged away on the surface drive.

"Shit," yelled the sheriff. His men jumped in their cars and proceeded to chase the car down the surface drive. One of the men asked, "Who are we chasing, Dale Earnhardt?"

The surface drive led to Silverbell Road and the Corvette turned right on the street and headed east. The action was now in front of the South Point Casino and Hotel and traffic became an issue. People that were watching the chase on television said it was like a Clint Eastwood movie. You couldn't script this kind of action. The Vette swerved around cars on the street and spun past the cars lined up to enter the Casino's parking lot. The sheriff's cars had fallen behind making sure they cleared the cars at the intersection.

The Nevada terrain quickly became an ally to the speeding Corvette. The area south soon would rise with jagged hills and rugged mountains that could hide a car easily. They had to catch the suspects before they got into the canyons ahead or it would surly get away.

Once Blair had explained the information to the guy

behind the desk in the marina he was more than cooperative. He brought out a chart showing her the arrivals and departures of all the boats in and out of the slips. Booth was still sitting in their vehicle getting an update on the car chase in Vegas for Salem Ellis' yellow Corvette. How he wished he was there. He could see that Blair was standing with the man inside and waving for him to come in. What could she want? He exited the car and walked into the office Blair proceeded to introduce him to the man in the office. Booth let her take the lead. She apparently found something important, why else would she want him to come in!

"Brandon, Jim here stated that there was a boat matching the description of the one we are searching for that just left here an about five hours ago. He said that it took on fuel and supplies and was met by two men and women who boarded it here."

Booth was excited that they may actually still be on track in the chase for Salem Ellis.

Blair continued to explain that the man could describe the people that met the sailboat. Booth was now asking questions.

"Did they left a vehicle behind?"

"Yes, it's in the lot."

Once he found out that there was a Cadillac Escalade in the lot he wanted to know if they got a sketch artist there could the man help with the identification of the people who boarded the boat. He was positive that he could.

"It was one of the things I was always good at. I'm better at faces then names," he told them.

Blair was calling the new information into Steve in LA and he said they were going to send a sketch artist by chopper up there. Now Steve wondered who the Vegas guys were chasing in the Vette.

Blair and Booth thanked the man and told him that someone from their office would arrive in a little bit. They asked if the boat had to leave a manifest with travel plans.

He told them, "It wasn't something that was required," and he pointed out where the Escalade was parked.

They thanked him and he suggested that they might want to go to the fuel station and check with the attendant. He might have more information on what supplies they picked up there.

Blair said, "This is a good idea, I'll check it out and then go to the fuel station and you could check the vehicle out." More leg work but at least they were back in some action.

The chase down Silverbell Road south of the city continued with more cars in pursuit. The sheriff vehicles were equipped with a high performance interceptor engines and catching up to the Corvette that had a big lead. Just then when it looked promising the flash of yellow left them in its dust. Thank goodness the channel 8 helicopter stayed on the chase. The Sheriff communicated with the television station and they agreed to send the cars co-ordinates back to his men.

The event had now been on television for over thirty minutes and the ratings would have made any Hollywood executive jealous. The Las Vegas Bureau now had sent a chopper of its own in pursuit. The suspects were heading up Salton Canyon Road. There was no way out. Why would they take that route? The chase continued with the five vehicles and two choppers and close to ten million viewers.

The speeding yellow blur left the road up ahead and made its way across the wilderness landscape. It was a desolate tract that led into the wasteland.

Officer's wondered why would they drive into a barren region? What was the driver planning? All the chase cars followed although they were far behind. The information from the chopper above kept them on track. The Corvette came to a screeching stop and a cloud of dust rose high above as it spun to a halt. Two people were seen running from the vehicle from the chopper and heading to an area that was covered with boulders and cactus. It appeared to be a man and a woman that ran from the Corvette. The chase vehicles slowed and pulled into a semi-circle in case there would be gun-fire. Where were they headed to? As far as the men knew there wasn't anything but desert there.

The officer's got out of their vehicles and moved behind them to devise a plan of attack. None of the men chasing the car realized they had been thrust into instant stardom on television. The chopper above radioed down that the two inhabitants of the sports car had taken a position about fifty yards up the raven behind large boulders. It wasn't clear if they had weapons but suggested that the chopper could hover above and create a massive dust storm to flush them out.

That sounded like a great idea. It would be pretty hard unless they were wearing mask to handle all the sand and wind that the chopper would drum up. The men on the ground cautioned the chopper pilot to be careful in case they had weapons. "Affirmative," he answered.

The television chopper was still filming the action although the dust made it close to impossible for viewers to make much out.

The police chopper descended about forty feet above the two people hiding in the rocky terrain and created a huge dust bowl. As the dust continued to fill the area the chopper moved down and the two were seen running from behind the boulders. The troopers and FBI personnel were able to grab both of them. One of the suspects was the woman who had answered the door at Isaac Ellis' house. She was covered in sand and coughing. The agents had their two suspects in custody and it was all caught on national television. Unfortunately neither person was Salem Ellis.

Blair walked into the fuel station on the dock and a young man from behind the counter sprang into action. The marina was very quiet and now he had a pretty good looking lady in the store. "Good evening, how can I help you?" he said.

Blair showed him her badge. "I need some information on a recent transaction by a certain group. The Harbor Master said you could help."

. "Yes Ma'am!" He was immediately impressed and at her service.

"We understand that there was a crew of people in here yesterday in a forty foot sailboat, named Jasmine, getting fuel and supplies. I need to know everything they picked up from here."

"Do you mean all the items the Jasmine purchased?" He asked.

"Yes, that will be helpful. Also fuel purchases."

"I can do that. We track everything by boat name," he told her. "It is easier because owners usually charge purchases. The Jasmine isn't unusual. It's a Hunter DS 41 footer and a pretty popular model." He quickly went back to the counter and pulled out a ledger. Blair followed him and saw that he was searching through pages of purchases made in the fuel center. "Do you log everything in there?"

He looked up and said that they were required to post all the purchases for inventory control. "We haven't gone to computerized records yet, so it was the only way to kept track and reorder without visually checking shelves." He kept checking and came to a page where he stopped and handed the ledge to her. "This is everything they bought." She started to review the information and thanked him for his help. "Can I get you something to drink," he asked.

"Sure that would be nice. Do you have a bottle of Spring Water?"

He moved over to the coolers and grabbed a bottle and handed it to her. She had pulled out a couple of dollars and gave it to him. "That isn't necessary, my treat."

Blair smiled and said thanks. There it was everything she needed in front of her. The number of gallons of fuel and supplies they loaded onto the sailboat. It was enough for more than a few days out to sea. "Can I use your copier?"

He took the book and laid it on the machine behind the counter. "How many copies do you want?"

"Only one do you also have a fax machine?"

"We sure do. Where do you want me to send it?"

She gave the number to the young man. She called the office and told the secretary that she was sending Steve an important fax. Blair left the fuel station and headed to where Booth was checking out the parked Escalade.

"Did you find anything," he asked.

"Oh yes, I sent Steve the list of items they purchased and got a copy for us."

He was impressed. Blair was the best partner he ever had. "Nothing much here," he told her. They both rummaged again through the Cadillac without finding even the identification of the owner. He told her to call it into the office. She dialed Steve and gave him an update on their findings. Steve in turn filled them in on the details from Vegas that had just culminated in the capture of two suspects in the car chase. When discussing the events they all figured that the address and eventual chase in Las Vegas was all a set-up. Guess Ellis was planning on sending us on a wild goose chase hoping to buy more time to escape. Steve said the forensic team that was heading to Santa Barbara should arrive within an hour and hopefully they can get some DNA evidence pinpointing that Salem Ellis was part of the crew there. The Coast Guard had been notified and would narrow their search area based on the new information. There wasn't much more that Booth and Blair could do now but wait.

Thirty-One

The Vegas Bureau had the two suspects in custody from the car chase and was questioning them at their headquarters. The young woman wasn't saying anything. She refused to answer their questions and sat silently during the entire interrogation. The man immediately asked for an attorney. They were at a standstill and when Steve called to inform them that they had a possible lead at the marina it was decided to put them in separate holding cells. The bureau chief said we'll contact their attorney when we feel that we have more information from the LA office.

It was becoming clear that the chase was a diversion. Salem Ellis must have thought that if the FBI came to the residence of Isaac, that they knew the existence of the sailboat. It appears he hoped that buying more time and leading the bureau around in different locations would assist his escape. The director was pleased that his teams were working so closely together. The Vegas and LA Bureaus were in complete communication and their agents were working as one team.

Steve studied the manifest that Blair had faxed to the office. It was an enormous number of items and the fuel amount told him that they could be at sea for a long time, especially since they had sails that would help preserve their fuel load. According to the details of the boat it only held fifty gallons of fuel. Guess they had reserves on board for the escape. They were able to pull up a full description of the boat from sales records found by the Provincial Police. All the information was being sent to the Coast Guard.

The Point Mugu Air Station from Thousand Oaks was already operating an air search and surveillance around the Santa Cruz Islands and National Park. The Navy Outlying Field at San Nicolas Island was handling the search from Los Angeles to the Mexican border. The Vandenberg Air Force Base was covering the area north and west of Santa Barbara. All the bases were covered and the director had full cooperation from the Navy and Coast Guards chiefs of Staff. With the high profile case of the Chief Justice of the United States murdered the president had asked everyone to be on the same page.

The southern search covered Catalina and operated from the Navy station there. It was conceivable that Salem Ellis could be headed to Mexico. The largest marinas along the coast were south of Los Angeles.

Blair watched the helicopter as it landed at the far end of the marina. She and Booth walked over to the three men and woman getting out. Two of the men were from the crime scene lab and planned to run fingerprint analysis on the Escalade. The woman was the sketch artist and was going to sit down with the people at the marina and hopefully get the identification of the people on the sailboat. It was all coming together. They didn't know the third man in the group. He introduced himself as Oliver Sands from Homeland Security Office. Oliver was sent at the request of the director and Head of Homeland Security to check on regulation at the marina. Since the events of 9/11 anytime the possibility of unsecure borders came up his department became part of the investigation.

The sketch artist was working with the man in the marina office and he told her that the crew had a total of four people. There was a man and woman that met the sailboat along with the two men that had sailed into the harbor. He was asked to describe the people that met the boat. They wanted to make sure Salem was on the boat.

There really wasn't anything left to do at the marina. Once the sketch artist was done and the forensic team checked the vehicle out they were done. Booth was hoping to get in on the action somewhere. Blair kept teasing him that he hadn't been able to shoot anyone yet. He reminded her that she could still be his next target. The two agents had built a great bond and teased each other during the case. Although they had only met a week ago in the LA office it appeared that they knew each other for much longer. Blair was the first partner that Booth felt this close to. He wasn't sure why but there was just something about her that clicked with him.

He was a little jealous that at first she had been so instrumental in the case. When they were in Vegas, Blair spent the time getting Corey to give her the details of the case against the Ellis brothers. He had told her that he felt a little left out. Until the search of the San Bernardino Mountains did he feel that he was important? She reminded him that he was the one who caught the assassin! She was right. He did chase and catch Assad Jacoby after the shoot out at the cabin. "You're right! Guess we just need to get our next order from Steve," he told her.

"I'll call," Blair grabbed her I-phone and dialed. The call back to the LA office for directions from Steve and what he wanted them to do next was simple. Two key elements had to be finalized before they left. Get the sketches with confirmation that Salem was on the sailboat and fax them back to the office. The marina manager could be crucial if there was a trial. Make sure the forensic team did a thorough check of the vehicle and the people at the Santa Barbara harbor were congratulated for their help in the case. They were reminded not to detail anything about the case. Just make sure they knew the information was important. Blair also made sure she had all the details on the two men in the marina for future reference. Never know when it would come in handy.

The director requested that the Atlantic City Bureau transport Omar Ellis to Washington. He wanted his investigators there to handle the case from this point. He would also planned to have Assad Jacoby flown to D.C. for the murder trial. If he could capture Salem Ellis he would be batting a thousand. The implications of the case would spur many other trials. There would be further investigations into the collusion of gambling interest and local politicians that may have been involved. With the Ellis brothers involved with casinos in Atlantic City, Detroit, Phoenix and Las Vegas who knew where the investigations could lead. The explosion of casinos in so many states opened the possibility of so many illegal activities.

John Franklin Martin had his best people on the case. His teams all around the country performed at the top of their game. He couldn't have been happier. The president was kept aware of the investigation and due to the nature of the murder of a Supreme

Court Justice the cabinet was kept appraised of everything. The director's star was rising higher among all the powerful men in Washington.

There would be follow-up investigations in many cities regarding the new casinos that were opened. When the laws changed allowing casinos to open with approval of local native tribes close to thirty states now had gambling houses. So much money brought a great deal of temptation.

Blair watched the sketch artist working in the marina. It was amazing to see how it was coming together. The man had a clear picture of the suspect in his mind and was able to relay it to the artist. Salem Ellis' picture was never in any newspaper during the investigation so it was important that he could identify him. No one could say that he just saw articles and pictures in the local papers. Once she had a finished drawing Blair knew it was Salem. His picture had been sent to all the agents across the western bureaus and Blair couldn't believe how accurate the drawing was. She ran out of the office and grabbed Booth who was standing at the Escalade with the forensic team. "It's him!" The man described Salem to a T. She was excited that they had confirmation.

Booth smiled. He knew their involvement was critical in the completion of the case. "We need to send it to the chief." He was right. In the excitement she left the drawing with the sketch artist and needed to go back and get it. The other people that would be drawn would help in the trial as accomplices. Just then the lead agent of the forensic team turned to Booth.

"Sir, we have definite DNA evidence of Salem Ellis in this vehicle. I will be taking it all back to the office."

So much had come together at the marina, now to find Jasmine with her crew on board. The sailboat won't be hard to spot with so many aerial and water crafts involved in the search. Booth wished he could take the chopper back to the office instead of driving back. It was late and he hated driving when so much work could still be done. It was late and he was sure that nothing else would happen today.

The Coast Guard had a dozen boats along with the seven

that the Navy had searching the shoreline of Southern California. There were close to fifty sea planes and choppers in the air and the bureau had agents aboard many small crafts operating in the search. Bulletins had been sent to every port from Mexico to Canada with a full description of the Jasmine and her crew. The search resumed at sunrise. The morning sun was rising in the east and activity on the water would be fierce. Streaks of blue appeared off the horizon and the fog was lying low along the coast. It would burn off fast and activity would begin. Sea planes, helicopters and ships from both the Navy and Coast Guard took off from their ports. The bureau had agents at every sea port in case their suspect was brought in.

Aerial activity had skirted the shoreline along the California coast from the Mexican border all the way up to San Francisco. Every resource was utilized in the search. With the timeline that the Santa Barbara marina furnished, it was easier to plot the furthest that Jasmine could have sailed. Reports were constantly coming in from the search teams and the results were updated and plotted. At twenty knots under engine power the sailboat could not have made it out of the area that the Coast Guard had circled on the map. Three boats matching the description of Jasmine had been spotted during aerial searches. Two of they were heading north. As the Coast Guard ships intercepted them neither one was carrying the suspects. The third ship had made its way past San Clemente Island and very close to the Baja Peninsula. This was a problem because it was in the area of shared waters with Mexico. It had to be intercepted before it crossed into Mexican waters.

The Coast Guard had sent two boats following the boat believed to be the Jasmine. It was important to wait for confirmation that Washington had sent a communication to the Mexican government that the United States was trying to apprehend a murder suspect along the coastline. Would their suspect be on-board? The team from Long Beach had their chase teams in position. Helicopters hovered over the vessel and confirmed that the ship carried the name Jasmine on the rear. There was a large marina at Ensenada, Mexico that would eliminate US Navy and Coast Guard from entering. Orders were given to try to divert the path the ship immediately.

The chopper made a pass over the top of the boat and the

people on board were pointing to it. They needed to act now. The closest ship was the Alex Haley and still fifteen minutes away. The Choppers pilot buzzed the nose of the sailboat almost hitting it and the man at the helm had to make a sharp maneuver to the right or the mast would have been sheared off. The Hunter DS was over forty feet long with a sixty foot mast unfurled. On the second attempt to change the boats course the blades of the chopper caught the rigging line on the jib and caused the helicopter's blades to bend and sent the chopper into a spiral motion. The pilot tried to gain control but the blades were taking the line off the sailboat. The lines were being wound around the motor of the helicopter causing it to crash into the water. It seemed to be happening in slow motion and the two members of the Coast Guard team scrambled to get out before it went under.

The people onboard the sailboat were also being thrust into a spinning motion as the choppers blades pulled them along until the rigging line snapped. One of the men was trying to hold onto the wheel when the mast spun and sent him flying into the water. There was panic onboard and another person was seen scrambling into the cabin to get out of the way of the lines. The action had all been caught by the Sea Plane that had been tracking the boat. They radioed back to report what had happened. The Sea Plane made a swing around toward the spot that the chopper had gone down and swooped along the water's surface making a soft landing to rescue the downed men from the chopper. The plane started to hoist the two men aboard when shots rang out from the sailboat. They were about fifty yards apart, half the size of a football field, and way too close to avoid the hail of bullets. Life preservers were dropped to the two men in the water and the plane pulled off from the rescue operation.

The helicopter had been on the Hamilton class cutter that the Coast Guard had used primary for counterdrug patrols. This ship was equipped with a helicopter flight deck and fifty caliber weapons. They had been called into action once the sailboat had been spotted. There were two USCG Blackfin ships about two miles away and closing fast. The Alex Haley was the closest to the scene and could travel twice the speed of the sailboat. It had mounted guns aboard and was ready for action.

With the rigging gone and the mast split the only hope the

sailboat had was its diesel powered engines. Once they had chased the Sea Plane off the Jasmine made a wide turn and continued south toward Mexican waters. They left the man behind that had been thrust into the water when the mast hit him. The Sea Plane circled back around and picked up the two men that had gone down in the helicopter. They searched for the man that had been knocked off the boat but there was no sign of him in the water. Their orders were to follow at a safe distance until the Alex Haley made contact. It had a surf boat aboard and a front mounted machine gun. The second Coast Guard Blackfin was also gaining on the sailboat and would block the sailboat from heading toward the shoreline. They hoped to move around and encircle the crew that was escaping. The trap had been set and there would be no getting away.

Once the boat had some separation from the Sea Plane and did not see any other Coast Guards units they had a false feeling of confidence. The Mexican border was less than four miles and Salem Ellis and his two companions were close to freedom. The front hull of the sailboat bobbed up and down as the waves crashed against the sides licking the Hunter sending it side to side as the seas turned rougher. The strong currents and high waves delayed the boats progress and it was much slower than it would be in calm waters. Salem was yelling to the man holding the wheel when off the horizon he spotted the Blackfin closing fast. It had launched the surf boat that was cutting off the sailboats forward path. Salem grabbed the wheel and jerked it sharp to the left and the boat dipped deep into the waters foamy surf. The white foam washed over the bow of the boat sending water down into the cabin as the woman below cried for help. She was tossed into the table and rolled to the floor. Blood splattered across her white slacks from the gash on her head and she soon lost consciousness.

The Alex Haley had caught the sailboat and was within one-hundred yards. The captain called out over the speakers, "Halt! United States Coast Guard." The sailboat answered with a volley of bullets that sprayed the front of the oncoming boat. Just then the Coast Guard cutter from the Long Beach port also came into view. Its massive hull of gray steel with red and white stripes and front mounted guns stood out like an impregnable wall. The surf boat with front mounted guns had closed from the front and now had direct aim at the crew. The call from the Blackfin again demanded a halt or they would blow the sailboat out of the waters.

Salem Ellis didn't plan on giving in. He was slow close to freedom. The man on the deck of the sailboat was yelling to Salem. "Boss, we ain't got a chance," he yelled. Salem turned and pointed his pistol at the man. He never saw the bullet. The blast sent him backwards into the wash of waves. Salem knew it was a do or die situation.

The Alex Haley pushed into the surf and was planning to ram the sailboat. It was the best way they would have on taking the suspects alive. Ram the boat, knock them into the water and hopefully fish them out. The escape had turned into a sea battle that the sailboat was not equipped for. The Hamilton cutter had cut the retreat off and the surf boat was in position to board them. The Blackfin was traveling at open throttle and charging on the port side at a rapid pace. Salem was trying to steer and only had a pistol to answer any gunfire. Sea Planes circled overhead and two choppers were off the starboard side.

It was hopeless. Salem was caught and pulled back on the throttle to kill the engines. He threw his hands up and the charging Alex Haley changed course as the surf boat pointed their weapons at Salem and boarded the Jasmine. The men on the surf boat took Salem into custody and heard the cries of a woman below. They found her lying on the cabins floor and bleeding. Another team from the Blackfin searched the sea's surface for the man that was seen falling off the back of the sailboat. When they fished him out of the water he had a bullet hole in his chest.

Thirty-Two

The news of the capture of Salem Ellis was greeted with cheers from everyone involved in the case. Steve and his team in Los Angeles would send agents to take the suspect into custody. The Coast Guard had captured Salem and his girlfriend on board the Alex Haley. She had been injured in the action and was being treated onboard. Her wounds appeared to be superficial although she had lost a lot of blood. Salem was indignant and had been restrained in the captain's quarters with armed guards at the door. The Blackfin headed to the Long Beach marina where it would be meeting agents. The woman would be transported to a local hospital for observation before being brought in for further questioning.

Steve knew that Booth wanted to be involved so he dispatched him and Blair to Long Beach to bring Salem in. The team was happy and waited with anticipation as the ship neared the shore. They were standing on the dock as the Alex Haley pulled into port. Only two members from the Jasmine were still alive. One was killed when the mast sent him into the sea and Salem killed the other one. It wasn't clear how the woman fit in but the key was Salem Ellis.

John Martin had all his suspects and he planned on having them in D.C. for a trial. He wanted the L.A. Bureau to transport Salem to the Capitol. The ensuing investigation would possibly last for a long time and who knew what else would be discovered. Everyone in Washington knew Martin could parlay this into a run for a Senate position. He made sure key details got to a local reporter, Gina Warren. He was hoping to make a friend in the press for the future. His accomplishments with the bureau and cozying up to the press could help to propel him in upcoming elections.

The investigation team had gathered critical information from Assad who was looking for a plea deal. Omar Ellis wasn't talking and they figured that Salem wouldn't either. If Assad could fill in the missing pieces of the murder it would put the nail in the coffin of the Ellis brothers. Teams in Detroit and Atlantic City were combing records for any other people involved. It might be years before it was all cleared up. The president had requested that details of Senator Albertson's personal involvement with Corey wouldn't be revealed unless necessary.

Corey Hart had given the investigation team all the names and details in the gambling syndicate case. Once the trail was over he would be relocated in the witness protection program. With a new identity and location his life would be as close to normal as possible. He would never know that Blair was an FBI agent.

On the trip back from Long Beach, Blair had secured Salem in the back seat with cuffs that were secured to a metal brace in Booths vehicle. The bureau had equipped all its agent's cars with the special bracket in the rear seat. It was developed so that the suspect was totally restrained. Their orders were not to question him. The director's team on Capitol Hill had special plans for that. Once back, Salem was delivered to LAX and taken by special jet to Washington.

The investigation into gambling connection around the country would continue as the bureau gathered more details from Corey and the other captured suspects. Everyone knew that Booth and Blair had been instrumental in the case. Brandon Booth was pleased with his partner. It was the first time he had someone that he connected with on the job. They thought alike and worked as one team. Once they had their suspect delivered back to headquarters they still had to write their reports. Steve knew that his newest special agent was going to be a real asset. The two agents were in the office and answering questions from the team members about the chase. Blair let Booth give them the details. She smiled at him and strolled over to her desk. For her it was all about being accepted and good at the job. She didn't need any praise, success was all she wanted.

Blair sat at her desk and Kathy and Chris surrounded her. "Tell us, what happened at the cabin?" Kathy asked. She shook her head and pointed to Booth sitting across the room. "Booth is much better at explaining it. He had some great ideas that panned out. I was just along for the ride."

They knew better, but appreciated her approach. Booth was the special agent in charge and she was the new person on the block. She would complete her report and hope to head home. It had been close to two weeks and so much had transpired. She was only able to contact her parents once but they knew that was how it would be. If she was on a case they would have to wait until it was over.

Salem had been transported to D.C. and the investigation would be directed from there. The team completed their reports and turned them in to their boss. Steve again congratulated his team and knew they could use some time off. "How about the two of you taking a few days off," he said.

Blair said, "I could use the time to finish unpacking." They both thanked him. Blair grabbed her briefcase and realized that she needed a ride home. Booth had picked her up at her apartment and her vehicle was still there. Things had quieting down in the office and it was getting late. She strolled over to his desk and he looked at her.

"Blair, sorry that everyone thinks I was the key in this thing. I kept telling them that it was your idea to head to the mountains."

Blair didn't care. "You're the Special Agent in charge. I'd rather be on the sidelines anyway. I've had all the attention I need for a long time."

He smiled at her. Booth appreciated his new partner even more. "What are you going to do with a few days off?"

"Well first I need a ride home!"

"Oh, shit! I forgot that you didn't have a car here. It seems so long ago that this all started." Booth jumped up and grabbed his jacket. "Do you want to go now?"

"I've got all my reports turned in to Steve and if you're done I'm ready too."

They headed to the elevators that would take them down to the garage area. The ride from downtown to Marina del Rey would take about an hour due to traffic on Highway 10. Many people that worked in town lived west of the city. The two agents talked about the case and joked with each other along the ride. They would be a great team and involved in many cases down the road.

Booth pulled into the parking lot of Blair's apartment complex. "You know I left all my clothes in Vegas at the apartment they rented for us." Booth forgot all about his clothes too. "I'm sure they will pack it all up and send it to us," he stated. She figured that he was right. He pulled into a guest parking spot and got out of the vehicle. The two stood in the lot for a few minutes and Blair reached out to shake his hand. "Booth, I appreciate everything you did for me on this case. I'm sure when Steve told you that I was tagging along you thought it cramped your style. Hope I helped!"

"You more than helped, every idea that you had was on target. I'm really happy that we're working together." He took her hand with both of his and looked into her eyes. "You know Blair Adams, you're pretty cool."

They smiled at each other and she said, "You're pretty cool too." There was something special about their time together. He knew it. As Booth drove off Blair stood in the lot, still with a smile on her face. She watched as he pulled out of the lot. One last wave and she headed back upstairs. She really liked Booth.

She was happy to be back home. How long had it been? It seemed much longer than it actually was. Her apartment was a welcomed sight. The home phone had so many messages from Jennifer and Linda that the recorder was full. She just wanted to fall into bed. Tomorrow would be soon enough to call them back. The four posted bed look very inviting and sleep was sorely needed. She would call them back tomorrow.

Sunlight broke through the blinds and the sound of birds chirping outside her window was so peaceful. What a change from the last few mornings. She almost forgot how great her new apartment was. It was Thursday morning and there wouldn't be many people on the beach. She planned on getting dressed and heading down there for a run. There was a great path along the marina that led to the fishing pier.

The weather report on television said it was 62 degrees with a slight breeze. CNN was on with Gina Warren giving viewers details of an amazing story out of Washington. The FBI had just announced that they had captured the man who murdered the Chief Justice and uncovered a corrupt gambling ring in the process. Blair smiled as she watched the reporter spin the details for her audience.

She grabbed her I-phone and put her keys in the zipper pocket of her windbreaker. The winding stairway led down to the parking lot and the quarter-mile jog would take her to the shoreline. The sun's rays glared off the surface of the water as she made her way along the path. What a great feeling it was to just feel the breeze at your back with the sound of crashing waves along the rocks. There were fishing trawlers and sailboats making their way out of the marina to the Pacific. Blair turned where the path curved and ran along the sand that had been packed down by the tide. Marina del Rey was the perfect spot to start her new life. Her I-Phone was playing *Perfect* by Pink and there were just a few people along the water ahead.

"Hello!" The young man was saying as she approached. She didn't hear him. "Hey! Hello!" Now he was waving and moved in her path.

She slowed down and recognized the surfer that she had met before on the beach. Blair pulled the ear plugs as *Bohemian Rhapsody* blared out. She thought it was one of Pink's best songs. God what was his name, she thought.

"Hey, where have you've been?" He was hoping that she would stop. "I've been down here every day and haven't seen you for over a week." He was standing next to his surfing gear.

She finally remembered, Connor! That was his name. She was glad she remembered. "Hello Connor," She remembered his invitation to teach her how to surf. She slowed down and walked toward him. He was now holding his surf board and had the wet suit handing from his waist exposing broad shoulders and muscular arms. He really looked like the stereo-typical California surfer. Great build fantastic sun tan and short curly blond hair. His blue eyes reflected the deep sea and she remembered looking back at him after their first meeting. He had a couple days stubble and it looked good on him. He put his board down on the sand near his windbreaker. A group of surfers behind him were gathering their equipment and packing up.

"I was asking where you have been. I was hoping you would take me up on the surfing lessons."

She stood there watching as the white foamy surf crashed

along the shore and gave him a big smile. "Just been around? Guess I've been too busy unpacking and all to head down here." *Can't tell him what I do,* she thought. Her job wouldn't allow for any type of relationships. Or would it?

"You can unpack anytime, the surf has been super," he told her. "You can't tell me you've been unpacking all this time?"

Blair thought for a minute and nodded her head. How do you tell someone what you do, without really telling them? "No, I had to show up at work, as well as finishing putting everything away in my apartment.

Connor said, "I'm still unpacking after two years at my place. Where do you work?"

"Downtown at one of those offices, you know one of those eight to five jobs that bore you to death." She hoped he would be good with that answer. They stood together talking as he started explained the surf board he was standing next to and motioning across the shore at the waves. It was obvious that he loved surfing.

Who knows, maybe she could have a relationship, but she knew it would be tough. What if the truth came out? How would she explain long periods of time away? They continued their conversation as the water washed across the beach.

"Come on let me show you how easy this is." He was leading her toward the water and excited that she actually seemed interested.

The sun was high in the sky and she could see along the shoreline all the way to the Malibu Mountains. She thought it was the most beautiful place on earth. Blair wondered what adventures lay ahead.

Little did she know that a man was standing on the Pier ahead with binoculars watching her walk along the beach? Who was he and what could he want?

About the Author

The Vegas Connection is the third novel in the Blair Adams Series of FBI Thrillers. Inspiration for the series had been developed after a family tragedy. Mr. Aued spins a story that is full of intrigue and mystery.

"Aued weaves a riveting tale that reads more like a motion picture than a novel," according to reviews by Sheila Yancy of The Times Herald in Port Huron, Michigan.

He has lived in various parts of the Midwest and Southeast and uses many of these locations in his writing. He returned to teaching, his first love, after a corporate career. He currently resides in Michigan with his wife Kathy and their dog Baxter.

Made in the USA
Columbia, SC
04 September 2023